NEW YORK REVIEW BOOKS
C L A S S I C S

3kp

16 95
10 50

RIDE A COCKHORSE

RAYMOND KENNEDY (1934–2008) was born and raised in western Massachusetts. In 1982, he joined the creative writing faculty at Columbia University, where he taught until his retirement in 2006. Kennedy's other novels include *My Father's Orchard*; *Goodnight, Jupiter*; *Columbine*; *The Flower of the Republic*; *Lulu Incognito*; *The Bitterest Age*; and *The Romance of Eleanor Gray*.

KATHERINE A. POWERS's column on books and writers ran for many years in *The Boston Globe* and now appears in *The Barnes & Noble Review* under the title "A Reading Life." She is the editor of *Suitable Accommodations: An Autobiographical Story of Family Life—The Letters of J. F. Powers, 1942–1963*, forthcoming in 2013.

D0974391

RIDE A COCKHORSE

RAYMOND KENNEDY

Introduction by
KATHERINE A. POWERS

NEW YORK REVIEW BOOKS

New York

THIS IS A NEW YORK REVIEW BOOK
PUBLISHED BY THE NEW YORK REVIEW OF BOOKS
435 Hudson Street, New York, NY 10014
www.nyrb.com

Library of Congress Cataloging-in-Publication Data
Kennedy, Raymond, 1934–2008.
 Ride a cockhorse / by Raymond Kennedy ; introduction by
Katherine A. Powers.
    p. cm. — (New York Review Books classics)
 ISBN 978-1-59017-489-0 (alk. paper)
 I. Title.
 PS3561.E427R5 2012
 813'.54—dc23

                        2012008640

ISBN 978-1-59017-489-0

Printed in the United States of America on acid-free paper.
10 9 8 7 6 5 4 3 2 1

CONTENTS

INTRODUCTION

During the last decade or so of his life, Raymond Kennedy would occasionally and ceremoniously roll out of Brooklyn in his Lincoln Town Car and travel to western Massachusetts where I would see him now and again. He was drawn there by the countryside and the hill-and-valley towns of his youth, the region that provides the setting for all but one of his eight novels, including this one, his comic masterpiece. He told me that the most arresting memory of his childhood was seeing an enormous boat carried overland, progressing in state slowly and hugely past his house along Enfield Road near the Quabbin Reservoir. He was only five or six years old and stunned by its size and the surreality of its presence before him. It was, it turned out, a police boat bound for the recently completed reservoir whose supply of water for faraway Boston had submerged four little towns, including Enfield, the one toward which this road once traveled.

It is not likely that the breathtaking sight of this vessel on its way to preside over four drowned towns shaped Kennedy's vision of the world, but it is just like him to recall it and its imperious journey with so much satisfaction. In his novels he is the master, usually celebratory, of the brazen, the impertinent and majestically presumptuous. And, as it happens, he liked especially to confer these qualities on his fictional women, creating as fantastic a bevy of dominatrixes as the world of letters has ever seen. From *Flower of the Republic* comes Pansy Truax, lubricious, titanic brawler, and Mrs. French, elderly, steely seductress; from *Lulu Incognito*, Mrs. Gansevoort, devourer of innocence, the very "flesh-and-blood epitome of a great destructive principle loosed upon earth"; and from this book, its turbulent heroine, Mrs. Frances "Frankie" Fitzgibbons.

Ride a Cockhorse, first published in 1991, is Kennedy's sixth novel. It is set in the autumn of 1987 in a small city in Massachusetts's Connecticut Valley where Mrs. Fitzgibbons, a widow and loan officer at a solid savings-and-loan bank, has gone mad, visited at the age of forty-five by sudden mania. Once kind, polite, and deferential, she is suddenly transformed into a powerhouse of ambition and a dynamo of sexual energy. She discovers in herself a "big thrilling voice," astounding powers of eloquence, and radiant sexual magnetism; these she wields to persuade and persecute with unhinged abandon.

Mrs. Fitzgibbons is the managerial version of Lewis Carroll's Queen of Hearts; arbitrary and vindictive, she is never more truly her own megalomaniac self than when calling for somebody's head. Her three-week reign of terror over the Parish Bank can be seen as a grotesque expression of the spirit that seized America in the 1980s, that of the ruthless downsizers and predatory takeover artists who annihilated jobs, and of the cavalier bankers who destroyed hundreds of savings-and-loan institutions. This wondrous, horrifying woman, amoral and insanely overreaching, is—as she herself might put it—all business. She revels in its buccaneer spirit, firing people willy-nilly, cutting multimillion-dollar deals, swiveling back and forth in her chair, "tossing out cliches in a quietly boastful manner." She is sexually aroused by financial waffle and flimflam, by the celebration of innovation and audacity. Her short reign encompasses the stock-market crash of October 1987, whose furious disarray relieves her twinges of fear and paranoia: "The reality of what was happening to certain big corporations out there was perversely reassuring. The telephone in her fist felt like a weapon, like a heavy black hammer, something solid and useful."

If Mrs. Fitzgibbons's charade of being a banker is a satire on banking itself, especially as it broke loose from government regulation to ravage the land, her rise to power and demented, despotic rule can also be seen as a version of Hitler's. That element is certainly there, handily inserted throughout in Mrs. Fitzgibbons's denunciations and tirades, and as she gathers her select forces around her. Still, *Ride a Cockhorse* is the furthest thing from an allegory. It is surreal, certainly, but it is also firmly seated in its location, a small New England city very much like Holyoke, Massachusetts, the once-proud manufacturing town in which Kennedy spent a portion of his youth. He is fond of its people; they are his characters, and he describes their personalities, appearance, and little ways with wit and precision. And he rejoices in their speech: the novel is spangled with such venerable ornaments of American slang as "jamokes," "galoots," "welshers," and "boogums."

We can detect, amid the comedy and verbal pyrotechnics, the author's nostalgic regret that American cities have lost their dignity. The Parish Bank, after all, is located on what was once the city's business main street: now no longer the self-respecting thoroughfare of its heyday but "revitalized" as an open-air mall. The atmosphere of a little burg's traditional amour propre pervades the novel, and, in fact, the floodgates of Mrs. Fitzgibbons's mania are opened by those stirring expressions of American civic pride: the high-school marching band and the triumphal, neoclassical architecture of banks of yore.

Kennedy's depictions of the bank's interior and of the marching band are exhilarating and, in the case of the latter, peerlessly so. The pages devoted to the rousing, uniformed splendor of the band as it comes swinging around the corner transmit to our own spirits a giddiness and buoyancy almost equal to that which infects the newly volatile Mrs. Fitzgibbons:

The spectacle overall, with its American flags and high school colors flying, its brilliant purple ranks and gleaming brass, exceeded description—as in the way, for example, that it turned the corner at Essex and Locust, with the inside marchers marking time very smartly, their knees snapping up and down in place, while the entire rank pivoted round them like a swinging dial, and then stepping forth proudly again, raising their horns to their lips. To Mrs. Fitzgibbons, the music and grand moving panoply of it all was nothing short of celestial, as though the Maker was showing His minions.

At the head of this magnificent assemblage is the "resplendent young drum major," eighteen-year-old Terry Sugrue; it is he, this "vision of martial beauty," who has unleashed the middle-aged widow's libido:

His head was up; he had a brass whistle in his mouth; the sun was in his face. Behind him, the row of majorettes had followed suit, their bare knees and white boots flashing up and down in perfect synchronicity with his own steps. The golden tassels of his prodigious baton blew and shimmered in the October air. Mrs. Fitzgibbons had an impulse to run into the street and wrestle him to the pavement. Suddenly the drums fell silent, the boy's whistle pierced the air, up shot the baton, there was a great clash of cymbals, and twenty trumpets sounded in unison . . .

"I'd like to change his diapers," said Mrs. Fitzgibbons.

Mrs. Fitzgibbons's iron-fisted seduction of this young man is only the first of her conquests. At the bank, energized by madness, the formerly mild-mannered employee finds her unfettered spirit in towering accord with the building's interior, the "great marble-columned room, . . . a magnificent, high-vaulted emporium, with its venerable dimensions, its twinkling dome, the long row of golden grilles of the tellers' windows—an almost celestial hall!" She usurps command through sheer willpower: it shimmers from her electrified presence and makes itself heard in vituperative riffs and wild fulminations, a heady verbal excess in which her creator clearly takes as much pleasure as she does.

She's got style. Bold, charismatic, and conquering, she moves up from a pitiful Honda to an enormous Buick commandeered from her hairdresser's boyfriend, Matthew, who enlists himself as her driver. With him at the wheel, the fabulous, frightening Mrs. Fitzgibbons travels big, her acolytes following behind in another car of despicable inconsequence: "The sight of the filthy compact following Matthew's gleaming, highly polished Buick down Dwight Street toward the business district was curious to the eye. It looked as though the Buick had snagged something under its wheels and was towing it to the city dump."

Mrs. Fitzgibbons's manic transformation into a juggernaut, ghoulishly funny as it is, is not entirely an antic affair; she is, in the first place, a genuine destroyer, gloating over the lives she ruins. Kennedy paints distressing pictures of those victims, their jobs annihilated by a force beyond reason or control. But then there is the case of Mrs. Fitzgibbons herself: she is tragically mentally ill. At times she glimpses this, feeling that she cannot quite control her thinking, at one juncture experiencing "the odd sensation that her brain had actually contracted; that the scope of her thinking was somehow attenuated, like water jetting from a nozzle." It must all end badly—in a macabre sexual *Götterdämmerung*. But when it does, and when the sun has finally set on Mrs. Fitzgibbons's regime, the novel finishes on an unexpected note of pathos that is truly moving.

Ride a Cockhorse is a brilliant, all-American oddity and its author, a one-man band. Somehow in these pages Kennedy has brought together surrealism, satire, and black comedy; affection, empathy, and nostalgia; astute characterization, inspired description, and astonishing linguistic brio. To quote Mrs. Fitzgibbons in a moment of sexual exultation: "This is the goods!"

—KATHERINE A. POWERS

RIDE A COCKHORSE

For Charles Drapeau

Ride a cockhorse to Banbury Cross
To see a fine lady on a white horse.
With rings on her fingers and bells on her toes,
She shall have music wherever she goes.

REVOLUTION AT MAPLE AND MAIN

ONE

Looking back, Mrs. Fitzgibbons could not recall which of the major changes in her life had come about first, the discovery that she possessed a gift for persuasive speech, or the sudden quickening of her libido. While the latter development was the more memorable of the two, involving as it did the seduction of young Terry Sugrue, the high school drum major, it was Mrs. Fitzgibbons's newfound ability to work her will upon others through her skills with language which produced the most exciting effects. By early fall, some of her fellow workers at the Parish Bank, where Mrs. Fitzgibbons was employed as a home loan officer, could not have helped noticing her growing assertiveness on the job. She was ordinarily very reasonable and sweet-tempered, the soul of polite discretion. Almost overnight, she had become more strident, even to the point of badgering customers on the telephone and lifting her voice to a level that was considered inconsistent with the usual soft-spoken manner of a courteous banker. She could also be quite tart and provocative with those working around her, as on the afternoon when she lectured Connie McElligot, the woman at the next desk, for fifteen minutes on the subject of how the escalating interest rates of the 1980s portended an economic crisis of global proportions. Moreover, while speaking, Mrs. Fitzgibbons let fall certain locutions that revealed her true feelings toward the other woman, which were deprecative and of long standing, as she likened Connie McElligot's ignorance of such perils to that of any layman walking in from the street. "What would you know about the connection between interest rates at the Fed and the collapse of commodity prices in South America?" she said. "Nothing. Not word one."

It was during these same days precisely, however, in the early fall, that Mrs. Fitzgibbons developed an unexpectedly lustful interest in the resplendent young drum major who led the high school band past her house. Every Saturday morning, at fifteen minutes to twelve, the big noisy ensemble came round the corner of Essex Street, not a hundred feet from her door, with flags and pennants blowing and the tall, sandy-haired Sugrue boy out front, high-stepping his way into view. It was a sight to behold. He flourished an enormous gold-tasseled baton. With his high purple hat, his fringed epaulets, and great chestful of gleaming brass buttons, he offered a vision of martial beauty. Behind the young drum major, like an amplification of his own youthful grandeur, came the band in perfect step, a colorful machine. First were the three flag bearers, followed by a gorgeous rank of prancing, bare-thighed, arrogant-looking majorettes, their batons twirling in unison in the sun. A half dozen cheerleaders followed, in purple-and-white sweaters, shaking pom-poms in both hands, and, last of all, the big, solid eighty-piece marching band itself, with trumpets and snare drums going. The sound was deafening. The spectacle overall, with its American flags and high school colors flying, its brilliant purple ranks and gleaming brass, exceeded description — as in the way, for example, that it turned the corner at Essex and Locust, with the inside marchers marking time very smartly, their knees snapping up and down in place, while the entire rank pivoted round them like a swinging dial, and then stepping forth proudly again, raising their horns to their lips. To Mrs. Fitzgibbons, the music and grand moving panoply of it all was nothing short of celestial, as though the Maker were showing off His minions.

Unfortunately, Mrs. Fitzgibbons's married daughter, Barbara, who often visited her mother on Saturday mornings, took an altogether different view of the noisy, militaristic display parading past in the street. Barbara Berdowsky was a person very much up to the minute in her social views, and in her manner of expressing herself associated a coarse tongue with the language of feminist liberation, environmentalism, and other such current enthusiasms. "They look like a bunch of fucking Nazis," she said.

Mrs. Fitzgibbons had not heard, however, as at that moment she was standing behind the leafy curtain of Dutchman's-pipe that ornamented her front porch, staring fixedly at the lean ramrod figure of the drum major himself. Terry Sugrue had halted smartly right in front of her house, holding his baton on a high diagonal from his chest, to signify, no doubt, the introduction of a new musical piece. He was marching in place. His head was up; he had a brass whistle in his mouth; the sun was in his face. Behind him, the row of majorettes had followed suit, their bare knees and white boots flashing up and down in perfect synchronicity with his own steps. The golden tassels of his prodigious baton blew and shimmered in the October air. Mrs. Fitzgibbons had an impulse to run into the street and wrestle him to the pavement. Suddenly, the drums fell silent, the boy's whistle pierced the air, up shot the baton, there was a great clash of cymbals, and twenty trumpets sounded in unison.

In tempo with the vigorous diagonal strokes of the drum major's baton, the band came past Mrs. Fitzgibbons's house. The noise was breathtaking. The drumming was indescribable. The purple-and-white uniforms lit up. The musical selection chosen by the bandmaster, Mr. Pivack (who wore a special beige-and-cream uniform and habitually skipped about on one side or the other of his talented assembly), became recognizable to the ear. It was the high school's own football fight song. Mrs. Fitzgibbons kept her eyes fixed all the while on the vain young drum major, as he high-stepped his way up the tree-flanked roadway toward the Franklin Street football field. The music was so loud that Barbara didn't hear her mother's remark, obliterated as it was by the grunting of the tubas going past. "I'd like to change his diapers," said Mrs. Fitzgibbons.

She never knew what had come over her, nor was she much

inclined to think about it, but for a week running, Mrs. Fitzgibbons dressed up for herself every night and went riding in her car. One evening, before going out, she caught an unexpected glimpse of herself in the hall mirror and was delighted to discover a stranger looking back at her. She was wearing the dark violet Charmeuse dress that she had worn to her daughter's wedding, and had accessorized with the silver and amethyst choker that her late husband, Larry, had given her one Christmas; her hair was tied back, and her face made up with obvious skill; even the lift of her own breasts struck Mrs. Fitzgibbons as the attraction of someone else. For more than an hour that evening, she drove around town in her dented Honda; she had the windows down and was listening to the Top 40 on the radio. It was the car that Larry had bought for them back in 1982, two years before he died. "Everybody thinks that the Chinese make junks," he used to say, "but the Japanese made this one." (Larry was witty. Mrs. Fitzgibbons never denied him that. On his deathbed, when he knew he was finished, he smiled at her, and said, "What were my last words?" That was Larry's farewell. He never spoke again.)

A few minutes before eight o'clock, after darkness had fallen, Mrs. Fitzgibbons spotted the Sugrue boy walking under the maples on Nonotuck Street, with his red nylon bookbag slung over his shoulder, his pale hair glowing under the streetlamp, and she pulled up next to him in the Honda. Her heart was thumping when he came over to the car window. She had signaled to him. As so often in the days to come, Mrs. Fitzgibbons hadn't a notion in mind what she was going to say before she actually spoke.

"I'm having motor trouble," she said. "It's skipping."

Obeying her instincts, she took an even franker approach. "You're the boy in the band! I know who you are."

She sat behind the wheel, with her elbow on the window, smiling at him.

"I'm the drum major," he said. He was tremendously vain, she thought. She liked that. She liked vain men. Larry, unfortunately, had not been that way.

"Don't I know it! The band goes past my house every week. You march beautifully!"

"Thank you," said the youth. Being tall, he was forced to lean over.

"I'm Frankie Fitzgibbons. My husband," she said, "was an alderman."

"Your name is Frankie?" said the boy.

Mrs. Fitzgibbons continued smiling. She couldn't help herself. She had never seduced anyone in her life. Larry had been like an appliance; he'd done what he was warranteed to do. The Sugrue boy was another animal altogether. Already she had intimations of success. She would tell him what to do, and he would do it.

"Do you know anything about cars?"

"I'm not good at mechanics," Terry answered. He was staring blankly at the dashboard.

"Can you drive?" Mrs. Fitzgibbons got into the passenger seat. "Drive it around the block," she said, "and tell me what you think."

As he climbed into the car, Mrs. Fitzgibbons admired his long blue-jeaned legs. He looked a little distressed at attempting to correct something for which he had no proficiency. "It sounds okay," he muttered softly.

"Well, it's not okay. It stalled on me twice." She was lying but gave no thought to it. "Drive it around," she said.

The drum major complied. He put the car in gear and started slowly up Nonotuck Street. Mrs. Fitzgibbons was watching him cannily. "What's your name?" she asked.

"Terry Sugrue."

"Is that the family with the murderer?" she asked.

"Murderer?" He looked at her.

"There was a Sugrue who killed somebody years ago."

"I never heard anything about that," said the youth.

Mrs. Fitzgibbons was improvising. "A man named Sugrue killed a bookmaker on a farm out in Granby and buried his body in the woods. He owed the man money."

"No fooling." He kept his eyes on the road.

"Do you know anything about carpentry?" She advanced an altogether new subject.

"Not much."

"You take shop classes, don't you?"

"I used to. A long time ago — in junior high."

"You can nail two boards together."

Terence laughed but continued staring at the road. He affected a keen listening attitude toward the engine, as he gradually speeded up the car. Mrs. Fitzgibbons was not watching the road. She was surprised by her own brazenness.

"I need a couple of boards nailed together," she said.

"Engine sounds okay to me."

"It's not."

"I think you'd have to ask a mechanic."

"You're doing fine. There! Did you hear that? It skipped. Now," she said, "it's going to stall."

The boy looked perplexed. "It's nice and smooth."

"Are you sure?" Mrs. Fitzgibbons assumed a doubtful air. "Ever since Larry died, I get a little paranoid." She sat back. "How is it you're still in high school?"

"I'm a senior."

"Because you don't look it." Mrs. Fitzgibbons addressed him in the way a school principal might. "You look about twenty. Did you stay back?"

"Me? I never stayed back in my life! I'm first honor roll."

"You are? I'm glad to hear that. Turn left on Northampton Street," she said, "and go a little faster. You're poking."

"Sometimes," he suggested, "it helps to gun the engine."

"Then gun it."

Terry shifted into neutral and raced the engine hard.

"That sounds better," she said, after Terry released the accelerator. "I think you did it."

"I didn't do anything."

"That sounds normal. What did you do?"

"I gunned the engine."

"That did the trick."

"I think you're worrying about nothing, Mrs. Fitzgibbons."

"Frankie," she said.

"Frankie."

"Gun it again."

"It doesn't need it."

"Gun it, sweetheart. Do what I tell you. I think you corrected it. Do you have a car of your own?"

"No, I don't."

"What do you do on dates?"

"Dates?"

"Dates," she said. "You can't go out without a car."

"Maureen, my girlfriend, has a car. Actually, it's her brother's car, but he works evenings at the junior college."

"Who is Maureen?"

"Maureen Blodgett."

"I know Maureen Blodgett," Mrs. Fitzgibbons lied. "*She's* your girlfriend?" She made a face.

"Well, sort of." Terry faltered, visibly disconcerted by the perplexed expression on the woman's face. They had stopped at a traffic light.

"She's a little young for you, isn't she?"

"Maureen? Maureen's nineteen. She's older than I am."

"Maureen Blodgett? Not the Maureen Blodgett I know. She looks like a kid."

"She looks a little young," Terry allowed, "but she's out of high school."

"I can't believe what I'm hearing. *You,*" said Mrs. Fitzgibbons, "and her? That is a surprise. If you had asked me to guess, I'd've picked somebody completely different from that. Somebody like that Salus girl, the pianist, the redhead, the one who goes to school in New York."

"*The concert pianist?*" Terry glanced in disbelief at Mrs. Fitzgibbons. For just a second, his eyes strayed to her breasts. Mrs. Fitzgibbons was sitting up straight, as though in a physical response to the shock of Terry's choice of young women. Her violet dress shimmered under the passing streetlights; she was conscious of the effect she had produced.

"What's so unusual about that?" she demanded, recalling hastily details from an article in the local *Ireland Parish Telegram* about the pianist. "She's in her twenties. She's beautiful. She has a future. You'd make a wonderful match."

"Me and her?" Young Sugrue couldn't believe his ears. The young woman in question had graduated high school five years earlier and had been known from an early age as a light of the community, a prodigal talent much written about in the local newspaper.

"Don't you think she likes men?"

"I suppose so," he said.

"Of course she does. You can speed up, by the way. We're not going to a funeral."

"I think the car is okay."

"You didn't answer my question. Do you honestly think that Lorraine Salus doesn't like men? Of course she does. It's hard for a girl like that to make a good match. People who are beautiful and gifted, like Lorraine, or yourself for that matter, find it hard in that way. To locate a proper mate, I mean. You can't just take anyone who comes along. I mean it. You may be underestimating yourself."

The look on the drum major's face, as he glanced round from the steering wheel at Mrs. Fitzgibbons, betrayed the deep core of vanity in him. He was listening intently. To be so susceptible to flattery, she thought, was really quite sad.

"It's your duty," she went on, "to make a good match. That's something that women understand better than men. Women judge men from a breeding standpoint. A woman always asks herself what kind of children she would have with this man. Men don't do that."

"That's very interesting."

"That's why Maureen What's-her-name is chasing after you. She wants to breed up."

"Breed what?"

"Up! It's instinctive. All females do that. They look to catch a male that is better than they are. It's called breeding up."

Terry regarded her with an ingenuous stare.

"It comes from nature. That's why wild animals fight in the breeding season. The males fight, and the females watch. And when it's over, the females go to the winner. It's as old as God. It's the oldest thing there is. I guarantee you, if Lorraine Salus saw you leading the band down to the stadium, she'd go crazy. Even I'm impressed. I'm very impressed. Anyone would be impressed."

"Maureen loves watching," he added.

"I should think she would!" Mrs. Fitzgibbons belittled the girl in a scathing tone. "You're her best chance. Who would take her out if she didn't have you?"

"I don't know."

"That's what I mean. She'd have to settle for some wimp who studies all night and couldn't get a girl if you set a pistol to his head." Mrs. Fitzgibbons cut the air with her hand. "Maureen wouldn't get anybody. I know who she is. I can see her problems. You have to face up to things, Terry. You can't let Victorian sentiments fuck up your life."

The sudden expletive from Mrs. Fitzgibbons's lips caused Terry to snap his head around. He was stunned.

"Use your skin," she said. "You have your whole life in front of you. You only get one good shot at it. The wheel goes around once, and that's it. You'll only be twenty once. You'll never see these days again. Some decisions," Mrs. Fitzgibbons stressed, electing to employ an impressive word, "are irrevocable. Where would you be five years from tonight with a girl like that?"

"Maureen is in college," he objected feebly.

"What college?"

The boy was putty in her hands. Mrs. Fitzgibbons could feel it. Each time he glanced round, his eyes darted to her breasts.

"Our Lady of the Angels."

"Your Lady of the Angels! What's she studying to be, a pope?" Mrs. Fitzgibbons laughed gaily. She was showing off her breasts now; he seemed to know it. He was just driving and steering. He wasn't paying any attention to the engine. He kept looking over at her.

"Why are you so dressed up?"

"Answer the question," she insisted. "Where would you be? I don't mean to be coarse, Terry, but someone has to wake you up to what's what. The best young women of your generation deserve a shot at you. You can't tie yourself up."

"I'm not tied up —" He hesitated at mouthing Mrs. Fitzgibbons's first name.

"Frankie."

"Yes. We're only friends, Maureen and I."

"What happens," Mrs. Fitzgibbons explained, adopting an analytic view, "with a girl like that, you have sex a couple of times, and they become totally possessive. That's the greatest danger of all," she added, as Terry's expression signified the correctness of her last thrust, not to mention her boldness. "They think it's everything. They think it's the purchase price of the rest of your life. *Is* she possessive?"

"Yes."

"Does she get jealous?"

"Sure. Sometimes," he said.

"I'll bet she's jealous out of her brainpan over those majorettes that march behind you in the band."

A look of guilt invaded his face. "She imagines things," he confessed.

Mrs. Fitzgibbons laughed mischievously. "Those girls are crazy about you. And I'll tell you something else. There isn't one of them that Maureen could keep up with. I know that for a fact. I see them going past my house. They're beautiful! Every one of them. They're arrogant! They're sure of themselves! They have beautiful bodies. Compared to your Maureen, they're like women from another planet."

"Some of them are beautiful," Terry conceded.

"They're all beautiful. They're tall, they're slender, they're vain, they know what they want. Can you imagine Maureen in that lineup?"

"She wouldn't look right."

"*Look right?*" Mrs. Fitzgibbons loosed a peal of laughter and set her hand over his. "And you wonder why she's jealous?"

"I don't make her jealous."

"Of course you do. How could you not? You would have to. Drive down Sergeant Street," she instructed. "I'm going to show you what happens to people who get roped into unhappy relationships."

By now, Terry was clearly enjoying the older woman's appreciation of his value and was not eager to suspend the pleasure. "Fine," he replied.

"And step on the gas. It's the pedal under your foot. You're making me nervous. I like a little wind."

Terry assumed a more mature tone. "You were right about the possessiveness," he said after a short silence.

"I'm right about all of it." Mrs. Fitzgibbons was sure of her intuitions about the young man and his girl. "Two or three sexual escapades with a college kid do not add up to a lifelong commitment. Some may say otherwise, but only because it's in their self-interest. Funny thing is, it's the stupid, inexperienced ones that hold onto an idea like that as though it were gospel. The less they know about something, the more scared and dogmatic they get. You must find it embarrassing."

Terry appeared unsure of the nature of her query and said nothing, but did capitalize on the moment to look across again at Mrs. Fitzgibbons's bosom.

"I would," she said. "It would make my skin crawl. I'm not saying that a twenty-year-old like yourself is supposed to have a hundred and fifty amorous entanglements, but the views of a little college girl, who is still wet behind the ears, add up to zero." She fiddled with the radio dial. She changed the station. She liked the look of her hand; her nails were shapely and pink, and the bracelet on her wrist twinkled attractively.

"I'm not twenty, Frankie," Terry reminded her.

She ignored him. "Maureen will find somebody else. Somebody of her own kind. You'll see. Tell me more about yourself. Let's talk about interesting people!"

"Well —"

"What do you do when you're not leading the band?"

Terry shrugged. "I don't know. I go to school. I wrestle at the Boys Club. I go to the movies with Maureen."

"You wrestle?" That interested her.

"I play golf sometimes."

"I play golf!" she said. "Larry belonged to the country club."

"No fooling."

"I still have his Wilson clubs. Do you have clubs of your own?"

"I have five or six old ones," he answered. "A wood, a couple of putters, and three or four irons."

"I'll show you Larry's. I'll bet you can hit the ball a mile. Are you on the golf team at school?"

"I haven't time for band and golf."

"I forgot about the band," said Mrs. Fitzgibbons. "I think you're better off with the band. Any dummy can play golf, but leading the band the way you do it, darling, is an art. It's one of the most exciting things I've ever seen. They ought to pay you a salary." Mrs. Fitzgibbons was smiling at him.

Terry flushed red. "I love leading the band."

"Didn't I know that already? You look like a dream out there."

"When did you see me?" The drum major couldn't conceal his feelings of pride.

"I told you. You go right by my house. I saw you last Saturday. With all those flags and drums, and your tall hat and that enormous baton. You looked like the Pied Piper of Hamelin, I swear to God."

"You ought to go to the football games, Frankie."

"I'm going Saturday," Mrs. Fitzgibbons shot back.

"No kidding." He looked at her.

"I wouldn't miss it for the world. Would you like that?"

"I'd love it."

"Who are we playing?"

"Springfield Tech. I could get you tickets, Frankie."

"Would you?"

"I'd love to."

"I'd only need one."

"You'd be going yourself?"

"I have a daughter, Barbara, but she's practically brain-damaged."

He laughed gushingly at Mrs. Fitzgibbons's remark, appreciative of the profane streak in her.

"Barbara thinks football is a game for rednecks. She hates bands, she hates sports, she hates bars, she hates pop music, she hates television and movies. She hates everything that's fun."

"I like all those things."

"So do I."

"What does she like?" said Terry.

"Causes," said Mrs. Fitzgibbons. "Barbara likes causes. Some-body over in Burma blows up the Burmese president in a plane, and that's a matter of great urgency to Barbara. She's never been to Burma. She's never going to go to Burma. She wouldn't know a Burmese from a Mongoloid idiot if she was lying in bed with him.

"I didn't spank her enough," she went on. "I should have whaled the daylights out of her. She's very serious. You're much more interesting. I hope you don't like politics."

"I hate politics."

"She wants to run for office. She wants to be an *alderperson*! It's enough to convulse a cat."

"How old is she?"

"Eighteen months."

Terry Sugrue burst out laughing, as Mrs. Fitzgibbons, also laughing, set her left hand lightly on his shoulder. "It's true, darling. She wouldn't get twenty votes. She should be locked up someplace. With her frozen dinners and her little yellow and pink vitamin tablets. Every time she comes in the door, I fill up with feelings of discouragement. You can read the bad news in her face. She and Eddie, her husband, subsist on frozen broccoli. They sleep on the floor on a futon. She hasn't put on lipstick in a year. I love cosmetics! Look at my nails." She set her hand illustratively on the dark satin of her lap. "Is that pretty, or is that pretty?"

"It's very pretty."

"Of course, it is."

When Terry stopped the car in front of her house and cut the engine, Mrs. Fitzgibbons was calculating rapidly what to do and say when she got him indoors. As she unlocked the door of her house, she blundered. "I haven't been with a man in three and a half years," she said.

She saw the look of shock register in his face. She was going too fast.

"Don't worry, I'm not going to attack you, darling. I'll save that for some pretty afternoon up at the country club," she said, "when you've hit the ball into the rough." She smiled at him in the half darkness. "I hope you like athletic women."

The youth colored pleasurably. "I don't know," he said. "Maureen is not at all athletic."

"I didn't think she would be." Mrs. Fitzgibbons switched on the foyer lights. She led Terry into the kitchen. "I'd guess that the women in your future probably will be. Follow me. I'll show you Larry's clubs."

While complying docilely, Terry returned the conversation to Mrs. Fitzgibbons's reason for his driving her home in the first place. "What were you saying," he asked, "about someone whose life was wasted by a woman?"

"When we were talking about Maureen?"

"Yes."

Mrs. Fitzgibbons deflected the question. She had opened the kitchen closet and produced a golf club. It was a wood. "Is this too short for you?" she asked.

Terry took the club in hand and set the head to the floor. "This is a beauty."

"It's like new."

"It's terrific."

"When we play, you can use them. If you like them, and if you behave yourself, I'll give them to you."

"I couldn't take your husband's clubs."

"My husband is dead."

Terry winced at Mrs. Fitzgibbons's brutal frankness. "That's what I mean," he said.

"Besides," she added, "you'll have earned them because you're going to help me with my game. We're going to play a week from Sunday." She enjoyed being bossy with him. The youth liked it, too. She could tell. "Put away that club and come into the other room. I've got a task for you." She led the way, conscious of the liquid shimmer of her dress. She smiled back at him. "I'm taking advantage of you."

"That's okay." Terry followed her obediently with a blank, ex-pectant look on his face, as though the "task" would reveal itself as something visible to the eye.

"I'm going to a reception tomorrow night," she went on, lying, "and I'm not sure what to wear. You're going to tell me."

"I am?"

She put on the living room lights and the television. "It's a party for a friend at the Canoe Club. My daughter's not going to be there, so I can wear something decent. Sit over there." She indicated the sofa. "I have a black satin party dress. I'll try it on."

"You're wearing a pretty dress right now," Terry pointed out.

"It's my favorite," said Mrs. Fitzgibbons. She was standing in the doorway, evaluating the way the sandy-haired youth was looking up at her from the sofa. A shiver went through her as she anticipated what was coming.

"You could wear that one."

Mrs. Fitzgibbons called to him from the next room while changing. "You have refined taste. I like your sleeveless argyle. Do you ever wear white trousers?"

"I have a pair of white duck pants."

"God, what you must look like in white pants! Wear them for me next Sunday. I like white on the golf course. And your argyle sweater. And a shirt and tie." Mrs. Fitzgibbons tossed her violet dress onto her bed and went to the closet.

Terry called back from the parlor. "I've never worn a tie playing golf."

"You will next week," she said, and stepped into her black dress. "Am I too bossy?"

"It's okay," he replied.

"You can call me Frankie."

"Okay."

"I'm almost ready." She was speaking to her image in the mirror. "I'm not really bossy," she explained. "I'm only like this when I'm paying compliments to someone who needs them."

Returning to the living room, she paused in the doorway, leaning a hand against the doorjamb while bending to slip on her high heels. "How do you like it?"

"That's beautiful." He was sitting on the sofa, his knees splayed, his hands on his knees. He was a trifle nervous.

Mrs. Fitzgibbons's dress had a sweetheart neckline and short, puffy sleeves. It was a cocktail dress that showed her figure to advantage. At intervals, she felt a nervous wave of excitement go coursing through her body. The drum major sat like an effigy, his face as blank as a dinner plate. Even his eyelashes were sandy.

"My greatest fear," she said, as she stepped into the room and looked at herself in the mirror behind the sofa, "is that some of the men I work with, who are going to be there, will assault me on the spot."

Terry said nothing to that. He sat fixated. She guessed he was quite scared. The profile of her breasts in the mirror was magnificent.

"I hate the men I work with. Fat, middle-aged bankers who talk from morning to night about football."

"What bank is that?"

"The Parish Bank. I'm a loan officer."

"I didn't know that."

"Is it too tight?" she asked. "In the thighs?"

"I don't think so, Frankie."

Pivoting, she looked over her shoulder at the mirror. "Also, they're all midgets. Even the chairman is a midget. I hate midgets. All men are crazy," she said, "but when a midget picks up the scent, a woman needs a revolver just to go to the bathroom."

The Sugrue boy gave a quick shout of laughter. Mrs. Fitzgibbons strode past him into the kitchen and returned with a bottle of Canada Dry ginger ale and two glasses. She was talking as she came and went. "I sometimes worry about my own son-in-law. When Barbara isn't around, he looks at me funny."

"Funny?" Terry was prepared to be shocked.

"You know, like he's expressing a secret language to me." She waved indeterminately.

"That's disgusting."

"It is disgusting, but it's true. My own son-in-law. He wants me. You're the only person I've ever told." Mrs. Fitzgibbons poured Terry some soda, then got herself some vodka from a bottle on the liquor cabinet. "You don't want vodka, do you, sweetheart?"

"A small amount would be nice." He reached up his glass, and Mrs. Fitzgibbons poured in a dash.

"Get us some ice cubes, and I'll tell you what happened with him. His name is Eddie. I'll tell you what aroused my suspicions." While Terry was in the kitchen, Mrs. Fitzgibbons poured him additional vodka. "You'll be the judge."

When he returned with the ice, Mrs. Fitzgibbons touched his glass with hers. "To golf," she said.

"Are we really going to play? Because I'd like to."

She flourished her glass. "To next Sunday morning, on the first tee, at ten o'clock. You'll wear your white ducks, and I'll give you Larry's clubs."

Terry couldn't get past her to return to the sofa. Instead, he leaned against the doorpost. Mrs. Fitzgibbons was getting more excited by the minute but was endeavoring to conceal it. She was controlling herself. Her thoughts were lucid.

"The last time Eddie was here," she began, "Barbara went outdoors to water the last of the marigolds, and while she was gone, Eddie asked me if I'd like to go on winter vacation this year." Mrs. Fitzgibbons grimaced perplexedly. "I said no, that picketing a nuclear power plant in the wilds of New Hampshire is not my idea of a vacation. Eddie said, 'But we'd go anywhere that you want. You decide. I,' he said in a secret sort of voice, 'will talk Barbara into it.' And he was looking at me very, very funny."

The youth was fascinated by Mrs. Fitzgibbons's bizarre recital. "That's very strange," he said.

"You agree with me, then?"

"Yes, I do."

"There's more." Mrs. Fitzgibbons paused to drink and waited till Terry had also drunk. "I shouldn't be telling anyone, but what the hell do I care? I didn't make the world," she said, "I just live here."

"What else did he say?"

"That was in early September, just before Barbara went to Boston to attend some pro-choice women's rally for abortion. After she was gone, Eddie called me on the phone. He said the pollen count was at a record, and could he sleep overnight on the sofa, because I have an air conditioner. He wanted to sleep in my house."

"Wow," said Terry.

Mrs. Fitzgibbons would have finished the fictitious story but had put her left hand on Terry's waist and had forgotten momentarily what she was saying. The thought of lying beneath the drum major's hard body disrupted her thoughts. She was just talking now, with no thought content.

"He's a bug," she said.

"He sounds it."

When Terry reacted to Mrs. Fitzgibbons's kiss by going pale and not moving a muscle, she shuddered perceptibly. Without hesitating, lest he find a reason to withdraw, she reached down and fondled him. She was whispering in a hoarse voice. "I'm not even going to that party tomorrow night. I hate men like that."

Terry managed to make a reply. "I'm glad," he said. He stood frozen against the doorjamb. She was clutching him through his trousers and had set the tips of her breasts against his chest. He was staring at her.

"Men like that are pigs," she said.

In short order, Mrs. Fitzgibbons had maneuvered him onto the sofa, her arms coiled about him, and was licking his ear. "I can tell you're experienced," she said.

"I'm not, very," he confessed.

"You're sensitive and intelligent," she remarked. "You don't try to rape a woman. You're one in a thousand. I could eat you alive."

The sight of Mrs. Fitzgibbons's creamy thighs above the line of her stockings, as she hiked up her dress, must have magnetized the boy's senses, for he gave out an amorous moan.

"You're finished with Maureen," she said. "Maureen belongs to the past."

"I think you're right," he said.

"You're going to be an adult now. Maureen is a child."

"She is, Frankie." Terry's voice quavered.

As easily as that, Mrs. Fitzgibbons had hold of Terry's penis in her fist and was squeezing and rubbing him with her fingertips. He was beyond turning back. She could say anything now.

"Next to you, she's an idiot," she said.

"I don't know." Terry was stressed.

"She comes from a family of idiots. All the Blodgetts are idiots." With her fingertips, Mrs. Fitzgibbons parted her panties, and rubbed and caressed him against herself. "Our Lady of the Angels! She won't even finish college."

"You may be right."

"She'll never finish!" she cried.

"I don't think so, either."

"She's a dead end, sweetheart." Mrs. Fitzgibbons was heating up tremendously. His head was beautiful; her left hand was behind his neck. "She belongs to the past."

"You're right about that, Frankie!" For the first time, Terence Sugrue's voice broke. He closed his eyes and grimaced acutely. He moaned again.

Mrs. Fitzgibbons denigrated the Blodgett girl. "She can't have you!"

"Oh, Frankie!"

"Tell me about her."

"*She's an idiot!*" he cried.

"Tell me again."

"Maureen's an idiot."

"I like hearing you say that. And do you know why? Because it's true, peppermint. That's why. Where does a lamebrain like that get off? She doesn't even know how to dress."

"She dresses like a bum, Frankie."

"She can't have a man like you."

"She really does."

With a deft maneuver of her hips, Mrs. Fitzgibbons introduced him inside herself. Terry's eyes widened incredibly. She wrapped her arms round him. "She'll find somebody else."

"She'll have to, Frankie."

"Somebody of her own stripe," said Mrs. Fitzgibbons. "She can't have you anymore. It wouldn't be fair to the others. It really wouldn't."

"You're wonderful, Frankie." Terry was breathing exaggeratedly; his eyes were wide as saucers.

"We're going to do this all night," she said. "We're going to do it ten times. We're going to do it and do it, till we can't even walk. How does it feel?"

"It's unbelievable," he cried.

Mrs. Fitzgibbons scissored her legs together underneath him and squeezed her thighs. "How about that?"

"Oh, God!"

"This is sex," said Mrs. Fitzgibbons. "This is the way it's supposed to be. This is how it feels to be with a woman."

"I love you, Frankie!"

"You're an adult, Terry. This is why people grow up. This is why I'm here. This is what I'm for. Can you feel my breasts?"

"Frankie . . . !"

"Can you feel my breasts, I said?"

"They're beautiful."

"They're for you now. They're yours, darling. Nobody else can touch them. Later, I'm going to put your penis between them. Would you like that?"

"Oh, yes!" His face was brimming with anguish. He was clutching Mrs. Fitzgibbons for dear life.

"They're going to be expressly for you. You'll give them hot, sticky kisses. You'll go crazy over them. You'll know I'm saving them for you."

"I love you, Frankie!"

"Tell me about Maureen."

"I hate her. I'll never see her again. . . . I'll say anything you want."

"Say something horrid."

"She stutters! She can't even talk right," he moaned. "She has no breasts at all. She goes to an idiot college. Her family are idiots!"

"Could she ever be a majorette in the band?"

"Never!"

Still fully clothed, Terence was moving rhythmically atop her; he was breathing hard in Mrs. Fitzgibbons's face.

"Is she as good as you are, darling?"

"No, she's not." Terry's head was up; he was staring into space in ecstasy.

"Say something worse."

"I will! I will!"

"Then do it," she commanded.

Terry's face was pained and sweated. "I'd like to throw her in front of a car!" he shouted.

TWO

For about a month, Mrs. Fitzgibbons's self-confidence had been surging, to a point where nothing of a reasonable nature seemed impossible to attain. Why should it? She looked about herself with new eyes, at the people she worked with at the bank — the ill-dressed secretaries and tellers; the stolid middle-aged loan officers toiling at their desks; even Mr. Leonard Frye, her boss, a pleasant, plodding, phlegmatic individual who never raised his voice in anger or excitement, who neither hectored nor encouraged his staff — and she marveled over her own long record of genial indifference to the way of things. During her fourteen years at the Parish Bank, which was located in the "revitalized" downtown open-air mall, Mrs. Fitzgibbons had floated along on the sluggish current of a workaday life, as a leaf being borne to the sea. Even Larry's death back in '84 had produced no remarkable effect upon her. It changed nothing in the real sense. Leonard Frye had kindly insisted, following her husband's funeral, that she stay home for a week; but in no time, upon returning, she lapsed once more into the same tiresome routine — doing her paperwork, smiling at customers, examining properties, seeking Leonard Frye's approval on mortgages.

In retrospect, what was real and ordinary took on, in Mrs. Fitzgibbons's agitated spirit, the aspect of a nightmare. It might all have been a frightening, portent-laden dream, of sitting at a shiny little desk inside a great marble-columned room, indeed a magnificent, high-vaulted emporium, with its venerable dimensions, its twinkling dome, the long row of golden grilles of the tellers' windows — an almost celestial hall! — surrounded by a collection of witless, pasty-faced people, all of whom, like herself, were involved in nothing more meaningful than growing one day older every day.

The very first occasion on which Mrs. Fitzgibbons had found her tongue, as it were, and spoken out in anything like an egregious way, had occurred three weeks ago, on a Monday afternoon, while talking to a woman on the phone about the delinquency in her mortgage payments. It was not Mrs. Fitzgibbons's job to dun customers for promptness in payment, but the woman in question had asked Julie Marcotte, the telephone operator, to connect her to Mrs. Fitzgibbons, who had arranged her mortgage in the first place, and whom she evidently trusted and liked.

"If you're looking for a sympathetic ear," Mrs. Fitzgibbons had disabused the woman at once, "you're barking up the wrong tree."

Remarkable as it might seem, with that one line, Mrs. Fitzgibbons put behind her years of futile, soft-soaping diplomacy. She was sitting at her desk in the home loan department, with Connie McElligot bent over the desk in front of her, and Felix Hohenberger at the desk behind. As Mrs. Fitzgibbons gave the woman a piece of her mind, she swiveled sidelong in her chair and looked up importantly at the pale, splintered sunlight trembling in the pretty windows of the ceiling dome thirty-five feet above herself. She was frowning with her lips set in an unhappy expression as the woman on the line sought to explain in detail the reasons underlying her tardiness of payment. Mrs. Fitzgibbons remembered the couple. The woman was a garrulous talker who was constantly producing documents from her handbag, as though trying to demonstrate her pedigree; her husband, a plumber or electrician, was content to sit back and let his wife carry the ball.

There was little doubt that Mrs. Fitzgibbons's agitated spirit had been coming to a boil anyhow, but it was facilitated by the soft, liquid, flattering tones of the woman working her on the telephone. The woman was appealing to Mrs. Fitzgibbons's vanity and good nature.

Suddenly, Mrs. Fitzgibbons interrupted the woman, speaking up in a voice that carried. If anyone was unsure whether Mrs. Fitzgibbons was speaking to a customer of the bank, she left no doubt on that score.

"I don't care," she started scolding boldly, "whether you're three months late with your payment, or thirty-three!" She looked around as she spoke at the startled faces of her fellow officers and the timid customers sitting here and there on solitary chairs. Everyone was looking at her now.

"I thought you would understand," the woman on the phone was replying in a chastened, quailing voice.

"Oh, I do!" Mrs. Fitzgibbons came right back in a rising, ironical voice. "I understand only too well. Whom do you think you're dealing with? Your local grocer? We're your bank!" She pivoted importantly to her left, then back again, in her swivel chair. She struck an arrogant listening air. She flicked an invisible fleck of lint from her knee.

Everyone in the vicinity had fallen silent. They listened with pained, embarrassed expressions. Ignoring all, Mrs. Fitzgibbons picked up a memo from her desk and gave an impression of perusing idly the words thereon, while the woman spoke. She turned slowly this way and that in her chair. She was the focus of attention in the home loan department. "No," she said, suddenly, in a stern voice, "that's *not* good enough. I've been very patient with the two of you. I've given you every break in the book."

The rather frightening picture that Mrs. Fitzgibbons presented here of the cold-visaged creditor threatening ruin to some woebegone, disadvantaged soul on the other end of the line was certainly outlandish with regard to what her superiors expected of her. She was violating every unspoken rule in the book. However, Mrs. Fitzgibbons had grown impatient with superficial niceties; it satisfied her very warmly inside to put a hypocrite in her place. She listened for a moment to the woman wheedling in her ear, then terminated the matter in a decisive way.

"That's not what you're going to do," Mrs. Fitzgibbons ordered in a harsh voice. "I'm not going to wait three weeks. You will make a double payment on the tenth of the month. And you'll make it in person. I want to see the two of you here at my desk on the tenth of October. We're going to have a talk about this."

Mrs. Fitzgibbons felt magnificent. A sensual thrill ran through her blood.

"I'll tell you why," she reacted with an even bigger voice. "Because you and Jed are going to have to convince me that you can get your act together. We're not talking about your snowblower or your refrigerator. We're talking about your house. If you can't show me good faith, I'll turn it over to Maloney and Halpern for foreclosure proceedings. You'll come in here at ten A.M., on the tenth of the month, and ask for me, Mrs. Fitzgibbons. Both of you." With an elegant gesture, she hung up the telephone and got to her feet.

Everyone was staring sheepishly as she hurried past Mr. Hohenberger's desk, touching her hair as she went, and looking very much the part of the capitalist banker, vain and ruthless, contemptuous of the hardship of others. To her fellow officers, as well as to other bank employees, however, Mrs. Fitzgibbons's outburst was extraordinary to the point of pathology. Not a month or two ago, she was esteemed by all who knew her for her competence and sweet temper; but if any of her colleagues had doubted the testimony of their senses in recent days, this outburst settled the question. Mrs. Fitzgibbons had gone beyond the bounds of propriety.

The very next day, Mrs. Fitzgibbons was summoned to the office of her superior, Leonard Frye, the vice president of the home loan department. Mr. Frye and Mrs. Fitzgibbons were relative old hands at the Parish Bank, going back to the early 1970s, and had worked smoothly together all that time. As employer and employee, they were notably compatible. Lately, though, Mrs. Fitzgibbons had begun taking a less charitable view of her boss, as she saw some of the man's virtues as handicaps from a business standpoint. She saw his smiling, self-effacing manner as detrimental to the needs of a modern financial institution. The loan officers on his staff got away with murder. Further, the man was apathetic, too willing to limp along in the same old way rather than firing up his workers to get new business. When Mrs. Fitzgibbons looked about herself at the great imposing edifice of the bank, with its palatial marble columns and floors and glowing dome, the idea that a man like Leonard Frye, moping about in his well-worn, shiny-trousered blue suit, should occupy a position of dignity and importance here struck her as a near obscenity.

Consequently, when Leonard Frye requested that Mrs. Fitzgibbons report to his office, she was only too eager to do so. She went in with a chip on her shoulder. Moreover, as soon as Mr. Frye detected Mrs. Fitzgibbons's abrasive manner, he looked disheartened. He remarked on it at once.

"What's wrong, Frankie?" he said. "You're not yourself lately."

Mr. Frye was sincerely trying to fathom the revolutionary component in Mrs. Fitzgibbons's behavior. He sat behind his desk, staring worriedly at her through his ancient, amber-framed glasses. While known all her life as the soul of tact, she had no desire this morning to show the big man in the blue suit her conciliatory manner. Also, on this morning in particular, his wheyish complexion gave him an unusually aged look, as though he had added about ten years to his life in a week. Mrs. Fitzgibbons felt very different from that. She was revitalized; she was attractive, ambitious, on the move.

"I won't pull my punches," he said, employing a figure of speech that brought a wry smile to Mrs. Fitzgibbons's lips. "You've been very outspoken lately. Lots of people have noticed it."

"What if they have?"

"You see?" Leonard Frye set down his pencil. He was genuinely perplexed.

Mrs. Fitzgibbons watched him with a puzzled smirk and said nothing. She had begun dressing in a more fetching manner lately and was curious to see whether Mr. Frye would lose the thread of his thought were she to pause and cross her legs in a deliberate way while showing him a fixed, smoldering look.

Mr. Frye faltered. He took off his glasses. "Frankie," he said, "you're going to have to tell me what the trouble is. Connie McElligot said you spoke rudely to her and that you raised your voice three or four times to Mr. Donachie, the security guard, scolding him for looking sleepy on the job."

"I didn't speak to him for being sleepy," said Mrs. Fitzgibbons.

"That is your own complaint, I'm sure. I happen to like Mr. Donachie, because he's never afraid to interfere when a customer starts to act up. I corrected him," she said, "because he had his service cap on the back of his head, and another time for a loose necktie."

"But that's not your responsibility." He shrugged placatingly, pleased to relieve her of unnecessary concerns.

"As for Connie, I want her off my case." Mrs. Fitzgibbons's retort took the form of a demand. "She sends me deadbeats. I've told her a dozen times to deal with her own deadbeat customers. A week ago, she interrupted a closing of mine in the conference room to remind my client's lawyer that the exterminator's report, which was required on that transaction, wasn't available yet. Does that make sense?"

"No, it doesn't," said Mr. Frye, looking demoralized.

"Where does she shine in?" As Mrs. Fitzgibbons straightened in anger, she noticed he averted his eyes from the upward inclination of her breasts.

"I'll talk to her," he muttered.

What Mrs. Fitzgibbons said next was a choice instance of the boldness and unpredictability of her newfound assertiveness and gift of speech. She flung out the words without a moment's reflection.

"Everyone knows," she said, "and has known since long before Larry died, how I feel about you, Leonard." The remark was sternly put.

Mr. Frye's reaction was that of a man struck a blow on the head. He actually lurched in his chair.

"How what?"

"I feel about you. It's no secret. And I don't mind, so long as certain fat-legged busybodies don't go running behind my back trying to discredit me in the eyes of one of the few people I know that I really like and admire." Mrs. Fitzgibbons had relaxed once more, sitting back, and was showing Mr. Frye the calm, level, intense sort of look characteristic of persons involved in, or at least intent upon, romance.

"You know, Frankie," he persisted politely, "we almost never have strife among the personnel. And we're having an excellent year."

"I," Mrs. Fitzgibbons corrected him, "am having an excellent year."

"You're having a fine year."

"I'm having the best year I've ever had. I've done more business in the past six weeks than any four of them put together."

"Is that," he queried in a discreet voice, "why you've gotten so outspoken? Because you're outperforming the others?"

Mrs. Fitzgibbons affected bewilderment. She couldn't control her tongue. "What a mentality," she said.

"I'm not saying that it is that!" he was quick to point out.

"Listen to me, Leonard." Mrs. Fitzgibbons felt an overpowering need to take command of the moment. "In the past couple of years, I've had four or five job offers from other banks. The South Valley has made overtures, and so has Citizens. I'm not here today because I'm desperate." She was lying, but was not troubled by the blatant fiction of her claims, as she felt that these statements offered a more accurate appraisal of her worth than any measurable criteria. The sight of Mr. Frye sitting before her, in his old blue suit, with the three points of his starched white handkerchief showing, left Mrs. Fitzgibbons feeling that the first forty-five years of her life constituted a terrible joke.

"You're a good loan officer, Frankie," he said.

"I stayed because of you," she lied even further. Sitting close to his desk, she laid her arm on the shiny olive wood surface, offering to view the prettiness of her wrist and bracelet and of her pink manicured nails. "I want Connie off my neck," she told him.

"I'll talk to her, Frankie."

"You do that." In a second, it had flashed upon Mrs. Fitzgibbons that Leonard Frye could not summon the courage to fire her if he had a million years to do it. She regarded him with dismay and pity. This was the sort of vacant, neutered force to which she had paid loyalty all these years, believing in the meanwhile that her personal welfare and livelihood depended upon it. It was a revelation to her. The man was a leader in title only. If put to the test, he would be swept from his post in a twinkling. "I won't stand for it anymore," she said.

She spoke with the power of law. He listened in trepidation. She could feel it. The sharpness and unpredictability of her tongue hypnotized him. Leonard Frye yearned for peace and harmony and would have conceded anything to maintain it. Mrs. Fitzgibbons was not like that, not anymore; nor could she respect anyone who was. Leonard was wishy-washy. He was manipulable.

"You're not being fair to me, to let her insult me like that."

"I'll speak to her," he said.

"You know what I think of you, Leonard, and how that must affect me."

The vice president's resolve to reprimand Mrs. Fitzgibbons and warn her of the possible unhappy consequences of her strident behavior lately had ironically lost force upon contact with that very thing. She was very much in charge of the situation and was enjoying herself immensely. Even when it had become apparent that Mr. Frye considered the matter closed, she made no move to get up.

"We've been together for fourteen years. We've been through thick and thin," she argued in a fibrous voice. "If you're going to favor somebody above me, I'll go to work someplace else."

"I won't." He was clear on that point. His eyes were watery and shone a pale cloudy blue as he polished his glasses.

"You made the chairman give me a Christmas bonus my first year on the job. That was important to me."

"I don't remember that," he said.

"You did." That too was a lie, and Mrs. Fitzgibbons knew it was a lie, but no one in his right mind can resist such blandishments. After that, the falsifications poured out unrestrainedly.

"When Zabac promoted you to vice president, who in all the bank was happiest for you? I was." She continued to regard him with a stern, recriminatory look. Once or twice, the vice president's eyes strayed to Mrs. Fitzgibbons's breasts, which were moving agitatedly as she spoke. "I talked about you so much Larry used to get jealous. 'What is he, some kind of god?' Larry used to say."

Hearing that, the banker muttered something in embarrassment, adding, "Larry was a wonderful guy."

Mrs. Fitzgibbons was not smiling. "He was sick with envy. He used to worry that I wouldn't come home at night. He said my dresses were too tight. He said I wore too much perfume on the job. He accused me of being restless in bed." Her imagination ran on without hindrance. "That was why I avoided you the morning of the funeral," she said. "Do you remember?"

"I don't," said Mr. Frye.

"You don't remember my husband's funeral?"

"Of course, I remember the funeral —"

"I intentionally avoided you. I didn't even look at you. I tried not to think about you all morning."

Mr. Frye passed his hand before his face. He touched his lips with his fingers. He picked up his amber eyeglasses. He was in a visible muddle, astonished and confused. Mrs. Fitzgibbons's lips were pursed incriminatingly.

"Larry and I were a mistake. He knew it, and I knew it, and," she said, "I think you knew it."

"I didn't," he said, his tone as soft as that of a penitent in a confessional.

"From the beginning," she added harshly. "From day one."

Leonard Frye appeared to be searching his mind for something to say to her. At the moment, he reminded Mrs. Fitzgibbons of a tongue-tied secretary whose boss was making a pass at her, and who was both frightened and thrilled, and couldn't speak up.

"I'm afraid," Mr. Frye brought out at last, "that some of your remarks have come as a shock to me."

Having said that, the banker lapsed into a painful silence; his pallid face admitted tiny wine spots of embarrassment. Mrs. Fitzgibbons was left shaking her head in wonderment. His ineptitude was indescribable. She decided to let him squirm.

The vice president cleared his throat. "I've been thinking a lot about the Howell-McCann account," he said, in an astonishing change of subject, "and whether we can put that together."

Mrs. Fitzgibbons couldn't believe her ears.

"We're not here to talk about that," she said, inflamed momentarily by his digression. She had a half mind to say something outrageous, as about his fat wife, or even unleash an obscenity or two. Still, his next remark left scope for debate.

"We're not going to be able to talk anymore in such intimate terms," he said. He stared at her with colorless eyes.

"How on earth are we going to do it, then?" she said.

"We're not." He was finding his voice now. "We're going to go on just as before."

For the first time, she actually enjoyed the line he was taking. It seemed coy. She found it provocative.

"Believe me, Leonard, it's not going back to the way it was."

"Yes," he countered, "it is."

"All we'd be doing is protecting somebody whose appreciation of you isn't worth five cents."

"Are you talking about Ruth?" he exclaimed, invoking his wife by name.

"I'm talking about someone who has done nothing to help propel you one inch in your career, except to let herself go to the devil. You shouldn't even *be* in a town like this. Not at your stage of life. You could have done anything. How old are you? Fifty?"

"Yes."

"In the big banks," said Mrs. Fitzgibbons, "like the Morgan Guaranty or Citibank, men who couldn't carry your briefcase are promoted at age fifty into positions that pay an annual fortune. Do you know what Wall Street bankers take down in a year?"

Mr. Frye chuckled appreciatively.

"And you think," she went on, "that I'm going to let the two of us slip backward, now that we've brought this into the open? That's not a solution. I know what I'm talking about."

Leonard Frye glanced nervously at the closed door of his office, and as before passed his hand before his face.

Mrs. Fitzgibbons couldn't restrain herself. She had a compelling impulse to shock him. "That is not going to happen. I'm not going to let it. I'm not going to be lying home awake nights, masturbating," she said, "while you're dying of neglect up on Vassar Circle."

This last remark produced the most ossifying effect imaginable upon Mr. Frye. He turned to stone before her eyes. Although Mrs. Fitzgibbons continued to speak a moment longer, remarking on Mr. Frye's professional chances with an institution such as Chase

Manhattan in New York, it was apparent he was not making sense of her words. She left him sitting there, staring into space, as she went to fetch Connie McElligot.

She stood over Connie's desk and addressed her crossly. "Go see Leonard," she said. "He wants you."

Mrs. Fitzgibbons was not through making waves for the day. That afternoon she seized her red ballpoint pen and inscribed a most remarkable memo to Mr. Louis Zabac himself, the chairman of the bank, whose big sunlit office on the second floor, with its oil paintings, bronze statuary, and luxurious Chinese carpet, was more like that of a great statesman or national leader than the headquarters of a small-city banker.

She had no more patience for beating about the bush. The pathos of the frightened blue-suited man whom the powers that be had designated as her superior directed Mrs. Fitzgibbons's hand as she dashed off a few choice words:

Isn't it time, her scrawled memo read, *that an executive change was made down here? This department has fallen asleep!*

She signed the note very carefully so there could be no doubt as to its authorship, then signaled to Mr. Donachie, the security guard, to come to her. She liked the idea of the note being delivered upstairs by someone in uniform.

"You don't mind." She dealt the guard the envelope.

"Not a bit, Frankie." Mr. Donachie liked Mrs. Fitzgibbons, even though she had overstepped herself twice by commenting tartly on the state of his dress. In fact, in the past two or three weeks, whenever Mr. Donachie had overheard anyone criticizing Mrs. Fitzgibbons behind her back about the way she was puffing herself up and shooting off her mouth, he was quick to defend her. He had begun to admire Mrs. Fitzgibbons. He said he liked the way she had begun to show the assertive hidden side of her nature.

"Must be important," he cracked pleasantly, and waved the envelope.

Mrs. Fitzgibbons flashed Mr. Donachie a reproachful look that was not devoid of feminine allure. "You're just supposed to deliver it, Alec."

When she left work minutes later, going out the rear door to

the vestibule and street, Mr. Donachie was standing at his post by
the outside door. As she came past, he smiled and touched the
visor of his cap with his fingertips in the way of a polite military
salute. "All serene," he said. "Mission carried out."

Mrs. Fitzgibbons swept past him, her heels rattling on the marble
floor, nodding as she went, acknowledging the genuine respect
behind the playful manner. Alec Donachie was someone she could
rely on in a pinch.

She stepped briskly across the open-air mall toward the parking
garage. It was a lovely October afternoon. The sun dropping low
behind the spires of the towering city hall sent shafts of yellow
light ricocheting from the store windows to the sparkling granite
fountain and igniting the colorful leaves that blew across the red
brick walkway that was once the main street of the business district. She was going to get her car. She always walked hurriedly
these days, impelled by an unknown urgency.

For all her recent outbursts, and whatever worrisome signs she
might have betrayed, the fact was that Mrs. Fitzgibbons had truly
always hidden her light under a bushel. She could not remember
one instance in all her years when she had been asked to show
what she could do. She had played the part that life assigned her,
of caring wife and mother, and of responsible employee, an un-
witting champion of the very things that had obscured her light.
She was just a name that appeared on papers; a person of no
special account or personal history — walking up the ramp to the
parking garage at Maple and Main.

Sitting alone in her Honda, behind one of the steel columns,
Mrs. Fitzgibbons surrendered to feelings of pity for herself; she
pressed a Kleenex to the corner of her eye. She was recalling, by
chance, an evening many years earlier when, for just a minute or
so, she had asserted herself. On a winter night in 1960, as a member
of the Holy Rosary High School debating society, she had astonished herself by suddenly speaking out in the midst of a heated
argument, and dominated the stage for an impressive interval with
a brilliant, impromptu rebuttal of an opponent. To this day, she
could remember the silence of the audience of parents and faculty,
the hush on all sides, as she held forth in a commanding voice.

The words had leaped from her. She could still recall verbatim her impassioned conclusion, and of the way she turned and pointed a finger about indiscriminately, at this individual and that, both on stage and in the audience, saying, "These are not concerns of the so-called general public, but are *yours* — and *yours* — and *yours*." There was applause when she sat. She was trembling inside, as though the soul within her were shaking its cage to be let out. As it happened, of course, in her subsequent life that episode was not repeated; her triumph was a little candle glow burning somewhere in the past, soft, wavering, impermanent.

Mrs. Fitzgibbons shivered in the car. She wiped tears from her eyes with the tissue and blew her nose.

THREE

In the week to follow, events took a turn, or rather a double turn, that even Mrs. Fitzgibbons, for all her surging optimism, could not have foreseen. The first and lesser of these two unexpected developments arrived in the form of an elegant, curly-headed young man who came to her desk to make application for a home mortgage. Mrs. Fitzgibbons knew him by sight. He operated a hairdressing salon and beauty parlor in the indoor section of the mall next door to the bank, an establishment she had patronized herself once or twice. The young fellow, whose name was Bruce, was just a trifle effete in manner and appearance. More important, he showed Mrs. Fitzgibbons an attitude of cordiality and polite deference which she could not help warming to, as it harmonized comfortably with her own mounting self-esteem.

"I've been waiting for you to return from lunch," he said. "I didn't want to talk to anyone else. I was here one day last week, and while waiting to see Mr. Hohenberger, I heard you talking to someone on the telephone about their late payments, and decided that you were the businesslike sort of officer I'd like to talk to."

Mrs. Fitzgibbons liked him instantly. She liked everything about him. She liked his neatness of person, the good taste of his herringbone suit, white button-down Oxford cloth shirt, and paisley necktie, and his darkly polished, tasseled loafers, not to mention the immaculate, manicured look of his hands. Mrs. Fitzgibbons sat back in her chair.

"You don't remember me," he started to introduce himself.

"Of course, I do. You're Bruce Clayton. From the mall."

Her quick retort ignited the young man's face. He was sitting as straight as a rule before her. "You know me?"

Swiveling toward him, Mrs. Fitzgibbons rocked backward at the same time and showed him an expression of executive gravity that she was sure in advance he would enjoy seeing in her. "How can we help you, Bruce?"

"Well," he began softly, "a friend of mine and I would like to purchase a property. It's an eight-room house up on Homestead Avenue. The asking price is a hundred thousand dollars. It's probably a fool's errand, as we only have a few thousand dollars in cash."

"I wouldn't be so sure," Mrs. Fitzgibbons remarked encouragingly. The elegant young fellow was leaning forward stiffly in his seat now, hands clasped, and was fixing upon her a hopeful smile. Something about Mrs. Fitzgibbons's authoritarian manner on the telephone the previous week, when she had badgered and scolded that woman about her late payments, had obviously attracted the young man's interest.

"Who has the money?" she asked.

"I beg your pardon." Bruce colored guiltily. He couldn't comprehend the thrust of the loan officer's question.

Mrs. Fitzgibbons pressed him more emphatically. "Who is your friend?"

"His name," said Bruce, "is Matthew."

"Matthew what?"

"Matthew Dean."

"And what does Matthew do?" Mrs. Fitzgibbons was holding a long yellow pencil horizontally between the tips of her forefingers, her elbows resting comfortably on the padded arms of her chair. She noticed how Bruce repeatedly stole glances at her black pleated dress and stockinged legs. He wanted her to be important and officious.

"He's a computer programmer for the city. He works for Mary Daly, the tax assessor."

The fact that Bruce's friend worked for a woman brought a smile to Mrs. Fitzgibbons's lips. "Who has the money?" she asked again. "You, or Matthew?"

As earlier, the handsome, curly-headed man blushed. "I wouldn't want to insult you for the world," he said, "but may I ask, Mrs. Fitzgibbons, what bearing, exactly, that would have on the application?"

"It's simple," said she. "If Matthew has the money, you're doing the sensible thing to come here as you are. If it's your money, you should apply for the mortgage yourself."

"Oh, I see." The candor of the woman, combined with her obvious effort to favor him in any possible arrangement involving his friend, appealed both to Bruce's vanity and common sense.

She was still examining him over the outstretched yellow pencil. "Whose money is it, Bruce?"

"It's mine," he said.

Mrs. Fitzgibbons opened her hands to signify the obvious and flipped her pencil onto the desktop. "I think we can do business," she said.

Bruce Clayton didn't pretend to be nonchalant in the face of Mrs. Fitzgibbons's airy reply. His astonishment and admiration showed in his face. "Are you telling me, Mrs. Fitzgibbons, that it's possible?"

"It's better than that," she came right back at him. "I like you," she said. "I'd like to do business with you." Moments like this gave Mrs. Fitzgibbons a warm, flushed feeling that she could not recall having often experienced prior to this autumn. The look on the young man's face alone was worth a thousand dollars.

"Explain to Matthew," she counseled him, "how it will have to be." She revolved slowly to and fro in her chair, while wagging the toe of her black leather pump and staring at her admirer with an expression on her lips that bespoke the need for firmness in the face of personal considerations. It was a condescending look. "Tell

him I said so. Put the burden of blame on me." Mrs. Fitzgibbons
let that sink in. "It's going to be your house, Bruce."

The young man looked pale. He was shaking his head in wonderment. "I was so afraid it was all a hopeless proposition."

"Not at all."

"Can you be certain of the outcome even at this preliminary
stage?" he said.

"We're going to do business," she said firmly. "This *is* the outcome."

Up until now, in dealing with a customer like Bruce, Mrs.
Fitzgibbons would have portrayed herself as a model of caution; she would have been polite, informative, and attentive to
detail; she would have elicited a wealth of background material,
got it down on paper, and sent the young fellow away with a
dozen different forms to fill out and return. Now she operated
differently. Instead of the great abstract institution of the bank
arriving at ultimate decisions, to the delight or torment of the
applicant in question, Mrs. Fitzgibbons did it herself. Bureaucratic
procedures were replaced by flashes of intuition. At this same
moment, Mr. Frye had come out onto the floor from his office and
was quietly discussing certain specifics contained on the piece of
paper in his hand, and Mrs. Fitzgibbons, spotting him, capitalized
on his presence near at hand to compel Connie McElligot to do
her bidding.

"You're not busy," Mrs. Fitzgibbons said, and handed Connie
the young man's preliminary application form. "Give Bruce what
he needs to make formal application for a single-family home
mortgage."

The bossy tone of voice, combined with the presence nearby of
Mr. Frye, who had just chastised her in matters concerning Mrs.
Fitzgibbons, caused Connie to take the paper in hand without
demur. The fact that Mrs. Fitzgibbons's dictatorial voice caused
the vice president himself to glance over in astonishment only
heightened the air of menace, and further encouraged the other
woman to do as she was told.

As Bruce got quickly to his feet, to follow Connie's pink blouse
back to her desk, Mrs. Fitzgibbons halted him with a word. "I

want an appointment at your salon," she insisted, "for a consultation and a shampoo."

"That would be wonderful," he replied, flattered. "I'm booked for the afternoon but can give you an appointment any time tomorrow, Mrs. Fitzgibbons, or any day thereafter."

Mrs. Fitzgibbons waved that aside. "I'll be in this afternoon at four o'clock sharp."

"This afternoon is fine," Bruce said, reversing himself on the spot without a hint of hesitation. "I can easily make time for you."

In fact, Bruce was waiting at the door when Mrs. Fitzgibbons, about ten minutes late, came breezing in from the mall and sailed past him and past two of his girls who were tending customers under dryers. Peeling off her coat, she made for the rear. Within a second, Bruce had Mrs. Fitzgibbons's coat and scarf in hand and was seating her with a show of ceremony that concealed nothing of his feelings toward her. He switched off the radio, skipped away, and was back in a flash with a little glass of ruby port. To provide an extra measure of privacy, he opened out a hand-painted silk room divider. A month or two ago, Mrs. Fitzgibbons would have colored to the roots of her hair if anyone had shown her such fawning solicitude; but as she was coming to regard herself as one of the movers and shakers, and recognized also the young fellow's obvious need to associate himself with such a figure, his brisk and obeisant manner reinforced her vanity. She liked Bruce Clayton, but her appreciation of him was a balanced one, tempered by common sense. While he was affable and polite, and doubtless artistic in his ministrations, he was not more than that. (She guessed in passing that Bruce had a very fashionable, authoritarian mother somewhere, who probably telephoned him nightly to listen for a half hour or so to soap opera updates on his love affair with Matthew, dishing back dollops of maternal advice.)

Bruce didn't mince words with Mrs. Fitzgibbons, either, as he surmised from his brief knowledge of the woman that she liked candor. "I don't have to tell you," he enthused, "that I'm thrilled you want my help."

"You act it," she said.

"I'm so transparent!"

"Does that bother you?"

"Being transparent?"

"No," said Mrs. Fitzgibbons. "Being thrilled."

"Oh, not in the least! I want you to know. Why shouldn't I?" He adjusted a lamp in order to deflect the light from her eyes. "Having a client like yourself has to be a joy. Say," he said, "it puts me on the map."

"Are you always this charming?"

"I'm usually horrible." He hovered at her side. "Would you like to rest your feet?"

"Please." Mrs. Fitzgibbons lifted her legs, as Bruce slipped off her shoes. "You realize that I'm going to put through your loan. I hope your friend is agreeable to our putting your property solely in your name. That's the way I want to do it."

"I already spoke to him about it," Bruce admitted.

"Was he upset?" Mrs. Fitzgibbons employed a truculent tone that implied the need to be steadfast in such matters.

"I would say that he was more surprised than upset."

Mrs. Fitzgibbons made herself comfortable. "When Matthew has the money, let Matthew buy his own house. This way, when the two of you have a lovers' quarrel, you'll have the upper hand."

Turning away, the hairdresser blushed furiously.

"Sentiment has its place in bed," Mrs. Fitzgibbons added, "not on the dotted line of a home mortgage."

In short order, Mrs. Fitzgibbons agreed to a complete makeover and rested herself enjoyably as the talented young man busied himself about her. He was talking all the while, remarking on Mrs. Fitzgibbons's skin and complexion, and the strong points of her face. She had classic cheekbones, he said, a smooth, high forehead, prominent eyes, and beautiful lips; her natural beauty was a cosmetician's dream. He rattled off the trade names of a hundred different skin care products, citing various foundations, blushes, moisturizers, and cortisone creams. He worked at close range to her face, his voice an intimate whisper. Mrs. Fitzgibbons was touched by the realization that this attractive man had grown oddly infatuated with her and that the source of his feeling was her forcefulness. Her dark blue eyes followed him as he worked on her with his brushes and pencils. His adoration of her shone in his face. "This is what I do best," he spoke softly. "You have a face. You have character."

When Bruce faltered, Mrs. Fitzgibbons helped him. "I do understand."

Bruce laughed nervously; he shook his head. He was gazing at some microscopic point of interest on her face. "I doubt that."

She took from his hand the mirror he was about to give her and regarded herself. The effect, in fact, was remarkable. The face in the glass was composed with such artistry, the eyes luminous above the perfect angles of her cheekbones and the seductive golden red coloring of her mouth, she couldn't look away.

"I knew from the moment I laid eyes on you," he whispered, "I could do my best work with you."

While inspecting the beautiful mask of her face in the mirror, she reached absently for her empty glass. "Get me some more port." She spoke pleasantly while continuing to marvel over the transformation.

Bruce was back in a flash with the decanter. "You should look like that every day. I'll darken your hair just a fraction, and that will be perfect."

The warm sensation coursing through Mrs. Fitzgibbons's veins could not have been explained by the small amount of alcohol she had consumed.

While pouring, Bruce couldn't restrain his excitement. "You have it all, Mrs. Fitzgibbons. Eyes, lips, nose, temples, hair, everything."

"You'd better not let Matthew hear you."

"Matthew would be in raptures over you. He knows I'm working on you right now. I told him you were coming. He . . . wished me luck."

His constant pandering to her vanity, in combination with the genuine surge of enthusiasm she felt over her reflection, displaced any feelings of pity that Mrs. Fitzgibbons might have felt for the young man. She handed him the mirror. "You're gifted, Bruce. If you're worried that I won't come back, you can stop worrying."

"Why don't you come in every morning on your way to work and let me touch you up. I wouldn't charge you a cent."

"Don't be an ass."

Bruce stopped what he was doing. "I'm never going to charge you." He was mortified at the thought of it.

"I will not come to you if I can't pay." A trace of surliness appeared in her voice. She showed him an adamant eye.

Bruce stood before her in his shirtsleeves, nonplussed, his hazel eyes sparkling. He was sincerely perplexed.

"You're not being fair," he said.

Mrs. Fitzgibbons recognized the hopelessness of her position.

"Finish me up, then," she said. "If I can't pay you, I'll take you for cocktails. I'll take you out. I'll take you to Toto's."

"And you will come in mornings? Before work?"

"I'll come," she replied, "when the spirit takes me." She regarded him steadily. She knew that he wished to be handled with affectionate deprecation.

"But you will come regularly," he persisted in earnest.

For the first time, Mrs. Fitzgibbons gave scope to her waxing egoism. She turned in her chair and stated imperatively, "I am *sitting here,* Bruce!"

The timeliness of Mrs. Fitzgibbons's grooming and rejuvenated looks was evident the very next morning when she came into the bank from Bruce's salon in the mall, her face and hair made up so subtly and artistically that she was scarcely recognized by Julie Marcotte, the receptionist in the home mortgage department, and found on her desk a sealed envelope bearing the imprint of Mr. Louis Zabac himself, the president and chairman of the bank. The typed note inside consisted of a single sentence. It said, "Please come upstairs to me, Mrs. Fitzgibbons, first thing this morning."

Being optimistic these days, Mrs. Fitzgibbons could only guess that the summons to Louis Zabac's plush second-floor office portended something salutary, as she walked briskly across the plum carpet and climbed the brass-banistered stairway at the back. Her appearance was, in fact, compelling this morning, especially to those who knew her best and were most accustomed to her usual neat, unvarnished look. Her hair was soft and fluffy, and moved about in an attractive way as she walked; her eyes glowed with a dark blue fire that no one had noticed before. On the second floor, Miss Mielke, secretary to the chairman, watched as Mrs. Fitzgibbons darted past her desk, and without even troubling to knock, opened Mr. Zabac's door, and strode right in.

Downstairs, everyone had paused in their early-morning preparations for work to comment on what they had just seen. For the first time in memory, Frankie Fitzgibbons had not offered a single good-morning, or even so much as glanced at anybody, before tearing open the envelope, scanning its contents, then going on a beeline upstairs. Her magnificent appearance, added to the mystery of Mr. Zabac's summons, focused everyone's attention. Felix Hohenberger shook his head ruefully at what he guessed was about to happen to her, for by then Mrs. Fitzgibbons's outspoken behavior had become a talking point in the office. It couldn't go on this way, Felix had said. Others, like Julie the receptionist, felt that Mrs. Fitzgibbons's occasional flashes of egoism were too few and too recent to have caught the attention of the man upstairs. Anyhow, Mrs. Fitzgibbons's glamorous looks were of greater interest to Julie than the implications of her trip to the upper floor.

Connie McElligot, who had never liked Mrs. Fitzgibbons, but now both feared and detested her, could not conceal her bitter point of view. Not long after Mrs. Fitzgibbons vanished up the stairs, Connie nodded knowingly. "Mr. Zabac knows what's going on," she said.

This remark was undermined to some degree, however, in the next minute, when there came from upstairs the distant muffled sound of a man's laughter, followed instantly by the higher-pitched echo of Mrs. Fitzgibbons's own laughing rejoinder.

Despite his various titles as chairman and president of the institution, Mr. Zabac was effectively the owner of the Parish Bank. Twenty-five years earlier, he had wrested control of the bank away from the Fergus Cameron family, and since then had resisted a score of attractive takeover offers from out-of-town institutions. He liked his present life; coming to work three or four mornings a week, taking pulse of what was going on; convening a meeting from time to time with his chief subordinates; then heading home to indulge his favorite pastime, tending the big flower gardens behind his picture-book house, particularly his rose garden, which had become the glory of his later years.

Physically, Louis Zabac was a very small man. Unknown to most people, Mr. Zabac was the spitting image of his own father, a tiny, knotty-boned little fellow who had come to Ireland Parish, Massachusetts, from Estonia in 1920, and for years worked the streets of the city as a junk dealer. The elder Zabac was the epitome of his trade. An enigmatic man, he spoke with an accent, and was familiar to all, with his horse and wagon, his good-natured haggling and penny-pinching, and, in time, his accumulated wealth in real estate. Louis looked exactly like him, in features and stature. When Louis Zabac stood up behind his massive tulipwood desk and came round to greet his caller, he seemed to increase his height by only a bare inch or two, but his manner was so cordial and impressively self-assured as to dissipate in seconds the shock of his ridiculous appearance. He was a paragon of executive charm.

Sitting opposite him, her legs prettily crossed, Mrs. Fitzgibbons was able to appreciate the diminutive man on a level she had not considered before. Till now, Louis Zabac was a very remote personage, rather like the dictator of some small, far-off country, as he came stepping his way into the bank each morning, his little shoes gleaming like glass, a benign glow to his face. He spoke to no one on the floor, but proceeded upstairs to his office with an air of propriety so complete that he seemed almost an apparition. Had he ever actually stopped and spoken to someone downstairs, that person — and Mrs. Fitzgibbons was no exception — would have been thoroughly discombobulated. It was known, too, that the chairman never lost his temper. He never raised his voice to scold or correct someone. He never got flustered. He dictated his desires in a clear, uncompromising manner, whether in ordering the dismissal of a hapless employee or in ordering an increase in someone's year-end bonus.

The fact that Mr. Zabac opened his interview this morning with a smoothly put pleasantry, remarking cheerfully on Mrs. Fitzgibbons's enchanting appearance, did not, she knew, guarantee happy

intentions on his part. The story of Mr. Zabac's having complimented the bank's erstwhile chief financial officer, Mrs. Ida Man-
ning, on her mathematical brilliance just a minute before firing
her was legendary in the bank. Mrs. Fitzgibbons's response to his
compliment was consistent with her own intention, however.

"You don't suppose I'd come up here looking like a shoeshine
girl," she said.

It was at this point that Mr. Zabac had given out the deep,
throaty laugh that registered with those working downstairs, and
which was followed immediately by Mrs. Fitzgibbons's own mirth-
ful outburst.

"How on earth you could have fixed yourself up like this in two
minutes," he said, "will remain a mystery to me, Mrs. Fitzgibbons."

"I don't fix myself up," she came right back. "Others do that."

The briskness of her retort fixated the man for a split second.
He rubbed his palms together lightly. "I see, I see," he muttered.
He was clearly unprepared for the prepossessing figure before him.
To aggravate matters, Mrs. Fitzgibbons, who was never lately at
a loss for words, now remained scrupulously silent. She eyed the
little man levelly. She didn't move a muscle.

"You and I have not had the opportunity to speak for quite a
long while," he remarked at last, agreeably.

"We've never spoken," said Mrs. Fitzgibbons.

"Never?" He affected surprise. "In all these years?"

As before, Mrs. Fitzgibbons allowed his remark to go unan-
swered, but in the interim changed her position in her chair, while
consciously regulating her breathing and making a point of lifting
her chin speculatively. She was studying him all the while, but had
already concluded that this godlike man, in his exquisite cadet-
size Italian silk suit, intended to please her in some way. Besides
his having received her trenchant little memorandum of last Friday,
she guessed that word of her more forceful behavior, not to mention the amount and quality of the mortgage loans amassed in her
portfolio, had finally caught his notice. She couldn't help herself,
but at the moment her estimation of the entire staff of bank employees working downstairs was that they were a collection of

knuckleheads. Waiting no longer, Mrs. Fitzgibbons spoke up. She didn't beat about the bush. She put the question firmly.

"What do you want me to do for you?" she said.

Mr. Zabac reacted with a nervous laugh and got to his feet. His diminutive silhouette against the big plate glass window that looked out on city hall struck Mrs. Fitzgibbons as both sinister and comic.

"I would like to get your impression," said Mr. Zabac, making the point with nice precision, "of the Parish Bank's current position in the mortgage market."

Mrs. Fitzgibbons brushed a thread from her skirt. "We don't do enough business," she said. "Some people ought to be fired."

The chairman glanced round instantly. "You believe that?"

"You know it as well as I do." The grimace that twisted Mrs. Fitzgibbons's lips bespoke a world of shared understandings.

"I am surprised."

Mrs. Fitzgibbons's manic capabilities here shifted into overdrive, enabling her to express herself without significant forethought. "I'm not happy with it," she said, "and you're not, either. If you were, I wouldn't be here. It isn't like a few years ago, when Sam Cochran was cracking the whip downstairs. People came to work with clean fingernails and their hair brushed and combed. Everything went off like clockwork." She reverted to the memory of the bank's most celebrated past employee. Her voice hardened. "Sam did business!"

As she grew accustomed to the daylight shining behind Mr. Zabac's head, she was able to make out the unworried smile on his face.

"Aren't you exaggerating?" he inquired gently, in a melodious tone of voice.

"Am I?" She had an impulse to stand up and give him some sound advice but checked herself. Instead, she offered Mr. Zabac an ironical observation. "Is our share of the market bigger than it was back then?"

Mr. Zabac lifted an instructive finger. His black silhouette against the white glare of the autumn light, with his finger up, was like that of a little mountain gnome cautioning a heedless traveler.

"The nature of the business has changed since then, Mrs. Fitzgibbons. Your point is well taken, but remember, there has been a significant relaxation of controls upon us at the federal level. Today there are a lot of players in the business whose questionable loans are no less safeguarded by the government than our own solid investments. They take chances with their deposits that would have been unconscionable in the days of Mr. Cochran's tenure."

"Would you have any coffee?" Mrs. Fitzgibbons's sudden interruption came out not as an avoidance of the chairman's considered opinion on changing bank regulations, but rather in the spirit of a trusted colleague settling in for a serious tête-à-tête. Sometimes she liked talking about banking; she was especially in the mood to do so right now, as she and the man before her had reached what seemed a proper appreciation of one another. She was quite used to the idea now that the remote chairman, with his austere ways and impeccable bearing, esteemed her satisfactorily. While he went to the door and told Jeannine Mielke to telephone the Phoenix Lunch, Mrs. Fitzgibbons had turned around attractively in her chair and was apprising him of certain timeless fundamentals in the business. She had decided that she would wait until Mr. Zabac had seated himself once more before getting up herself and speaking on her feet, as she did not want to embarrass the little man.

"No matter what takes place at the Federal Reserve, or the Federal Home Loan Board," she said, "or in the back rooms of our unscrupulous competitors, there's no excuse for sloth and incompetence downstairs. In the end, efficiency makes the difference. That's always true, and you know it." She liked the fine timbre of her voice as she articulated this truism. "Efficiency alone," she stressed, "will win us back our share of the market."

Mr. Zabac could not conceal the charm he felt at Mrs. Fitzgibbons's surprisingly hard-nosed views and obvious good horse sense, as well as the results of her glamorous grooming. While he was returning to his desk, stepping blithely across the carpet on the balls of his feet, Mrs. Fitzgibbons smiled to realize how the sight of their coffee being carried up the hallowed staircase would impress those working below. She pictured Connie McElligot staring stupidly before her, the alarm writ big on her face.

"I would not have guessed, Mrs. Fitzgibbons, that you held such firm views on these matters. Is it your belief," he inquired in a soft, musical voice, "that the Parish Bank is on the slippery slide?" Mr. Zabac smiled pleasantly, his furry eyebrows going up, as he seated himself once more behind his big shiny desk.

She didn't mince words. "You know what's going on better than I do. There are some people here who ought to be fired."

Each time she expressed her hard line, Mr. Zabac's features contorted, and he stared at her acutely.

"I wouldn't fire them all in one day," she conceded. "You wouldn't want a panic down there. But I'd certainly frighten them into getting some work done."

Truth was, in all her years at the bank, Mrs. Fitzgibbons had never once adjudged the staff of the Parish Bank to be anything but typical of a firm of its size and type, nor certainly did it occur to her that Mr. Zabac might himself have harbored some worries of this very sort. Her next remark was inspired. "When everyone," she said, "is underperforming, no one notices it. How could they?" She waited with a frozen visage and set lips for Mr. Zabac to respond to that unanswerable conundrum before elaborating. "They all think they're doing wonderfully well down there."

Two or three times, Mrs. Fitzgibbons had mouthed the expression "down there," characterizing the workers toiling below as beings of a lesser dispensation than herself and Mr. Zabac. The soft colors and spaciousness of Louis Zabac's daylit office, with its racing prints and luxurious cream-and-blue Chinese carpet, only further emboldened her. She could understand why the natty little chairman never invited any of his tasteless fellow employees to join him up here; she imagined Leonard Frye standing as limp as a dishrag in front of the boss's big tulipwood desk, trembling in his shoes. As for herself, after only ten minutes in his company, she couldn't have felt more comfortable.

"I'd start with the tellers," she said, "the two De Maria brothers. I'd let them go first thing."

Mr. Zabac, after gaping momentarily, nodded sadly, as he acknowledged the wisdom in Mrs. Fitzgibbons's choices.

"We do have two or three tellers," he confessed, "whose tardiness, errors, and resultant late hours are costly."

Mrs. Fitzgibbons's confidence mounted apace. "I'd throw them both out." She was tempted to call Mr. Zabac by his first name but thought better of it. "Incompetents like that spoil our good name."

"Both of them?" said Mr. Zabac, unsure of himself.

"If you keep one, he'll only be bitter over our axing the other one."

Mr. Zabac winced at the word *axing* but could not dispute the woman's insight into the matter of sibling loyalty.

Mrs. Fitzgibbons added to the increasingly violent mood of their discussion, saying, "They should be sacked today, at three o'clock."

The little chairman took a deep breath, then laid his two hands flat on the desk before him. He looked regretful. He loved his employees. "I've been very patient with the De Marias," he said, "patient and forbearing. But when I asked you to come up here, Mrs. Fitzgibbons, it wasn't to discuss firing people."

"I'm not suggesting a reign of terror," Mrs. Fitzgibbons tossed out lightly, although, in truth, she would have liked nothing better than striking dread in the hearts of everyone in the place, "just some selective dismissals."

"At the moment," Mr. Zabac continued, recovering his smooth presidential manner, "while the home mortgage climate is robust enough in this region, I feel we may not be writing our share of the business."

"We're not." Mrs. Fitzgibbons reacted with characteristic certitude. Her instincts counseled a brutally frank manner. "Five years from now, when we're flat on our backs, we can blame this past year for it. Why," she snapped, "we're losing business left and right!" For the first time, a note of anger appeared in her voice.

When Jeannine Mielke entered the bank president's office, bearing a carton with their coffee containers, the luscious look of Mrs. Fitzgibbons sitting slantwise in her chair near the center of the room startled her noticeably. What was more, Mrs. Fitzgibbons was staring at her.

"There are two teacups in my desk downstairs, Jeannine. Get them for us, will you," Mrs. Fitzgibbons instructed.

Visibly shocked at being told what to do, and so arrogantly, by anyone other than the exalted chairman himself, Miss Mielke flashed Mr. Zabac a protesting glance. But the man behind the desk, mulling over Mrs. Fitzgibbons's last comment, was lost in reflection. Jeannine Mielke left the room with burning cheeks. As the door closed, Mrs. Fitzgibbons stood up. She wanted Mr. Zabac to understand that the views she was expressing were not the issue of an abstract mentality, but of her whole flesh-and-blood person. She stepped to the window where she shifted the heavy curtain sideways to kill the light on his desk. "I'm willing to do whatever's necessary," she said.

As before, Mr. Zabac attempted to steer the interview back to his original purposes. "Your own department," he said, "under Mr. Frye, has had, it is true, only a marginally successful year."

The sudden introduction by Mr. Zabac of her own boss's name prompted a spontaneous reaction from Mrs. Fitzgibbons. "Leonard is a nuts-and-bolts man."

"Nuts and bolts?" Mr. Zabac followed her with his eyes as she strode past his desk to her chair.

"He's good with numbers. Banking procedures, paperwork, back-room details." Sitting, Mrs. Fitzgibbons went further. "Leonard is good at overseeing stuff that is already in the pipeline."

The look of sad resignation that passed like a shadow across the little gentleman's face at this instant told Mrs. Fitzgibbons all she needed to know. "I'm not saying he should be let go," she conceded importantly, "but something drastic is in order."

"That," Mr. Zabac admitted, and he nodded, "is why I asked you to come up here."

"I know that." Mrs. Fitzgibbons made a face to signify the needlessness of overt explanations. At this time, anyone else would have kept silent in anticipation of the employer revealing his intentions, but Mrs. Fitzgibbons felt no such need to be tactful. "What are we going to do?" she said.

The exchange that followed evidenced Mrs. Fitzgibbons's capacity to cope with fast-moving developments:

"He is a loyal and capable officer," said Mr. Zabac.

"He should be kept," said Mrs. Fitzgibbons, nodding her instant agreement and showing her willingness to accept a quid pro quo.

"I've been thinking along the lines of giving our various loan officers greater autonomy. A freer hand," he continued.

"It won't work."

"Mrs. Fitzgibbons" — the chairman smiled pleasantly — "you haven't heard me out."

"They need a boss down there."

"May I?" He smiled patiently once more. "What I foresee is a greater sharing of authority."

"It won't work."

Lifting a diminutive pink hand, the chairman signaled once more for patience. "It might be preferable to certain alternatives. These, Mrs. Fitzgibbons, are the questions I've been pondering for a month."

"You can't demote a man by just a little bit, and then hope for the best."

"Am I imagining it, Mrs. Fitzgibbons," said the other, "or do you suppose that I asked you up here this morning to offer you Mr. Frye's post?"

"I know why you asked me."

"You do?"

"You're not happy. You want some results."

"For a week or two, I considered interviewing possible candidates from the outside."

Mrs. Fitzgibbons discharged that possibility with a sweep of her hand, knowing that he would surely not have told her that if he still intended to do it. She also guessed that he was enjoying the frankness of her opinions; her determination to make changes reassured him. He had not realized that he had such a knowledgeable and resolute figure downstairs. The look of satisfaction on the chairman's rather sallow face convinced Mrs. Fitzgibbons that all she needed to do now was to reach out and take what he had in hand for her — which she proceeded to do.

"This is my suggestion," she said. "Leonard and I will exchange posts. He'll go to my desk, and I to his. I'll do my best to cushion the shock by explaining that his technical skills aren't matched by anyone in the department, and so on, and so forth."

Louis Zabac was gazing across his desk in silence at the apparition of Mrs. Fitzgibbons sitting before him; he looked genuinely relieved to hear his new vice president taking such an empathetic attitude toward her fallen predecessor.

"I'll talk to him," Mr. Zabac added compassionately.

"Naturally." She sat back in her chair.

She would have said more, but Jeannine Mielke returned just then with their teacups and saucers. Besides, Mrs. Fitzgibbons thought it prudent to direct their discussion away from business matters for the moment, as the chairman was obviously distressed at having to demote Leonard Frye.

"What I would enjoy," Mrs. Fitzgibbons remarked graciously, while watching with an absent eye as Miss Mielke poured the coffee carefully from the containers into the china teacups, "would be to drive out and see your gardens one of these days. What are they like in the fall?" She drew her chair forward and positioned herself by the side of his desk next to her teacup.

"A proper garden," said Mr. Zabac, with pride, "is a treasure to the eye year-round."

"I've heard that said," she answered thoughtlessly, and dealt Mr. Zabac's secretary an icy, unfriendly smile. Jeannine was pouring the steaming coffee with maddening exactitude. Mrs. Fitzgibbons lost patience with her. "That's coffee, not nitroglycerin," she said. "Pour it into the cup."

No one in memory had spoken to Jeannine Mielke in so contemptuous a manner; the woman's proximity to Louis Zabac had long ago assured her inviolability; most employees trod softly in her presence. To Mrs. Fitzgibbons, however, who had herself always avoided contact with the quiet, officious woman, a new day had dawned. A new order was in place. Miss Mielke was a glorified clerk typist! But Mrs. Fitzgibbons concentrated on the little man in the Italian silk suit and turned to him.

"When would you like to show off your gardens? A Saturday would be convenient. I usually golf on Sundays."

"You amaze me, Mrs. Fitzgibbons."

"Golfing is good for business, even if," she amended, "I'd like to see the country club golf course developed for some luxury housing."

"It's a magnificent property," Mr. Zabac agreed.

"Magnificent isn't the word. It's the most spectacular acreage this side of Tibet."

"I'm afraid our local preservationists would raise an objection or two on that score." Mr. Zabac spoke with sweet reasonableness, his hands folded properly before him. He was enjoying her company.

"Preservationists!" Mrs. Fitzgibbons ridiculed such interests. It pleased her to sit in the bank chairman's office, his anemic-looking secretary hanging on every word she said, and show her contempt for such civic-minded do-gooders as might wish to oppose the destruction for profit of a golf course. She could picture her own daughter picketing the site. "When the bulldozers come, they change their tune."

Mr. Zabac laughed lightly at her wit, his bushy eyebrows bristling like two caterpillars.

"They see those steel treads churning up the grass and knocking over trees," she said, "and the little woodchucks and field mice running for their lives, and that's enough to convince even the dumbest among them. I'll give them preservationists."

The chairman and Mrs. Fitzgibbons reacted gaily to the comic picture she drew of environmental protesters fleeing tractors. When Miss Mielke departed the room, however, pulling the door silently shut behind her, the little man sat forward once again. He addressed his new vice president in his best businesslike manner.

"I hope, Mrs. Fitzgibbons, that you will not contemplate any impulsive moves, and, surely, that you will make no decisive steps without consulting me first."

"Not to worry, I'm not like that." She was stirring the sugar round and round with her spoon. "You do know that it's going to reflect well on all of us to have a woman as your chief home loan officer."

"That," he smiled, angelically, "was a factor, I must confess, in my deliberations, Mrs. Fitzgibbons, as well, of course, as your steadily improving record over the years with us. But I am happy to add that I was not nearly so convinced of the merits and rightness of my view yesterday as I am this morning, after hearing you out. I hadn't known you held such sound, strong views on the matters that we've taken up. But you seem," he said, "to have anticipated me. You knew what I desired from the outset."

"I knew what you needed." She raised her teacup to her lips. "I was surprised you didn't call on me sooner."

Mrs. Fitzgibbons rattled on about how she had been taking the pulse of the bank every day and was confident that he would summon her sooner or later; but she was thinking about how she would dress on the day she drove out to see his gardens. Mr. Zabac's wife had been invalided several years earlier, and Mrs. Fitzgibbons could imagine the poor thing sitting up in bed as Mr. Zabac introduced the two of them, and of how frightened out of her skull the woman would be at the great sight of herself wrapped up in some splashy concoction of a dress, with her longish legs, and her breasts pushed out scarily.

"I'll talk to Mr. Frye today," the chairman concluded with a note of regret. "I'll convince him of the necessity of the step, the wiseness of it, and, at the same time, of his own secure role in the new arrangement. He will understand."

"He'll have to."

"Now, now," said the chairman, smiling, exhibiting his even, godlike temperament, but revealing too his acceptance of her adamant remarks. "He's as solid as a rock, you know."

Mrs. Fitzgibbons was holding her saucer in one hand, her teacup in the other. She responded with visible forbearance. "If you insist on keeping him, I won't argue." Her open-mindedness on this point was as obvious as her soaring self-esteem. She wanted Mr. Zabac to know that she could accommodate him in the matter of her former boss, if only as a sop to the little man's softheartedness.

"Leonard can stay," she said. That was final.

"Shall we discuss salary?" he asked.

"Later will do," she said.

FOUR

Few individuals, probably in all history, have felt such a surge of pure egoistic excitement over their accession to power as that experienced by Mrs. Fitzgibbons as she descended the narrow marble staircase and glanced out over the great sprawling emporium of the bank. The symmetry of its tasteful yellow-shaded lamps glowing amid the double row of great, mottled marble pillars, the long rank of gleaming brass window grilles, the mahogany rails, and grand churchlike windows — all of it — summoned to her senses an impression of grandeur consonant with her bounding fortunes. The usual collection of early-morning customers was milling about in lines at the windows, under the watchful eye of the security guard standing casually before the ornate brass doors. As Mrs. Fitzgibbons made her way through the maze of desks and lamps, all eyes were upon her; but she noted with satisfaction that everyone looked down quickly as she came hurrying by. She had already decided not to wait for the chairman sitting upstairs to notify her predecessor of his demotion, but pushed open the door of Leonard Frye's office and walked in.

For a split second, Mr. Frye didn't even recognize her. He had not yet seen her this morning and was as unprepared as Mr. Zabac had been for the dramatic transformation that Bruce had brought to pass. However, if the vision of Mrs. Fitzgibbons was a happy one for the loan officer in the blue suit, the pleasure was fleeting.

While Mrs. Fitzgibbons was in an ebullient mood, with her color up and her physical movements charged with energy, she was not in a frame of mind to waste words with her fallen superior. Within ten minutes, Mr. Frye was sitting out in the loan department at Mrs. Fitzgibbons's desk, looking shell-shocked, while his secretary, Anita Stebbins, went about the melancholy business of transferring the contents of both desks. The exchange of posts was meanwhile naturally invigorating to Mrs. Fitzgibbons. She was exultant. At the same time, though, her manic, rapid-fire behavior suggested forethought, as in the way she instantly called to her office Julie Marcotte, the department's receptionist and telephone operator, and promoted her on the spot.

Mrs. Fitzgibbons was sitting behind her new desk, opening and shutting drawers, when Julie entered. "You're going to be my new secretary."

The girl in question had betrayed on occasion a sycophantic streak that appealed to Mrs. Fitzgibbons, a trait that Julie had unwittingly reinforced not an hour earlier when she had gasped with admiration at Mrs. Fitzgibbons's new look. Mrs. Fitzgibbons didn't need to ponder it. The telephone girl had just the sort of polite, smiling, deferential manner that the new head of the home loan department associated with streamlined efficiency on the job.

"You'll be responsible to me."

Startled by her stroke of good fortune, Julie's cheeks colored. She was thrilled.

"More responsibility," said Mrs. Fitzgibbons, "more work, and more money."

Anita Stebbins was in Mrs. Fitzgibbons's new office at the moment and couldn't help blurting out, anxiously, "Where will I go?"

"Mr. Frye will not have a secretary of his own." Reaching, Mrs. Fitzgibbons lifted an immense sheaf of papers from the bottom drawer of her desk and cast it into the wastebasket. She stood up. Anita Stebbins's fate at the Parish Bank was a nettlesome point.

"Go work for Mrs. Baskin with the part-time clerks. And clear out your desk. You have to make room for Julie," she said. "Julie, take down that hideous calendar and throw it out, and throw out that plant, and get rid of those two chairs. And put a brighter bulb in my desk lamp."

"Yes, Mrs. Fitzgibbons!"

"And tell Jack Greaney I want to see him."

"I'll send him right in, Mrs. Fitzgibbons." Julie was breathless over her sudden promotion to private secretary and was exhibiting the contagious effects of her superior's high-speed way of doing things. She started out the door at once but came back momentarily, blushing still with disbelief. "I'm so happy to work for you, Mrs. Fitzgibbons."

"And something else," Mrs. Fitzgibbons pointed a finger at the retreating back of Anita Stebbins, who was carrying Mr. Frye's personal effects to him in a cardboard box, "if I ever catch that girl, or anyone else, for that matter, in my office, you'll go to the wall."

Julie's eyes gleamed brightly with happiness. "Don't worry."

"I won't."

"No one will set foot in your office while I'm here."

"And don't put through any calls to me without telling me first who's calling."

"I understand." Julie faltered, then came back a step or two into Mrs. Fitzgibbons's office. "You know," she hesitated, "I can't type very well, Mrs. Fitzgibbons, or work a computer."

"Did I ask you if you could?"

After having just demolished Mr. Frye with news of his humiliating reversal, it gratified Mrs. Fitzgibbons to be able to make somebody happy, as Julie Marcotte was right this instant. She sat down in her comfortable leather-backed chair and gazed about the old-fashioned office, with its mahogany paneling and spacious dimensions. If Mrs. Fitzgibbons had given any thought whatever to the question of her authority over the tellers — which authority she had certainly not obtained from the president upstairs, nor which her predecessor had ever been permitted to exercise — the only form it took was her spontaneous rejection of its opposite.

"You wanted to see me, Frankie?" Jack Greaney, the head teller, who poked his head in at the door, was a slender young redhead, with a toothy smile and an amiable, ingratiating spirit, who had never made an enemy in his life. To Mrs. Fitzgibbons's mind, he had always seemed like an overgrown altar boy. Jack was light-complexioned, freckled, and lanky. He usually wore a bow tie, and he smiled from morning till night.

While she chafed at the idea of being called Frankie, Mrs. Fitzgibbons let it pass. She addressed him instead in the manner she would employ with all of them in the future. "Sit down, Jack," she enjoined him in a friendly tone. "I want to talk to you."

In fourteen years at the bank, she had never spoken thus to anyone on the staff, not even the handymen or the boy who worked afternoons in the mailroom.

Jack Greaney was grinning broadly, if sheepishly, with pink lights in his cheeks, as he sat. "Congratulations on your promotion!"

Mrs. Fitzgibbons waved aside the young redhead's felicitations.

Like everyone else, Jack Greaney was fairly astonished by the changes that had come over the woman sitting behind Leonard Frye's desk. It was as if she had generated a new personality; loquacious, where she had been soft-spoken and reticent; bold and very self-assured, where she had previously been unassuming; and most noticeable, quite beautiful, in her hair, makeup, and attire, the reverse of the woman he was used to seeing every day. In the moments to come, the look of astonishment that invaded Jack Greaney's features, as Mrs. Fitzgibbons instructed him in the method by which the two De Maria brothers were to be fired from their jobs at closing time, was so unimproveable that a camera would have recorded little more than an open mouth imprinted on a white plane.

"He's firing them?" Jack, referring to Mr. Zabac, was clearly taken off balance by the news.

"You needn't inquire where it's coming from," said Mrs. Fitzgibbons, feeling a rush of enjoyable spirits radiating upward within her, as Jack reacted appropriately to her dictum. He sat in his shirtsleeves on the edge of his chair, grimacing toothily.

"Both of them?" he said.

"You'll use Mr. Donachie. Have him on hand while they're collecting their things, and see the two of them personally out the back vestibule to the street. I want you to do that for me," she added unnecessarily, in a flash of vanity.

"But what did they do?" Jack countered.

She ignored the question. "The others can take notice that we won't be coddling idiots here any longer." Mrs. Fitzgibbons stressed the noun. "This is not a thrift shop, or some fly-by-night motel. We're going to be marching to a new drummer." Mrs. Fitzgibbons allowed the young fellow to digest her meanings and to gaze a moment longer on her sober, immobile face before completing her thought. "This is a bank!" she said.

Before the day was out, the entire staff had arrived at the obvious, if flawed, conclusion that Mrs. Fitzgibbons had known about her promotion all the while; that was why she had become so outspoken and assertive in recent days and would certainly have explained why she had come to work looking like a million dollars this morning. Who could argue with the logic in that? Madeleine LeClair, one of the tellers, predicted in a whisper that Mr. Frye was certain to resign, as no one, she said, could endure such a painful comedown; however, Pauline Smith, the elderly lady working the next window, disagreed in dismal tones, asking where a man of his age would be able to go. Later in the day, Mrs. Fitzgibbons called Connie McElligot into her office and sailed into her. She gave Connie a solid piece of her mind. Mr. Zabac had gone home for the day, so Mrs. Fitzgibbons felt no need to keep her voice down. On the contrary, dozens of people could hear her scolding of Connie through the open door.

Mrs. McElligot remained motionless throughout the tirade, looking stupefied in her chair. A red band of color traversed her forehead. She was at heart a bully, and like many of her kind was herself rather easily hectored. To Mrs. Fitzgibbons, the exercise was wonderfully cathartic; it crowned a day of triumph. Her mind jumped from subject to subject.

"Another thing. Three weeks ago, you were in here selling raffle tickets for the Blessed Sacrament's women's solidarity movement. Last summer," she said, "you were recruiting people for a church choir. I wouldn't be surprised to see you come huffing and puffing in here, pushing your big church organ in front of you!"

Connie was long known at the bank as a woman who couldn't open her mouth without boasting about her music and her position as organist at the Blessed Sacrament Church; she was oddly hypnotized by this line of attack, therefore, and looked upon the woman pacing methodically before her, with her creamy face and beautifully mascaraed eyes, as though Mrs. Fitzgibbons were the devil on earth.

"The nuns and priests of this world can stoke their own boilers," said Mrs. Fitzgibbons.

She would have said more, but Julie entered, carrying a basket of flowers with an enclosed note from Bruce. The word of her advancement was spreading. At this same time, Mrs. Fitzgibbons got a congratulatory call on the in-house line from Howard Brouillette, the vice president whose responsibility was to reduce the bank's loan risk by selling mortgages into the secondary market. Mr. Brouillette worked by himself at the opposite side of the bank, in a little cubbyhole office behind Mrs. Wilson's auto loan section; and on the strength of his rumpled, bespectacled appearance and his wizardry with technicals, was characterized by many of his coworkers as something of a geek. While Mrs. Fitzgibbons might have acknowledged the importance of other officers, like Neil Hooton, who was treasurer of the bank, or Mrs. Wilson, Howard Brouillette was *infra dig*. "I can't speak to you now," she said to him.

"You must be on cloud nine," Howard persisted in a gushing voice, but Mrs. Fitzgibbons hung up.

For the final hour, her office was a beehive of activity. After sending Connie back to work, she telephoned the local newspaper and told Sherman Resnic, who occupied the city desk and was a friend of hers from childhood, of her promotion at the bank. While on the phone, she sent Julie across the floor to the tellers' windows, to tell Jack Greaney to put his jacket on and to keep it on. At one point, she actually had three different employees in her office at the same time (as it happened, not a single one of them responsible to her) and was giving out suggestions that amounted to orders from on high, as from Mr. Zabac himself. One of these was the bank guard, Alec Donachie, who was kindly disposed toward Mrs. Fitzgibbons, anyhow, and appeared to enjoy everything about her these days, not the least of which was the way she had suddenly replaced her own boss and was now generating some excitement in the place. A dark, meaty blush came to Mr. Donachie's cheeks when Mrs. Fitzgibbons told him to go out and get himself a new uniform, something more "eye-catching," as she put it.

"Go to the uniform store in the mall. I don't want you looking like that." She frowned and waved a pretty hand at his faded gray jacket, his near-creaseless twill trousers, and the rather ugly sight of the tips of a pair of lumpy brown Oxford shoes. "I want you noticeable, but not as a duffel bag."

"You've got some right ideas, Mrs. Fitzgibbons."

"You look like you lost a war. The person who put you into those things should be shot dead."

"He is dead," said Mr. Donachie. "They belonged to old Bobby Bresnahan, remember?"

Mrs. Fitzgibbons couldn't conceal her liking for the stout, balding guard and flashed an agreeable smile at the way he fell in naturally with her high-handed remarks. He clearly welcomed her treating him with a steely affection that was both imperious and reassuring.

"Find something in black," she said. "They used to have a black uniform in the window that had a very smart cut to it. I want you in it. That's what I want. That and a black-visored cap, white shirt, black shoes polished like glass."

"Could I wear a little American flag pin in my lapel?" he was eager to know.

"Go back to your post now, but don't get lost out there. I have an important assignment for you this afternoon. If you show a little snap in the days to come — some style, Alec — I'll get you a raise."

"No fooling," he said, impressed.

Mrs. Fitzgibbons returned to her desk and sat down. She was

having a wonderful time, and, what was better, saw no conceivable end to it.

"You could do that?" he said.

"Go back to work." She didn't look up, but reached for her pen and appointment calendar.

At the door, Mr. Donachie turned back. He had straightened his cap and pulled ceremoniously on his lapels but appeared perplexed.

"What, exactly, is the nature," he inquired, "of the important assignment for this afternoon?"

"You'll be called when the time comes." She looked at him with a blank face that both challenged and dismissed his curiosity.

Interestingly, in the next thirty minutes, Mrs. Fitzgibbons forgot all about it herself. At about ten minutes after three, with the doors locked, as the bank staff settled down to complete their end-of-day computations and paperwork, Mrs. Fitzgibbons departed her office for the day. As she strode across the gleaming marble space adjacent to the tellers' windows, her path intersected with that of the security guard and the head teller. Jack Greaney and Mr. Donachie had just emerged from the ornate glass door that led into the tellers' work space, and between them were the two De Maria brothers. The two brothers wore dolorous expressions, their oval balding heads shining with an olive hue, their lips compressed. Jack Greaney was leading the way and was plainly uncomfortable at being forced to carry out the task of firing and expelling two of his men, while Mr. Donachie brought up the rear.

"Why us?" said Laurence De Maria, the stouter and more effusive of the two. He was staring with hatred at Mrs. Fitzgibbons, as she came striding past them. "What'd we do? Kill somebody? . . . What am I, an embezzler?"

Mrs. Fitzgibbons showed a look of disgust at the indecorousness of the man's remarks and went on elegantly before them toward the door.

"Thinks she's a bigshot," said Morris De Maria, the younger of the two, whose eyes were reddened and inflamed with tears.

"Who told you you could run a bank?" Laurence De Maria called after her viciously.

"Thinks she's a Rockefeller," said the other.

"Well, she's not!" Laurence was furious. His dark eyes bulged ominously. "You can't run a bank!" he shouted.

Worse luck, Mrs. Fitzgibbons had to stop at the rear door and wait till Alec Donachie came forward and unlocked it. The De Marias were right at her elbow. Laurence was fit to be tied. His swarthy cheeks glowed purple. He continued to lash away at Mrs. Fitzgibbons while leering at her. Mrs. Fitzgibbons, who was significantly taller than the De Marias, waited with a pinched, arrogant expression and stared at the door while Mr. Donachie fished out his key. Not long ago, she had looked on the De Maria brothers as a playful, likable pair, a couple of chatty practical jokers who leavened the formal atmosphere of the bank on quiet days with their harmless high jinks. As the guard inserted the key in the door, Jack Greaney stood to one side, clasping and unclasping his hands; he was wearing his suit jacket now; a sickly smile twisted his lips; he was mortified by his role in the events.

"Why don't you shoot us?" Laurence shouted at her.

"She can't fire people."

"We want our severance pay, lady. I'm not kidding you."

Mr. Donachie held out his arm in such a way as to obstruct the brothers from preceding Mrs. Fitzgibbons out the door. Alec's deference was not lost on Mrs. Fitzgibbons; she nodded fractionally as she stepped past him. "Throw them out," she said.

Hearing that, the De Marias came scampering after her in the vestibule that led to the street. The newsdealer in the lobby stared up at the sight of the two gnomish brothers chasing the elegant woman.

"*Throw them out!*" One of them mimicked her in a high-pitched voice. "You'll be hearing from us!"

"We've got rights."

"Look at her, with her fancy-ass way of walking all of a sudden. A fancy ass! *Throw them out?*"

A scattering of yellowed poplar leaves blew past with a scratching sound on the red-brick pavement of the open-air quadrangle. The granite fountain twinkled in the sun. Mrs. Fitzgibbons walked with her head in the air.

"Thinks she's in the movies."

"We've got benefits coming, lady."

As Mrs. Fitzgibbons lengthened the distance between them, Laurence loosed an obscene parting shot. "She's got her snatch out for everything that moves."

He followed her partway up the ramp to the garage. "Big-shot lousy cunt! We want our severance pay!"

FIVE

For a day or so, Mrs. Fitzgibbons concentrated her attention on some of the more superficial aspects of her new job, such as sending Julie to the stationery store to order new letterhead and giving her signed approval to mortgage loans that Leonard Frye had already endorsed. Her only business decision came on Thursday afternoon in response to Felix Hohenberger's description of a garden apartments project on Lower Westfield Road which he wanted the bank to fund, but the soundness of which Mr. Frye had questioned.

"Do it, Felix," said Mrs. Fitzgibbons. "I like it."

"Zellan and Downey are pretty good businessmen," he explained, prepared to repeat at length the arguments he had earlier expounded to Mrs. Fitzgibbons's conservative predecessor. Mrs. Fitzgibbons was having her afternoon coffee, which Julie had brought to her on a pretty black-and-red-lacquered tray, and the last thing she wanted to hear was Felix Hohenberger enlarging for twenty minutes on the character and creditworthiness of his borrowers. She dismissed him with a wave of her teacup, in a manner Felix was not used to. "I want it, Felix. Write it for me," she said.

The backs of Felix's ears glowed like two tomato slices as he went out the door, a reaction that Mrs. Fitzgibbons was quick to notice. Her officers did not seem to understand, evidently, that their tenure was a day-to-day proposition. Mrs. Fitzgibbons sent Julie into the mall then to get her some stockings at Fogel's, a mother-of-pearl compact she had admired at Stearn's Jewelers, and some herbal teas at the specialty food store, and, while the girl was gone, returned a call from Sherman Resnic at the newspaper. Sherman had heard more about the "Parish Bank shakeup," as he called it, and asked Mrs. Fitzgibbons to comment on the extent of the changes. He wanted to write it, he said.

"Send a reporter," Mrs. Fitzgibbons replied.

"I was too busy to talk yesterday but was happy to hear the good news. I'll give you a nice spread, Frankie."

"I'm glad. Send a photographer with him."

"That's automatic. What time?"

"Eleven," she answered. She could picture Sherman sitting at his desk at the *Ireland Parish Telegram,* and remembered him from childhood as a polite, studious, wet-lipped young lecher who followed women in the street and was actually arrested for it once in the lobby of the Victory Theatre. Sherman was known for his off-color puns, one of which he retailed at this moment.

"I'd like to come myself," he said.

"Please," Mrs. Fitzgibbons cut him off, "I haven't got time for this."

On Friday morning, before the newsmen arrived, Mrs. Fitzgibbons sent Julie upstairs with a written request that would empower her to enforce a dress code on the entire staff of the bank. Julie returned right away, saying that Mr. Zabac had not come in yet. Later, Mrs. Fitzgibbons sent her to the second floor again, this time bearing two requests. The second typewritten note asked the chairman to grant Mrs. Fitzgibbons authority over staff personnel in the vague but important area of bank-customer relations — that is, the code of conduct which bank employees were expected to observe in dealing with depositors and loan applicants. With such seemingly innocuous powers in hand, Mrs. Fitzgibbons felt confident that she could quietly extend her authority across departmental lines, and thus undercut the authority of certain important officers, such as Neil Hooton and Mrs. Elizabeth Wilson, whom she now regarded as her adversaries. When Julie came back downstairs with the requests in hand and stated that Mr. Zabac would not be coming to work today, Mrs. Fitzgibbons was greeting the men from the newspaper.

If, until now, the brilliant transformation in Mrs. Fitzgibbons's attire and grooming had been such as to attract the notice and admiration of others, those efforts were nothing compared to the results on parade this morning. She was wearing a very costly Emanuel Ungaro wrap dress that Bruce had helped her select the previous evening. It was poison green, and gave Mrs. Fitzgibbons a slender, luminous appearance that even she might have thought impossible. (In his salon that morning, Bruce went into raptures at the sight of her; he actually set his hands flat to his face when she peeled off her coat and sat down to be worked on.)

Spotting the memos in Julie Marcotte's hand, Mrs. Fitzgibbons seized the opportunity to exhibit her newfound authority in the presence of the newspapermen.

"Tell Jeannine Mielke to get down here," she said.

"Yes, Mrs. Fitzgibbons." Julie darted out the door like a messenger in combat.

Without preamble, Mrs. Fitzgibbons launched into an account of her promotion to vice president and the reasons underlying the chairman's decisions. As she explained it, though, it sounded as though her advancement owed more to destiny than to any person overseeing such changes. "The time had come," she said. "We had to put forward more aggressive leadership, a change on the executive level that would make a difference. Mortgage banking isn't what it used to be. Today," said Mrs. Fitzgibbons, as she closed her office door, "you have to find a way to be both cautious and daring."

She liked the sound of that. It had come to her lips without hesitation. Clearly, the ability to speak out confidently, without a slip, or without even having to think concentratedly, was on the order of a minor miracle; a gift locked away inside her all these years. With the proper encouragement, these energies should have been released long ago. Sometimes, such as now, her performance excited vital sensations, a satisfying tautness in her leg muscles, a tingling in her breasts, a sudden hormonal rush that compelled her to get up and move about. She paced across the room to her desk.

"We're serving notice on everyone, from Albany to Boston, that we're going to be major players here. If that weren't the case, I wouldn't be standing in this office today."

"That sounds like a mandate." The reporter spoke jocularly. He had begun writing rapidly in a long, narrow notebook.

Mrs. Fitzgibbons laughed with great charm. "My mandate is to smash the competition."

"And will you?"

"I will do just that. Any bank," Mrs. Fitzgibbons specified very firmly, "that is not operating in our region today, will come into our region over my dead body." Mrs. Fitzgibbons looked genuinely determined and flashed her eyes belligerently to dissuade the reporter from interrupting her (as to ask perhaps about the trend among certain invasive big-city banks). "On that point, I will not give an inch. I'll tell you something else. The region in which we operate, and which we intend to dominate and protect, is forty-percent bigger this morning than it was yesterday afternoon."

"That is news," piped the reporter, who was a cheerful soul, and was transcribing her words to paper with lightning speed. At the same moment, the photographer took his first picture of Mrs. Fitzgibbons. "Sounds like a war," the newsman put in genially.

"It won't be war," said Mrs. Fitzgibbons, reverting to her lighter, more winning manner. "We're just going to play ball on a bigger field."

"In which direction will you expand? Springfield?"

"No. Not right away," Mrs. Fitzgibbons said, responding firmly on subjects she had not thought about for a minute. "There are a hundred towns north, east, and west of us, up in the hinterlands, waiting and praying for us to come up there."

"There are also banks up there," the newsman cracked.

Mrs. Fitzgibbons gave a derisive shout. She liked the reporter. It was clear from his ironical remarks that he appreciated the loaded quality of her statements.

"There are banks and there are banks," she remarked sarcastically, and then continued to delineate her views, as the photographer took a series of seven or eight shots of her. "We're going to bring those people some relief from the shoddy business practices they've been getting up there for about a hundred years. I'm going in," she said, "and I'm going to get what I'm after, and consolidate it, and then I'll look around for bigger opportunities. I don't want to pick a fight with a bank in one direction while forty or fifty unprincipled little fly-by-nights are bilking my friends and calling me names behind my back. You can quote me on that."

"I'm quoting you on everything," he said, and laughed.

"We've outgrown the competition," said Mrs. Fitzgibbons, "and we've outgrown the sleepy managers, here and elsewhere, who sit on their hands, and fart and burp, and —"

The photographer convulsed with laughter over Mrs. Fitzgibbons's unexpected vulgarism.

"I won't quote you on that," said the reporter, just as a rap came to the door and Julie peeked in.

"Miss Mielke is here." She widened the door to reveal the figure of Mr. Zabac's private secretary standing next to her. The bony, blond woman from upstairs stood with her mouth ajar, stunned at Mrs. Fitzgibbons's temerity in summoning her, but perplexed as well by the sight both of the newsmen and of Mrs. Fitzgibbons's radiant attire.

"Where is Mr. Zabac?" Mrs. Fitzgibbons rapped out, even though Julie had already informed her.

"He won't be in today," said Jeannine Mielke.

"Why did you return my memos?" Mrs. Fitzgibbons was demonstrating to her two guests from the media how underlings get talked to in a modern-day financial institution — and at the same time exorcising some devil in herself which had led her to believe in past times that she was no better than this anemic, phony-assed excuse for a human being who stood gaping in at her.

"Well," Miss Mielke retorted, a trifle apologetically this time, "he said he wouldn't be in."

"Put them on his desk! Use your head!"

After Mr. Zabac's secretary had hurried away, Mrs. Fitzgibbons remarked, "That is what you get these days for eight bucks an hour — an appliance who leaves her batteries at home."

"Mrs. Fitzgibbons," the reporter spoke up curiously, "would I be right in concluding that you are, in fact, the new chief executive officer of the Parish Bank?"

"I'll explain the situation. Louis Zabac is the finest, smartest, fairest banker in the Commonwealth of Massachusetts — in all New England — besides being a marvel to work for. The man is varsity. He's a prince." She imagined the chairman sitting at home in his little Giorgio Armani suit, reading these extravagant accolades in tomorrow's newspaper. She had turned to the photographer to permit him some good frontal shots. "Louis is my hero. I'd go to the ends of the earth for him. He's what I'd want my son to be like, if I had a son."

"You have a daughter, don't you, Mrs. Fitzgibbons. A teacher?"

"My daughter believes that glass pyramids have supernatural powers in them and that you can generate a sixth sense by listening to synthesizer music while chewing Sen-Sen. Barbara is so liberal that she cleans up behind her dog with her bare hands. If you so much as include her name in this article, I'll close both your savings accounts. Do you *have* accounts here?"

"I do, he doesn't," answered the reporter, chuckling.

"You're not a depositor?" Mrs. Fitzgibbons turned on the man with the camera and showed him a look that advertised better than anything so far the artistry of her cosmetician. Her face glowed like alabaster. She pouted.

"I'm not, but I'm going to be," came his singsong reply.

"I should hope so. Julie," she called, "get this gentleman an account application from René. The Golden Access application."

"Could I get a shot of you leaning against your desk?" he said.

"Why not." Already, Mrs. Fitzgibbons's interview with the *Telegram* was pleasurable to all. She could feel their enthusiasm. They wanted her to be witty, to boast, be aggressive and outspoken. Mrs. Fitzgibbons came round the desk once more, leaned her buttocks against it, and continued with vivacity about the new administration, while the cameraman backed up to the door and took full-length shots.

"We're going to promote like the devil, but we're going to do it with taste. If you walk out of here with a toaster, it will be because you walked in with one. If our growth curve doesn't take off for the moon," said Mrs. Fitzgibbons, parroting words she had come across that morning in the *Wall Street Journal* while Bruce was blow-drying her hair, "if my quarterly projections aren't met, I can promise you, heads will roll." She waited for the reporter to get it down. "I'm here to double and treble our results. I'm not going to tolerate more of the same."

"Mrs. Fitzgibbons," the reporter interrupted, as before, "are you, in fact, the chief executive officer of this bank?"

"I am," she said, decisively, at last.

"You are."

"Yes."

"Well, that is news," he sang, while scribbling in his leather-bound pad.

Mrs. Fitzgibbons's outrageous assertion, although thrown out impulsively, was not altogether impromptu; the idea had been flitting in and out of her brain for a few minutes, so that when the words actually left her mouth, she felt relief, a sense of having kicked a senseless obstacle from her path.

"Are you aware," said he, "that you are the first woman to serve as chief executive officer of a bank in the entire area?"

"How could I not be?" she countered. "Mr. Zabac is a pioneer. The man is progressive. He knows what he wants, he knows what's right, he's not sexist, or small-minded, or parochial in any way. He wants the best he can get. I'm going to give him what he wants."

Mrs. Fitzgibbons's invoking of Mr. Zabac was a conscious lie, the recognition of which only fueled her indignation; she was alive to the fact that she was seizing the post, and would deal with her enemies and detractors as they came to her.

"Will you be bringing in new blood?" asked the reporter.

"I'm the new blood!"

"Zabac retiring?"

"Louis will never retire. Behind the quiet facade, the man is a powerhouse. He'll live to be a hundred. He'll bury us all." Mrs. Fitzgibbons couldn't stop talking.

While she was revealing at some length the unpropitious fate that lay in store for the banks nearer at hand, that is, the chief competitors in town, Mr. Donachie, the guard, came to show off his new uniform.

"Those are the institutions," Mrs. Fitzgibbons was saying, "that are most imperiled by what is happening here today at Maple and Main."

"Look, Mrs. Fitzgibbons." Mr. Donachie signaled from the doorway, then gestured with his chubby fingertips at the outfit he had just acquired. The effect *was* eye-catching. The black uniform he wore, and the glistening black cap that shaded his eyes, formed a faintly sinister picture that was ameliorated very little by Mr. Donachie's swelling paunch or by the little brass American flag on his lapel. Mrs. Fitzgibbons didn't pause to comment on Mr. Donachie's satanic appearance, or even to look twice, as she was caught up in her own train of thought.

"They're the ones that will feel the pinch," she promised. "They're the ones for whom insolvency could become more than just a word."

Both the reporter and photographer were staring at Alec Donachie.

"Mortgage finance is my business. I'm committing us to growth. I intend to increase incoming deposits and the depth of our loan portfolio by more than thirty percent this year. Now, that's going to hurt somebody. It's got to. Let's be realistic. Our capital-to-assets ratio is the envy of the region. We have the muscle." Mrs. Fitzgibbons recalled a statement made by Mr. Brouillette in a recent conference. "For a year now, the spread between the cost of funds and the yield on loans has been under severe pressure. Those that can endure the pressure in the months ahead will survive, and over the long run will actually prosper at the expense of others. The day of reckoning" — Mrs. Fitzgibbons felt angry juices in her blood — "is coming fast for our competitors. I won't mention their names, but I have the wherewithal to drive them into a corner! — *and* I have the will."

Mr. Donachie had gone back to his post. The reporter was scratching furiously in his notebook. While being photographed, Mrs. Fitzgibbons was leaning against her desk, gesturing with her fist. The words bubbled forth with spontaneity.

"We've waited patiently for this day," she said.

"You have known for some while, then," the reporter prompted, "that you were to be named CEO."

"We don't jump impulsively. When the time is ripe, as it is now, we like nothing better than to take off the gloves. Our competitors are not cost-effective. They're already headed into the red, and, believe me, it's going to get much worse. They're going to be dripping in the stuff! The red'll be coming out their ears!" she exclaimed hotly, causing both newspapermen to glance up instinctively.

She had a vision at that moment of Mr. Curtin Schreffler, president of the nearby Citizens Savings Bank, a man of exquisite tailoring and a rather sniffy hauteur, being dragged out the front door of his bank by a couple of shirtsleeved, big-bellied city marshals and thrown into an unmarked sedan.

"It's not going to help them to discover, today or tomorrow, what's in store for them." Mrs. Fitzgibbons ridiculed her enemies. "The people I speak for, and I speak for every prudent, honest-minded human being that lives and works in this valley, and every person, young and old, and the not so young and not so old, who are entitled to home ownership and a decent yield on their hard-earned money — the people I speak for are fed up with the shady dealings, the nosiness, the extra charges, the impoliteness, the inconsistency, the mathematical errors, the stupid late-night television advertising, the deaf and dumb tellers, the insensitivity" — Mrs. Fitzgibbons was in high gear and could have gone on like this all afternoon — "the rudeness, slovenliness, and incompetence that these local-yokel operators *purvey*" — she waited for the reporter to catch up — "as their ordinary day-to-day bilk-the-other-guy way of doing business."

"Wow," the photographer put in.

"I'm getting it," said the reporter. "We're fine, Mrs. Fitz."

"I'm going to overrun them!" she said.

Until now, Mrs. Fitzgibbons's oratorical skills had been just a memory, a winter's evening in high school when she had suddenly taken the floor to dominate a debate. Julie and two or three others had collected outside the door, blinking in unison each time the camera flash went off. Mrs. Fitzgibbons had the wind up, her blood coursing with excitement.

"I'm not going around them, I'm going to roll over them."

While speaking, she saw Mr. Neil Hooton go treading softly past her door. He peered in at her suspiciously, then glanced away. Of all the officers at the bank, Mr. Hooton had always best satisfied Mrs. Fitzgibbons's idea of what a successful banker ought to look like. A portly man with a headful of snowy hair, he wore little gold spectacles far down on his nose and had a taste for colorful suspenders and bow ties. Since her first days at the bank, she had admired him; she had sought his help and approval on a thousand occasions, even though his responsibilities as treasurer and director of the capital markets desk differed categorically from her own. Moreover, since the start of the monumental bull market that got under way in the summer of '82, with the Dow averages surging higher and higher year after year, Mr. Hooton's star had risen commensurately, to a point where it was generally recognized that any sort of emergency at the bank that might have incapacitated Mr. Zabac, as to require his staying at home, would have seen Neil Hooton mounting the marble staircase to take his place.

Later on, as Mrs. Fitzgibbons was showing the newspapermen out of her office, Mr. Hooton came back the other way. The stock market in New York was down significantly that Friday afternoon, and the man was pulling a long face. He strutted past her with an angry frown. Tiny pinpoints of paranoia assembled in Mrs. Fitzgibbons's pupils, as she stared daggers at him. That quickly, the stoutish man had materialized as her most dangerous adversary. She stared fixedly in the direction of the treasurer's office long after Mr. Hooton had passed from view.

Julie was waiting patiently nearby for Mrs. Fitzgibbons to acknowledge her presence. Anita Stebbins was standing next to Julie.

"Mrs. Baskin doesn't need Anita," Julie said, unable to conceal the satisfaction she was experiencing at treating Mr. Frye's former secretary as a basket case. Anita was gaping at Mrs. Fitzgibbons. The flash of resentment she had shown yesterday on being removed from her job had given place now to a helpless, simpering expression.

"Mrs. Baskin said I was overqualified." Anita smiled ingratiatingly.

"Is that a fact?" Mrs. Fitzgibbons was still smoldering inside over the spectacle of Mr. Hooton marching past like an important financier, so that the sudden opportunity to fire somebody presented itself as a cathartic relief; in fact, it aroused physical sensations in Mrs. Fitzgibbons that she would have been ashamed to describe.

"What are you qualified to do?" she asked harshly.

"I know word processing."

"Come along, speak up. Tell me what you can do." Mrs. Fitzgibbons snapped out the words with great impatience.

"I type seventy words a minute, I know word processing, I've helped Jacqueline Harvey do payroll — I've been secretary to Mr. Frye since May of eighty-six — and back in the summer of —"

"You're superfluous staff!" said Mrs. Fitzgibbons, unable to hold back a second longer. "I see no place for you here."

"Please, Mrs. Fitzgibbons." Anita was a pretty, dark-haired girl, who had never made an enemy.

"You're finished." Mrs. Fitzgibbons was implacable.

"But I understand the bank."

"Well, you go understand another bank." She dismissed Anita in an even bigger voice, her eyes widened in consternation at the girl daring to answer her back.

"But, why?" Anita implored to know.

"Hold on, now," exclaimed Mr. Donachie, stepping suddenly out of nowhere into the breach between Mrs. Fitzgibbons and the secretary, raising his hands to signify the uselessness of further objections.

"Take her to her desk for her things," said Mrs. Fitzgibbons.

"I don't have a desk!" cried Anita.

Unfortunately for Miss Stebbins, this last protest produced a humorous effect. Marcel, the part-time boy from the mailroom, and Julie laughed, while others in the vicinity stifled their amused reactions. Only Mr. Donachie showed a sober countenance; with his head in the air and his eyes bulging with voluptuous satisfaction under the leather bill of his black hat, he led Anita away by the elbow.

Mrs. Fitzgibbons explained later to Julie the necessity of eliminating certain "elements" among the staff. "When the boss goes, his loyal flunkies are left unprotected. They have to go. That's how it works. When you take over authority at the top, you have to lop off some heads. If the man before me had understood that, and had had the testicles to scare people, he'd still be here. He'd still be chief. Leonard has no fight in him."

Julie followed Mrs. Fitzgibbons into her office. She remarked in a soft, thrilling voice on Mr. Frye. "He keeps *staring* at you," she said.

"Of course he does. You're surprised? He wants me to jump his bones."

"*Mrs. Fitzgibbons!*" She raised her hand to her face.

"He depends on my good nature now. He works for me. He doesn't want to be scolded or fired. He wants me to drive him out to the forest, to some leafy ditch, and show him that he's attractive to me."

Julie shrieked with delight over Mrs. Fitzgibbons's outlandish cracks.

Mrs. Fitzgibbons chimed in at once. "Show him that I like his body!" she cried, and loosed a peal of laughter that could be heard in the street.

When Mrs. Fitzgibbons arrived home that Friday afternoon, her daughter and son-in-law were just pulling up to the curb in their gray compact. Eddie was behind the wheel. If Mrs. Fitzgibbons had had any admirers in the past three or four years, her son-in-law was one of them.

"Wow, look at your mom," he said, as Mrs. Fitzgibbons strode up to her door in her poison green dress with her coat over her arm.

Barbara was repelled at once, however, by Mrs. Fitzgibbons's glamorous looks. She ridiculed her mother at the first opportunity. "What on earth have you done to yourself? Have you gone insane? You look like a high-class tramp."

Mrs. Fitzgibbons did not put her key into the lock, but paused at the door with an expression of wry forbearance. At close range, the beauty of her face and her dark, almost navy-blue eyes had magnetized Eddie Berdowsky. She looked taller than usual, too, and her hair glowed lustrously.

"What a change," Eddie said. "You look super, Frankie. Look at her dress."

"I have a date," said Mrs. Fitzgibbons. "I can't talk now."

Barbara's gray gooseberry eyes, magnified unnaturally behind her big shiny glasses, shone with alarm. "What is she talking about?"

In fact, Barbara and her husband looked no more impressive in Mrs. Fitzgibbons's presence than a pair of domestics reporting for work. Eddie was still wearing his faded blue uniform shirt from the electronic-game company where he worked, a long-sleeved shirt with the crisscross emblem of a baseball bat and hockey stick stitched on the pocket. Barbara wore a shapeless floral dress, a cardigan, and walking shoes with brown-and-white laces. They followed Mrs. Fitzgibbons indoors.

"I've been promoted at the bank, and I have a dinner engagement," said Mrs. Fitzgibbons. "Why don't the two of you go off to the Gulf of Mexico and save some endangered birds?"

"What a comic!" Eddie loved his mother-in-law.

Ignoring them, Mrs. Fitzgibbons went into her bedroom to change. She was scheduled to pick up Terry at six o'clock. She spoke to Eddie and her daughter through the partially closed door, remaining out of sight. When the phone rang, and Barbara went to answer it, Mrs. Fitzgibbons pulled open the door. Eddie couldn't credit his eyes.

Mrs. Fitzgibbons was wearing only her shoes and underclothes. "Was that the telephone?" she said.

Eddie stared up at her from the sofa with a sickly smile on his lips. She had changed into a pink brassiere; she was removing a skirt from a hanger. Eddie was speechless. Barbara never wore brassieres. She called such things "harnesses." Women, Barbara said, were not draft animals. Moreover, Barbara was not built like her mother.

At length, Eddie spoke up. He was sitting forward with his legs apart, his elbows on his knees. "We came with news. Barbara thinks she's pregnant."

Mrs. Fitzgibbons stopped toying with the hanger. "Please," she said with disdain, "spare me."

"She does, Frankie."

Reaching, Mrs. Fitzgibbons closed the door between them. "Make sense," she said.

"It's true. That's why we're here. It's ten to one, Frankie. Barbara thought you'd be thrilled. Hey, I thought so, too."

Eddie had come now to her door and was speaking through it in an intimate tone. "Who are you dating?" he asked quietly. He was staring at the doorjamb suspensefully. "Who's the lucky guy?"

When Barbara came back from the foyer, Eddie was pressed against Mrs. Fitzgibbons's bedroom door, smiling crazily. "I told her about the baby," he said.

"And?"

"I think she was not thrilled."

Mrs. Fitzgibbons emerged then in a new gray angora sweater and black skirt. She was clasping a bracelet onto her wrist.

Barbara watched her mother with a grim, thin-lipped expression. "Someone named Terry is on the phone," she said.

"Tell us about your new job, Frankie." Eddie hovered close to Mrs. Fitzgibbons. He turned to Barbara. "Your mom has a date tonight."

"What's this about a baby?" said Mrs. Fitzgibbons.

"Is that all you have to say?" Barbara's anger was transparent. "Why aren't you ever home lately?"

"You can't even take care of yourselves." Mrs. Fitzgibbons eyed the mirror behind the sofa. "Look at the two of you."

"We thought you might help us now to get a mortgage," Eddie said. He glanced at Barbara, whose face was an angry mask. "The way we talked about it — you know —"

Mrs. Fitzgibbons looked at them with genuine amazement. "You what?"

"You know," Eddie blushed, and made a wreathing movement with his hand, "at the bank."

Without pausing, Mrs. Fitzgibbons invoked the businesslike tone of one transposing a polite conversation to a less frivolous level of discourse. "You two are barking up the wrong tree. I run a business. We don't show favoritism," she said. "This is mortgage financing. This is not Monopoly. You have to have money. You have to be creditworthy."

Instantly, Barbara exploded. "You conceited bitch! I knew she'd say that. When the time came, I knew it! I hate your insides!"

Mrs. Fitzgibbons watched with stern calm as Barbara squeezed and shook her fists in frustration.

"I wish my father could have lived to see the day!" Barbara cried. "You're shaming me. He would turn over in his grave."

"The only thing that would make your father turn over in his grave would be if the television set was behind him."

"I'll never talk to you again!"

Eddie sought to mollify his wife. "Don't be rash."

"Who's on the phone?" said Mrs. Fitzgibbons.

"You sicken me," said Barbara. "I hate and despise you." She waved her fist in her mother's face. "You'll live to rue this day. I'm shamed!" Barbara departed the house with her gray eyes bulging scarily. The front door slammed.

Eddie offered his mother a mitigatory interpretation of his wife's tantrum. "It's because she's pregnant," he said, shrugging.

"Don't be a jackass."

"She says she is."

"It takes more than saying. You're not that naive."

With Barbara gone, Eddie reverted to his intimate manner. "You look really exciting, Frankie. Is that your date on the phone? You know," he said, in a tone suggestive of a long-standing mystification on this point, "I was always surprised that you didn't date. I could never figure that out." He followed Mrs. Fitzgibbons to the telephone in the foyer. "A woman like you," he added ardently.

Outdoors, Barbara was blowing the car horn for him. Mrs. Fitzgibbons held the telephone receiver to her collarbone. "You run along now. I want to talk to this man."

Realizing he had followed her to the phone, Eddie colored embarrassedly. "You still want me to come over and clean the cellar one of these days?"

"Go with Barbara. Go play mommy and daddy," she said.

Eddie clapped a hand to his head and laughed insanely at her words.

*   *   *

When Mrs. Fitzgibbons came back at midnight with Terry, she was feeling her champagne. Within minutes she was in bed with her drum major and was displaying an aggressive style of love-making, which was not distasteful to the eighteen-year-old youth. She was very full of herself, a sensation that was only exaggerated by the look of infatuation in Terence's eyes whenever she complimented him. The boy was in love. Mrs. Fitzgibbons saw him as one of the perquisites of success. She had noticed over dinner at the Canoe Club how he listened in raptures when she talked about doing things for him in the future, or how he smiled in coy embarrassment when she talked about buying him some new golf clubs, or a pair of those pigskin perforated gloves that looked so stylish on the fairways.

In bed, she chided him amusingly. "It's a good thing you don't work for me," she said. "I'd fuck your eyes out twice a day."

"I wouldn't mind that, Frankie. I really wouldn't."

Mrs. Fitzgibbons was on top of him, holding his face and chin in her left hand, while reaching back with her right to excite and frustrate him. "You wouldn't be worth a nickel to anybody else."

"You're right about that, Frankie!" he said.

"You fell into the honeypot. A boy like you shouldn't work at all. You should be set up in a hotel room someplace, down at the Roger Smith, taking bubble baths and prettifying yourself for the evening."

"I don't know what to say to that." The pitch of Terence Sugrue's voice rose with his mounting excitement.

"I'll do the talking, peppermint."

"Don't you need protection, Frankie?"

"Not if Dr. Doodles is right."

"Doodles?"

"Alvin Donnelly, my gynecologist," said Mrs. Fitzgibbons, "the dirtiest-minded physician since Freud himself. When I told him I hadn't ovulated for four months, he told me the cradle may be gone but the playpen is as good as new. He billed me sixty-five dollars for that. God Almighty," she yelled, "this is exciting."

"I love you, Frankie."

"Keep still." She was sweating now. Her breasts swung pendulously before him. She couldn't stop talking. "I'm going to buy you everything, beautiful things, argyle sweaters, dress shirts, cologne, jewelry. That's how I want you to look." She had thrust him inside herself and was moving atop him with vigor. The look of romantic helplessness that blanched Terry's face was extreme. For a second, he didn't even look human. Mrs. Fitzgibbons lost control of what she was saying. The words came out in a spate of manic ebullience. "This is what you do. You're my boy! I'll take you away weekends. I'll buy you a car." At one point, she actually whooped. Terence was moaning and staring at the ceiling. Mrs. Fitzgibbons was clutching him by the biceps. She was biting her lip. "This is life! This is the goods!" she shouted. "Up, boy — up, boy — up, boy!"

Nor were Mrs. Fitzgibbons's requirements anything close to satisfied in the first full hour of such exactions; at thirty-minute intervals thereafter, with Terry Sugrue blurting his love, she could be heard disporting herself upon him. ("You've been discovered! . . . Up, boy!" etc.) It was no wonder that the comely boy fell at last into a magnificent slumber, sprawled picturesquely across Mrs. Fitzgibbons's bed in the lamplight, where he slept till morning.

To worsen matters, Mrs. Fitzgibbons was in no frame of mind to comfort the young drum major when he awoke in a panic. The Saturday edition of the *Ireland Parish Telegram,* arriving at her front door, contained a complete transcript of her interview at the bank. When Mrs. Fitzgibbons saw it, she gave a triumphant shout. As she entered the room, she threw aside the front part of the newspaper and was holding up the "Local News" section, the front page of which was always produced in color on Saturday. The entire page was devoted to her. It centered upon a full-length shot of Mrs. Fitzgibbons standing importantly in front of her desk at the bank, looking incredibly resplendent in her poison green dress. She had not seen such a magnificent photograph of anyone in all her life.

Across the top of the page ran a full-length banner head in dark blue ink, which read:

A NEW REGIME FOR OUR OLDEST BANK

The effect on Mrs. Fitzgibbons was sensational. While Terry was hurrying into his clothes, worried sick at not having gone home the night before, she was exultant.

"I've got band!" he said. "Today is game day. My mother'll kill me!" He was practically in tears. "What am I doing here? What am I going to tell them?"

"I've done it! Let them try something now." She read aloud the caption underneath the big six-by-eight-inch photo of herself in the paper. " 'Newly installed executive vice president of the Parish Bank speaks out on the need to run a tight ship in these perilous, fast-paced times.' " Mrs. Fitzgibbons was so worked up over the full-page article that she threw the paper onto the bed, then immediately snatched it up again. "They'll never get me out," she said. "Not this year, or next, or ever."

She had never seen her words in print before. Her eye darted about the page, picking out subheads. " 'Calls Chairman a Prince!' 'Woman with a Will!' 'Fitzgibbons Throws Down Gauntlet!'

"This battle is over even before it started," she said. "What a way to hit them! It's glorious. Look at the size of it. I didn't even leave them a leg to stand on."

As the Sugrue boy rushed out to keep his appointment with the marching band, Mrs. Fitzgibbons called after him in joyous accents: "Wait till Louis Zabac claps eyes on this picture. If he's not forking off in ten minutes, he'll be beating up on his gimpy wife."

SIX

Still, she was not insensible to the fact that she had overstepped herself on Friday and knew very well that Mr. Zabac might react with great annoyance. She had not lost her senses. The fact that he did not telephone her over the weekend to congratulate her on the great windfall of publicity that her article had won for the bank could be construed either as ominous or as an example of the little man's respect for the privacy of his second-in-command.

Monday morning, while Bruce Clayton worked on Mrs. Fitzgibbons's face and hair, she sought to anticipate the various lines of approach that the chairman might take. To begin with, she rejected the more extreme possibilities. He would neither dismiss her out of hand, nor accept her seizure of authority without some protest or struggle. In effect, she had presented him with a *fait accompli*; all that was required was for her to stand up to him, to stand on her decisions and show resolve. If he fired her, he would make himself the laughingstock of the city and of the local banking community. If he scolded her severely for taking too much on herself and insisted that she quietly back down, she would

refuse, but not without hearing him out and offering him reasonable reassurances, reasonably voiced, that the grand spread in
Saturday's newspaper was just a foretokening of the exemplary
good work that she would do and upon which she should be
judged. If, however, Mr. Zabac took the harder line and began to
upbraid and threaten her — which was the bleakest and ugliest of
the alternatives — then she would take him head on. She would
give him a piece of her mind! By raising her voice to him in such
a way as to prefigure her getting up and walking out, he would
be completely outflanked. To allow Mrs. Fitzgibbons to resign her
post was precisely the same as firing her; and that he could not do.

"What time is it?" she said.

"It's after ten," said Bruce.

"Finish me!" she commanded. Bruce enjoyed being talked to
like that.

"I am trying," he argued, politely.

"I've been here for an hour."

Over the weekend, Bruce had mounted Mrs. Fitzgibbons's big
colorful newspaper article in a Victorian walnut frame, and had
hung it in a prominent setting between mirrors in his salon. He
fussed sedulously at her side. He was crazy about her. Mrs. Fitzgibbons accepted his bowing and scraping with a voluptuous,
stern-faced air of self-importance which left her feeling very safe
and warm inside.

"On Saturdays and Sundays," he said, "I'll do you at home."

When Mrs. Fitzgibbons came sailing into the bank at ten-twenty,
darting in at the front door past Mr. Donachie, the tails of her
raincoat flying, the bank was unusually busy. The level of activity
was brisker than on most Mondays. Had it been the third of the
month, when depositors lined up in droves with their government
checks, she might have seen the cause of it; but today was the
nineteenth. All eight teller windows were open, and the line of
patrons sprawled about the floor like a snake. Mrs. Fitzgibbons
made a circuit to her right, going round them, and made directly
for her office. Before Julie could put her boss's coat away, she
apprised Mrs. Fitzgibbons of important developments taking place
elsewhere.

"Have you heard the news?" Julie said. "The stock market is crashing!"

"What are you talking about?"

Julie took Mrs. Fitzgibbons's coat to the closet in her office. "They're all talking about it. It's fallen hundreds of points."

To ascertain what was going on at the windows, Mrs. Fitzgibbons got Jack Greaney on the line. Jack assured her that nothing of a ruinous or extraordinary nature was taking place.

"Well, what on earth is happening?"

"Nothing," Jack answered on the phone. "We're just doing business. It is very busy," he allowed.

"They're not withdrawing?" Mrs. Fitzgibbons had never lived through a financial panic, nor ever suspected anything like a bank run, but the atmosphere was electric. She experienced a stab of paranoia.

"Not at all," Jack replied. "In fact, we've opened a significant number of new accounts."

Mrs. Fitzgibbons stepped to the door of her office with the phone to her ear and looked across the loan department and the tops of a row of glass cubicles to where Jack was standing. He had the phone to his ear and was looking back at her.

"What new accounts?" she demanded.

"Just that, new accounts," came his muttered reply.

Ever since the previous week, when she fired the De Marias, Mrs. Fitzgibbons noticed, the slender redhead, Jack, had shown her a timid face whenever they met. In previous years, by contrast, there was no person in all the bank who had been more outgoing and amiable toward her than Jack Greaney. Mrs. Fitzgibbons guessed he was scared stiff.

In his next breath, Jack cleared up some of the mystery. "I think," he offered, softly, "it has to do with your article in the paper. It's bringing in a lot of business."

All at once, the realization of what was transpiring dawned on her. The grand full-page article in the *Telegram* had produced an unexpected wave of new patronage. The sudden awareness of what she had done, especially as she had not anticipated anything of the sort, produced an intoxicating effect, which was evident at once in the angry thrill of her voice. "*Get over here!*" she said to him.

Jack's explanation was correct. Mrs. Fitzgibbons determined that fast. Almost all the new depositors had seen the Saturday news story.

"There's a lot of talk among the tellers," Jack added, as though to explain his own initial uncertainty over the brisk pickup in business at the windows, "about what's happening on the New York Stock Exchange this morning."

"You tell those hunchbacks to concentrate on what they're doing." She handed her scarf to Julie.

"They're all working hard, Mrs. Fitzgibbons. They really are. I have my eye on them."

Jack didn't even blink at Mrs. Fitzgibbons's rude language, and for the first time stopped addressing the new vice president as "Frankie," as he had been accustomed to doing for years. Mrs. Fitzgibbons noted the change with satisfaction.

"You tell them to keep their mouths shut and tend to business."

"I will," said Jack.

"You do that."

She could have enjoyed talking to Jack like this for an hour or two but was even more excited by the press of new depositors milling about out front. With Jack Greaney following her, she strode out to the windows. Her appearance on the floor this time removed any last doubt. People standing in line pointed at her. She saw it herself. She smiled back at them. An elderly woman in a frayed red coat reached out and clasped Mrs. Fitzgibbons by the elbow. "Good for you, dear," she smiled toothlessly. "I'm proud of you."

Mrs. Fitzgibbons stopped at once and turned her attention to the grinning well-wisher. The woman's complexion was doughy, and her eyes sparkled like two sapphires in the wrinkles of her good-natured face. Compared to the little lady in the red coat at her side, Mrs. Fitzgibbons looked like a designer's idea of a high-powered, up-to-the-minute woman of affairs. By this time, everyone standing in line was beaming at the two of them. Even the tellers paused in their transactions to look out at Mrs. Fitzgibbons and the little woman holding her arm. Mrs. Fitzgibbons was not so puffed up by her recent ascendancy, or by the manic pressures bubbling inside her, to have lost her lifelong natural cheerfulness. She knew exactly what to do.

"You come with me," she commanded the woman, and led her out of the line with a show of ceremony. "I'm taking you straight to the window," she said.

As she did so, several customers spoke up enthusiastically. "Congratulations, Frankie! Proud of you!"

"These aren't the most decent people in the world for nothing," Mrs. Fitzgibbons explained, waving at all assembled. "Everyone will wait one extra minute while you go first."

The thin, bony woman in the red coat grinned foxily at the others as Mrs. Fitzgibbons paraded her to the front of the line and on from there to the first available window. She glanced at the woman's deposit slip as she passed it under the grille and announced to the teller in an official tone:

"Gertrude Bollenbach is here on business."

The happy effect on all was predictable. As Mrs. Fitzgibbons strode back past the admiring throng, the triumph of her public relations coup in the newspaper, not to say of the imagination and boldness she had shown in stealing a march on everyone, on friends and adversaries alike, seemed reflected in their faces. Who could have blamed her if she tossed her head as she walked?

"That's the new president."

"We love you, Frankie!" someone called.

"She's some looker."

"You were there," cracked another.

Mrs. Fitzgibbons was feeling so buoyant that she actually snapped her fingers at Julie on entering her office. "In here, girl."

There was much to be done. To begin with, Mrs. Fitzgibbons determined beyond a doubt that a disaster of historic proportions was unfolding by the minute in the nation's security markets. Word from the back office was that Mr. Hooton, along with Lionel Kim, his young Taiwanese assistant, were glued in horror to their computer screens, watching as the flow of luminous digits reflected enormous blocks of common stock changing hands at plummeting prices. Panic was setting in. Mrs. Fitzgibbons could scarcely credit the fortuitousness of it all. The little bombshell she had dropped on Friday, by appointing herself chief executive officer of the bank, had become, all at once, like a tiny twinkling light in a fire storm spreading across the country. Although the debacle in the markets did not affect her directly, she was very pumped up. She couldn't sit still. Twice she dispatched Julie to the back of the bank to report on conditions in the treasurer's office, and twice she telephoned Jeannine Mielke upstairs, asking if Mr. Zabac had come in.

"No," Jeannine said, "he hasn't."

"Has anyone called him?" Mrs. Fitzgibbons insisted.

"At home?" Mr. Zabac's secretary was startled by the outlandish idea. "*I* certainly haven't," she said.

Julie Marcotte reported back as before. "They're just sitting there, staring at their machines. They look, you know, like paralyzed."

Mrs. Fitzgibbons saw herself as equal to the circumstance. In fact, the sense of developing ruin in the world's financial markets actually dissipated certain secret fears she had experienced that morning before coming to work. She had had some very paranoid thoughts. The reality of what was happening to certain big corporations out there was perversely reassuring. The telephone in her fist felt like a weapon, like a heavy black hammer, something solid and useful. When Mr. Zabac picked up his telephone at home, she didn't mince words with him. "Has Neil Hooton called you?" she said.

Mr. Zabac sounded very cold and distant. He recognized her voice. "What do you want, Mrs. Fitzgibbons?" His tone was laden with menace.

"Haven't you been informed what's happening? He hasn't called you? He's invested up to his neck, isn't he? I can't believe he hasn't called." She affected amazement at Mr. Hooton's dereliction in not notifying Mr. Zabac of the Wall Street panic. She spoke of him as of a low-level functionary who would require punishing. Mr. Hooton had become overnight iniquitous to her eye, an adversary to be hounded and demolished. "The stock market is crashing!" She announced the news in a thrilling, timbral voice. "It's down hundreds of points. There's no end in sight. He must have called you. He's sitting back there like a block of stone. The man is terrified! I can't believe he didn't notify you. You've got to come right in."

The silence on the line indicated the chairman's shock as he strove to come to grips with the sensational news, as well, perhaps, as with his reactions to Mrs. Fitzgibbons herself. Mrs. Fitzgibbons was not eager to get off the phone, as it was exciting to communicate the downward tide of great events. "Wall Street is trying to get the President to address the nation," she said, repeating a report that Julie had overheard minutes before.

Here Mr. Zabac broke in frustratedly. "Mrs. Fitzgibbons, we are not an investment bank."

Clutching the black receiver to her ear, Mrs. Fitzgibbons continued, undeflected. "That isn't all," she said. "We're taking in tens of thousands in new deposits. That's the good news. We've opened dozens and dozens of new accounts this morning." Mrs. Fitzgibbons felt a surge of contempt for the man on the other end, picturing him sitting in his pajamas in a breakfast nook overlooking his gardens. "It's because of that article of mine, the full page I gave to the *Telegram*. That's what's done it. We're having our biggest morning in the history of the bank. They're lined up all the way to the street!" Her voice took on a sharp, victorious rasp as she recounted these last developments.

By now, however, Mr. Zabac's ability to assimilate the torrent of news, with its admixture of calamity and triumph, compelled him to conclude the call. He assured her that he would be on hand at the bank in twenty minutes.

"I'm glad!" She said it just like that. She wanted to leave no doubt in the man's mind that his new chief executive officer was equal to the crisis. "We're going to come through it in good shape," she said. "I'll see to that."

"We are not an investment house," he repeated acrimoniously. He was very angry.

"I can't believe," Mrs. Fitzgibbons continued, shrewdly side-stepping the little chairman's riposte, "that man didn't notify you. That's unforgivable in my book." With that, Mrs. Fitzgibbons banged down the receiver.

For the next half hour, she capitalized on the prevailing tension by issuing a stream of instructions, directing them in particular to individuals who had no clear understanding of her authority, except as they might have believed the account of her promotion in the Saturday newspaper. Mrs. Wilson, head of the auto loan section, received a typewritten, stiffly worded memo that typified Mrs. Fitzgibbons's spate of orders. "Instruct your employees," it stated imperatively, "to STOP gabbing among themselves about today's stock market. We are NOT an investment bank! Let them tend to business!" Mrs. Fitzgibbons signed this memo with an extravagant flourish of her pink felt-tip pen and dispatched it by hand with Julie. Minutes later, Julie could be seen running to the office of Mr. Brouillette with a request that he set to paper a quick and succinct estimate of the effects to be expected in the secondary market as a consequence of the developing crash. Mrs. Fitzgibbons had no true understanding of the question she was asking but knew Howard Brouillette as an eccentric type, who would gleefully undermine his own position and virtually demote himself, in order to show off his knowledge. That done, Mrs. Fitzgibbons phoned Jack Greaney and told him to count up the number of new accounts opened that morning and to get her an estimate of the total dollar amount of the new deposits.

Jack called back in short order, but Mrs. Fitzgibbons made him wait on the line while she took an outside call from a building developer who offered his congratulations on her promotion to CEO. By that time, Mrs. Fitzgibbons's phone was ringing a lot, mostly from well-wishing business associates of the bank, lawyers and accountants, and from several prominent outside firms, some of them located miles away. In each case, Mrs. Fitzgibbons acknowledged their felicitations with businesslike terseness: "It was sweet of you to call. I'm in conference right now. I'll get back to you."

"There are forty-seven new accounts already," said Jack on the line. "Mostly of all sizes. Although one of them is big. The total is well over a quarter of a million." His voice contained both pride and admiration.

"That includes our branches," Mrs. Fitzgibbons assumed.

That remark left Jack speechless momentarily. "I haven't called the branches," he confessed in a faltering tone.

This is what Mrs. Fitzgibbons liked. This called for a tyrannical outburst.

"Jack!" she shouted, as though he were a boy. "What earthly use are you to me if you don't get things straight? This is just the sort of blundering, thoughtless incompetence that has been the ruin of this place. What do you think I'm all about?" she cried. "What do you think I've been complaining about over and over?"

In her forty-five years on earth, she had never known how much fun a day's work could be. She spoke huskily into the phone. "I fire people for less than this."

He answered softly. "I'll call the branches."

"You get them on the phone!" she said.

Mrs. Fitzgibbons sent Julie to get the radio from the ladies rest room. Julie plugged it in on the floor by Mrs. Fitzgibbons's desk and tuned it to the local news station. After that, the voice of the broadcaster droned on and on about the sickness of the stock market. Recorded interviews with government officials, economists, even the president of the New York Stock Exchange, were aired at regular intervals. The market was going down in a long, frightening cascade of selling. Computerized trading programs, it was said, were continuously introducing tremendous new offerings, massive block trades to be sold without hesitation at market prices. Many specialists on the floor, it was known as fact, had already been wiped out. Now and again, Mrs. Fitzgibbons stopped to listen but understood next to nothing about the workings of the securities industry, or, indeed, of what constituted a Wall Street catastrophe.

Later on, after Mr. Zabac had gone upstairs to his office, she saw Neil Hooton making his way past the row of glass cubicles toward the rear staircase. He looked shaken. Seizing her felt-tip pen, Mrs. Fitzgibbons scratched out a note to Mr. Zabac, summarizing in a sentence the good news from the tellers' windows, as she thought it wise to pass this cheerful bulletin along to him while Mr. Hooton was sitting right there in front of him looking like death. "Mr. Z: By the end of the day we'll have one hundred new accounts and far in excess of a million in new deposits."

For all her bravado, however, her confidence began to take a downward turn. Maybe it was the voice of the man on the radio, groaning in the background like the voice of fate itself. Or it might have been the knowledge that the hour of reckoning impended, when the little godlike master on the floor above would summon her. She was not so self-absorbed, after all, as to have missed the cold vein of anger in his voice on the telephone, or to blithely assume that her bold stroke in the pages of the local paper had carried the day for her. She imagined Louis Zabac standing redfaced behind his desk, shaking with fury. How he would shout at her in a big dwarf voice! He would order her back to her old desk. Mr. Frye would supervise her. They would slash her pay. She would be the laughingstock of everyone. And then it would get worse. Mr. Hooton would want her head. Mrs. Wilson would savage her left and right. Julie would be fired; Mr. Donachie would be demoted to a porter!

In the past month, Mrs. Fitzgibbons had suffered acute paranoia attacks, but none so gripping as now. Her scalp was damp, her pulse cold and drumlike. When Julie knocked on Mrs. Fitzgibbons's door and looked in, she found Mrs. Fitzgibbons staring at her with dilated eyes.

"He's come out," she whispered. "He's coming downstairs. He looks terrible, Mrs. Fitzgibbons."

In seconds, Mrs. Fitzgibbons was out on the floor. She hadn't reflected on it whatsoever but acted on an impulse that she later regarded as outrageous under the circumstances. She put herself in Mr. Hooton's way. Just as he came round the green-and-black-marble pillar, shuffling forward between desks with his head down, a manilla envelope and clipboard in hand, she obstructed his path. He could not get by her.

"Well," she exclaimed wryly, "what are we doing? Are we selling?"

Mr. Hooton reacted unpleasantly. "I beg your pardon!" He eyed her in disbelief. As always, he wore little gold spectacles on the tip of his nose. His eyebrows were like two white caterpillars; color invaded his cheeks.

She strove with all her faculties to remain calm, but her heart was racing. "What's the plan of action?" she persisted airily. "Are we in, or out?"

Certain that Neil Hooton's response would betray what had happened upstairs, Mrs. Fitzgibbons struggled to hold her ground. The man could not continue to where he was going without pushing her aside. His belligerence was not reassuring.

"Would you mind," he said, superciliously, in a gruff, dismissive tone of voice, "if I went back to work?"

Again, she did not move. She summoned everything within herself to face him down. "I want to know what we're doing. That's a reasonable question. Are we in or out?"

"Is it necessary for you to know? What has it to do with you? The markets are in disarray from here to Frankfurt —"

"Is that what you call it?" said Mrs. Fitzgibbons, heartened by his unwillingness to reject out of hand her questioning. She breathed deeply and showed Mr. Hooton an obstinate eye. "That means we're still in."

Once more, Mr. Hooton countenanced the question. He did not push past her, nor turn about and go the other way, as he surely would have done if Mrs. Fitzgibbons's extraordinary interview in the Saturday newspaper had already spelled her doom.

"If you must know," he said, his voice dripping with dislike of her, "we're holding on."

Mrs. Fitzgibbons stepped aside and allowed him to pass. Mr. Hooton went off muttering to himself. Mrs. Fitzgibbons returned to her office with a stunned look.

"I got it out of him," she said.

"What's happening?" Julie asked softly.

"I insisted on an answer, and he answered me. He hasn't a leg under him. Nothing happened upstairs. How could it? Look at the business out there!"

"What did Mr. Hooton say?"

"They didn't talk about me," Mrs. Fitzgibbons added. She

reached and shut her door. Instantly, her attack of unreasoning dread gave way to buoyant spirits. She mimicked him. " '*We're holding on!*' He's shaking in his shoes. I'll drive him from pillar to post! I'll hound him to the ends of the earth. The market's down a million points, his entire portfolio's going down the sewer, and I'm going after him. I have the will," she said, "and nobody is going to stop me. Nobody."

"Nobody would dare do that," said Julie, her pink-faced sycophancy offering a mirror to Mrs. Fitzgibbons's egoism.

"I'll grind him into the floor. I'll beat his balls into a powder."

Her resurgent spirits set her striding to and fro in front of Julie. "Everyone on the planet is selling his stock. In every city in America, in every country in the world, from Turkey to Poland, what's everyone doing?"

"They're all selling."

"He's holding on." While stepping vainly about, Mrs. Fitzgibbons raised a pedagogical finger. "He's standing up to them. A disaster of global proportions is taking place, and only one individual money manager on earth has the brains and guts and stamina to stick by his guns, and that man works for us. He wears a blue-and-yellow bow tie, and big yellow suspenders with little blue ducks printed on them, and he, of all people, knows what to do, because he gets a handsome fat bonus every winter, just for knowing what to do when everyone else also knows what to do." In an access of irony, Mrs. Fitzgibbons slapped her palms together in rhythm to her words: "It's going to go down, and down, and down, and he's going to hold on. He's going to wait, and wait some more, and watch it sink further and further, hour by hour, until it hasn't anyplace else to go, and then," she said, "he's going to crack. As God is my witness, he'll liquidate everything he can get his hands on. He's going to sell."

Julie Marcotte had never seen anyone work themselves into such a hypnotic trance.

"That's what's going to happen. I promise you. The man is petrified. I saw it in his eyes. Today, sometime before closing, his nerves will fail and he'll sell the whole kit and caboodle."

"I'm sure you're right."

While many of Mrs. Fitzgibbons's longtime colleagues at the bank had begun to wonder if she was not experiencing some form of delusional dislocation in recent days, others of more recent acquaintance, such as Julie, were inclined to construe the woman's showiness and fiery outbursts as nothing more than the outward signs of a dramatic business success. When Mrs. Fitzgibbons began a tirade, Julie shrank with apprehension.

"I am right! And out there, at the windows, I'll be opening new accounts all week. You'll see. Telephone Bruce. Tell him to meet me at the hotel. I'm going to lunch."

"What if Mr. Zabac calls?"

"I don't want to see him till the disaster is complete. You call me when you hear Hooton is selling."

"But, Mrs. Fitzgibbons, how will *I* know —?"

"You'll find out. You'll just do it."

Mrs. Fitzgibbons darted across the vast main floor of the Parish Bank, pulling on her raincoat, nodding politely to customers in line who recognized her from the newspaper. The public's adulation was spontaneous.

For the next ninety minutes, Mrs. Fitzgibbons sat in a corner banquette at the Roger Smith Hotel and entertained Bruce with a rush of verbal pyrotechnics that returned again and again to the theme of Neil Hooton's cowardice and of her own vaunting bravery in coping with crises. "Credit me," she said. "I have the man in my hands."

At two o'clock, Mrs. Fitzgibbons came hurrying back to her office. Not only was Mr. Hooton selling — "Alvin Bray said that he's been on the phone to Shearson for twenty minutes," said Julie — but Mr. Tom Pesso, the anchorman of the local WKYN television news team, had telephoned for an on-camera interview with Mrs. Fitzgibbons.

SEVEN

When Mrs. Fitzgibbons started up the back staircase to see the chairman, she was in a very determined frame of mind. She intended to wrest from him nothing less than full authority over every soul on the payroll. While Mr. Zabac was owner and titular head of the bank, to Mrs. Fitzgibbons's mind his function now was to hand over the reins of power.

She strode past Miss Mielke's desk, rapped on the chairman's door, and walked right in. Mr. Zabac was waiting for her. He was standing at the big semicircular window, with his back to the door, gazing worriedly out at the spires and pink-and-gray-slated roof of the city hall. Not a man to beat about the bush, he started in at once.

"I can't imagine what possessed you to do such a monstrous thing. It's unheard of. It's grotesque. It's the worst kind of insubordination. Mrs. Fitzgibbons," he cried in a thin voice, his cheeks shaking, "what possessed you? How could you say those things?"

"Mr. Zabac —" she started to respond.

"How could you publish such lies? What were you thinking? What did you think I would say?" His eyes rounded with disbelief as he leaned toward her. "How could you put me in such an impossible situation?"

The chairman's distress was evident as well in his clenched fists; nevertheless, his anger was in check. He spoke to her in a voice that he wanted no one else to hear, including his secretary. It was soon apparent that Mr. Zabac had convinced himself that the woman before him had not comprehended the scope or implications of her actions and that she had not acted in deceit. That Mrs. Fitzgibbons had become a perplexity to him was obvious. For these reasons, Mr. Zabac modulated his manner toward her.

"You didn't know what you were saying," he pointed out. "Your statements have been interpreted in ways you could not have guessed. I honestly believe that you don't understand what you've done."

The daylight was in Mrs. Fitzgibbons's face, as she stood in front of him. She was staring down at him with a hint of a smirk on her lips, her eyes narrowed shrewdly.

"You have frightened and offended a half dozen of my officers downstairs," he said, "the ablest employees I have. If it wasn't for all the excitement today, they would be tendering me their resignations."

"Where would they go?" Mrs. Fitzgibbons demanded with a truculence that belied the prettiness of her appearance.

"You see?" he exclaimed. "I'm right. You don't understand."

"Where would they go?" she repeated firmly. "The South Valley Bank is in a coma. The Citizens Bank is reducing staff. We," said Mrs. Fitzgibbons, employing the no-nonsense air of a chief executive officer, "are the only viable thrift in this neck of the woods."

Mr. Zabac showed Mrs. Fitzgibbons a raised hand, but he was visibly pleased by her characterization of the competition. "Let me explain something to you. You are a home loan officer." He paused. "That's what you are, and that's what you have been. You have an adequate grasp of that. In fourteen years, you've established a creditable, even enviable, record. You're pleasant," he continued, "you're honest, you're helpful. All that is true. You tend to business. You're loyal and hardworking." Unable to desist, he alluded to Mrs. Fitzgibbons's revolutionary looks. "You have a fine, dashing appearance, also, that I find to be both businesslike and reassuring. People like that. But this is a big bank, Mrs. Fitzgibbons. It has taken me half a lifetime, more than thirty years, to comprehend the complexities and risks in this business. You don't understand these things."

For the first time, Mrs. Fitzgibbons felt anxiety; it moved about her insides like something with cold legs. Mr. Zabac's head was drawn down toward his shoulders. His little shoes gleamed icily, and his cheekbones, glimmering with tiny hairs, darkened to the ominous color of raw meat. Had Mrs. Fitzgibbons not learned lately how to confront danger, and had instead succumbed to her long-accustomed habit of accommodating authority by smiling placatingly and quailing before it, she would have faltered fatally at this moment. It was her proven ability to hold forth in a bright and inspired manner, the words coming unbidden to her lips, the seeming issue of a lifetime of reticence and shyness, that fueled her response.

"If you're going to insult me," she said, peevishly, "I'll hand in my resignation on the six o'clock evening news."

"What are you talking about?"

"Tom Pesso and his camera team from Channel 6 are on their way to see me right now. He's coming to interview me for the evening news program."

The chairman looked as though he had been tapped on the top of the head with a heavy tool.

"The people at WKYN are interested in the fact that ours is the first bank in the region to give a woman a meaningful promotion." She tossed out this last invention with no regard for its validity.

After listening intently, Mr. Zabac emerged from his momentary stupefaction and returned the discussion to its original subject. "Mrs. Fitzgibbons," he said, "do you, or do you not, understand the harm you did to me and this institution in your newspaper article?"

"I do not."

Of the two, Mrs. Fitzgibbons was now the more reasonable and self-collected. When Mr. Zabac showed signs of frustration or uncertainty, as he was doing now, a warm, almost sexy feeling

ran through her limbs. Nevertheless, she backtracked diplomati-
cally. She did not wish to corner the man.

"I told them you were a prince," she said, "and you are. I would
do anything for you. You know that," she brought out with sudden
heartiness. "Why shouldn't I?"

"I have no doubt," said Mr. Zabac, in an even more conciliatory
way, "that you meant no harm to me personally, or to the others."

"What others?" she interrupted sharply.

Mr. Zabac ignored her this time and went on. He stepped away
from the window and paced thoughtfully to his desk. "Nor," he
conceded, "can there be any question, Mrs. Fitzgibbons, that your
newspaper story has produced a very happy effect today on the
popularity and reputation of the bank."

"No one would argue that!"

"That's what I said." Up shot the stubby pedantic finger.

Mrs. Fitzgibbons was in no mood to be lectured. "The deposits
are pouring in."

"I am not unaware of it."

"It's the biggest single day we've ever had." She kept interrupting
him, determined to steer the discussion to her own purposes.

"In that way," he said, nicely, "you have shown some considerable skill." By praising her, he hoped to regain the upper hand.
"You have talents."

"Some of the deposits are enormous," said Mrs. Fitzgibbons
sternly.

"You have talents that were not known to most of us."

"What is Neil doing?" That quickly Mrs. Fitzgibbons swung
the discourse onto her adversary.

The chairman didn't like it. "Mrs. Fitzgibbons! Please. I insist."

"Did you tell him to sell his holdings?"

"We are not going to talk about that. Our exposure in that area
is not great."

Sure of herself, Mrs. Fitzgibbons persisted. She spoke in the tone
of one autocrat addressing another. "I'm glad," she said. "I'm
relieved that you didn't. Only a moron would eliminate holdings
at this stage."

Like a cardplayer, on discovering each incoming card to be even
more welcome than the last, Mrs. Fitzgibbons knew in a flash by

the painful wince in the chairman's face that he was not in sympathy with Mr. Hooton's decisions. Unable to quell her joyous feeling, she turned and paced to and fro on the big Chinese carpet. "That's all we'd need," she continued invidiously, feigning ignorance of what Mr. Hooton had just done. "To have our treasurer make us the laughingstock of the entire state — on the very day when every depositor who saw my picture in the paper, and who read what I had to say, is lining up at our windows."

While stepping about, she gestured modestly with her fist. "They liked my interview," she said. "Everyone did. It gave them confidence in us. That's why they're pouring in here this morning. They wanted to be told that we're up to the minute and not just some roadside, drive-in pack of money-grubbing amateurs risking our money on deadbeats."

"That's not the point," he argued.

"That we're going to be sleek and dynamic," she added. "That our competitors are in for a fight now. They're feeling sick this morning. A week ago," Mrs. Fitzgibbons fired at him, as though citing the most incredible of facts, "the public didn't even know our name! That's criminal. After what we've done for thousands and thousands of them. They know it now," she said. "I gave it to them."

Once again, although despairing somewhat, Mr. Zabac endeavored to broach and thrash out his objectives; but Mrs. Fitzgibbons turned and faced him.

"Someone had to tell them. Tell me I did wrong."

She would like to have said much more but decided it was time to present the dapper little chairman with a picture of the beautiful, self-assured figure to whom he would presently be entrusting total power downstairs. She was standing very straight and holding his gaze without a blink. She studied him with her midnight blue eyes as he strove to summon the necessary courage.

"I see only one way out for us," he said at last, with finality. "You will have to make known to everyone that while you are my director — you may use the word *director* — of our home loan department, any *greater* implications that have been erroneously disseminated —"

"That's ridiculous." Mrs. Fitzgibbons's snappish response

sounded more like a wife refuting her husband over some minor domestic squabble than of a bank executive intent on seizing authority. "It was in the newspaper," she reminded him.

"But don't you see," Mr. Zabac cried, "you put it in the newspaper."

She calmed him with a raised hand. "No one should hear us. Otherwise, there'll be no stopping the rumors."

In the face of Mr. Zabac's sudden resentful outburst, Mrs. Fitzgibbons's self-control was a thing of beauty. "This is my plan," she said. "I'll go on television in an hour, and I'll bring you on with me. We'll go on camera together. We'll be on the evening news tonight. And I don't mean for a few seconds. They'll guarantee us sufficient air time, or I'll refuse to do it."

The abrupt shift in subject to that of the WKYN news team silenced Mr. Zabac, as he appeared both alarmed and enchanted by the prospect. "You needn't worry about having to say very much or answer a lot of questions," she said. "I'm comfortable with it and will keep the ball rolling nicely. That's my forte. That's my job. Let's don't worry, Louis, about tromping on the toes of some people downstairs. They'll be sitting home watching us on television, just as a hundred thousand other people will be doing, and will know that the bank is on the move." Mrs. Fitzgibbons continued more robustly. "You gave them every chance. What are you supposed to do, massage them to sleep at night? The publicity will be worth a fortune. It isn't even measurable!"

Mrs. Fitzgibbons's vigorous recital was accompanied by attractive movements as she gestured prettily and turned her head this way and that. She felt his eyes glued to her. If her gathering moral ascendancy over the man involved a sexual component, what was the harm in it.

Mr. Zabac tried again. "I admit that you did wonderfully in your interview, Mrs. Fitzgibbons. I was impressed by the length of the article, by its prominent position in the paper, and by its obvious results."

"Only I could have done that."

"Please." He protested the interruption.

But Mrs. Fitzgibbons had an inspiration. "I hope that Mrs. Zabac saw it," she exclaimed.

"She did, I assure you."

"I hope she read every word. I hope she was proud of you. What did she say about your appointing a woman like myself?"

"She couldn't imagine who you were. She couldn't believe you had worked for me all these years."

Here Mrs. Fitzgibbons decided to seize the nettle. Until now, her instincts were unerring. It was time for Mr. Zabac to vacate the field of dispute.

"Between ten o'clock this morning and noon," she said, "I received two very attractive job offers. I turned them both down. I intend to stay here. The only way I would leave is by being compelled to leave." Again, she regarded him with a level stare. "I can't go home today without knowing exactly where I stand. I can't function in a cloud. It's essential I have the proper authority to do the things I want to do."

Mr. Zabac listened carefully to every word. If Mrs. Fitzgibbons's locutions sometimes involved the language of violence, it only served to dramatize her resolve.

"They will carry me out dead," she said. "There has to be somebody downstairs to crack the whip. And I'm not talking about" — she raised her voice — "people in bow ties who go to pieces at the first sign of trouble." Mrs. Fitzgibbons looked adamantine. "The head of your capital markets desk has a foot-wide yellow stripe down the middle of his back, and is downstairs whimpering like a baby, and doing, I'm sure, the worst thing he could possibly do. The man is liquidating everything in sight!" she cried. "You know it, and I know it. I'm not like that!" Her contempt for her adversaries suddenly shone through. "These fair-weather dandies! With their little spectacles and clipboards and fake Gucci loafers. Why, it's enough to constipate a cat. They'd take me out of here on a slab before I'd back down." She was very close to him now, showing him the beauty of a truly determined woman. "You're going to have to fire me, Louis. You're going to have to do it today." She put her face close to his. Her navy blue eyes flared. "You're going to have to cut my head off."

"No one is talking about firing."

"This place is my life. It's everything to me. It's meat and drink to me. I know what I'm doing."

"I don't want to demote you, and I don't want to fire you. After all," he protested, "I'm not simpleminded."

"I need full authority to do what needs doing."

"You're unreasonably impatient," he exclaimed. "It's only days since we moved you into Mr. Frye's post."

"And look what I've done. That's all the time it took me to do it. I didn't need more than a few days, any more than I needed more than five minutes this morning to bring Tom Pesso and his cameras right into your office. That's the way it should be." Mrs. Fitzgibbons gave a name now to the position in question. "Your chief executive officer should always have her chairman's best interests in mind first, and she should be capable of doing good new things. It isn't enough just to plug away like a little drudge behind a desk and shiver in your timbers when the going gets rough."

Mrs. Fitzgibbons, at the moment, looked truly magnificent. The excitement in her blood brought a bright light to her eyes and set her whole body aglow with animation. She sensed Mr. Zabac's growing inability to stand up to her and instinctively modulated her discourse — not, however, without treating the point at issue as a resolved fact. "I'm not going to be making waves by firing people, either," she said (a statement that might have left many a psychiatrist shaking his head). "In fact, I won't dismiss a soul."

"A senior vice president," the man offered with a sigh, "must be expert in all areas of finance."

"As often as not," Mrs. Fitzgibbons returned smoothly, "there are more important things. I don't have to understand everything there is to know about the Federal Home Loan Bank Board, or about inverted yield curves, or any other such mysteries, as long as I know who *does* know. What does the president of this country need to know about interstate highways? Or the price of a Venezuelan barrel of oil, for that matter? Leadership is different from that. Leadership downstairs!" Her bracelets tinkled as she pointed a long arm significantly toward the lower storey. "Those people need someone to be accountable to. Someone with some backbone to her."

Just as Mr. Zabac appeared to resign himself to Mrs. Fitzgibbons's single-minded onslaught, a smile of relief came to his lips. "My goodness," he exclaimed, charmed anew by the phenomenon standing before him.

"No one down there will defy me," said Mrs. Fitzgibbons. "I have the willpower."

"If you get out of hand, even in the smallest way, I shall ask for your resignation. You understand that."

The chairman's sudden capitulation had an instantaneous effect on her, as the severe drain on Mrs. Fitzgibbons's constitution gave way to relief. "You'll never be sorry! I promise you. If we're here a thousand years, you'll never regret it, Louis. Never," she said. "Never."

Mr. Zabac laughed genially. "And you're not going to fire Mr. Hooton." He made a joke of it.

"You have my word."

"And," he went on, evidencing relief himself, with a light-spirited note, "all of this with the understanding that your chief tasks will be in administration" — he looked at her squarely — "and in public relations?"

Mrs. Fitzgibbons was thinking lucidly. "As long," she insisted, "as your official memorandum naming me as chief executive officer doesn't say so."

Mr. Zabac nodded. "It will be our understanding, yours and mine."

"Then I agree." Her eyes were expanded and concentrated. "And you'll never be sorry."

"You already said that."

"Never," said Mrs. Fitzgibbons. "I swear it on the head of my dead husband."

"That's not necessary," he returned mildly.

An observer looking in would have seen Mr. Zabac smiling like an enchanted dwarf while Mrs. Fitzgibbons stood over him vowing eternal fidelity in a frightening voice.

"I swear it on Larry's head. On all that's holy." With that, Mrs. Fitzgibbons went quickly to the door and called in Mr. Zabac's secretary. "Bring your steno pad," she said.

While Mr. Zabac sat forward in his tall leather armchair and dictated notice of the appointment of Mrs. Frances Fitzgibbons to the post of senior vice president and chief executive officer of the bank, Mrs. Fitzgibbons stood behind Jeannine Mielke's chair and watched with unconcealed satisfaction as the secretary's pencil scratched quickly across the lined pages. When the secretary completed the last page, Mrs. Fitzgibbons dictated the conclusion. "Effective immediately," she said.

"Effective immediately," agreed Mr. Zabac.

While the natty little chairman might not have noticed Mrs. Fitzgibbons's expression, the secretary, upon rising from her chair, and stealing a quick, curious upward glance at the bank's newly appointed senior officer, found herself the target of a pair of liquid blue eyes gloating with menace.

The transaction in Mr. Zabac's office affected Mrs. Fitzgibbons's breathing and nervous system for many minutes afterward. Once or twice, she stopped to take a deep breath. The stimulation and sense of triumph left her feeling very anxious, like someone who had been handed, or had just stolen, a valise full of money. Her voice was steady, though, when she spoke. "It was like taking candy from a baby," she said to Julie. "I should have had this job years ago. *He* knew what he was doing. He knew exactly what he was doing. Somebody's going to feel it, too. Won't I settle an account or two. Won't I? They'll see if I won't."

A quarter hour after closing, when Julie Marcotte looked in to notify her that Tom Pesso had arrived with his associates, Mrs. Fitzgibbons collected her wits instantly and came out. She met Mr. Pesso in front of her office. The perfection of her grooming and her attractively draped figure brought a quick appreciative smile to the announcer's face, as the woman standing before him was nothing less exciting in person than in the big color photo in the paper.

Mrs. Fitzgibbons turned to Julie, who stood blushing with pride, and sent her upstairs with a flick of her hand.

"Tell Mr. Zabac I want him," she said.

From that first moment, as she turned to face the television crew, Mrs. Fitzgibbons knew she was in wonderful fettle.

EIGHT

"And Louis trying to hide behind me the whole time!" she was saying that evening, very pleased with herself.

"And didn't you let him," Bruce attested, with a victorious shout.

"Naturally, I did. It was me they came to see."

Because Bruce had had the foresight to record on video cassette Mrs. Fitzgibbons's television appearance that night on the Channel 6 evening news, he had captured the most memorable seven minutes of her life on film for all time. To savor better her triumph, Mrs. Fitzgibbons came to Bruce Clayton's home that evening for dinner. When she arrived at the apartment on Brown Avenue at eight o'clock, the sedulous politeness lavished on her at the door by her beautician and by Matthew Dean, his friend and housemate, was fitting of royalty. And when Mrs. Fitzgibbons, pushing her way in, in her best cocktail dress, remarked approvingly on the crowded, comfortable, artfully decorated rooms that Bruce and Matthew shared — with mysterious glimmerings of crystal lights twinkling behind white voile draperies, the walls covered with a striking collection of sconces, hangings, medieval-looking tablets, and prettily framed watercolor paintings, not to say a luxurious amount of great soft pillows thrown everywhere — both the young men made an open show of their relief, as though their lives had depended on her approval.

"I had a horror you wouldn't like it," Bruce said, as he raised both hands to receive Mrs. Fitzgibbons's scarf.

"It's delightful," said Mrs. Fitzgibbons, who had never expressed herself with such cinematic hauteur, or had ever even cared much about furnishings or tasteful arrangements. Settings were more important to her now.

"It's priceless."

"Do you think so?"

"Just what I hoped for and expected."

As Bruce pivoted and handed her scarf to Matthew, Mrs. Fitzgibbons marched past him through the shadowy foyer and proceeded with an expectant look on her face through a doorway consisting of a narrow arch of velvet draperies into the almost tentlike dining room. The ceiling was hidden behind voluminous swags of dark velvet. At the center of the small, mysteriously lighted room was the dining table, with settings of china, crystal, and silverware gleaming on a field of white linen. At the head of the modest-sized table stood an impressive Savonarola chair, on the seat of which was placed a gold-tasseled pillow of regal proportions. Bruce had prepared this place of honor for Mrs. Fitzgibbons only minutes before her arrival; he hurried forward and drew back her chair. It was plain to see that Bruce wanted and was encouraging Mrs. Fitzgibbons to be spoiled and imperious.

"I should have gone to get you in the car," he said.

While being seated, Mrs. Fitzgibbons was still showing an interest in the velvet draperies overhead, the miniature chandelier, and the orderly assemblage of the dinner service before her. The centerpiece, bracketed by chocolate-colored candles in silver sticks, was a spray of flame red gladiola.

Bruce was speaking all the while. "Matthew has a magnificent old Buick. It's ten years old, but very posh inside. You'd love it."

"It sounds very comfortable." She looked at the two of them. She liked making some new friends.

"It rides like a dream."

"And it's very roomy in back," Matthew put in.

"I could enjoy being driven sometimes," Mrs. Fitzgibbons confessed. "I haven't been spoiled enough in my adult life. I detest driving."

Positioned at the head of the table, with the soft light converging upon her, Mrs. Fitzgibbons glowed like a picture. As Matthew Dean set about removing the cork from a bottle of champagne, she sat back in the candlelight, looking both beautiful and executive.

As soon as she had her champagne flute in hand, Bruce played the video of her Channel 6 news interview at the bank. All three laughed lightly at various points in the broadcast, beginning with the moment when Mr. Zabac, looking ridiculously short standing beside her, and revealing visible discomfort in the glare of attention, stepped back — and she, clearly the center of attention all along anyhow, stepped forward and took over. Mr. Zabac simply vanished behind her shoulder. In truth, Mrs. Fitzgibbons was herself quite amazed at her composure before the cameras, and at the facility of her tongue.

"How wonderful!" Bruce cried.

"Interviews are a piece of cake." Without looking, she dealt Matthew her empty champagne glass. Bruce and Matthew stood on either side of her chair. Matthew was eyeing her in raptures. Mrs. Fitzgibbons was very full of herself.

Bruce had stopped the video and backed it up, and all three laughed again as Mrs. Fitzgibbons unleashed one of her clever ripostes.

"You're already an inspiration to many, many women," Tom Pesso said.

"I'm a banker," said Mrs. Fitzgibbons, *"not a woman."*

"That sounds quotable."

"Women don't need inspiration, Tom," Mrs. Fitzgibbons was explaining with charm. *"Women are not Hottentots living in the wilds of Borneo."*

More laughter ensued after that, with Mrs. Fitzgibbons herself appearing the most delighted of all. Her own laughter excited a second merry outburst. She looked very beautiful on the screen.

"Is it true," Tom went on, *"that you're going to serve as grand marshal of the great Anniversary Day parade next March?"*

"That is not true." Mrs. Fitzgibbons showed Tom Pesso a placid but rather forbidding expression. Her earrings flashed majestically. *"I was telephoned by someone on the committee, but I'm not prepared to accept. I'm a banker, not a drum major. If you want a drum major, why not ask that handsome young Adonis who leads the Ireland Parish High School Band? Young Terence Sugrue!"* she piped. *"He'd be a wonderful marshal!"*

Mrs. Fitzgibbons lurched forward in her chair and gave a shout of laughter. Bruce Clayton and his partner chimed in at once, as Mrs. Fitzgibbons's sexual liaison with the tall, sandy-haired high schooler was known to both of them.

"He could lead it with his pecker out!" she said.

"Now, you're being shocking!" Bruce spoke up with delight.

"You two would never be the same. You've never seen anything like it in your life. It's a work of art. You couldn't dent it with a hammer." Mrs. Fitzgibbons had been suppressing her urge to mouth an obscenity all day. "They could start a whole new universe with it. Put on some music," she said. "If I'm going to process a mortgage for you two lovebirds, I might as well keep you hopping. What kind of soup have you made?"

"It's mushroom barley," said Matthew, "with vegetable stock, garlic, and a world of basil."

"I love it. It's going to be a wonderful success. Bruce, shut off the VCR. We'll watch it again later. I'm starving. Where's my napkin? Let's have dinner."

While Bruce stood at her side and unfolded her starched napkin, she called through the door to Matthew in the kitchen. "Bring the tureen to the table. And some café-grind pepper, if you have it. You're both wonderful. I love you both. I need people I can trust."

Leaning, Bruce extended Mrs. Fitzgibbons's napkin across her lap. His infatuation was marked. "I'd do anything for you."

"And well you may," said Mrs. Fitzgibbons, looking hungrily at the big blue bowl of steaming soup that Matthew was transporting ceremoniously to the table. "I'll tell you what you're going to do." She apprised Bruce of her desires without detaching her gaze from the tureen in Matthew's hands. "You're going to dig up some dirt for me. You're going to do some local research. On enemies of mine. People who would like nothing better than to see me brought down."

"Enemies?" Bruce stepped in front of Matthew, took up the china ladle, and began to serve Mrs. Fitzgibbons her soup. "You haven't an enemy on earth."

"I," she said, "shall be the judge of that. What effect do you think today's coup has had on my rivals?"

"But Mr. Zabac appointed you."

"An appointment is nothing."

"She means," Matthew suggested helpfully, "that other officers coveted the post also and are probably resentful."

"Exactly."

"I never thought of that." Caught in the dilemma of wanting to be innocent in Mrs. Fitzgibbons's eyes while keeping Matthew in his place, Bruce's eyes twinkled in frustration.

"The real struggle," Mrs. Fitzgibbons stated with authority, "is just beginning. You can't be a bleeding heart. That's where others go wrong, by being sweet and grateful and trusting, while some treacherous little heel with big ideas is sneaking up behind you with a knife in his hand. That's not going to happen to me."

"Maybe," Matthew Dean suggested, "they'll more or less accept the new arrangement, now that it's done, though."

"They won't." Mrs. Fitzgibbons tasted her soup, as her hosts sat down on either side of the table, Bruce to her left, Matthew to her right. "But I have the power. They don't. I can make things happen. My options are real. I can terminate people. I can demote them, transfer them, reduce their wages, or eliminate them altogether. While they're skulking around in the dark, I can operate in the open. That's what my appointment means. Nothing more and nothing less. All I need is a little dirt to make my job easy. You'll find it for me, too. Worms leave a trail."

"She's right about that!" Matthew said gleefully.

"I'll try," said Bruce.

"You'll do more than try, darling. Every person in this world is either a liar, a crook, or some kind of lecher or cheat or drunkard — or gambler or drug addict, or just some twenty-five-cent fink who beats up his mother." She waved her soup spoon. "Look at the two of you," she said.

Surprised momentarily by her allusion to their own relationship, Bruce and Matthew reacted with laughter.

"Bruce was right," Matthew said. "You're wonderful, Mrs. Fitzgibbons."

"I'll smear them, if I have to," she continued. "The public wants to believe the worst about people, anyhow."

While dining, Mrs. Fitzgibbons explained to her two young men something of the cold-blooded nature of human affairs on the executive plane. "You will never know what it was like in there. If I hadn't had murder in my heart all day, I'd be in ruins now. I'd be at the mercy of tyrannical little underlings like Elizabeth Wilson, who makes her girls show her their fingernails. Disgusting creatures who want to get you under their heel. I'd be a basket case. I'd be dead. If I had faltered for a second, just once — if I had shown weakness — I wouldn't be here tonight. I wouldn't be on television, I wouldn't be the new chief, I wouldn't be a thing. My future wouldn't be worth a penny. You only see the surface," she explained. "You see the little chairman standing behind me on the six o'clock news and assume it had to be that way. It didn't."

"I'm sure she's right," said Matthew.

"I've learned to be hard in a crisis," Mrs. Fitzgibbons boasted. "I have more courage than other people. I take the fight to them. I did it today." She was sitting up in the candlelight. She moved her hand in a lateral gesture. "I won total authority. And I'm going to keep it. I'm not going to dribble it away. They'll never get me out! Not Hooton, or Wilson, or Brouillette, or any of them. I have them in my hands. Now," she promised, "you'll see what cowards they are."

If Mrs. Fitzgibbons's warlike egoism struck Bruce or Matthew as excessive, neither one showed it.

"You're right to consolidate your position," Matthew concurred.

"Of course, I am." Mrs. Fitzgibbons was empyreal on that point.

She turned to Bruce with a simpering expression of exaggerated tolerance on her face, as though disabusing a child of infantile notions.

"I didn't disagree." Bruce protested feebly the sudden unfair concert of criticism leveled at him.

"Machiavelli said, 'All men are vulgar,' " Matthew was pleased to point out.

"They are." Mrs. Fitzgibbons was directing herself regularly now to Matthew, as though he were the man of the house, the more practical and worldly of the two. She was aware, too, that Matthew was stealing looks at the fullness of her breasts, swelling and ebbing behind the soft silk of her dress, and at her makeup and hair. Despite his efforts to emulate Bruce's artistic sensibility and more sophisticated mannerisms and outlook, Matthew seemed the coarser and more masculine of the two.

"Everyone fears a strong hand," said Matthew. "Keep them guessing."

"Exactly."

"I think you should treat your enemies with great suspicion," Matthew added.

"I think you should shut your mouth!" Bruce exploded in a paroxysm of anger that astonished both Mrs. Fitzgibbons and Matthew. He was shouting at Matthew. He was very pale and shaking. "What do you know about business? You're just a clerk! You're nothing but somebody's little gofer. Didn't I warn you an hour ago to keep your mouth shut? Mrs. Fitzgibbons came as my dinner guest, not to be lectured at by some three-hundred-dollar-a-week, city-employee ass kisser. Talking about Machiavelli!" Bruce's eyes flashed with menace. "What in heaven's name do you know about someone like that? You were quoting me," Bruce shouted. "I told *you* that. The night you came crybabying home from Mount Tom with your tail between your legs. And *I* took you in." For an instant, Bruce mastered his embarrassing outburst, as he looked down in consternation at his plate, then to the left and past the gladiola, with his lips together. Then he lost control again.

"You shit," he cried. "You presumptuous, two-faced, penny-pinching shit." Bruce turned in desperation to Mrs. Fitzgibbons. "He begged me to let him make dinner tonight. He knew how important it was to me. He knew it meant everything to me." Bruce's voice cracked with these words, and he cast up his napkin. "Now, it's all spoiled."

"Nothing is spoiled." Mrs. Fitzgibbons was instantly affected by Bruce's distress.

"Well, it is," he said, and got up from the table. "For me, it's spoiled."

Bruce stood stock-still behind his place at the table. His features were distorted. Then, dreading the humiliation of actually shedding tears, he hurried from the room.

Mrs. Fitzgibbons was appalled by the sudden sequence of events. She had never seen such a furious altercation erupt over such insignificant cause. She got up from her chair and followed him. She went out through the draperied doorway into the foyer; but Bruce was nowhere to be seen. Without knocking, Mrs. Fitzgibbons opened a door nearby and let herself into the adjacent room. It was shadowy inside. The room was dominated by a canopied bed of luxurious proportions, a wonderwork of gauzy materials floating down from the ceiling. Bruce was in the room. She could barely make him out. He was leaning against the wall, with his fingers to his lips.

He was crying quietly. "I knew he would do that."

Mrs. Fitzgibbons closed the door behind her. "It wasn't serious," she remarked softly.

"To me it was." He spoke in a troubled whisper.

The sight of the young man standing pale before her, leaning against the wall with his head averted, aroused Mrs. Fitzgibbons's sincerest sympathy. She felt a surge of affection for him. "You're too sensitive, darling," she said.

Bruce shook his head and made as if to speak, but no words came.

"Matthew is not like you," she added in a tender voice. She touched him on the shoulder. "You're different, Bruce. You're not like everyone else. You're special."

At these last words, Bruce stifled a choking sound and put his hand over his face. The look of him, with his cuff links and neat dotted necktie, put her in mind of a troubled schoolboy she had once known in grammar school, a delicate boy named Howard Ellert, who was the butt of much childhood malice. Impulsively, Mrs. Fitzgibbons reached and put her arms around him. Her own heart was drumming. "Being different," she counseled him softly, "takes courage."

Bruce replied under his breath, after a moment elapsed. "I know."

"That's why I'm surprised."

"I was jealous. Now, I've spoiled everything."

She felt the warmth of his flesh through his shirt, and placed her hand behind his head. "I love you, Bruce."

His shoulders trembled as the feelings welled up in him; Mrs. Fitzgibbons divined readily the much deeper reservoir of unhappiness that underlay this reaction. She kept talking while holding him.

"I love you, too," he said.

"I want you to." She spoke earnestly to him, their voices conspiratorial in the darkened room. "You're my right hand. . . . You're my good luck." Mrs. Fitzgibbons uttered words that she had spoken long ago to Larry. A phrase came back to her. "You're my brightness," she said.

They stood thus, in the shadowy room, for an extended length of time. His collapse, she knew, was of a general nature, deeper than the moment, like waters forcing a rupture in cellar walls. Nor was she surprised later, after insisting on taking him out to dinner, to hear Bruce reproaching his friend in the dining room in rather violent terms. Looking in, she saw Matthew sitting stonily behind the table, exactly as they had left him, his face as white as the linen. "You can eat your own dinner!" Bruce was saying, while buttoning his double-breasted suit jacket and arranging his polka-dotted pocket square with elegant flourishes. "Your own little masterpiece. You're not fit for civilized company. I hope you choke on it."

"But, Bruce —" the other began.

"Shut your mouth!" Bruce snapped hotly. "Don't speak to me.

Mrs. Fitzgibbons and I are going to the Hofbrau House. I'll settle my differences with you when I come back. Why, you're nothing but a little Tartuffe. A little snake in the grass. Come on," he said, and snapped his fingers rudely. "The car keys."

During the ride downtown in Matthew Dean's Buick, Bruce continued to deplore his friend's behavior as "unmannerly," "boorish," "simpleminded," and as a want of good breeding in "a working-class stiff." While stopped at a light on High Street, he begged Mrs. Fitzgibbons to forgive the unintended insult. "What made me think that a common rowdy, a city clerk who hasn't read six books in his life, wouldn't revert to barbarism, I can't say."

By now, however, Mrs. Fitzgibbons felt that her friend behind the wheel had salved his feeling sufficiently to be treated once again the way he enjoyed being treated.

"The light is green, Bruce. Let's step on it. I don't want to hear about your dirty linens. Save your smut for the beauty parlor. Drive me to Ann Taylor. The mall is still open. I want to look at some clothes. And remind me to watch the eleven o'clock news tonight. I'll be on again, you know."

"I'll remember." Bruce was now very much himself, a picture once more of the efficient aide-de-camp.

"That's what I pay you for," she said playfully. "To keep me happy."

"I won't forget."

"Where did you two deviants get that big bed?" she said, suddenly. "I'd like to use that myself sometime."

"You'd be welcome to," he exclaimed.

"It looks like something from a Persian whorehouse."

With Bruce Clayton as consultant and as an earnest advocate of her acquiring a more dramatic wardrobe, Mrs. Fitzgibbons was fitted at the women's fashion store for a smart pin-striped peplum suit, a black and silver-lamé cocktail dress, and a rather spectacular winter cape that tied at the throat. She wore the cape and lamé dress out to the car. Bruce hurried along at her side, marveling at the ease with which Mrs. Fitzgibbons had plunked down more than two thousand dollars in twenty-five minutes, and was impressed, if not actually intimidated, by the way she had ordered the saleslady about. The more manic and overbearing Mrs. Fitzgibbons got, the more Bruce appeared to adulate her. By ten o'clock, when they entered the restaurant, Mrs. Fitzgibbons was on her high horse. She even complimented Bruce for the way he interceded with the maitre d', an elderly white-haired man named Liebeck, to instruct him in the importance of showing Mrs. Fitzgibbons to the choicest, most visible table. If the lady standing by the reservations desk, drawing considerable attention to herself in her cape and silver-and-black dress, did not fit Mr. Liebeck's conception of a banker, she certainly suited his notion of what a celebrity should look like. The stately manner in which the white-haired man led the two of them to a central table resembled that of an impresario leading a renowned performer and her accompanist onto the stage.

Once seated, Mrs. Fitzgibbons waved away the waiter at her side without looking at him. The attention of diners nearby gave her a very warm sensation inside. She actually felt herself to be the scintillating heart of the big, tastefully lighted dining room. She made a glittering appearance. Magnificently composed, the words flowed from her lips without the slightest hesitancy or any sign of mental deliberation.

"I'm not a psychiatrist," she tossed out. "I can't tell you why people think the way they do, or, for that matter, what's so fascinating about me and what I'm doing, that they can't get enough of it."

"People love a success story," Bruce managed to interject.

"Well, of course, they do. I don't fault them for that. My secretary thrills to my successes as much as I do."

"So do I," said Bruce.

"Naturally," said Mrs. Fitzgibbons. "But I wasn't talking about people who stand to gain from what I do. Let's be honest. A good session of ass kissing makes sense if you stand to profit by it. I wasn't talking about that. I was talking about the brain-damaged, about the man in the street who can tell you Wade Boggs's batting average. He's the same boogums who comes in and tells me how to run my bank. Larry was like that."

Mrs. Fitzgibbons's reference to her dead husband was a trifle perplexing to Bruce; he remained silent a moment.

"You must miss him," he said.

Mrs. Fitzgibbons nodded idly. "I missed him for a while," she said. "He had some unusual characteristics. For a year or so, I missed the way he could move around in the dark. Larry was a regular bat. He could actually see in the dark. Our bedroom wasn't just dark, it was pitch-black. Larry was brought up as an altar boy. For him, the precondition for love was total, absolute, leg-breaking darkness. Lovemaking was something that was supposed to take place under a log in a swamp. If you've ever seen my daughter, Barbara, you'd know what I mean."

Patrons sitting nearby had been careful to conceal their interest in Mrs. Fitzgibbons's entertaining discourse. This remark ignited laughter on all sides.

"You know what I'm talking about," Mrs. Fitzgibbons addressed herself cheerfully to a woman on her right, then turned at once to another on her left. "What disappointment on earth can equal it? That's why they have doctors and nurses there. If it was just me and the child, only one of us would have left the room alive."

Mrs. Fitzgibbons would have said more, but her attention was drawn elsewhere in the room. Those watching her saw a look of consternation on her face, as she straightened in her seat and directed a sudden fiery look at the back of a busboy working to clear one of the tables. "What is he doing here?" Mrs. Fitzgibbons demanded to know.

The busboy in question was wearing a mustard yellow vest with a white shirt and black bow tie; he was piling serving dishes, dinner plates, and half-drained teacups atop a tray, working quietly at his job. Sensing the attention of others, however, he turned round and saw the woman in the glittering silver-and-black dress glaring up at him. She was sitting not ten feet distant. Of all the people he had ever set eyes on, no one was as frightening or loathsome to his senses as she. The sight of Mrs. Fitzgibbons hypnotized him. The busboy in question was none other than Laurence De Maria.

"What is he doing here?" she said then in a big, angry voice.

"Am I being made a fool of?" She turned to Bruce. "Is he going to dog me to my grave? This is the same blundering idiot that I fired last Wednesday. Now he's here. Where I go, he goes! What," said Mrs. Fitzgibbons, "is that boy doing here?"

The effect of Mrs. Fitzgibbons's vicious attack upon the balding busboy was mesmerizing. He leaned forward from the waist and gaped at her with his mouth open. Her face was alight with anger. Her eyes were wide. At that moment, Mrs. Fitzgibbons, by some standards, was perhaps technically insane.

"This is your living example of the very thing I've been talking about." She vilified the De Maria brother in a harsh voice. "This is just the sort of oily, mealymouthed parasite — this reptile," she went on, "this yellow little reptile — who comes sneaking out of his hole at the first sign of a crumb on the floor. He can't dress himself. He can't add up a column of figures. He has a vocabulary of about four hundred words. But when no one is looking, this little Latin bag of tricks will walk off with your silverware, your umbrella, your tables and chairs, and your life savings!"

As Mrs. Fitzgibbons lashed away at her ex-employee, she maintained a rigid posture and a very drained expression. The restaurant had fallen silent on all sides, especially as the target of Mrs. Fitzgibbons's wrath stood transfixed in horror before her. Laurence De Maria's fear passed description. He couldn't move.

Bruce endeavored to dissuade Mrs. Fitzgibbons from continuing; he set his fingers lightly on her hand but lacked the audacity to speak up. She turned to him.

"I threw him out," she said. "I personally saw him to the street. What happens? He pops up someplace else."

Having heard the disturbance while talking on the reservations phone by the front door, the maitre d' came at once and mercifully interposed himself between the glamorous lady and Mr. De Maria. Taking him by the arm, Mr. Liebeck guided his badly shaken busboy across the dining room of the Hofbrau House toward the kitchen. Satisfied by his removal, and vindicated in her objective, Mrs. Fitzgibbons directed herself to those about her.

"They think they can't be found," she said, and smirked to signify the folly of criminal behavior. The dining room remained noticeably subdued, even though Mrs. Fitzgibbons appeared to regain her equanimity almost instantly. In fact, she changed the subject with startling swiftness, and for many minutes thereafter entertained Bruce with a catalog of amusing anecdotes about her daughter and son-in-law and the activities they pursued in the name of environmentalism. She sipped her wine and dined with obvious relish on her lobster thermidor, while remarking jocularly on the plight of baby seals, or on how spraying for Dutch elm disease was destroying the ozone layer. Her behavior was so airy and genial, in fact, that many, including Bruce, might well have wondered if Mrs. Fitzgibbons was not justified in the vicious attack they had all just witnessed. Orderliness is often its own justification.

Much later, however, in the parking lot behind the restaurant, as Mrs. Fitzgibbons led the way past a row of automobiles to Matthew's Buick, an incident transpired that had an enduring effect on Mrs. Fitzgibbons's outlook and policies thereafter. Out of nowhere, a figure materialized. There was a sound of running footsteps on the gravel, followed by a glimpse of something shapeless in violent motion on the near side of a bank of evergreens. In the space of a second or two, Laurence De Maria was rushing at the two of them from behind, waving a very long two-by-four plank high above his head. The actual blow, delivered with unrestricted force and a warlike scream, was intended to transfer Mrs. Fitzgibbons instantaneously to the land of her ancestors.

Bruce threw himself between them and flung up his arm. Had he not done so, the blow would certainly have fractured Mrs. Fitzgibbons's skull. As it was, his elbow deflected the seven-foot-long beam near its mid-point, and was followed by a cracking noise as the upper portion of the plank struck his forehead a glancing blow. Mrs. Fitzgibbons retreated in astonishment as Bruce and the gold-clad Laurence De Maria went down on the gravel in a twisting, grappling heap. "Save yourself!" Bruce was screaming at her, as he wrestled with the fifty-year-old busboy. "Run, Mrs. Fitzgibbons!"

Laurence De Maria was himself in a frenzy. "I'll kill the bitch! I'll kill the bitch! I'll kill the bitch!"

When the chef and a waiter came running through the darkness from the kitchen, Bruce had his opponent pinioned to the gravel with the two-by-four against his collarbone.

"Here we have an individual," Mrs. Fitzgibbons explained to the police at the station house, "who can't do his job, is dismissed by his superior, and in less than a week, not seven days, sets out to kill her."

Mrs. Fitzgibbons's cape swayed impressively as she moved about in front of the booking desk, discussing what had happened in a wonderfully lucid manner.

"I would be dead. That's a provable fact. If it wasn't for my young assistant, who put himself in the way, I'd be lying in a pool of blood. The latest victim of another senseless killing."

"You were very fortunate." Lieutenant Rollins sought earnestly to comfort her.

"Is that what you call it?" she snapped, by way of rebuttal. "I see nothing fortunate in being attacked by a twisted maniac who conceals himself in the bushes with a big piece of lumber in his hands just because somebody looked at him funny. If that's fortunate, I hope my good luck has run out forever." She spoke bitterly while pacing. "Don't think this wasn't an education for me. This puts me on my guard. This was a day when the stock markets of the world were practically destroyed, but I didn't expect to be killed in the process."

She returned to Bruce, who was sitting on a long, spindle-backed wooden bench, holding a bloodied handkerchief to his head. "I'm taking you to the hospital."

"That won't be necessary. I'll drive you home, Mrs. Fitzgibbons." Bruce was very gratified by Mrs. Fitzgibbons's repeated allusions to his courage and loyalty. He had taken off his jacket and necktie; he leaned forward with his elbows on his knees. His shirt front was badly torn.

Turning on her heel, Mrs. Fitzgibbons waved her gloves at Bruce. "This is another kind of human being altogether. I thank God," she said, "for the day I found him."

Laurence De Maria had already been arrested and locked up for the night. Before Mrs. Fitzgibbons left the police station, she made it clear to Patrick Rollins, the lieutenant on duty, that should Mr. De Maria come to grief during the night she would be the first to come forward and corroborate any convenient fiction concocted to justify his death. Mrs. Fitzgibbons's remarks elicited chuckles from the several cops in the room. During the ride home, while sitting back against the passenger door of Matthew's sedan, she enlarged on her sanguinary views. "He ought to be beaten to death in his cell," she said.

By now, however, Mrs. Fitzgibbons's frame of mind was such that she took pleasure in dwelling on the violent incident outside the Hofbrau House. The fact that someone had made an effort on her life was a fitting corollary to the magnitude of the events that day in which she had shown her mettle. It was agreeable to her self-esteem. Mrs. Fitzgibbons looked both excited and pale as she sat back with her cape spread over her lap.

Bruce winced from time to time at the extremity of her views. "The courts will know what to do with him," he suggested amelioratively.

"Oh, I'd know what to do with him. I'd have someone take him down to the railroad yards and put a bullet in his head. *And* in his brother's head. And anyone else's who's mad enough to think that I'd take this lying down. This is what I get for being a soft touch. I go out to dinner with a friend," she recited once more, almost verbatim, her earlier words, delineating the reasonableness of her position, "I want to relax and enjoy myself at the end of a strenuous day, and a busboy, a nobody, one of the feckless, anonymous millions, jumps out of nowhere and tries to assassinate me." She gestured ironically and raised her voice. "Say, maybe this happens to everybody. Maybe I'm the deluded sap. People see you on television, they know you're somebody, and something clicks in their heads. You're not supposed to live anymore."

"Thank God you weren't hurt."

"Your personal aide jumps in the way at the last second and is beaten black and blue, left on the ground bleeding from the head, and it's the most ordinary thing in the world. People around here think nothing of it. In some parts of the world, they hang assassins on meat hooks. Here" — Mrs. Fitzgibbons made a face — "it's business as usual."

Mrs. Fitzgibbons slept that night in Bruce's peach-and-green canopied bed. Bruce expelled Matthew from the apartment in a rude, flagrant manner, then set about making her comfortable. At home, the full extent of Bruce's injuries was apparent. His left arm above the elbow was swollen and discolored. A cake of dried blood showed in his hair just above the ear. His knuckles were skinned red. Since he took such obvious pride in the badges of his bravery, however, Mrs. Fitzgibbons did not spoil him unduly. She compelled him to help her prepare herself for bed. Sitting back against enormous pillows, with a cup of herbal tea in hand and the bed sheet drawn above her breasts, it struck Mrs. Fitzgibbons that she had missed the late evening news broadcast on WKYN and was quick to point out Bruce's failing.

"I take him to dinner, I buy him the choicest wine in the place, and here I am," she said, "at fifteen minutes to midnight, sitting here like an idiot, and I've missed myself on television."

Her reproach injured Bruce. He sought to mollify her with reason. "I have the entire broadcast on tape, Mrs. Fitzgibbons." He stood by the bed with a pained expression.

"Is that what I asked you?" Mrs. Fitzgibbons stared fixedly before her at the pretty peach-and-green voile draperies hanging in delicate swags over the foot of the bed. An enjoyable feeling coursed through her veins as she pursed her lips sternly. Bruce remained speechless. She had never scolded him before. "Because if it is, I must be unbalanced," she said.

After that, Mrs. Fitzgibbons remained silent for the longest time. She neither looked at Bruce nor spoke to him. She sat perfectly still, with a direful expression on her face, a picture in the flesh of the brooding tyrant.

THE TERROR SPREADS

NINE

Of those who knew her well, none but a handful would ever have doubted Mrs. Fitzgibbons's generous nature. She had possessed from birth a kindly, tolerant disposition. All her life, she had shown herself to be the sort of person who saw her own failings in the weakness and ineptitude of others, and was more apt to forgive than censure shortcomings. It figured in Mrs. Fitzgibbons's likability, even from her earliest days. As a schoolchild, she would have been about the last one present ever to ridicule or torment a pathetic classmate. She wasn't like that. If as a wife and mother, she had been secretly disappointed in the direction her life was taking, and to some degree even in the persons with whom she shared that life, she attributed it, as most do, to the unrealistic expectations that take root in the young and that naturally wilt as time goes by. If her successes in recent days seemed to involve a repudiation of her virtues, Mrs. Fitzgibbons saw it as nothing more than a response to circumstance. On Tuesday morning, the day following both the stock market panic and the murderous attack upon her at the Hofbrau House by an ex-member of her own staff, Mrs. Fitzgibbons was able to put into words some trenchant insights on the subject of her struggle. "You can have the loftiest ideals in the world," she said, "plans that stand to benefit everybody — you can spend more than forty years preparing yourself — and the instant you stand up to show others the way, somebody clubs you on the head. You could be the Virgin Mary."

While Bruce worked on Mrs. Fitzgibbons in his salon, she enlightened him on the dynamics of power. She had often wondered herself how historic figures had been able to bear the constant trials and perils of leadership. Now she knew. "They don't have a choice," she said. "I've learned more about history in the past three days than old Sister Stanislaus could have taught me in a lifetime."

Bruce was working on her eyelids with a sponge applicator, imparting to each fluttery eyelid a layer of pale blue eye shadow. Unknown to Bruce, Mrs. Fitzgibbons was experiencing nervous spasms in her stomach. It didn't show, but her nerves were jangled. Every few minutes, her heart rate speeded up. In the full light of day, Mrs. Fitzgibbons did not expect some demented attacker to come rushing in from the mall and assault her on the spot; but gathering feelings of a paranoid nature had established themselves in her system.

"You can't turn back," she said. "There's no place to hide. You can stay forever buried in the mass, as long as you keep quiet and grin and swallow what they feed you, but when you start to fight, you have to defend yourself around the clock every day of the year. And you can only do that by attacking and destroying your enemies."

"By keeping up the pressure."

"Exactly, darling. It's a never-ending struggle. If you stand still," she said, "those behind you will smash the life out of you."

Despite Mrs. Fitzgibbons's anxious state of mind, her magic was more than evident this morning. The three women who worked for Bruce crowded around her, all talking at once, praising her for her Monday evening television appearance. On Maple Street, as she went from the salon to the bank, people recognized her in the street. Moreover, the bank itself was even busier than it had been the day before. When Mrs. Fitzgibbons entered through the re-volving doors — wearing a very dark, gun-metal blue leather coat she had appropriated from Bruce, with its epaulets and trim styling, which lent her a brisk, military look — the crowd inside was un-precedented in size. The people standing in line were also noisier than usual, as if they imagined themselves participating in some-thing exciting, as in the sudden rise to prominence of one among their number. As she darted in among them, the highlighting around her cheekbones and temples shone to create a very deter-mined expression. She ignored the felicitations thrown at her from all sides. There was a genuine aura about her. She radiated purpose. Everyone noticed it.

The first thing she did that morning was move her office. As a proper site for a chief officer, she selected the big conference room adjacent to Mr. Hooton's department at the rear of the bank. The elegance of the room, with its beamed ceiling and full mahogany paneling, reflected nicely, she thought, on her newly won authority. More important, being deep and spacious, it would produce a frightening effect on anyone called into it. The conference table was removed, and Mr. Klopfer, the head of maintenance, was instructed to position Mrs. Fitzgibbons's big desk in the far corner of the room. In this way, anyone summoned to her office would be required to march across twenty feet of open carpet just to reach her desk, a requirement that she guessed would abash the stoutest heart, especially if the summonee were then left standing in limbo for a while as she continued to busy herself with her desk work. Mrs. Fitzgibbons was not insensible to such subtleties.

Mrs. Fitzgibbons was a fountain of nervous energy this morning. While Mr. Klopfer and his assistant, Marshall Moriarty, relocated her desk, files, and personal effects, she was everywhere at once, and kept Julie on the run as well. Spotting Jack Greaney, Mrs. Fitzgibbons collared him on the floor and gave him a task that astonished him. She wanted a secret memorandum prepared, she said, on the subject of Laurence and Morris De Maria, a compi-lation that included everything that could be discovered about them.

Young Jack, who looked nervous whenever Mrs. Fitzgibbons

was in his presence, listened in stupefaction as she gave him the law; she cited examples of what she wanted. "Who hired them, who their references were, where they worked before, whom they married, where they live, where they work now — all of it — in a confidential report to me. The whole putrid mess," she said. "I'm going to get to the bottom of those two," she added, setting a gloved finger in front of Jack's face.

"What did they do?" Jack was concerned to know the cause of the bank's enduring interest in them.

"What they did is a matter for the courts of law. I'm going to put them in jail, Jack. I'm going to put them away."

Backed up against a glass cubicle, his face as white as a parsnip, Jack listened as the new senior vice president of the Parish Bank eyed him with a scary intensity.

"I want to know who they lunched with while they were here, who their closest friends were, their neighbors, their doctors, their children, their wives' maiden names, their parents, everything in the book."

"But we don't have information like that," he countered helplessly.

"Because if you don't do that for me," she went on, "you'll be a stock clerk at K mart. You'll be working for the sanitation department. You'll be peddling your body down at Race and Main to little Puerto Rican men with mustaches. I'll fire you, Jack." Mrs. Fitzgibbons looked genuinely scary, very even-eyed and soft-voiced, as she enunciated her threat. "You were their superior. Your neck is on the line."

By this time, even the more indifferent, workaday employees of the bank were convinced that Mrs. Fitzgibbons's administration presaged a dynamic new era in the history of the bank. Depositors opened new accounts in impressive numbers. Mr. Zabac came to work a little earlier than usual and betrayed a certain bounce in his footstep at the sight of the continuing press of new business, as he mounted the stairs with his usual stiff-backed, godlike dignity. Ensconced in her new office, Mrs. Fitzgibbons took congratulatory calls one after the other, only interrupting herself long enough to get Leonard Frye on the line to approve three separate home loan applications he had sent to her desk. Twice, while coming and going outside her office, she encountered Neil Hooton; she ignored him both times, sweeping past him with a regal, impatient expression. The stock market was in pieces. She showed him her contempt, while remaining mindful in her heart of the man's hatred of her and of the need to ruin him at her earliest convenience.

Her most enjoyable communication that morning came from a man named Nahum Solomon, a highly placed loan officer at the Shawmut Bank in Boston, who called to wish Mrs. Fitzgibbons the best of luck in her new post. He had seen an Associated Press article that morning in the *Boston Globe,* he said, which included her photo and an account of her promotion to the senior position. Then, in the way of greeting Mrs. Fitzgibbons to the greater banking community, Mr. Solomon inquired if Mrs. Fitzgibbons might be interested in joining what he referred to airily as "a little consortium of banks" being assembled to finance a modest, very low risk, state-sponsored industrial park in the Worcester area.

"Not only am I interested," said Mrs. Fitzgibbons, sitting back in her chair, savoring the first deserts of her P.R. wizardry, "but I'm positively delighted you thought to call me."

Julie had started into the office, but Mrs. Fitzgibbons waved her out with a brisk cut of her arm.

Nahum Solomon had a deep, wonderfully prepossessing voice that was fashioned by nature to make small of big things. "Then I think we'll do business," he crooned pleasantly.

"I'm sure we will." She revolved in her chair and compressed her lips thoughtfully. "In effect," she explained, with self-importance, "this is my first full day in charge of operations here. I'm not too busy to talk, Mr. Solomon —"

"Call me Nate."

"I'm Frankie," she said. "I'm not too busy to talk, Nate, but I couldn't come out Worcester way this week."

"It's a real plum," added the other softly, under his breath. "You'll like it."

"We'll make medicine on it, I'm sure."

"I'll send a car for you one day soon."

Mrs. Fitzgibbons brushed a thread from her skirt. "Let's try next Monday."

"Monday noon would be choice," said he.

"You were a grand sport to call me." Mrs. Fitzgibbons looked about at her magnificent office. "When I get something that's too big for us to handle, I'll know who to telephone."

"I'm always here."

"Till Monday," she said.

Life had never seemed so bountiful. After hanging up, Mrs. Fitzgibbons sent Julie to the news dealer in the rear vestibule for several copies of the *Globe*. Julie was back in a twinkling; her cheeks were pink with excitement as she spread open the paper on Mrs. Fitzgibbons's desk. Right off, Mrs. Fitzgibbons sent a copy upstairs to Mr. Zabac, then settled back to read, and reread, the glowing, condensed version of her appointment as chief executive officer. The article concluded with the words, "Mrs. Fitzgibbons is one of a small but stellar handful of women to attain executive control of a New England bank."

This last development, coming atop so many others, filled Mrs. Fitzgibbons with such a sense of pride in herself that she couldn't control the urge to act out her feelings of personal triumph, as by giving somebody nearby a good dressing down.

"Who was that young man with Emile Klopfer?" she demanded of Julie. "The assistant from the maintenance department who helped to move my desk? What's his name?" Mrs. Fitzgibbons felt better already. The instant she made up her mind to do something, the anxious tightening in her chest began to dissipate.

"Oh, him," said Julie, amused at the individual in question. "That's Marshall Moriarty." She laughed. "He's the one they call the Most Beautiful Man."

"They?"

"The women in the ladies lounge. They talk about him. He comes to work at seven, they say, wearing a suit and necktie and carrying his work clothes in a briefcase, and then changes into them."

Mrs. Fitzgibbons knew the man by sight very well and had noticed herself how neat and immaculate he was and how he bore himself with exquisite posture and a smiling, diffident expression. Marshall was the only maintenance worker who troubled to wear a necktie with his blue shirt, and was, as Julie implied, noticeable for his handsomeness. Mrs. Fitzgibbons snatched up a yellow pad, scratched Marshall Moriarty's name on it, and signed it with a flourish of her initials. She dealt it to Julie. "Get him," she said.

When Julie came back, Mrs. Fitzgibbons was on the phone with her daughter. Barbara had heard from a friend in the police department about the "incident" in the parking lot of the Hofbrau House. "People hate your guts!" Barbara was scolding her mother mercilessly. "You're shaming me to death. I can't live here anymore. I dread being seen in public. You're behaving like a maniac."

Mrs. Fitzgibbons hung up on her daughter and told Julie to get a dictation pad. While Marshall Moriarty stood in her doorway with the yellow slip of paper in his hand, Mrs. Fitzgibbons dictated her latest new policy idea to Julie. It concerned the Christmas bonuses, which were to be disbursed in a few weeks. The idea came to her on impulse. She searched her mind for the best wording. "This year's holiday bonuses," the memo began, "will aggregate a 5% increase over last year's total disbursement" — Mrs. Fitzgibbons paused while Julie wrote — "but will entail a 10% increase for all employees other than officers, without exception."

The restructuring of the year-end bonuses was such, the memo made clear, that the senior officers were going to take it on the chin.

Marshall Moriarty accepted Mrs. Fitzgibbons's invitation to pull up a little chair in front of her desk and make himself comfortable. Mrs. Fitzgibbons was leaning forward on her elbows with her hands folded, following the young maintenance assistant's movements. She wore a pretty expression, a benign candor. She was feeling a lot better, relaxed inside and composed, now that she had someone in front of her upon whom to train her subsiding anxieties.

Before speaking, Mrs. Fitzgibbons looked him up and down with a favoring eye, from his starchy blue shirt and necktie, and pressed jeans, down to his gleaming black shoes. She noted his manicured nails and marveled at his ability to keep himself in such

an impeccable state. Most arresting of all, however, was the shape
and clean-carved angularity of Marshall Moriarty's head, not to
say the profusion of curly golden hair crowning it. Mrs. Fitzgibbons recognized the justice in the epithet given him by the women
of the bank, *viz.*, the Most Beautiful Man.

"Would you mind closing the door?" she said, and then waited
as he got up and marched all the way across the carpeted floor
and then all the way back again.

"You and I haven't had an opportunity to talk." She disengaged
her chin from her hands and sat back in her leather chair. She was
toying with a yellow pencil while examining her perfectly shaped
nails. Whatever was keeping the handsome young man a maintenance assistant, it was already clear to Mrs. Fitzgibbons, had to
be mental.

She did not, therefore, bandy words, but struck at the heart of
the matter. "Tell me about your schooling. You're not, I take it,
college-educated?"

Because of his size, which was that of a professional athlete,
and the absurd smallness of the chair on which he sat, Marshall
Moriarty appeared suspended in space in front of her desk. He
shook his head incredulously.

"I have never gone to college."

"High school?" Her voice climbed inquisitively. "What high
school did you attend, Marshall?"

"I was a member of the class of 1970 at Ireland Parish High
School."

Mrs. Fitzgibbons reacted with amazement. "How old *are* you?"
she cried.

"I was thirty-six in July."

"You look ten years younger. What on earth do you eat? Baby
foods? I thought you were a boy."

"Everyone tells me that." He colored sheepishly.

As she questioned him, Mrs. Fitzgibbons couldn't help pausing
from time to time to show him a steely eye. It was the rather
gloating look of the executioner appraising his victim, and produced an unnerving effect on Mr. Moriarty. Other times, despite
the age of the Most Beautiful Man, she communicated a tender,
maternal disposition. "Aren't you old, Marshall, to be working as

assistant to one of my handymen?" She spoke softly to him, as though to keep between them something that was rather shameful. "That's a job for a boy. That's an entry position."

Marshall was not slow to respond. "When Mr. Klopfer hired me, to help him mornings with maintenance, and to help Mr. Taylor after lunch each day with repair calls on the floor, he told me I would be promoted."

Mrs. Fitzgibbons affected an expression of great wonderment. "He had no authority to say that."

"He said that I would take over for the first person who quit or retired, except for Timmy Lyons, of course, who is a licensed electrician." Marshall waited expectantly for her to reply to that.

But Mrs. Fitzgibbons was shaking her head still, with a look of sadness. "He had no authority to say that to you."

The dilemma stated by Mrs. Fitzgibbons left Marshall speechless. He sat there, with his beautiful Viking head looming in the air before her and nothing to say. As for Mrs. Fitzgibbons, she couldn't help relishing what was coming, not just the frightening effect that selective expulsions had upon others at the bank, but the act itself. She was not unaware, either, from minute to minute, that she could change her mind at any time. That intensified the excitement. She could send him back to his duties and call in some other benighted employee.

"You must have misunderstood your superior's words. Only I," she stressed, very softly, "have that authority."

"I thought he did."

Mrs. Fitzgibbons closed her eyes while shaking her head slowly to and fro. "He doesn't have any such thing." She rose and came round and perched herself casually on the front corner of her desk. She wanted to show that an executive of the highest reaches, even the supreme officer herself, was not too busy to explain basics to someone of the rank and file, to a spear-carrier like himself, a nonentity.

She ticked the shining surface of her olive wood desk with a fingernail. "All authority comes from here. All promotions, all salary decisions, bonuses, holidays, suspensions, dismissals, everything. It all comes from my desk. It all comes from me."

Marshall's face lighted, as he perceived a fissure in Mrs. Fitz-gibbons's logic. "That was a year ago, Mrs. Fitzgibbons. Mr. Klop-fer promised me my promotion when you were still —"

She silenced him with a hand. "Mr. Klopfer is a glorified porter, Marshall. He is of no importance here whatsoever. He was doing a trip on you. A mental loop-the-loop. Oh, I could promote you," she said heartily. "Imagine that you were very ambitious, that you wanted to get ahead, that you had excellent work habits, and had, besides that, a background in real estate finance, or a degree or two from a master's program in business administration, or even first-rate accounting skills —"

"I like working with people," Marshall said, and faltered, "and I like a challenge."

Mrs. Fitzgibbons turned sidewise from the waist and buzzed for Julie.

"Where did you work last?" she continued.

"Until June of eighty-six, I was on temporary duty with the Parks Department."

"Oh, my." Mrs. Fitzgibbons actually winced over this reply. One might have guessed that it was the very last thing she expected to hear. She spoke with obvious dismay. "This is not going to work out," she said, and seemed genuinely sorry to impart this information.

Marshall's response suggested, however, that he had not grasped the essence of her remark. "I don't need to be promoted," he said. "I'm happy with my work."

The look of sad tidings on Mrs. Fitzgibbons's face following this last response was only intensified by the tender concern in her voice. "It isn't going to work out, Marshall." She stood with her hands clasped before her. She was a picture of feminine solicitude. "I'm not going to be able to keep you."

Julie came in the door then. Not only had she gone downstairs to get Marshall's briefcase, which she was lugging in her hand, but had already put Mr. Donachie on standby alert outside the office. Until now, Mrs. Fitzgibbons had not appreciated how really clever the girl could be, and couldn't imagine anything more suit-able to her desires than the sight of Julie plopping the briefcase down on the table next to the vestibule door. As Mrs. Fitzgibbons directed Marshall Moriarty to the table, she signaled the bank guard to join them. Mr. Donachie entered her office and closed the door gravely behind him.

"Look through your things," Mrs. Fitzgibbons commanded, and all three stood round and watched with blank expressions as Marshall opened and examined his case. Principally, it contained a glen plaid suit neatly folded, a white dress shirt, socks, and a necktie. He fumbled nervously through them.

"All shipshape?" said Mrs. Fitzgibbons.

"Yes." Marshall looked stupefied.

Mrs. Fitzgibbons nodded, and indicated with her eyes that Mr. Donachie was to accompany the Most Beautiful Man out the back door to the vestibule and street. Julie jumped past them to yank open the door, then watched with suppressed excitement as they marched by. Marshall came first, moving past her with the carriage and complexion of the walking dead. Behind him came Mr. Donachie, staring at the back of Marshall's neck. The guard's eyes glowed like gray agates under the leather bill of his black police cap. (Gossip on the floor in recent days suggested that Mr. Donachie had undergone personality changes matched only by those of Mrs. Fitzgibbons herself. The bank guard never smiled anymore, was quick to show people a censurious eye, and in conversation repeatedly referred to Mrs. Fitzgibbons as the Chief. "Don't let the Chief catch you doing that!" "If that's going to the Chief, I'll take it!" "Things are different under the Chief!" "When the Chief says no, she means no!" That Mr. Donachie was transformed by the new regime was reflected in a joke making the rounds. It was said that Mr. Donachie would work like a slave for his wife, but that he would kill for Mrs. Fitzgibbons.)

Taken in its entirety, Mrs. Fitzgibbons was thrilled by the beauty of the operation. The elimination of Marshall Moriarty on an impulsive, whimsical basis had assuaged her nerves to an extent she would not have thought possible, and at the same time would introduce an element of fear in the staff. The De Marias and Anita Stebbins were genuinely superfluous types, incompetents with whom others could not readily identify. With the sudden dismissal of the beautiful man from the maintenance section, however, all that was changed. Now, no one would feel safe.

"God, was he scared!" said Julie, her hand to her face, thrilling to Mrs. Fitzgibbons's power.

"Well, why shouldn't he have been?" As she stepped importantly about the office, even swaggering a little, Mrs. Fitzgibbons couldn't conceal her happiness. Her thinking was a trifle deranged, but she somehow knew it. "I don't send for people in order to have a sociable chat. A dismissal from time to time makes the others sit up. They realize I mean business. That's why I'm here. We're not the bank we used to be. I'm fast-forwarding us," she said.

"It's a very exciting bank," said Julie. "The tellers are going like mad out there. The phones are ringing —"

Mrs. Fitzgibbons acknowledged the point. "That's my strength. If I didn't generate new business, I wouldn't be able to build the power and influence that I need to make the changes that I want. I go on the air, I put myself before the public, and in seventy-two hours, I have an organization in place that they're talking about in Boston. And don't think," Mrs. Fitzgibbons added, "that I'm not going to smash up some banks around here."

"Like the Citizens Bank?"

"That's one."

"South Valley?"

"Anyone," she explained, "whose territory touches or infringes on mine is a candidate for Chapter XI. I'm not the Easter bunny. I'm going to obliterate them." She paced purposefully to and fro as she spoke, her eyes dilated abstractedly. "I'll make pretty little cooing noises to two or three of them, while I'm smashing the fourth, until there isn't so much as a grease spot left to any one of them."

"Will you be firing others?" Julie asked hopefully.

"Are you joking? There are people here who hate my insides. Who'd betray their own mothers just to get at me."

For ten minutes, Mrs. Fitzgibbons discoursed on the perfidiousness of her detractors and enemies, until even Julie herself was showing signs of exhaustion.

"I have the willpower," said Mrs. Fitzgibbons. "This broom

sweeps clean. I'm going to fumigate the place. I've accomplished more in five or six days than all those jimokes were able to do in fourteen years."

If Mr. Zabac had not phoned for her to come upstairs, she might have vapored on for an hour. Nonetheless, on the way upstairs, she intuited trouble. She was relieved to find Mr. Zabac waiting for her with a smile on his face and coffee set out on his desk in her own two teacups.

"My goodness," Mr. Zabac spoke up in greeting, "how agitated you look, Mrs. Fitzgibbons." He then addressed a remark to her that he had evidently rehearsed in advance. "I hope that you will learn the lesson stated long ago by Marshal Joffre of the French army. 'The higher one is promoted, the easier the job becomes.' "

Mrs. Fitzgibbons responded affably and moved her chair closer to his desk before sitting. "You were wonderful on television, Louis. Everyone says so. My hairdresser said you reminded him of Claude Rains. You made quite a hit."

Unable to hide his pleasure, Mr. Zabac gestured modestly. "Oh, I preferred just to say my few words," he allowed politely, "and make way for you, Mrs. Fitzgibbons. I thought that appropriate. After all, the newsmen were here to see you. I thought you handled yourself with distinction."

"Thank you, Louis."

"You have a flair for it. You have a speaking gift, Mrs. Fitzgibbons. I never knew that." As was his custom, the chairman expressed himself in measured accents. "You've been hiding your light." He reached for his teaspoon. "If anyone had told me three months ago that you and I would be on television together, I would not have believed them."

"You deserve to be showcased. There's going to be more of it. I intend to keep us in the news."

"Are you aware," inquired he, "that we are having another magnificent day downstairs?"

When Mrs. Fitzgibbons looked up in reply, she saw in his face for the first time a look of rapt attention. He was staring at her in a puzzled, inquiring way, as though trying to fathom the secret of the woman who had sprung to life like a wizard right beneath his feet. On his desk lay a copy of the *Boston Globe,* turned open to the page with her picture on it.

"I don't calculate the money at the windows. I'm here," she said, "to publicize us, to generate excitement. The Shawmut Bank called this morning — Nate Solomon — to ask if we'd like to participate with a few other banks in funding an industrial park in Worcester."

"Worcester?"

"A state-backed, low-risk arrangement that the bigwigs throw to the fat cats."

"But that's fifty miles away." Mr. Zabac was doubtful.

"He saw my photo in the *Globe*. They're tossing us some tenderloin, Louis." Mrs. Fitzgibbons enjoyed expressing herself in this way, portraying a cynical, sophisticated demeanor.

"We don't do multimillion dollar deals," Mr. Zabac cautioned her. "We're prudent. We spread our risks. We keep ourselves in step with the health of the region."

Mrs. Fitzgibbons nodded wryly. "We're not going to do anything rash. This isn't the sort of prospect that I'd entrust to Leonard, or Felix, or Connie, or anyone else out there. I'll look into it myself. Nate is sending a car for me in a few days." Despite the warm, voluptuous feelings coursing through her body, Mrs. Fitzgibbons thought it proper to accustom the little man to his figurehead status; to the realities of her prerogatives. "If I like what I see, we'll get our feet wet."

Seeing him wince at these words, she returned the subject to something brighter. "I'm not an egomaniac, Louis, but it's obvious that the media want me. It's a simple equation. The media give out the news. If they don't have news, they have to make the news. That's when they turn to people like me. Once it's obvious that the public wants you, you have the media in your hands. I know what I'm talking about," she added in a harsh voice, and showed him a challenging eye.

"Well, I'm convinced you do."

"What do you suppose would have happened," she went on, while crossing her legs and balancing her teacup delicately on her knee, "if they had interviewed someone like Neil Hooton instead of me? Can't you just picture it? Mumbling gobbledygook under his breath about transportation stocks and hedges against inflation, while the market is coming down around his ears." She threw her head back and laughed gaily.

"Now, now," said Mr. Zabac.

"We'd have had a run on the bank."

"Mr. Hooton is not to blame for the crack in stock prices."

"The man is yellow." Mrs. Fitzgibbons showed the chairman a look of blushing contempt for her adversary. The disdain was so withering that the chairman chose not to object. "Why," she said, "he doesn't know word one about Wall Street. Do you honestly believe that he understands what's happening? He's a little lamb!" Again, Mrs. Fitzgibbons blushed and revealed discomfort at having to discuss the merits of a fool.

"Many investors," Mr. Zabac reminded her softly, "were caught unawares. The market fell five hundred points. We must be fair."

"The man sold out at the bottom. And it's going to get worse. The market will rally, and he'll be left with his pants down."

Mr. Zabac nodded unhappily. "It's rallying now."

"*I* have to take the heat!" she said arrogantly. "I'll have to answer for him, you know."

Mr. Zabac realized that she had not heard his remark. In her brief, two-day tenure as chief executive officer, her temper had already become something to be avoided or appeased. Like many others, Mr. Zabac chose not to upset her. When she saw the way he was trying to mollify her, Mrs. Fitzgibbons's nipples actually tingled. The thought of suddenly pulling Mr. Zabac out of his chair and throwing him down onto the floor set her smiling. The daylight pouring in through the big window illuminated her features in a compelling manner.

"Well," the chairman faltered, "he might have been a little cowed by events yesterday, Mrs. Fitzgibbons. I wouldn't gainsay you on that point."

To Mr. Zabac's surprise, she burst out laughing. Her eyes were fixed steadily upon him. She was joyous at the little gentleman's diplomacy. "Louis, you're the end!" Her laughter filled the room. "If you aren't the living picture of the successful banker. I swear,

you should be in the movies!" Her voice dripped with affectionate
sarcasm, as she lifted her cup of coffee to her lips. "I can understand
why your employees love you too much. You have a good word
for everyone. You wouldn't harm a fly. Now," she said, "I can see
why you've given me my head. You want someone who'll get the
job done."

"You are wrong, Mrs. Fitzgibbons."

"Oh, I'm sure you don't know it," she countered.

"Believe me, it was not my intention, Mrs. Fitzgibbons, that you
should effect any dramatic changes that I would not willingly carry
out myself."

"Don't agitate yourself," she teased him, and widened her eyes
playfully. "Nobody is going to be taken out to the cloakroom! I'm
not going to spank anyone."

"The reason I asked you up here," Mr. Zabac continued, "concerns a complaint I've received from a rival institution." He held
up his small hands. "I'm not chastising you. We're on the same
side, Mrs. Fitzgibbons. But Mr. Curtin Schreffler, the president of
Citizens, found some of your remarks provocative."

"Did he?" she cried. She flushed angrily.

"I only tell you," Mr. Zabac was quick to placate her, "as it's
my duty to apprise you of such information as it comes to hand.
If persons of consequence out there take offense over your views,
or the way you utter them, I feel it's wise to inform you."

Mrs. Fitzgibbons had turned and was staring intensely out the
big semicircular window at the city hall. "I'm going to grind him
into a powder," she swore quietly.

At these words, a thorn of fear entered Mr. Zabac's heart. His
face showed it. Mrs. Fitzgibbons had begun to scare him.

"I'll hang him up by his heels," she said. She pictured in her
mind the man in question. "Here we have an Ivy League fancy
Dan, who dresses like a French gigolo, who went away to school
to avoid being contaminated by the rest of us, whose father died
of some foul, unspecified disease and left him an entire bank to
get off on, and he finds me objectionable." Mrs. Fitzgibbons truly
could not abide criticism these days. "I'll pin him to the wall. I'll
bankrupt him. I can't believe what I'm hearing."

When Mrs. Fitzgibbons stood up to leave, Mr. Zabac followed her to the door. He thanked her for coming. She didn't answer him. At the top of the stairs, however, the sight of the big bank sprawled beneath her, with its pretty geometric arrangement of yellow-shaded lamps and dark, mottled columns, restored her sense of well-being. Descending the steps, her heart beat proudly, as she contemplated the view of scores of workers toiling diligently at their tasks. Felix Hohenberger kept his head down when she went past his desk. Mrs. Fitzgibbons liked that, the tacit understanding that his behavior toward her bore directly upon the economic welfare of his family. Not a second later, Laura Stathis, a girl from payroll, blanched in fear at the sight of Mrs. Fitzgibbons coming straight toward her, turned on a dime, and hurried away in the opposite direction. Such, Mrs. Fitzgibbons concluded, were the salutary effects of an administration that was not incapable of making up its mind.

TEN

It was a case of the wish made real. When Mrs. Fitzgibbons came darting out of the bank that afternoon, full of confidence in her ability to work her will upon others, to mold and shape events according to a plan that was no more complicated than telling other people what to do, her quick string of achievements was already producing real shock waves in the banking community. Not ten streets away, an emergency meeting was in session on the third floor of the South Valley Bank. In all of its seventy-seven years of doing business, a span of time that had included some very trying years, the South Valley had never experienced anything on record as puzzling as what had happened these past two days. Deposit dollars were being withdrawn at an alarming rate.

That morning, when Mrs. Fitzgibbons had mentioned to Bruce her intention to play some golf this afternoon with Terry (her "boyfriend"), Bruce offered her the use of Matthew's Buick. The car was to be parked at the curb, with the keys over the visor. However, when Mrs. Fitzgibbons came out onto Maple Street, she found Matthew himself standing on the tree belt by his car. In fact, the instant he spotted her, he turned and opened the back door for her. Mrs. Fitzgibbons's reaction to this gracious touch illustrated the ease with which she was able to accommodate the solicitude of lesser beings. "Why, thank you, Matthew. What a wonderful surprise," she exclaimed, as she swept past him and entered the rear of the car. "I'm going to the country club."

As Matthew guided his automobile through the late-afternoon traffic, Mrs. Fitzgibbons took notice of the spotless interior of the car, with its plush upholstery and freshly vacuumed carpet. She sat back with her coat open, her legs crossed, and a severe but not angry look on her face. Stopped briefly for the traffic light at Essex Street, she was completely unmindful of the fact that they were halted directly in front of the South Valley Bank, nor had she a clue that an emergency meeting was convened upstairs, in which her name was being repeated with dismaying frequency.

While the officers and directors of the South Valley Bank were careful that afternoon not to invoke the language of panic, the seriousness of the matter did inspire some telling phrases. No one at the conference table demurred, for example, when William Daviau, one of the directors, characterized what was happening downstairs as "a temporary hemorrhaging of funds." Nor would the leadership of other neighboring banks have objected to it. These were financial institutions of a size that could not withstand such an onslaught. In truth, the flight of funds was taking place on a near-ruinous scale. With nothing more to explain her advent than a single full-page newspaper article and seven minutes on the evening news, Mrs. Fitzgibbons had befallen these little sister institutions like an early winter storm.

As in all such developments, change worked a reciprocal effect upon its agent. That is to say, Mrs. Fitzgibbons's triumphs not only left her feeling successively more important, and did nothing to slake her thirst for further victories, but caused her to depreciate all other people at a proportionate rate. She had never been the sort of human being to depreciate a person for living in conditions that they could not overcome, especially a youngster of eighteen, but when Matthew Dean stopped the car outside Terence Sugrue's house on the corner of Nonotuck and Spring, and Mrs. Fitzgibbons winced at the sight of the derelict clapboard structure (with a rusted refrigerator parked on the front porch and wild vines and shrubberies running riot everywhere), her subsequent view of the Sugrue boy was severely abbreviated. She saw him as a vain, "back street" sort of boy, someone to be good-timed and discarded at her convenience.

This view was strengthened for her by the way the young drum major looked about in awe at the inside of Mrs. Fitzgibbons's chauffeured Buick. He turned pink with embarrassment at the luxurious setting, not to mention the look of Mrs. Fitzgibbons sitting in the opposite corner with her legs crossed.

"Matthew, forget about the country club," she said. "Drive me up to Jarvis Avenue."

"Right you are," he said.

Terry was sitting on the edge of the seat, blushing uncomfortably at the way Mrs. Fitzgibbons ordered the man behind the wheel to comply with her desires. He blushed, too, at the overtly concupiscent look that she turned upon him, examining him up and down.

"We'll drive around some of the back roads up there and have a little talk," she said to Terry. She was staring at him now with open sensuality, but without having moved a muscle. "The joy of being young," she said, "is that you can butter up people without annihilating your self-respect."

For the most part, Terry was perplexed by her words. Matthew stole looks at the two of them in the rearview mirror, while driving along slowly under the twilit trees.

Downtown at the South Valley Bank, as the hour of dusk drew a gray light through the city streets, Mr. William Daviau was put through on the telephone to Alita Lindberg, the publisher of the local newspaper. Mrs. Lindberg's replies to the bank director's complaints about her coverage of Mrs. Fitzgibbons in the Saturday issue of the *Telegram* were obviously rehearsed, a certain indication that he was not the first banking official to lodge a grievance that day. However, the earnestness in Mrs. Lindberg's prepared responses took account of the obvious gravity of the situation. According to Mr. Daviau, who was very angry, the *Ireland Parish*

Telegram was responsible for what he elegantly termed "an increasing destabilization of the local economy."

Alita Lindberg reminded him that on the occasion of South Valley's seventy-fifth anniversary, in the summer of 1985, the *Telegram* had given the South Valley Bank an enormous three-page spread, including photographs of the original limestone bank building, its founders and present officers, and several shots of its current facility and branch locations. Mr. Daviau was not appeased.

"I don't think you realize what you've done. You people have created a situation that must be rectified. You've inflicted some serious damage out here."

"Personally," the publisher responded, "I don't even know Mrs. Fitzgibbons. I know literally nothing about her. All I know is that our reportage has been fair and accurate."

"By boasting and innuendo, she's made the rest of us sound like a pack of rank amateurs, whereas, in fact, it's she," he insisted hotly, "who is the amateur. The article you printed was nothing more than a vehicle for a big-talking publicity hound!"

"Mr. Daviau."

"She has no background in banking. No schooling in it. No true experience. She's just a woman shooting off her mouth — appealing to a vulgar streak in your readers. She's a home loan officer."

"No," said Mrs. Lindberg, chafing at the man's sexist remarks, "you are wrong. Mrs. Fitzgibbons is, in fact, the chief executive officer of the biggest bank in this city. And she certainly is news. What are you proposing? That I blackball her?"

"I know beyond a doubt," said he, "that every one of our several local savings institutions is suddenly under pressure. If it weren't for what's going on in the stock market, and the worry it's causing to people out there, this would not be happening."

"That's open to question."

"The developments are coincident, Alita. How can you deny it?"

"If they are, Mr. Daviau," she paused to emphasize the formality of her reply, "you can't blame me. If they are not, then you must blame yourselves. The article stands." Abruptly, she terminated the discussion. She gave Mr. Daviau her last word. "There will be no retractions, no amendments, no apologies. I will, however, if you wish, send my city desk man himself, Sherman Resnic, to your offices tomorrow morning. What's more, I will print the interview in full. I will print your objections to the Saturday article word for word. I should caution, however," she advised, "that a vitriolic attack on Mrs. Fitzgibbons, especially if it makes small of her being a woman, or so much as suggests that her position is inconsistent with one's expectations of a person of her sex, could produce results that would be" — Alita Lindberg hesitated a split second to find the word she wanted — "would be retrograde to your desire."

"It's obvious, Mrs. Lindberg," he came right back, "that you really don't appreciate the extent or possible permanent effects of the damage that's taking place."

William Daviau had no wish to end the conversation in progress. His fellow officials sat round the conference table, staring at him, as he strove to make the publisher see the peril and injustice in it all. No one present had even thought to get up and switch on the lights, even though a cool, wan glow had spread throughout the room; the water glasses on the table and the folders and scattered sheets of paper took on a cold aspect. The people sitting in the room seemed to be losing substance at the rate that their endeavors were losing force.

A mile to the west, on a lonely stretch of Jarvis Avenue, far from the bitter telephone dispute taking place downtown, Matthew was driving along slowly, as instructed. The back seat of the sedan was cast in a twilit gloom. The leafless trees at roadside moved slowly past. Mrs. Fitzgibbons was querying Terence on his future, employing honeyed tones.

"Would you like to go into banking?" she asked in a softly melodious way.

Not used to thinking seriously about his future, he presented an abstract countenance. He seemed unaware that Mrs. Fitzgibbons's skirt had ridden up on her thighs; the sides of her gun-metal leather coat were thrown wide.

"I've never thought much about anything like that," he confessed genuinely.

Mrs. Fitzgibbons came back in the same hushed accents as before. "Aren't you ambitious?"

"Oh, I'm very ambitious."

"And don't you suppose I knew that? Of course, you are. Everyone wants to get ahead, to afford the good things in life, travel, expensive clothing, racy cars. You're no different."

"Do you," he asked, curiously, "flatter people?"

"I don't have to," she remarked. "I run my firm."

He sat staring at her. His hair glowed like a crown of gold.

"You're just starting out. You have to put yourself under somebody's wing."

"Do you know," the Sugrue youth answered very thoughtfully, after pondering the woman's advice, "I think that being nice to Mr. Pivack last year helped me to become the drum major."

"Well, there you are. My point, exactly."

Terry colored slightly. "I sort of knew I was doing it, too."

"You should never be ashamed of success, or," she added, "of how you went about getting it. We like that," Mrs. Fitzgibbons added, speaking for executives in general. "We prefer employees who aren't ashamed to make themselves attractive and useful to us and who know exactly what they're doing when they butter up."

Terry actually gushed a bit when he laughed over her last comment. "I can tell you right now who's going to be drum major next year! The Ireland Parish band is going to be led by a girl for the first time in its history!"

"Oh?"

"This redhead? Rita Crowson? She's a junior, and you should see her laying it on!" Terry clapped a hand to his head. "Every time Mr. Pivack turns around, Rita is right there, showing him everything she's got. And she's got everything. Rita," he said, waving his hand, "has no shame at all. She's got a lock on the job."

Mrs. Fitzgibbons appeared interested. "Is she fucking him?"

Terry's face fell. "*Mr. Pivack?*" he cried.

Mrs. Fitzgibbons had just spotted a cart road a few yards back and instructed Matthew to turn about and drive back.

"Where are we going, Frankie?" Terry asked.

"I used to ice-skate in here as a girl," she explained.

Matthew steered the long black automobile slowly in through a natural gateway formed by the burnished red leaves of overhanging sumacs, and up a bumpy incline. From the crest of the hill, not a hundred feet in from Jarvis Avenue, there stretched before them patches of cattails and the gleaming black waters of a stagnant marsh. In politeness to her driver, Mrs. Fitzgibbons suggested that Matthew get out and walk about for a while in the dusk.

In less than a minute, she was clutching the drum major's head to her abdomen and had commenced in a quiet voice to soothe him and to allay any anxiety he might feel over the matter at hand. In all her life, Mrs. Fitzgibbons had been sexually serviced in only the most traditional manner, a want of experience that she attributed to having had, in Larry, something of a wet blanket for a husband, as well as to her own uninterrupted fidelity. Mrs. Fitzgibbons had planted her right foot atop the front seat, and was encouraging Terry to acquaint himself with the long slice of white thigh she had thus revealed to view above the top of her stockings. "We're not going to be here all day, cupcake. This is a good time and place for you to begin. You don't make fifty thousand dollars a year by starting at the top."

The drum major responded in a muffled, worried tone. He was showing himself surprisingly resistant to her urgings, and even shook his head once or twice, although continuing all the while to plant soft kisses on the exposed flesh of her thigh. "I just don't know," he muttered, and shook his head.

At Essex and Maple, the bank director had by now concluded his talk with the publisher of the *Telegram* and hung up the phone; but within a minute, he was on it again, ringing up Mr. Curtin Schreffler at the Citizens Bank, a man he didn't even like very much. In the conversation that followed, the two bankers spoke with greater candor than either of them had used in addressing

Mrs. Lindberg. As before, William Daviau alluded to the "hemorrhaging of funds," but on this occasion talked also about "shrinking capital," "balance sheets," "bottom lines," "capital standards," "net worth," and the like. On the other end of the line, Mr. Schreffler confessed to a point of special vulnerability at his bank; it concerned a multimillion dollar loan to a development company that had been shared by four different banks, including his own and Zabac's. The loan was in serious default. "If Zabac calls it in —" Mr. Schreffler suggested ominously.

"If Mrs. Fitzgibbons calls it in!" Mr. Daviau corrected him angrily.

"That's what I mean," the other admitted. "We have to think about that in the background. If this outflow continues, even for a few days, she's going to be dictating terms!"

"Goddamned fascist!" said Mr. Daviau. His cheeks shook with anger.

"Although I doubt she knows what she's doing."

"Are you a moron?" In his frustration, Mr. Daviau lashed out at Curtin Schreffler on the phone. "Are you simple? Do you suppose that Louis Zabac doesn't know that he's loosed this fast-talking populist hotshot in the midst of a nationwide financial crisis? Is that what you're pretending to dismiss?" The volume of the director's voice in the big, dusk-lit room reverberated round the pale figures of his seated associates with godlike resonance. "They don't know what they're doing?" he cried.

"It seems too sinister."

"You poor little lamb. She's a demagogue!" he said. "The woman's a rabble-rouser. She works on people's fears. She plays to the balcony. Who do you suppose is behind her? Where did she come from? Who's behind her, if it isn't himself? Donald Duck? Use your brain. He turned her loose!"

"I can't believe that." Curtin Schreffler had not been raised to suspect villainy in the hearts of his neighbors; of the two, he remained the more placid. "I believe it's a fluke. It's just a two-day panic. The market has made people jumpy."

"Then why," Mr. Daviau demanded to know, "aren't their depositors coming to us?"

"They are," the other replied feebly.

"How many?"

"Several," said Mr. Schreffler.

"Four?" Mr. Daviau was clearly in an ugly mood. As the conversation flagged, his expression darkened further. His eyes protruded unnaturally in the failing light. "Three?"

"Well, I'm not at liberty to divulge statistics, but —"

"*Statistics?* You call that a statistic?"

"It will be better tomorrow. Mrs. Fitzgibbons has had her hour in the sun."

"She wants blood," said the South Valley director, invoking the sort of sanguinary vocabulary relished by Mrs. Fitzgibbons herself.

"Mr. Daviau," the other man protested.

"Now, I see it. It wasn't till I spoke to you that I realized that." Mr. Daviau's voice was oily with sarcasm. "You've made it clear to me. Everybody's going to the sacrificial altar. That, finally, is what she's all about. She's out for blood." He addressed the persons sitting nervously about him: "Everything is going to be better tomorrow. Curtin Schreffler says so. She has his collar size, the name of his florist, and a jug of formaldehyde under her desk, but everything is going to be all right tomorrow."

Mr. Daviau returned the receiver to its cradle without a word of farewell to the president of Citizens Bank. A spectral figure nearby spoke up. It was a woman's voice. "Somebody should call Zabac," she said. "It can't hurt."

By then, Mrs. Fitzgibbons had already departed the marsh with Matthew behind the wheel once more. They were tooling north along a dark stretch of Jarvis Avenue. Ever since Matthew had gotten back into the car, he had been more than scrupulous not to glance into the back seat, as he had good reason to suspect what was going on. Mrs. Fitzgibbons was sitting up just as before, but the young drum major could not be seen. She was holding his head between her legs.

At one point, it had been necessary for Mrs. Fitzgibbons to show the youth a flash of temper. He had not witnessed her anger before. "Listen!" she broke out. The resistance of a blushing, high school pretty boy who was on the make with an important banker exhausted her patience. "I'm not asking for the world!" That was when she seized and clutched his head to her loins. "Stop grousing and crybabying. Get busy! I want my bubble!" she shouted. "I want it now."

She could not tell for sure, but it seemed once or twice that the unwilling youth was sobbing softly while ministering to her needs. Even after Matthew had started up the car, she continued to express bewilderment over his distaste for the task.

"It's not a horror show," she complained, as she began to undulate and rock her hips. She stared with a glazed, hypnotic expression out the windshield at the yellow stripe unfurling on the asphalt ahead. She had Terence's head clamped comfortably below her. Matthew sat like a robot at the wheel. He was driving very slowly. "Nobody's going to snap your picture. This is what grown-ups do for one another. Listen to him. He's in pure clover, and he's sniffling like a baby."

Later, after Matthew had turned back down the mountain road in the dark, and Mrs. Fitzgibbons had begun undergoing rhythmic spasms that sent shudders up and down her body, she naturally gave off talking. But for the moment, she even included Matthew in her discourse.

"This is what came of their famous sexual revolution. This is what these youngsters learned. This is what all the shouting was about." Mrs. Fitzgibbons had changed position. She had her knees up, her ankles lying crisscrossed on the small of Terence Sugrue's back. "They know as much about sex as the mother of Jesus."

"You're right about that," said Matthew.

"Of course, I am." She kneaded and caressed the drum major's golden head in rhythm with the thrust and retraction of her hips. "This little majorette is the envy of six states. Do you know what I could do for a boy like this?"

"It staggers the mind."

"Anything I wanted. I could send him to college if I wanted. I could send him to work for Nate Solomon at the Shawmut Bank in Boston. I could hire him as my personal assistant and pay him a tidy fortune! I could do that at a stroke of the pen."

"He doesn't understand that."

"I could talk myself blue in the face. With a vibrator, you throw a switch and it comes on. You don't have to climb a mountain. The beauty of using a human being is in their gratitude and eagerness. You'd think he was on the rack. I'm giving him pure honey. You'd think it was cyanide. It's enough to paralyze a crow." Mrs. Fitzgibbons laughed gaily as she rearranged his head beneath her hands. "I pick him up in my car. I take him in the back seat with me. We go out to the woods. I'm in the midst of a busy time, signing off on sixty different deals, taking a hundred phone calls, keeping a hundred employees honest, reaming them, docking their time, firing them, running up and down stairs — and he — who has no future, not a prayer — hasn't sense enough to suck a lollipop. This is what I'm saddled with. *Come on!*" she cried. "Do me. Yes. That's more like it. That's better. That's good! Come on! Come on!"

From the mountainside, the city of Ireland Parish lay stretched out below, with spangles of countless lights scattered about the dark like something luminous that had been shattered at a blow.

Struck dumb by the unexpected fury of the onslaught taking place behind him, Matthew stared in blank embarrassment and trepidation at the road ahead, as it curved downward between two walls of black trees.

"It takes work," she was saying. "You've got to give. I'm coming, come on! This is your night!" Mrs. Fitzgibbons reiterated this last phrase then, over and over, for a full minute — "This is your night!" — until it attained a hypnotic cadence that transformed the interior of the Buick into something almost strange to man.

ELEVEN

Unknown to all, Mrs. Fitzgibbons had instituted a policy conceived to protect her new powers from the usual jealousies and intrigues that attend a new regime. Her intention was to strike fear in the hearts of all by firing people on a purely capricious basis. The instrument of chance that she seized upon was the old-fashioned metal index wheel on her desk, a cylinder of small manila cards, containing the name, job description, and nearest telephone extension number of every soul in her employ.

On Wednesday morning, after toying with the wheel on her desk for two or three minutes, while on the telephone to one of the bank's accountants, Mrs. Fitzgibbons set the wheel spinning in earnest. Her fingernail came to rest on the card of a branch office employee whom she had never heard of. That was unfortunate, and explained why Mrs. Fitzgibbons fired two people that day in the span of twenty minutes; for the need to act in a vigorous way also required confronting the poor soul in person. In less than a minute, Julie had Betty Hurley, the branch manager on the line, and Mrs. Fitzgibbons was instructing her what to do.

"You have an employee named Simmons?"

"Carol Ann?" said Mrs. Hurley. "Yes, Mrs. Fitzgibbons. Carol Ann is at the South Street branch today." Mrs. Hurley's breathless politeness was all but palpable on the line. "Is something wrong? She's filling in for Doug MacDonald for the rest of the week."

"She won't be here the rest of the week," said Mrs. Fitzgibbons. "You'll discharge her this afternoon at five o'clock. You'll say nothing to anyone about it. No one is to know until she's gone."

"I see." The woman's voice was a bare whisper. Clearly, she could not fathom the cause of the action, but wise enough to know by Mrs. Fitzgibbons's tone of voice and her much-rumored volatility not to press for an explanation. Mrs. Hurley acquiesced without protest. "I'll let her go at five sharp."

"You do that," said Mrs. Fitzgibbons.

However, the best example of Mrs. Fitzgibbons's want of prejudice in calling people onto the carpet and eliminating them from the bank, occurred in the case of Mr. Desmond Kane. When Mr. Kane's name showed up on the wheel, she felt a stab of remorse. Desmond was not only the senior teller in terms of his years of service, but was also the most elderly employee in the firm. A diffident, yellow-toothed man of advanced age, Desmond had suffered the loss of an arm in the fighting for the Philippines in World War II, and was always accorded an extra measure of respect by all. The choice threw Mrs. Fitzgibbons into a quandary. For as long as she could remember, she had felt a special warmth for Mr. Kane. During her first year at the bank, back in 1973, he was always there to help. In the days following Larry's death, no one anywhere had been kinder to her, or more solicitous over her loss than he. She knew from the start that she was going to fire him, however, as it would have been folly to corrupt the impersonal workings of fate by showing favoritism. Also, by now, Mrs. Fitzgibbons prided herself on her capacity to master inner weakness. In sum, she saw her own hurt feelings as a necessary part of the sacrifice that was required in exciting fear among her charges. It was in this maudlin state of mind that Mrs. Fitzgibbons sent Julie Marcotte with a little yellow summons to fetch Mr. Kane.

As matters evolved, however, the man selected for the ritual firing was not nearly so willing to be separated from his job as she had anticipated. She started in on a genial enough tack, explaining to the one-armed gentleman that her new position required her to implement decisions that were not always in accordance with the dictates of her heart. As she explained this dolorous truth, her emotions began to move in sympathy with her words, until Mrs. Fitzgibbons felt a little saddened by what was coming. Yesterday, in firing Marshall Moriarty, the so-called Most Beautiful Man, she had rather enjoyed leading him hither and thither by the nose, first exciting hope, then apprehension, then hope anew, only to end it all with a sudden swing of the axe.

"You see," she was explaining to Mr. Kane, preparatory to dismissing him, "we're changing direction as an institution. That's the key to everything that's happening around here this week."

As she went on, Mr. Kane showed no emotion whatever, but sat stonily in his chair, with the left sleeve of his suit jacket folded neatly into his side pocket, and an expression of wry scorn etched on his lips. As long as he remained thus, Mrs. Fitzgibbons continued to elaborate on her views. If necessary, she could have talked like this till the cows came home.

She swung back in her chair, gesturing languidly and tossing out clichés in a quietly boastful manner. "We're a deposit-driven institution. We don't originate loans until the funds are in. We keep our risks down. Now, because of that, our growth requires a dramatic infusion of new funds. That's how I make sense here. That's the single most revolutionary change to have taken place, you see. Because with me at the helm, we're not going to sit on our hands any longer. We're not just going to hope," she flung out disdainfully, "that everybody out there will be nice to us and let us survive. That attitude was acceptable years ago. Today, we have a more challenging environment. I wouldn't last a month," she added, "if I were to conduct business as usual."

Desmond Kane continued to regard her with the imperturbability of a gargoyle. She had never seen him in such an obstinate frame of mind, and guessed that he had divined his termination and was resolved to take the blow with stoic forbearance.

"You can't imagine the kind of pressure that I put myself under, Desmond, in order to make the changes here that should have been made years ago. Believe me, it isn't enough just to take the public by storm, to create a stampede of new business through my front doors. I have to consider a hundred and one other things." Sometimes, when boasting like this, Mrs. Fitzgibbons felt a surge of excitement in her blood. She actually felt her body heating up. "I even have to watch the securities markets." She threw her pencil onto her desk. "I'm sitting on eighty million dollars, and the future of it, and of everyone in this place, is riding on my back. It's easy for a secretary or a teller," she said, ridiculing Mr. Kane's position and forty years of service at the bank, "to give me a day's work in return for a day's pay, and think nothing more of it. I'm the one who has to control costs." Mrs. Fitzgibbons decided to give Mr. Kane a peek at the scary decision that trembled in the offing. "I'm the one who has to reduce expenses and streamline the staff."

Hard as she tried, though, Mrs. Fitzgibbons could not get a rise out of the man. Moreover, the gray stony set of his face was beginning to get on her nerves. To worsen matters, there materialized in her mind's eye an image of the ugly stump of Mr. Kane's severed arm dangling uselessly inside his folded sleeve, a vision that revolted her.

To her relief, Julie Marcotte put through an important telephone call. It was from a top executive at the George Hitchings Corporation, a Hartford-based developer well known in banking circles along the Eastern seaboard. Mrs. Fitzgibbons loved this part of the job. She liked talking to highly placed executives, especially of powerful firms that had never solicited business from the bank before. The man on the line told her that Nate Solomon had spoken highly of her.

Mrs. Fitzgibbons leaned backward in her chair, with her breasts up in the air and the phone tilted prettily in her hand, as she addressed herself at first to the ceiling. While the consequence of her business call from the man at the Hitchings Corporation was fifty times as important as her dealing with the one-armed teller, Mrs. Fitzgibbons was conscious all the while that the picture she was presenting to Mr. Kane would point up to him his own insignificance; he would be able to relax now in the knowledge that her decision to get rid of him was based on considerations too lofty for him to comprehend.

"Nate is a gentleman," she was saying. "It was grand of him to mention me. It's quite true that we're interested in proposals that originate outside our region. If the fundamentals are good, we're ready to play." She had turned and was staring abstractedly at Mr. Kane now, but gave no indication of seeing him. She was staring through him. "I expect to be in Worcester the next few days," said Mrs. Fitzgibbons, fictitiously. "What I'd like to do is send down my assistant, Leonard Frye. He's my nuts-and-bolts man, anyhow. If you could take an hour with him."

"Sounds perfect," said the other with an altogether agreeable air.

"Give him the lay of the thing to bring back to me. Would you do that?" Mrs. Fitzgibbons shivered over the excitement of executive power. "If I like it, and if a meeting is desirable to you, you and I could get together."

By the time Mrs. Fitzgibbons had arranged a meeting for Mr. Frye in Hartford and had hung up, she had stopped feeling sorry for the doomed man sitting in front of her. She even concluded that Desmond Kane had treated her kindly over the years only in order to flatter himself by treating a loan officer as an equal. He had probably secretly despised her all along. Now that she had climbed to stratospheric heights and become superior to everyone, and could no longer gratify his vanity, he lapsed into a moody, churlish silence.

She gave him one last chance to show a spark of appreciation, a sign of his comprehending the wonders she was working here, and of the fact that his future was hers to enhance or mangle. She pivoted in her chair to face him head on. "My instincts tell me," she said, smiling pleasantly, "that you don't have a solid grip on the sort of changes I'm bringing about here."

Mrs. Fitzgibbons waited, but Mr. Kane made no reply. The wryness in his face was sculpted in granite.

"You wouldn't know what a loan portfolio is," she said, "let alone what it means to increase deposits by four percent in three days, or be able to boast a twenty-two percent return on average equity. How could you? You've been a teller here since the War of 1812." She raised her voice, but not in anger. "You're one of my tellers, Desmond. Your job is mechanical. It's like being a piston or the exhaust pipe in a car. A piston," she explained, "functions without regard to where the car is going, or how fast, or in what direction, or whether it's moving at all. The car could be going over a cliff."

"It probably is," said Mr. Kane.

The unexpectedness of Mr. Kane's voice arrested Mrs. Fitzgibbons in the midst of her metaphor, and even required her to think for a second about what he had said. She sat forward, laid her arms flat on the desk, and eyed him incredulously. Before she could respond, Mr. Kane spoke again.

"That's what cliffs are for," he said.

Some of the nearby staff workers who had seen Mr. Kane cross the floor and vanish into Mrs. Fitzgibbons's enormous office like a sleepwalker entering an unexplored cave, had just begun to take heart in his prospects, when, out of the blue, Mrs. Fitzgibbons started to shout. The torrent of fury that erupted behind her door had no precedent in the hundred-year history of the venerable bank at Maple and Main. To exacerbate matters, Mr. Kane interrupted with more to say.

"I don't think you're doing that well," he said.

On her feet, Mrs. Fitzgibbons looked about swiftly for some heavy object. She couldn't credit her ears.

"I want to know why this is happening to me," he added in a controlled manner. "I want an explanation."

But by then, Mrs. Fitzgibbons had drowned him out. Like many people born with native oratorical talent, Mrs. Fitzgibbons had a pair of lungs. When she got really angry, her voice actually dropped half an octave and took on a rasping hoarseness. It was deafening. "*Get Mr. Donachie in here!*" she hollered with incredible volume. "*I want my guard!*"

Mrs. Fitzgibbons ran across the room and flung open her door. Her voice filled the entire bank. "I WANT HIM IN HERE!"

The actual expulsion of the one-armed teller — to worsen matters — involved a brief physical altercation at the door of her office between himself and Alec Donachie. Mr. Kane thrust the bank guard aside and, showing his yellow teeth, commanded him to stay put. However, the deep, morbid desire in Mr. Donachie to throw himself into action for Mrs. Fitzgibbons, the woman responsible for uniforming him in his black police clothes and for elevating him to a position of respect, triggered a spontaneous reaction. In a twinkling, Mr. Donachie had twisted Desmond Kane's surviving arm behind his back and was propelling him with force toward the back door of Mrs. Fitzgibbons's colossal office, in the direction of the vestibule. He was clutching the collar of Desmond's suit coat in his left fist while thrusting him before him. "Nobody sasses the Chief," he said. "You're gone, mister. You're out of here!"

If there was one thing Mrs. Fitzgibbons could not brook, it was criticism. Alone in her office, she sat, heart beating. Her nerves were in riot, her pulse fluttering. The revelation that her firing policy had turned up, by chance, an actual detractor, someone who questioned and despised her, left her shaken. She felt sorry for herself. She showed Julie a suffering face. "This is what comes of being fair-minded."

"Mr. Kane was very stupid to say what he did," Julie said comfortingly to Mrs. Fitzgibbons.

"He's lived off us for a hundred years. We gave him a pleasant corner to work in, benefits, holidays, a weekly paycheck, year after year, but when it's time for him to go," said Mrs. Fitzgibbons, practically in tears, "then the ugliness comes out. It was there all along, and now it comes out."

"It was a disgusting thing to say," said Julie.

"Here is a man," said Mrs. Fitzgibbons, still pitying herself, "who can't zip up his fly, but can sit in front of me, with an ugly look on his face, and question what I'm doing. Oh, and I was polite with him. I tried to show understanding. I kept my voice down. I called him Desmond. I was prepared to treat him like a human being. I would have given him compensation. He has the heart of a rat, and I was going to give him the world on a platter."

Mrs. Fitzgibbons accepted a pocket tissue from Julie and touched it to the corner of her eye. She was truly hurt. For a quarter hour thereafter, she struggled to make sense of the secret motives of subordinates.

"It was stupid of him," said Julie.

"It wasn't stupid," said Mrs. Fitzgibbons. "It was vicious."

"It was the most vicious thing anyone could say," Julie agreed. "I'd like to see something horrible happen to him."

Mrs. Fitzgibbons sniffled angrily and wiped her nose. "I swear to Jesus," she said, "if anyone ever speaks to me that way again, I'll have him beheaded."

For the rest of the hour, Mrs. Fitzgibbons remained in a guarded state of mind. She experienced the odd sensation that her brain had actually contracted; that the scope of her thinking was somehow attenuated, like water jetting from a nozzle. She felt restive and menaced, and refused to take an entire sequence of phone calls. She closed her door and busied herself with her paperwork. It was no coincidence, therefore, when Mrs. Fitzgibbons later detected something suspicious in passing that aggravated her paranoia. She had just come to her door to give Julie a letter to type, when a young woman from Mrs. Wilson's department went past Julie's desk on her way to the rear vestibule. Mrs. Fitzgibbons caught a glimpse of something extraordinary under the half-open flap of the girl's rumpled tote bag.

Mrs. Fitzgibbons accosted her on the spot. The young woman halted and looked about in bewilderment. She was a plain, stooped figure dressed in a woolen jumper and Indian-print blouse. Her sponge-soled shoes, which laced up like a man's, accentuated the pigeon-toed posture of her feet.

"You!" Mrs. Fitzgibbons brought her to a halt with a word and pointed to her door. "Go into my office."

The color drained from the young woman's face. She was frightened out of her wits. She preceded Mrs. Fitzgibbons stiff-leggedly across the endless expanse of carpet.

Before following, however, Mrs. Fitzgibbons stopped to say something to Julie; she was certain that if the girl were guilty and given an opportunity, she would attempt to conceal the evidence. When Mrs. Fitzgibbons went in and closed the door behind her, the girl in the jumper stood as quiet as death before her. She had closed the flap of her tote bag, though, and had shifted the weight of it behind her back.

"Where were you going?" Mrs. Fitzgibbons inquired with a

factitious airiness. Her musical tone of voice was belied by a narrowing of her lips and the penetrating glaze of her eyes.

When the young woman opened her mouth to respond, she revealed a gap between her front teeth. "To the store," she managed to croak out. "For a bottle of aspirin."

"And what is your name?" Mrs. Fitzgibbons asked in that same frightening, melodious pitch.

The girl was quaking visibly. "I'm Emily Krok."

After a little silence between them, Mrs. Fitzgibbons turned with a grim look and pointed her finger. "Empty your bag onto my desk."

Emily Krok's eyes shot up to the ceiling. "Oh God!"

"Go on," Mrs. Fitzgibbons instructed her. "Do as you're told. I know what you're up to."

In seconds, Mrs. Fitzgibbons had the object in hand, a little blue-and-white box containing a typewriter ribbon of the sort used by bank secretaries. The cellophane was still sealed. "Well, now," said Mrs. Fitzgibbons, in a throatier tone, "you're just a little thief."

"Oh, please," the girl brought out. In her distraction, she looked mindless. "I've never stolen anything."

"You just stole from me." Mrs. Fitzgibbons refuted the claim.

"I've never stolen before."

"What are you talking about? You've been stealing all your life." Mrs. Fitzgibbons looked the quailing girl up and down. "What do you do with this property of mine?"

"Please, Mrs. Fitzgibbons. It's true. I swear it." Emily begged to be understood. "I've never stolen before."

"Where do you sell these?"

"*Sell them?*" Emily's voice climbed in horror.

"The things you steal. The umbrellas that have been disappearing, the scarves, Mrs. Lawrence's wallet, the stationery. You're going to spill your guts out. I have you red-handed." She flourished the blue-and-white box. "Have you ever been arrested?"

"God, no."

"I want to know," said Mrs. Fitzgibbons, insisting, "what you've stolen and how you dispose of it. Because I know who you are.

You're one of the ones who talk behind my back." The thought of it set Mrs. Fitzgibbons's temples aflame.

"Don't have me arrested." Emily's voice broke, and she started to sob. "Don't call the police. Do anything but that. I'm begging you."

"You're going to confess."

"I'll confess to anything if you don't have me arrested. I'll say anything. I'll do anything."

Mrs. Fitzgibbons was not moved by the young woman's pleadings, even though Emily Krok's want of good looks was rendered even more apparent in her distress. The girl looked very wizened and misshapen, with her head jutting forth, as she pleaded.

"You can start by admitting that you're a little kleptomaniac who can't keep her grubby fingers off my property."

Emily, true to her word, nodded miserably.

"Come along."

"It's true," said Emily.

"If it isn't bolted down," Mrs. Fitzgibbons insisted, "you walk off with it."

"Yes." Emily was clutching her head with one hand.

"You cheat and steal and tell lies about me behind my back."

"No!" Emily replied. "I can't bear this any longer. What am I going to do? Help me. What am I going to do?" Her balled fists shook now.

"Why, I've had you on report for a month." Mrs. Fitzgibbons drew attention to a pile of folders on her desk, as to the dossiers of criminals. "You and a dozen others, including your own boss. Elizabeth Wilson talks about me. I have it on paper, in black and white. Tell me I'm lying."

"You would never lie, Mrs. Fitzgibbons." Emily wiped her nose with the back of her fist.

"Then tell me what you heard."

"It's true, Mrs. Fitzgibbons. She talks about you."

"You heard it with your own ears."

Emily nodded, the tears shining on her eyelashes. "Mrs. Wilson said you were too big for your own boots. I heard her say it one morning to Mr. Barrett, when he brought her her Danish and coffee. She said that somebody would cut you down to size. She said you were crazy as a bedbug!" Seeing the look of shock on Mrs. Fitzgibbons's face, Emily immediately excepted herself. "I couldn't believe my *ears!*" she said. "I thought I was dreaming."

"Then, it's true."

"It was something about the Christmas bonuses. How the officers were going to get less money this year. We all love you, Mrs. Fitzgibbons!" Emily saw her opening and broke out in a spate of passion. She was clasping her hands together fervently. "You should hear the way the girls talk about you in the rest room — about your hair and makeup, and the way you stand up for us, and how wonderful it is to have somebody tough in charge of the bank. We'd die for you! We really would. You should hear them."

"Go back to your job."

"I'd do anything for you," Emily added, not hearing. "You're fair to everybody. You're honest and beautiful. Ever since you changed, we're all behind you."

"Since I changed?" Mrs. Fitzgibbons appeared puzzled.

"When you became different," Emily explained. "When you changed. When you started talking out — scolding people for this and that. When you were in the newspaper. When you were on television. We were so proud of you. I was so proud of you. I could have killed Mrs. Wilson that day."

Transformed by her own words, Emily Krok was left gazing abjectly at Mrs. Fitzgibbons. The light of reverence showed through her distorted features. She wanted to say more. "You ought to wring her neck."

Mrs. Fitzgibbons reached with a fingertip and brushed a tear-stain on Emily's cheek.

"You ought to break her back," Emily said.

"Don't worry, sweetheart," Mrs. Fitzgibbons soothed the girl. "I'll destroy Mrs. Wilson."

"She should be chain-sawed. She should be killed in her sleep."

"You'll work for Julie from now on. You're going to be Mrs. Fitzgibbons's little spy."

"I'd like that. You're beautiful. In every way," Emily added, in raptures.

"Julie is very loyal to me, and so will you be. You'll keep your eyes and ears peeled and report to me in secret everything that's going on. This afternoon, I want you to go up to my house and give the place a good cleaning." Mrs. Fitzgibbons got her purse from her desk. "It hasn't been touched in a month. Make everything sparkle and shine. I'll be home at five."

With Mrs. Fitzgibbons's house key in hand, Emily paused in the rear doorway of the office, her knees bumping and the toes of her sponge-soled shoes turned inward. She reminded Mrs. Fitzgibbons of an old painting she had seen of a knot-faced medieval peasant, stooped with hardship, her body afflicted with premature age. She was the exact opposite of how Mrs. Fitzgibbons saw herself, a stylish modern-day woman commanding the fortunes of a powerful institution. "Go along, darling," she said, with charity for the pigeon-toed girl hunched in the doorway in her forest green jumper. "I know how miserable you are."

Emily stared back with a fixated expression. "I'd do anything for you, Mrs. Fitzgibbons. Honest."

"Start in the kitchen," said Mrs. Fitzgibbons, "and work your way toward the front of the house."

By closing time that Wednesday, when she called Leonard Frye into her office to brief him on his Hartford assignment, Mrs. Fitzgibbons had regained her confident outlook. The ghastly look of Mr. Frye standing in her doorway startled her. It did not occur to Mrs. Fitzgibbons that the man whom she had replaced and demoted half expected to be fired, or, for that matter, that Mr. Frye, in the interim, had developed a severe middle-aged crush on his boss.

"You look like you've donated a gallon of blood. Shut the door behind you. I have an important assignment for you."

She regarded him across the lamplit, dark-grained surface of her big desk and shook her head in dismay at the notion that two weeks ago this fellow was overseeing her work and giving her orders. The impression was unsettling.

"You're not ill, are you?"

"Not at all." Mr. Frye glanced about for a chair, but Mrs. Fitzgibbons had ordered Julie to take the chair out of her office following the episode with Desmond Kane. No other employees would abuse their welcome by remaining seated after she had finished with them if there was no chair for them to sit on in the first place.

"This will only take a minute," she said, and instructed him then on the matter of his visit to the George Hitchings Corporation.

"You want me to do that?" Mr. Frye was clearly impressed by the size and reputation of the firm she was talking about.

"I think you can handle it."

Ironically, of all the employees who had felt the impact of Mrs. Fitzgibbons's regime, it was Mr. Frye, her fallen predecessor, who appeared most convinced of the validity of her success. It showed in his face.

"Look your best," she told him. "Be personable down there. They know you're a good technical man because I told them you were. We're looking for bigger game," she boasted. "Under me, Leonard, everyone on my staff is going to get an equal chance to show me what they can do. Everybody starts at go. And don't think I won't be cracking the whip."

"You're doing a fine job," he put in quietly.

"I'm going to increase the spread between costs and yields if it kills me." Her spine tingled. "Everything rides on my ability to do that." She touched off essential points on the fingers of her left hand. "Unprecedented publicity, lower operating costs, low-cost funds in volume, low-risk loans with a solid yield, and a lean, hard-hitting staff underneath me."

For the first time, Mrs. Fitzgibbons detected the distinct look of romantic infatuation that left Mr. Frye's temples tinged with pink. The realization embarrassed her and led her to address Mr. Frye in a manner quite different from her earlier suggestion about his career possibilities in New York.

"You're not twenty-five years old, Leonard. I have to be shown that you can still cut it. This is your retirement job. You can't pack up and run off to Hawaii. You can't decide overnight to become an oceanographer or a pineapple grower. You're over fifty," she said, "and you've got yourself a hard-driving boss." Mrs. Fitzgibbons could restrain her tongue no longer. For two hours, the compulsion to mouth an obscenity had been building within her. "Don't think for a second that I can't be one motherfucker," she said.

Mr. Frye swallowed hard over that one, but succeeded at maintaining his balance and an unruffled expression.

"I'm your future." Mrs. Fitzgibbons swung round to face the door, as Julie entered with a folder in her hand. "What is it, sugarplum?"

Across the face of the manila folder, in bold black letters, was the legend, "Background Report on Laurence and Morris De Maria. Confidential to Mrs. Fitzgibbons, from J. Greaney."

"What have we here?" Mrs. Fitzgibbons peeled open the folder and regarded its contents with a self-satisfied smirk.

"Has something happened with the De Marias?" Mr. Frye had caught sight of the lettering on the folder and spoke up instinctively.

She ignored him, as she turned a page of the carefully typed report and began scanning the section titled "Current Activities, Employers, Organizations, Social Acquaintances." Mrs. Fitzgibbons felt a voluptuous thrill over her power to commission such a detailed document on such short notice. She liked, too, the way Jack expressed some of his findings in the secretive language of undercover intrigue. The last sentence of the first paragraph read, "A 'friend' of this institution reports that the latter, Morris De Maria, was refused employment at the firm of the Nicholson Wire Co. over his inability to explain the cause of his dismissal from his previous post. Our 'friend' reported further that Mr. M. De Maria and his wife, Marie, later engaged in a vicious shouting match in their car outside the wire plant."

"This is exactly what I wanted!" Mrs. Fitzgibbons slammed shut the folder and rapped on her desk for Julie. "Tell Jack I'm pleased. Tell him I'll thank him tomorrow. Tell him to get in here in the morning." She turned to Mr. Frye. "I'm going to put Laurence De Maria in jail. I'm going to put him in state prison. I'm sending him to trial," she said, "and he's going to jail."

To Mr. Frye, the woman behind the big lamplit desk looked genuinely scary. The flesh of her face was drawn back with masklike tautness. Her blue eyes flared and sparkled.

"He'll rot in there," she said harshly. "And don't think I won't have a couple of million-dollar lawyers pressuring the district attorney. I can afford the cream of the crop. I'm going to lock him up. I'll put him away for years."

"But what did he do?"

"He can beg for mercy till he's blue in the face," she said.

TWELVE

W hen I come into the room," Mrs. Fitzgibbons instructed Emily in a kindly manner, "always step to one side. It's impolite to stand in my way."

Emily Krok watched as Mrs. Fitzgibbons glanced cursorily about the kitchen at the gleaming floor and appliances and stepped on into the next room. Outside, darkness had fallen, and a cold autumn rain was coming down. The rain increased in intensity, hitting the bedroom windows, while Mrs. Fitzgibbons changed clothes. She wanted something sporty for a change, and settled on a black turtleneck and black pants. Both Matthew and Julie were waiting outdoors in the Buick. Mrs. Fitzgibbons didn't want to eat alone tonight. She had made plans to meet Bruce for supper out at the Monarch Club, a rustic gin mill three miles north of town, but then decided to invite the others, as well. She wanted to be surrounded by her intimate circle.

"Julie told me that you had a chauffeur," Emily said, flashing an obsequious, gap-toothed smile, while watching Mrs. Fitzgibbons change.

As she pulled on her turtleneck, Mrs. Fitzgibbons was both

conscious and understanding of the way that the poor girl stared at her. Emily had a short-legged, blockish build, with an arched neck and flat breasts, which added up to something gnomish, even a little malevolent in its ugliness. She had reddish skin and rough hands. Mrs. Fitzgibbons could appreciate how her own womanly form, with its curves and softnesses, not to mention the perfection of her head and throat, could inspire awe in the other. Outdoors, the rain hammered away at the side of the house, buffeting the windows, and kept up a steady rushing noise in the rhododendron leaves. Twice, while dressing, Mrs. Fitzgibbons heard a distinct cracking sound from outside the bedroom window. She was sitting at her dressing table, touching up her makeup, while Emily stood at her elbow, with Mrs. Fitzgibbons's black raincoat folded over her arm.

Presently, a sudden sharp splitting sound brought Mrs. Fitzgibbons to her feet. It was the sound of a bough snapping in two, but was followed instantly by a cry. In the same second, something heavy hit the side of the house. "What the devil?"

"Somebody's out there." Emily put down the raincoat.

Never a coward, Mrs. Fitzgibbons darted to the window and pulled back the curtains and shade, just as there arose a sound of scuffling footsteps in the mud, and the whomp of a body hitting the clapboards. In the crescent of light shining from the window, Mrs. Fitzgibbons saw the back of Matthew's head disappearing downward into the wet rhododendron leaves. He was wrestling someone to the ground. "That's Matthew!" she said. "He's caught someone."

"Someone's peeping at you!" Emily astonished the other woman as she dropped everything and ran to the front door. Mrs. Fitzgibbons followed, pulling on her raincoat. In her haste to help Matthew, Emily Krok left the front door thrown wide behind her. From the porch, Mrs. Fitzgibbons detected the pale oval of Julie's face, staring out the back window of the Buick. The rain was blowing across the sidewalk. By this time, Emily was around the side of the house, out of sight, and was shouting angrily. Her raucous shouts were frightening in themselves. "Hit him with something!" she was yelling. "Club him! Club him!"

In no time, the three of them came around the corner of the house. Matthew was clutching Eddie Berdowsky in a headlock and propelling him forward in the rain with skilled violence. Emily had thrown herself into the struggle and was holding Eddie's shirt collar in one fist, and the seat of his trousers in the other. For his part, Eddie was pitched forward at a dangerous angle, as Matthew shot him along in the rain.

"Wouldn't you know it," said Mrs. Fitzgibbons, recognizing her son-in-law as the intruder at her window.

"It's a peeping Tom!" Emily confirmed triumphantly.

"You'd better call the police," said Matthew.

"Take him inside," said Mrs. Fitzgibbons, clearly disgusted.

Satisfied that Mrs. Fitzgibbons knew what she was doing, Matthew thrust the rain-soaked man up the steps and into the house. Eddie gaped with bulging eyes at Mrs. Fitzgibbons as he rocketed past her. Emily, not wishing to lose her grip on Eddie's collar and trousers, crashed hard against the doorjamb on the way in. Julie came running from the car. In the front foyer, Eddie's feet were slipping from under him at every step. A little Persian carpet flew sideways as Matthew maneuvered him roughly into the parlor. "Jesus Christ," Eddie said.

Matthew Dean was incredulous on learning the identity of the other man. Eddie was sitting on the hassock now, gasping for breath. "He's your daughter's husband?"

Mrs. Fitzgibbons stood over her son-in-law. His trouser legs were plastered with mud. He avoided looking up at her.

"Where is Barbara?" she wanted to know.

Eddie held up a staying hand, while regulating his breathing. He couldn't reply for a moment. "Origami class," he said, finally.

"She's folding birds, you mean."

Eddie nodded. A spray of rhododendron leaves clung wetly to his shirt.

"This is what I'm saddled with." Mrs. Fitzgibbons gestured disdainfully.

Julie came into the room, staring aghast at the sight of the man in the drenched blue factory shirt on the hassock. "What happened?"

Mrs. Fitzgibbons commenced to castigate her son-in-law in rhythmic locutions, patting the flats of her hands for emphasis. "I go into my bedroom to change my dress, and, lo and behold, somebody's watching me. Somebody's out in the dark peeking in my window. Somebody," she stressed, "who couldn't impregnate a woman if he had the stuff in a petri dish, wants to watch his wife's mother take her clothes off."

Eddie showed Matthew a sickly smile. "I lost my key," he said, pathetically.

Emily Krok hovered close to Eddie, eyeing him with a menacing grimace. "I'd like to tattoo him real good."

"I run a bank from nine to five," Mrs. Fitzgibbons's voice climbed, "I come home to dress for dinner, and my daughter's husband is forking off in the bushes outside my window. Because that's what you were doing. We're not children!"

"Frankie!" Eddie protested her words energetically.

"What's more, you can't call the police," said Matthew.

"That's my point," said Mrs. Fitzgibbons. "That's what I mean. That's the beauty of it, I suppose. I can't call the police, I can't have him pinched, I can't even tell Barbara."

"I hope you won't," Eddie said sincerely.

Mrs. Fitzgibbons turned instructively to Julie Marcotte and Emily. "This is the adult world. This is what you've got to look forward to. The day he married Barbara, he had a pair of my panties in his tuxedo pocket."

Eddie colored instantly. "That was a misunderstanding."

Matthew, unable to check himself, began laughing. Mrs. Fitzgibbons laughed, too, and so, to some extent, did Eddie. "Somebody put them there," he explained lamely. By now, though, the sight of Mrs. Fitzgibbons standing over him in her slender black raincoat, turtleneck sweater, and pants, had begun to work a hold on Eddie. He was staring at her in thrall.

"You're not fit to keep polite society," she said.

Never in the entire three years of his marriage to Barbara had Eddie presented himself to Mrs. Fitzgibbons as obsequiously as now. In the minutes to come, Mrs. Fitzgibbons called Eddie every name in the book. He was a toady, she said. He was a pervert.

His parents were demented. Eddie nodded with philosophical resignation as Mrs. Fitzgibbons characterized his entire family as Neanderthals. "It isn't true?" she said.

"It's true," Eddie agreed.

"That was why Barbara married him," she cried. "She didn't want to upset the ecosystem, the balance of nature. Tell me I'm lying."

"It's true." Eddie picked wet leaves from his shirt.

"These are orangutans," said Mrs. Fitzgibbons. "This is the missing link. He can talk, he can drive a car. He puts on his own pants. He can tell a condom from a balloon. There isn't a zoo in the world that wouldn't take him."

Julie and Emily screeched with laughter as Mrs. Fitzgibbons lashed away at her son-in-law. Oddly, however, when she turned and marched out of the house to the car, with her retinue following, and Julie holding an umbrella over her head, Eddie tagged along. He got into his own car and followed the Buick down Essex Street all the way to the river and across the bridge in the rain to Hadley Falls. The rain was very icy now. The trees in the parking lot of the old Monarch Club dangled ice-laden branches over the two cars and made light clashings on their rooftops. The club was empty, save for Emil, the barman, who sat on a stool, watching television. Sitting at the head of the oak table by the windows athwart the bar, Mrs. Fitzgibbons offered a bona fide picture of the genial dictator relaxing on off-hours with her chums. She entertained them with wit and charm.

"What I like about you four," she said, putting aside her gloves, "is that none of you is bringing me documents to sign!"

"We're too dumb for that," Eddie said, laughing.

She signaled imperatively to the barman. "Give them what they want. Bring me mineral water and a menu."

"Four mineral waters," said Eddie, whose deference toward Mrs. Fitzgibbons was getting so slavish, it was beginning to draw cynical looks from the others.

"Five in all," Matthew concurred unhappily.

Even before Emil could return with their menus, however, something happened to produce a most animated effect. Oddly, it was

Julie Marcotte who noticed it first. "Chief," she said, "look who's on television. That's the South Valley man, isn't it?"

The look of intensity that gripped Mrs. Fitzgibbons's face that second, and the suddenness with which she got to her feet, created a noisy stir of excitement at the table. Everyone followed suit. Even Emily Krok stood up. The evening news was being shown on the big color set above the bar, and Tom Pesso, the head of the Channel 6 news bureau, was about to conduct a live interview with the man whom Julie had recognized. It was Mr. William Daviau himself, the South Valley Bank director who had expressed such indignation over the media exposure accorded Mrs. Fitzgibbons.

The newsman was speaking. "Mr. Daviau has requested this chance," he said, "to rebut certain statements — or to correct unfair impressions, I should say — that he feels were aired over this station on Monday night, by Mrs. Fitzgibbons, the new chief executive of the Parish Bank. I would like to thank you," he said to the other, "for coming to the studio."

In the seconds to follow, only the sound of the cold rain hitting the windows of the tavern could be heard, as Mrs. Fitzgibbons and her cronies waited for the man to speak. She had come round in front of the long table and was staring up at the television, her face as pale as murder. For the longest while, nothing happened. William Daviau stared at the newsman in obvious fright. He was tongue-tied. Mr. Pesso tried to help him. "Where would you like to begin, Mr. Daviau?"

The South Valley man wet his lips nervously and opened his mouth to speak, but, as before, nothing came out. The bank director was suffering from a case of stage fright that was rapidly evolving into a living nightmare. Two or three times, he started to speak, but managed only an "um," or an "ah," after which his eyes glazed over again, and the silence came back more profoundly than ever.

Mrs. Fitzgibbons's anxiety gave way in a flash to a joyful outburst. Mr. Daviau was still on the screen, stricken with fear; the newsman was posing questions now conceived to elicit simple yes or no replies, but the bank director appeared virtually mindless. His face contorted in pain.

"The voice of the opposition!" cried Mrs. Fitzgibbons.

"That man should run for president," said the bartender.

"Let's have a round of beer," said Matthew.

"Hey, Chief!" Eddie Berdowsky put on an idiotic face, rolling his eyes and lolling his tongue, and stammered out an imperson- ation of the pitiful Mr. Daviau — "Ah — um, um — ah, blah, um blah" — while turning and stamping about in a circle, his body limp with amusement; a piece of inspired buffoonery that sent the others into howls of laughter. The floor shook beneath Eddie's feet as he marched round and round.

During the next half hour, Eddie put on such a display of sy- cophancy that even Julie and Emily were shocked by the son-in- law's shameless behavior. Mrs. Fitzgibbons couldn't open her mouth without Eddie gaping at her with a shiny face and a craven smile. He consumed two mugs of beer and began to sweat pro- fusely. "Did you hear that?" he would cry. "Didja hear what the Chief said? What a sense of humor! Oh, Chief! That's a hot one!" Eddie banged his beer mug on the table and, flinging back his head, gave out with a sudden horselaugh.

Sadly, for the others, Mrs. Fitzgibbons made no attempt to discourage Eddie. She took his servility in stride. This had the effect of encouraging the others to emulate him. He hung on every word she uttered. He sponged up the little water rings on the table before her with his napkin. When the barman brought a basket of bread rolls, Eddie snatched it and set it before her. Through it all, he never took his eyes from her, nor wiped the fixated smile from his face. The only time that Mrs. Fitzgibbons looked at him reproachfully was when Eddie, in a transport of delight over some- thing she had said, clapped his hand to his head with such force that the blow sent his sweat flying in a shiny spray.

By the time Bruce arrived at the Monarch, Mrs. Fitzgibbons's quiet Wednesday evening supper had evolved into a lively, joyous affair, with a great deal of laughter, and her friends banging their glass mugs on the table over practically every remark she made. Mrs. Fitzgibbons cut a fine, boastful figure at the head of the table. Indeed, the spectacle of William Daviau on television had not only embarrassed him, but by contrast illuminated her own rhetorical gifts. For no one could gainsay the brilliance with which she had used the media to capture public attention. Emily Krok spoke up at one point to suggest that Mrs. Fitzgibbons send a funeral bouquet of white carnations to Mr. Daviau's house, but Mrs. Fitzgibbons replied that "persons who dig their own graves should bring their own flowers."

Bruce had come dressed to perfection, peeling off his raincoat and revealing himself in an elegant chalk-striped gray suit, offset by a pearl-and-black necktie and pearl pocket square. As he advanced across the room, Mrs. Fitzgibbons silenced her friends with a snap of her fingers and gestured for him to take Eddie's place close to her. Bruce received her kiss before sitting.

From the moment he sat, it was clear that he had a matter of importance which he was eager to communicate. Mrs. Fitzgibbons listened with a cold expression as he apprised her of his discovery. It concerned an officer at the bank. As before, the sound of the icy rain striking the roof and windows of the rustic bar lent an ominous counterpoint to the matter at hand. Mrs. Fitzgibbons sat as straight as a rule in her chair, clutching her glass of mineral water; her dark hair and black turtleneck exaggerated the paleness of her face. "Get to the point," she said.

"His name is Howard Brouillette." Bruce was intent on presenting his findings in logical sequence. "One of the girls in my salon learned about it."

"About what?" Mrs. Fitzgibbons's pupils darkened. "What did he do?"

"It isn't like that." Bruce shook his head. "Nina, who works for me, went to school with Mr. Brouillette's wife. They went to the Metcalf School together. His wife's name is Dolores. She and Mr. Brouillette have been married about two years."

"I know, I know," Mrs. Fitzgibbons snapped impatiently.

From the inner pocket of his suit jacket, Bruce extracted a folded newspaper clipping. Mrs. Fitzgibbons took it in hand at once. With everyone watching, she opened it. It was a printed photo of a naked woman, her face obscured by a black bar of ink across her eyes and nose. The caption below the picture read "The Queen of Kink."

"Her name is Dolores," Bruce repeated unnecessarily. If he had expected an amused response from Mrs. Fitzgibbons, he was rapidly disabused.

"This," she said, "is Mrs. Brouillette? This is his wife?"

"I'm afraid so."

The anger in Mrs. Fitzgibbons's face discouraged the others from reacting. "Do you have any idea what this could do to me? My vice president in charge of secondary financing is married to a whore?" In an access of fury, Mrs. Fitzgibbons shouted at Bruce. "Where did you find this?"

Mrs. Fitzgibbons got to her feet before he could answer. "I'll be a laughingstock! This slut could destroy me." She looked about herself in frustration. When she got this way, Julie and the others shrank into their seats.

"I hadn't thought of that," Bruce muttered.

"My name and reputation will be dragged through the mud in every paper and news broadcast from here to Hoosac Tunnel."

Emil, the barman, was so riveted by what he saw, as Mrs. Fitzgibbons clenched and flexed her fists and flung acid remarks about, that he ignored the ringing telephone.

The man in question, Howard Brouillette, was an individual whose behavior bordered on eccentricity. Known to his coworkers as a young man who wore the same cheap suit of clothes to work every day, Howard talked incessantly to anyone who would listen and employed a technical jargon that bewildered the uninitiated. He talked about his triumphs in the secondary market in terms like "inverted yield curves," "Euroyen," "basis points," and about "segmented markets" and "globality." At his most loquacious, his face took on the glassy-eyed expression of a fanatic. Until now, Mrs. Fitzgibbons had looked upon the skinny, bespectacled man as nothing more than a harmless specialist who had found his place in life at the refinancing desk of the Parish Bank; she had never liked standing close to him, though, for there was something repellant to her in the combination of his bug-eyed appearance and the constant nervous agitation he generated.

As quickly as it had begun, Mrs. Fitzgibbons's harangue came to an end. She told Eddie to get her raincoat, and then signaled for Matthew to get up. Before anyone realized what was happening, Mrs. Fitzgibbons was in her coat and headed for the door. In fact, Bruce and the others were still sitting at the table when the sound of a car engine starting up gave them to realize that she was leaving.

As Matthew drove through South Hadley, past the college, Mrs. Fitzgibbons sat very austerely in the back seat and railed away in a harsh undertone on the unluckiness of her fate. "I could have been a social worker or a schoolteacher," she said. "This is what I get. This is my fate. I'm going to be chopped up and spiced and fried in my own fat. This is what you get for showing courage, for doing what has to be done. I could have left it to others! I'm going to be lambasted in public. I'm going to be butchered. Here is this disgusting little geek, an absolute gem if ever there was one — a pimp! — because that's what he is — and I'm going to take the fall. This is what I get. A knife in the back."

With blanched temples and a grim, fixated expression, Mrs. Fitzgibbons cited her grievances in an eerie monotone, all the way home.

THIRTEEN

The effect of the startling news concerning Mr. Brouillette's wife was evident the next morning in Mrs. Fitzgibbons's manner. When Matthew drove her to work, she was surly and uncommunicative. Bruce noticed the change also when he saw her coming through the mall toward his salon, in the rigidity of her posture and the humorless set of her face. At the bank, Julie must have sensed the change; she gave Mrs. Fitzgibbons a wide berth that morning. Even Mr. Zabac himself got a taste of Mrs. Fitzgibbons's harsh tongue when he telephoned down to ask if she had seen Mr. Daviau humiliate himself on the Channel 6 news the night before.

"What did you expect?" she snapped at the chairman. "You were surprised?"

It was obvious by now that Mr. Zabac saw his new chief officer as a sort of miracle worker, an indomitable figure who had sprung full grown from the pavement at Maple and Main. Consequently, when she was short with him, Mr. Zabac made allowances. He had no desire to rock the boat.

Mrs. Fitzgibbons hung up on him. As far as she was concerned, the bumbling man on television could as easily have been Louis Zabac as the other fellow. At the moment, Mrs. Fitzgibbons's thoughts were focused obsessively on persons nearer at hand, on subordinate officers among her staff, like Mrs. Wilson, Neil Hooton, and Brouillette; persons under her own roof who thirsted after her ruin. At one point, Mr. Hooton stepped soundlessly past her office door and glanced in at her with a look of disgust on his fleshy face. He was wearing wide yellow suspenders over his ample belly; his little gold glasses rested far down on his nose. Of them all, he was the arch renegade. The mere sight of the man set Mrs. Fitzgibbons's stomach shaking. In the back of her mind, however, an obscure plan was already forming, a secret scheme by which she would endeavor to link the fates of Mr. Brouillette and Mr. Hooton.

At noontime, she sent Julie to get Howard Brouillette. But when the girl returned to report that he had gone to lunch with Elizabeth Wilson and Neil Hooton, Mrs. Fitzgibbons's paranoid fears were confirmed. This piece of intelligence was the culminating provocation.

"So, there it is," she said.

"They've gone to Schermerhorn's Sea House," said Julie.

"Now it's out in the open. I'm not in power here four days, and the three of them go marching down Suffolk Street, big as life, just like that, to a secret lunch. They know that I know they're there," chanted Mrs. Fitzgibbons, "and it doesn't mean a thing to them. And I'll tell you why. Because they know exactly what's going to happen, and when, and in what form, and how it's going to happen, because they're the ones making it happen. They're not in hiding," she chanted on. "They're sitting at a table down at Schermerhorn's."

Emily Krok came into the office while Mrs. Fitzgibbons was expatiating on the mind-set of traitors. Emily was carrying a stack of computer printouts. She worked for Julie now, and held Mrs. Fitzgibbons in such awe that she was chary of addressing her directly. "Where would Mrs. Fitzgibbons like me to put these?" she asked.

"Keep quiet!" Julie snapped at the homely, misshapen girl.

"You work like a Chinaman for fourteen years to get where you are," Mrs. Fitzgibbons went on with her recriminations, "you do what you're supposed to do, you do it better than anyone else this side of J. Pierpont Morgan, and before the Thursday lunch bell rings, you've got a full-fledged conspiracy on your hands. My hours are numbered," she said. "Because nobody is that dumb. Anyone else would meet in secret — at *night*," she said, "in some lonely, out-of-the-way place. But not these little killers. They're down there dining on brook trout and caviar. They're washing it down with champagne. Because I'm finished. It's a *fait accompli*. It's a done thing. I'm kaput."

Emily was staring at her with alarm when Mrs. Fitzgibbons turned on her and ordered her to search Mr. Brouillette's desk.

"Turn it inside out," she said. "Close the door behind you, and lock it, and turn that desk inside out. I want the goods. Smutty newspapers, personal notes, letters, sex paraphernalia, everything."

"I'll find it, Chief."

Mrs. Fitzgibbons was already commanding Julie on what to do. "Get a roll of that yellow-striped packing tape from the mailroom, and when Emily is finished, tape shut his desk drawers." Mrs. Fitzgibbons was in an excited, agitated state, as she called after them. "If you don't find anything, invent it. I want results."

While waiting for them to return, Mrs. Fitzgibbons was called on to discuss a delinquent home mortgage loan. Connie McElligot came in person to Mrs. Fitzgibbons's big office with the pertinent paperwork. Connie herself wished to extend the sorry couple an additional month of grace.

Mrs. Fitzgibbons was in no mood for softheartedness today. "Get them out!" she said.

"What with winter coming —" Connie began.

Mrs. Fitzgibbons cut the air with her hand. "I want that house. I want it today."

"Mr. Sadakierski has just been called back to his job," Connie explained.

"Do you understand English?" Mrs. Fitzgibbons grabbed the papers from Connie McElligot's hands, planted them on her desk, and scrawled her signature in big red ballpoint letters at the bottom of the page. "I don't care if they freeze to death! Those deadbeats owe me money!"

Connie McElligot's fingers and jowls shook as she returned to her desk. Mrs. Fitzgibbons frightened her.

Within ten minutes, Mrs. Fitzgibbons was holding in her hands a species of evidence that was so damning, she could scarcely credit the sight of it. Julie and Emily stood on either side of her desk chair, leaning over her and watching in breathless fascination, as Mrs. Fitzgibbons went methodically through a stack of glossy, eight-by-ten, black-and-white photos that depicted Dolores Brouillette in various poses of undress. Most of the photographs were candidly pornographic. Each time that Mrs. Fitzgibbons moved one of the big black-and-whites to the bottom of the stack in her hands, revealing still another naked shot, the girls behind her gasped anew.

For her part, Mrs. Fitzgibbons was not herself visibly moved by Emily's dramatic discovery, but maintained something more of the air of a judge or police official who had long ago seen everything illicit and was merely mulling over the value of the evidence at hand. When she was finished, she tapped the stack of photos on her desk, straightening them, and returned all to the white envelope in which Mr. Brouillette had concealed them in his desk.

"You did good," said Mrs. Fitzgibbons.

"Did I?" Emily was thrilled.

"Very," said Mrs. Fitzgibbons.

"I can't believe that woman is Mr. Brouillette's wife," said Julie.

"She's really good-looking." Emily was impressed with the photos.

"She's not bad-looking," Mrs. Fitzgibbons allowed pleasantly.

"Mrs. Brouillette must have a couple of bolts loose," said Julie.

"What a body," Emily said. "I wish I had a body like that."

Julie turned on her. "She's a lowlife! What are you talking about?"

"You can be a lowlife and still have a tremendous body on you."

"She looks like a streetwalker!" Julie spat back.

"Not to me she doesn't," Emily persisted. "She's expensive. Did you see that fur jacket and the jewelry on her? I'll bet she charges an arm and a leg."

While the two girls argued over her head, Mrs. Fitzgibbons thought. She tapped her pencil. Oddly, the big stack of pictures had had the effect of dissipating her agitation. She felt much better. She was not listening to Emily Krok and Julie.

"I'll bet she makes videos, does shows, things like that," Emily said. "If she doesn't, she should."

"I suppose you would." Julie was tiring of Emily's impertinence and sneered at the girl's cheap Indian blouse and strange shoes.

"I didn't say that," Emily replied. "I can't imagine what it'd be like to look like that."

"You wouldn't feel any different."

"Ho! That's what *you* think!"

"I'm trying to think," Mrs. Fitzgibbons remarked. "Will you two stop chattering?"

"I'd feel *very* different," said Emily. "To see myself in the mirror in a body like that? I wouldn't feel different? Are you loco?"

"Don't speak to me like that," Julie reproached her. "You work for me."

"But Mrs. Brouillette doesn't. That's my point."

Mrs. Fitzgibbons broke in on them, but was clearly in a much-cheered frame of mind. "This isn't a bank, it's a bordello. We just pretend to be bankers. Our securities portfolio is down about three million, the typists are stealing every supply that isn't nailed down, and the vice president for secondary financing is running an escort agency. I thought we were the fastest-growing bank in the world. Not at all. I'm running a whorehouse."

Emily continued to argue with Julie. "Mrs. Brouillette is a professional."

"Oh, shut up," said Julie.

"I pay this ding-a-ling fifty thousand a year to spread our risks, peddling mortgages to the secondary market, and his wife's home spreading her legs to supplement the family income." Mrs. Fitzgibbons had worked herself into a surprisingly happy state of mind. "Julie," she said, "tell Mr. Donachie to post himself in Howard Brouillette's office and to bring him straight to me the moment he returns."

While Mrs. Fitzgibbons was denied the satisfaction of witnessing Howard's shock at seeing his desk drawers sealed shut with the garish tape, and of the bank guard staring at him with a lascivious look from beneath the black bill of his cap, the spectacle of Mr. Brouillette being marched through the auto loan department was observed by many, not one of whom was likely to forget it; for if death ever walked the earth on two feet, it could not have imparted its nature more spookily than that writ on the face of Mr. Brouillette.

Before addressing Mr. Brouillette, Mrs. Fitzgibbons signified with a nod that Alec Donachie could go. She waited for the door to close.

"I hope you don't mind my having had your desk taped," Mrs. Fitzgibbons started in, while reaching and moving the big envelope of photos to one side on her desk in such a manner as to draw his attention to it. "It's just a precaution," she said, "in the event that our interview doesn't turn out the way I'd like it to."

Mr. Brouillette smiled crazily at that. A sticky white froth appeared on his lips. "Our interview?"

"Our talk, Howard," said Mrs. Fitzgibbons in a robust tone. "We're going to have a talk."

"Oh," he said, "I see." He stood inertly before her desk; his spectacles glittered.

"I thought you should have your lunch first."

"That was thoughtful of you." Time and again, Mr. Brouillette's eyes flicked nervously to the envelope of photos on her desk. He reached up with a bony hand and adjusted his eyeglasses.

Mrs. Fitzgibbons sat forward at her desk. She looked quite beautiful, the lamplight glowing softly on her hair and illuminating the planes of her face. "The three of you," she inquired, pleasantly, "did you meet at Schermerhorn's, or did you walk down there together?"

Howard shifted his weight nervously. "I believe we met there," he said.

"I see. Did the conversation at lunch surprise you?"

Mr. Brouillette made as if to express his confusion over the question, then thought better of it. "Do you know, Mrs. Fitzgibbons, it did," he replied.

"They're not your sort of people, Howard."

Like a lost man descrying a point of light in the distance, Howard groped forward. "In fact," he confessed, "I was very surprised."

"I'm not going to ask you to repeat everything that was said, and I'll tell you why." Mrs. Fitzgibbons rocked backward in her chair, if only to demonstrate to a hapless subordinate the ease and casualness that destructive power is capable of indulging without depreciating itself. "With the two of them, Howard, I'm just biding my time."

"I'd be happy to tell you."

"Not at all!" Her melodious response showed her to be supremely indifferent to gossip.

"But I would," he insisted.

"You see, I," Mrs. Fitzgibbons pointed out, "knew that you were there in my interests."

"I was," said Howard, whose moral condition by now was already that of a man in dread of being taken down to the dungeon.

"I knew it whether you knew it or not."

Mr. Brouillette, an adept at chess, must have read Mrs. Fitzgibbons's move instantly, for he replied without hesitation: "But I did know it."

For a moment, Mrs. Fitzgibbons regarded him with a soft, endearing expression.

"Why else would I have gone?" he cried, and laughed eerily. The pale eyes in his long, moribund face glittered; he wetted his lips at frequent intervals.

The sight of the angular, ill-dressed figure standing before her, in his seedy blue suit and cheap maroon tie, inflamed Mrs. Fitzgibbons's ego. "*These little mice!*" she suddenly exclaimed, and flung herself forward in her chair. "You people are going to harm me? You would have to be mental to pick a fight with me!"

Mr. Brouillette's face fell. He gaped at her with a fixated smile that creased his pocked face.

"Your wife is in show business, they tell me."

"My wife?"

"Your wife! Mrs. Brouillette."

"I don't think so."

"I have it on sound authority that Mrs. Brouillette is a celebrity."

"No," he managed to reply. "I would not call her that."

"Then my sources have failed me. Who would know better than you? How long have you and Dolores been married?" Mrs. Fitzgibbons waved at the envelope.

"Two years," he replied drily, and coughed nervously into his fist.

"Don't misunderstand me," Mrs. Fitzgibbons put in. "I admire people in the entertainment business. Do you manage her?"

"No." He met that query with promptitude.

"From what I hear, Dolores is very talented. A rising star. Beautiful and photogenic. You must be very proud of her, Howard. I don't blame you for not trumpeting her successes around the bank, though. Some people have old-fashioned ideas about showgirls and movie actresses, and how you can't mix that sort of thing with business and finance. Does Dolores have her own automobile?"

The sudden changes of subject kept Howard off balance. "Yes, Mrs. Fitzgibbons, she does."

"What model is it?" came the sonorous rejoinder.

"She has a new Toronado."

"That's wonderful. Toronados are very pretty. I hope she financed it with us," Mrs. Fitzgibbons teased.

Mr. Brouillette hesitated. "Do you know," he concluded, with uncertainty, "I don't think it ever was financed."

"You do understand," Mrs. Fitzgibbons got to the point of her interview, without lifting her voice, "that I'm in a position to ruin you."

"You said?" Howard's jaw dropped.

"You understand," Mrs. Fitzgibbons repeated for emphasis, in a louder voice, "that I can smash the life out of you."

"Oh, absolutely." Mr. Brouillette reacted at once to her clarification.

"That I could have my guard come in and drag you out of here by the seat of your pants."

"I know that."

Mrs. Fitzgibbons stood now and showed Howard Brouillette a very stern expression. "You do know what's coming for your friends."

"I can imagine."

"They'll be waiting tables at the Puritan Diner. They won't know what hit them. I'm in the newspapers," said Mrs. Fitzgibbons. "I'm featured on television. The calls are backed up on my phone lines for an hour and a half. The question now is what I'm going to do with you. Isn't it?"

Howard showed her a penitential expression. "We all know you're fair."

"It isn't a question of being fair." Mrs. Fitzgibbons went past him in a little gust of perfume. "If I were fair, I'd send you and your movie-actress wife to jail. I'd have you beaten with a broomstick. I'm not trying to be fair. The banking business," she said, "isn't fair. If life were fair, you'd be working for yourself. You people don't work for yourselves. You work for me."

"I'm behind you foursquare, Mrs. Fitzgibbons."

"Some stupid skills picked up in a night school someplace mean nothing to me. You business grads are a dime a dozen. I need specialists who are personally devoted to me."

"Makes sense." Howard rewetted his lips.

"Who would go to the wall for me. That's how people get ahead here."

In the way of illustrating her authority, Mrs. Fitzgibbons turned on her heel and snatched up her telephone. "Julie," she said, "put me upstairs to the chairman."

Mrs. Fitzgibbons waited importantly for Mr. Zabac to come on the line, while relishing the way that Mr. Brouillette was gaping at her.

"Louis!" she said, and launched into one of her spur-of-the-moment promotional ideas. "I'm going to ask Nate Solomon of the Shawmut to come to lunch one afternoon next week, to give an informal talk to our loan officers about changes going on in the marketplace. I'm certain he'll come. In fact, he'll be flattered. I'll have the news people here in force! It's important you be here." Mrs. Fitzgibbons's manner was clearly that of the executive in charge. "We'll aim for Friday," she said, and hung up the telephone.

"That's banking," she explained, and snapped her fingers rapidly, five or six times, to show the accelerated pace of the new regime. She reached then and took up the envelope containing the thick stack of pornographic pictures of Mrs. Brouillette, and with an indifferent flourish, tossed it to him. "Where is Dolores performing?" she said.

The suddenness of the gesture left Mr. Brouillette thoroughly addled. He was holding the envelope.

"You can talk to me. I'm not the Pope," said Mrs. Fitzgibbons. "What sort of engagements does she have? Stage shows? Private parties?"

"Mostly," Howard managed to answer, "she's free-lancing."

"House calls?"

Howard grinned sickishly over that one. "Outcalls," he croaked, "yes."

"Outcalls? Is that how you put it? Well, it all sounds very lucrative. I'd like to meet this film star." Again, Mrs. Fitzgibbons's eyes went to the envelope in his hands. "Why don't you bring Dolores to dinner at the Canoe Club tonight at eight o'clock. Ask for me at the reservations desk."

"That would be wonderful," he said.

"I like your work, Howard. I've been watching you carefully. Since taking over here, by cutting out some deadwood, I've trimmed our total annual salary outlay by a hundred thousand dollars. Those funds are now available to me, you see, to reward people who march to the new music. I have the resources to reward loyalty."

The light on Mrs. Fitzgibbons's phone flashed repeatedly. On this occasion, she took up the receiver.

"What is it, lamb?"

"Mrs. Fitzgibbons, your daughter wants to see you."

"You tell Barbara I'm not to be bothered. I'm discussing wages with my financial officer."

Julie dropped her voice to a whisper. "She looks very distressed, Mrs. Fitzgibbons."

"Tell her to wait." Mrs. Fitzgibbons returned her attention to Howard Brouillette, who, in the preceding five minutes, had begun to show his superior an expression of the most intent fascination. He reached up many times with his index finger to wipe the perspiration from his hairline. Mrs. Fitzgibbons went on with her recital without missing a beat. "Money talks. I have the wherewithal. I have the power. With this fund, I'll put an end, once and for all, to any final pockets of resistance." She couldn't help preening as she boasted. "I can't offer you a new title, Howard, but I can increase your salary by an appreciable margin."

Mr. Brouillette was genuinely stunned by the sudden turn in his fortunes. "I wouldn't even know what to say to that."

"Oh, it's going to happen. I'm putting you in for it today. Why do you think I called you in here? To discuss Regulation Q? To pass the time of day?" She waved her hand at Howard's clothing. "Buy yourself a couple of new suits. You look like an immigrant. You're one of my vice presidents, not some carnival shill trying to guess people's weights. Have Dolores select something for you. I'm sure she has lovely taste."

"Dolores has wonderful taste."

"Something conservative and expensive. And, remember," Mrs. Fitzgibbons cautioned him, "if I catch you so much as talking to those two luncheon companions of yours, I won't just take away your rattles and teddy bears. I'll chop your spine off."

"I don't associate with people like that."

"I mean it," she promised, with a narrowed eye. "I'll put you in prison."

Mrs. Fitzgibbons showed him to the door. Outside her office, on a metal chair next to Julie's desk, Barbara sat waiting for her. Mrs. Fitzgibbons's daughter wore a plaid lumberjack coat and faded blue jeans. No two women could have been more dissimilar in appearance and bearing. As soon as she admitted her daughter and closed the door behind them, Barbara started in.

"You perfect bitch," she said, in a thin, suppressed wail of a voice. "You're ruining my life. What are you doing to me?"

"Barbara." Mrs. Fitzgibbons showed her daughter the face of reason. "I have a world of work to do. I haven't time for infantile temper tantrums. This is a bank. I'm chief executive officer here. I'm not Sigmund Freud," she said. "I'm not Captain Kangaroo."

Barbara mimicked her mother's repetition of the first-person pronoun. "*I — I — I!*" she shrieked.

"I have a dozen appointments. I have money market calls to make. I have loan proposals to study." She gestured about herself. "This is the actual world. There is no hole in the ozone layer here, or baby seals being murdered, or anything like that. We're not African killer bees. We make loans to people to buy things."

"You're sick," Barbara shot back. "You don't know what you're talking about. You've lost your mind. You can't afford those clothes. That awful makeup, that hair! Who told you you could be glamorous? I'm dying inside. Are you listening to me? Eddie stayed out half the night. He's in love with you! He's infatuated with you!" Barbara put her hands over her ears. "It's sordid and disgusting. Who ever heard of a man talking to his wife about the shape of her mother's breasts?" Barbara turned this way and that; her eyes flew about distractedly.

"He said that?"

"Why are you doing this to me? Why is this happening? Why?" She clenched her fists. "Why?"

Mrs. Fitzgibbons grimaced. "He was talking to you about the shape of my breasts?"

Barbara was staring with blank gray eyes at the wall behind her mother. "I tell you, I can't bear it anymore."

"Is he demented?" said Mrs. Fitzgibbons. "You have the gall to come in here, in the middle of the day, to tell me a story like that? I warned the two of you not to marry. I said it at the time. One of the two of you had to find someone better."

"You said nothing. You're raving."

"Look at you. You look like a forest ranger."

"Everyone but you knows what's happening," Barbara cried. "You've gone crazy. You're destroying people. Don't you realize that? Desmond Kane stopped me in the street —"

"That one-armed bandit —"

"You," Barbara hollered, "*fired him!* He hasn't a job now. What's he supposed to do? Where is he supposed to turn? All because of you. He said you've become a lunatic. He recognized the symptoms. You're out of control."

"I'm not out of work," said Mrs. Fitzgibbons.

"Desmond is unemployable now."

"That's hardly a qualification for me to employ him." She showed Barbara a smile of irony. She attempted to cheer her daughter. "Don't fret about things you can't control. We're all capitalists, Barbara. We're all guilty of dirty tricks from time to time. There's no lasting harm in it. How would you like to be living in Borneo?"

She opened her office door. "Look out there," she said. "Everyone is working in this place. People are lined up at the tellers' windows. Telephones are ringing. We take in twenty dollars for every eighteen dollars and sixty cents that we pay out. The difference between the two, by the end of the year, is enormous."

"I hate you," said Barbara.

"Seven percent stays here." Mrs. Fitzgibbons pointed illustratively at the floor under her feet.

"I hate your insides." Barbara suppressed the fury in her voice. Her eyes behind her glasses twinkled malevolently. "I hate your guts. I hate everything about you. I hate every memory of you. I hate the sight and sound of you."

"Well, you aren't alone," said Mrs. Fitzgibbons, surveying the great bank and the dozens of employees bent industriously to their work, as supplicants in a temple.

"I don't own a house," Barbara complained. "I have a husband who lusts after my own mother. He says that your signs are compatible. He actually said that to me —"

For the second time that day, Mrs. Fitzgibbons was abruptly brought face to face with her most daunting adversary, as at that moment, Mr. Neil Hooton came out of his office and paraded as big as life past the copy machines not twenty feet from where she stood. As before, the portly officer was conspicuously contemptuous of Mrs. Fitzgibbons. She was no more important to him than a little bug on the wall. That was plain to see. He went on his way with a disdainful swagger, his head back, his little eye-glasses riding on the tip of his nose. In her secret heart, Mrs. Fitzgibbons still feared the man. He alarmed her. She could not rid herself of the feelings of awe with which she had always looked upon him. It set her insides churning. Her forehead turned cold. Her eyes shone with blue venom.

FOURTEEN

Mrs. Fitzgibbons's string of triumphs had not only affected her own bearing, as in the proudness of her walk, or the rather impressive set of her jaw, it had also produced a similar result on some of her closest followers. Julie, for example, who was at heart a genial soul, and never wished to make trouble, was showing herself to be quite acid-tongued when dealing with staff members. Like a miniature edition of Mrs. Fitzgibbons, she too walked about in a brisk manner, stiff in her posture, head up and shoulders straight, and often a pinched, querulous expression painted her lips. She clearly enjoyed being the messenger of dire tidings, and couldn't help sometimes but to snap at people. Mrs. Fitzgibbons's power and her disposition were contagious.

Matthew, who served as Mrs. Fitzgibbons's driver both in the early morning and again in the evening, was not immune to the bacillus of authority. He wore a severe-looking navy suit every day now, with a starched white shirt and dark, navy necktie, and had begun to affect on his bony face an expression that could only be described as bellicose. Sometimes, while waiting for Mrs. Fitzgibbons by the door of his Buick, he fell into the habit of cracking his knuckles while showing passersby a mocking sneer.

Of them all, though, probably the most comic manifestation of this growing tendency was found in Emily Krok, who showed up for dinner this evening wearing an old bomber jacket and a motorcyclist's cap, giving her the appearance of an out-and-out hooligan. Emily appreciated Matthew more than she did any of the others, because of his amateur boxing as a boy, no doubt, but also because he never batted an eye when she made one of her cracks about "breaking heads" or "kicking them all blue."

For supper, Mrs. Fitzgibbons had engaged a two-room suite on the upper floor of the Canoe Club. When she arrived with Matthew, the others were already there. Bruce Clayton was responsible for all the arrangements and had made sure that the table was properly decorated with crystal, flowers, and candles, and had instructed Mrs. Kelliher, the lady in charge of the waiters, that Mrs. Fitzgibbons was the well-known banker whom everyone was talking about these days, and of how this chief executive was a stickler for form, and that efforts to pander to her vanity could only redound to the credit and future prospects of the restaurant. In response to that, Mrs. Kelliher smiled embarrassedly; but when she turned to walk away from Bruce, she found herself face to face with Julie and Emily Krok. They were both staring at her, and they were not smiling. It was Emily who spoke up. She pointed a bruised fingernail at Bruce and addressed the woman in an ugly voice. "That man is talking to you," she said.

One might almost have thought the plan that had been forming in Mrs. Fitzgibbons's mind all that day was somehow known to the others; for there was clearly in the air that evening the sort of relief that human beings feel once a decisive order has been issued. That was not, of course, the case; for their superior had not said a word to anyone. Yet a relaxed, festive sense prevailed from the start. When Mrs. Fitzgibbons came up the stairs and entered the prettily appointed Victorian dining room, Eddie spouted aloud, "Here's the Chief!" and everyone stood and applauded.

Mr. Brouillette had arrived with his wife not five minutes earlier, and was standing beside her in front of the big bay windows that looked out onto the night-lit river. Dolores was blessed with a magnificent mane of rich brown hair, had a flawless complexion, and naturally dressed in such a way as to draw some attention to her physical dimensions.

In minutes, the wine was flowing freely. Mrs. Fitzgibbons was a trifle less talkative than usual and content just to occupy center stage, with her companions gathered about her, clinking glasses, laughing, exchanging small talk. She had not troubled yet to remove her leather coat, but stood beneath the lighted chandelier, basking in the currents of affection and respect flowing from her court. Even Dolores Brouillette, who was a stranger to all of them, looked upon Mrs. Fitzgibbons with a warm glow in her eyes, as it was Mrs. Fitzgibbons, after all, who had that day hiked her husband's salary by a big increment.

Howard raised his champagne flute. "The first lady of banking," he said.

"I'll toast to that," said his wife.

"To the Chief!" Eddie cried.

Everyone touched glasses. Mrs. Fitzgibbons acknowledged the tribute with a curt nod, and raised her own glass to her lips. She didn't like alcohol very much but enjoyed the happy effects it produced on those about her. She was exulting inside, very at one with herself and her accomplishments. A waiter, clad in white jacket and black trousers, came bustling in, bearing a broad silver tray replete with delicacies, at the heart of which was a cut glass server decorated artistically with slices of yellow peppers and glistening black olives. Behind the waiter came Mrs. Kelliher, hurrying forward to greet and welcome Mrs. Fitzgibbons. As she did so, she could not help but notice the dark, leering looks that Emily shot at her. Emily hovered nearby, closing and flexing her fingers. Her squat, misshapen figure, tilted forward, contained a powerful feeling of the grotesque.

"Did you see how she looked at Emily?" Julie cried out in merriment, after Mrs. Kelliher had departed. Julie bugged out her eyes in mimicry.

Everyone looked at Emily, in her leather cap and bomber jacket. "I'd like to punch her lights out," Emily said.

"She was shaking all over," Julie said.

"Who wouldn't shake?"

Even Mrs. Fitzgibbons laughed heartily now at the sight of Emily eyeing the doorway with her lips drawn back.

"I'd be shaking," said Eddie Berdowsky, who had arrived uninvited.

"Yes, and I'd give you a good creasing, too," Emily told him. She was already betraying signs of having had too much alcohol. "With a word from the Chief, I'd tattoo you good."

"She's just teasing me," Eddie cracked happily to Dolores, including her in the banter, while stealing a peek at the pronounced lift of Mrs. Brouillette's white sweater behind her open jacket.

"Eddie is a peeping Tom," Matthew explained pleasantly.

"Oh, I see!" Dolores brightened happily over that.

Only Emily Krok remained grim and unsmiling. She showed Eddie the skinned knuckles of her two fists. "From punching cinder blocks."

Eddie downed his champagne and gestured merrily at Emily. "What a fruitcake! The day she was born, God was on unemployment!"

Sensing the party was getting too raucous, Bruce encouraged all to come to the table. Everyone stood at his or her place while Bruce took Mrs. Fitzgibbons's coat and seated her at the head. Mrs. Fitzgibbons was a picture. The twinkling lights from the chandelier and candles played iridescently in her hair and sent magical streams of light in sudden rainbows up and down the surface of her black dress. Her face was lit to perfection. While the others had enjoyed a few moments of relaxation among themselves, it was more than clear at the table that none save Mrs. Fitzgibbons would speak out without prompting. Consequently, a full five minutes passed without a word uttered, as Mrs. Fitzgibbons led the way in partaking of the vichyssoise. The silence was impressive. From the fireplace at the far side of the room could be heard the hot showering sounds of flaming brands disintegrating, followed by eruptive cracklings. When she did look about the table, which was infrequently, she did not make eye contact with anyone. The effects of her commanding presence were thus compounded by the minute, which imbued Mrs. Fitzgibbons with a very pleasurable sensation.

Not until the entree was served would she reveal to her little gathering of loyalists the thrust of her latest strategem. Prefatory to that, however, Mrs. Fitzgibbons thought it wise to display something of her firm manner and persuasive tongue, if only for the sake of Mrs. Brouillette, who was unfamiliar with the indomitable character of the Chief. She began by explaining how some of her enemies stood in complete ignorance of the dark forces collecting about them.

Everyone at the table smiled sinisterly at the hidden menace in her words. "What do you suppose they're doing to prepare themselves for me?"

Mrs. Fitzgibbons paused for the waiter to refill her water glass and then depart.

"They know I'm coming," she said. "They know I'm not going to shut my eyes as long as there's one of them left to interrupt my plans, or to strike at me from behind. I've been civil. I've been more than that. I've been cordial and pleasant. They've had more than a week," she stated, "to show me a decent attitude. More than a week."

"That's true," Julie breathed out in a soft voice, and nodded with sad understanding to Bruce, sitting opposite her.

"I've been the soul of patience and goodwill. I've given them a dozen examples of my intentions." Mrs. Fitzgibbons paused here to break bread. Her tone was that of the reasonable leader whose tolerant nature was being ignored by ingrates. "I have promoted deserving people with this hand, while chopping out deadwood with this one. The lesson doesn't take. They continue to defy me."

"The beat goes on," said Eddie.

"All that was necessary," Mrs. Fitzgibbons made clear, speaking now to Howard Brouillette's prostitute wife, while continuing to hold up her two hands, "was for such a subordinate to come to me, sit down in my office, congratulate me on my victory, and say, 'You have my complete support and loyalty. I *recognize* your authority, I can see with my two eyes the results you're producing, and I'm going to join you in doing my level best, so help me God, to carry out your programs.' The chairman," Mrs. Fitzgibbons fired out in a much harsher, more strident tone of voice, "is scared to death of me. *They're* not. He is, they're not. To them, I'm like a little autumn rain shower."

Dolores was listening raptly, her dark eyes focused on Mrs. Fitzgibbons. Her fork was poised in the air. "They must be stupid."

"They know I'm going to smash them, and they continue, hour after hour, day after day, to oppose me." Mrs. Fitzgibbons paused to show her assembled dinner guests the face and silhouette at the head of the table of the implacable destroyer. Then she reached for her wine. "Now we're going to play according to some new rules."

Silently, Eddie raised his two fists.

"This is what I'm reduced to doing. To bringing together, in the nighttime, in an out-of-the-way place, this little collection of happy-minded thugs — because that's what you are — just to effectuate these changes that should have taken place in the normal civilized course of things."

Mrs. Fitzgibbons's friends laughed spontaneously in unison over her characterization of them. Of them all, Julie was the most enthralled by Mrs. Fitzgibbons's inflammatory proclamations. Her face shone with a bright pink glow, her love of Mrs. Fitzgibbons as transparent as could be.

"Until today, I would have forgiven them," said Mrs. Fitzgibbons. "Had they come to me like human beings and showed a little remorse and a willingness to salve my offended feelings, I would have buried the hatchet. I would have pardoned them. Don't misunderstand me. I would have been angry, and maybe even a little punitive, but I'd have taken them back. Now," she said, bitterly, "that hour has passed."

As often happened when Mrs. Fitzgibbons contemplated her plans for her detractors, her language took on a violent edge. "Believe me," she promised, "only the most extreme measures remain open to me from this hour forward."

Instantly, she shot up her hand to forestall the display of enthusiasm which her companions were eager to offer. "Oh, I know what you all want. I'm not an idiot. But as you all know, all I asked from the start was a peaceful accommodation."

"And that," said Eddie, significantly, to Matthew at his side, "is not to be."

"Indeed, it is not," she said.

"Mrs. Fitzgibbons has waited day after day after day for them to come round," Julie attested, thoroughly drawn into the spell of Mrs. Fitzgibbons's darkening mood.

Sitting bolt upright in her chair at the head of the table, Mrs. Fitzgibbons offered a very fetching picture of the dictatorial figure who is not reluctant to deal with malefaction and will not shrink from using whatever weapons come to hand.

"Tonight," she said, "I'm ordering Dolores out to Hampton Ponds, to a certain lakeside cottage out there, where she'll begin to pave the way for the comeuppance of a man who has not only squandered millions of hard-earned dollars entrusted to his care, but who has been unrepentantly vicious toward me. Not just toward me personally," she added, "but toward the dignity of my office."

Perplexed by the sudden reference to his wife, Mr. Brouillette straightened in his seat. Dolores, equally bewildered, reacted with a foolish smile. "Where am I going?" she inquired amiably.

"Simple justice isn't enough," Mrs. Fitzgibbons went on. "Up until now, I've played according to Hoyle. If you please me, I promote you. If you fail me, I fire you. Those are the rules of civilized behavior. They are not the rules for dealing with a slick, pompous mountain of flesh who exhausts the life savings of others in the hopes of pulling down a fat bonus every December."

"I knew a man like that," said Eddie.

"Keep quiet," Julie scolded.

"Those aren't the rules for dealing with a high-ranking official whose salary I pay and whose office consists of three or four of the most disgusting, bootlicking brownnosers the world has ever seen. Playing by the book is out the window."

"It's about time," said Matthew, his face and eyes glowing from the alcohol.

"This is no small-time chiseler," she said. "This is no downtown penny-ante Puerto Rican hustler working a street corner in Ward Two. This man was advantaged. I," she reminded her friends, "came from nowhere. I spent years in the trenches. I started at the bottom. I know every dirty trick there is. I'll tell you a story. The day I took over total authority, that little man upstairs made me promise that I wouldn't act rashly — that I wouldn't hurt the feelings of the man I was replacing."

Everyone laughed over the cynicism Mrs. Fitzgibbons employed in her remarks, as she smirked and opened her hands to signify a tolerance of naiveté.

"I gave him his lollipop. Why wouldn't I? I knew what I was going to do. I had the power. I went downstairs and in ten seconds flat took that sad sack by the neck and flung him out of his office!"

For the first time in many minutes, the table erupted boisterously. Emily thumped the tablecloth with the heel of her fist.

"I was expected to run that place, to manage the lives of all those people, with my hands tied behind my back. Not two days later, I gave that little man upstairs my solemn word that I wouldn't fire anybody. We all know what happened to that!"

Of those present, only Bruce showed an anxious reaction to Mrs. Fitzgibbons's egotistical outburst. He watched her fuming away at her imaginary enemies with a worried look on his face.

"I didn't call that meeting," she was saying. "I didn't take a poll. I don't govern by committee!"

Mrs. Fitzgibbons spoke uninterruptedly for ten minutes, while the food turned cold on their plates. The only interruption came when the waiters appeared to clear the table. Just as dessert was about to be served, Dolores Brouillette paid Emily an unintended insult that set off gales of laughter. Dolores had just learned Emily's name, but thought that she was being kidded. She didn't believe that anyone was named Emily. "That's a little piggy name," she said.

Emily, who was sitting next to Mrs. Fitzgibbons, with Mrs. Brouillette on her left, had turned to the prostitute and was gazing at her with a very hurt look. Next to Dolores, Emily resembled a creature of an inferior species. She was scrunched up in her chair, staring into Dolores's face as if it were an immense searchlight that had suddenly located her.

Dolores was blushing, as she believed she was being teased by her new friends. "Emily is a piggy's name," she said.

"Not to me, it isn't," said Mr. Brouillette, in an effort to release Emily from her agony.

"What are you talking about? Am I an idiot?" Dolores was beaming, enjoying the attention that Mrs. Fitzgibbons had drawn to her. She enjoyed being looked at. She turned her head and regarded Emily once more; her face was still heated from the sensation of being kidded along. Emily was transfixed. "What's your last name?" Dolores asked.

Emily's eyes were on a level with Mrs. Brouillette's breasts and the delicate rope of pearls that draped forward on the soft up-swelling of her white cashmere sweater. She gaped at the wine glass in Mrs. Brouillette's fingers. Emily moved her jaw from side to side before replying. "Krok," she said.

Dolores's face came alive instantly, as she reached and set down her glass. "Is somebody tweaking me?" she cried gaily.

Even Mrs. Fitzgibbons enjoyed the merriment, in particular the picture of Emily's face twisted into a knot of misery.

"*Crock?*" Dolores let out with a shriek. "Wouldn't you just kill yourself?"

Over dessert, Mrs. Fitzgibbons detailed the part that Mr. Brouillette's wife was expected to play in the unfolding drama. Dolores was game for the plan right off the bat, but was slow at divining what precisely was expected. Matthew tried to clarify it for her.

"Mrs. Fitzgibbons wants you to compromise someone," he explained.

"Oh, I'd like that," replied Dolores, sitting up and straightening her torso, conscious of the admiring looks and attention of all.

"You'll be remunerated," said Mrs. Fitzgibbons.

"I couldn't take money!" Dolores was clearly put off by the offer, but after a moment of stunned silence, during which interval everyone looked round at everyone else in disbelief, she modified her objection. "I mean, for this job," she said.

"You'll take what I decide to give you."

As Mrs. Fitzgibbons instructed Mrs. Brouillette in the particulars of her assignment, Howard revealed some obvious symptoms of discomfort. He was hunched forward over the table, his hands pressed flat between his knees, and had taken to scraping his feet back and forth on the floor. His face was sweaty; he was smiling insanely.

"He won't be expecting you," said Mrs. Fitzgibbons, "so you'll have to inveigle your way in."

"What is inveigle?" Dolores inquired.

"Show him some leg," said Eddie.

"Matthew will drive you out to the lake house. It's Thursday night. I know he won't be going home from there till nine or ten o'clock."

"Can *I* drive Dolores?" said Eddie.

"All right." Mrs. Fitzgibbons acceded to her son-in-law. "You drive."

"Will the rest of us follow them?" Matthew inquired.

"Not tonight. Let him have some rope."

"This is exciting," Julie said, as Dolores and Eddie stood up and went for their things. Eddie made an elaborate act of helping Mrs. Brouillette into her coat.

"As for you," Mrs. Fitzgibbons instructed Eddie, "you'll park about a hundred yards back on the road and get out of the car. That way, if Hooton is not alone in his cottage, Dolores can say she's having motor trouble and lead him out to the car."

Dolores was tying a silk kerchief about her throat. "Do you want him to score?" she asked bluntly, evidently reveling a little in her cool professionalism.

"Whatever it takes," said Mrs. Fitzgibbons. "I want him primed for tomorrow night."

"That's my specialty."

"I'm sure it is."

"It really is," Dolores repeated, happy to cite her strengths. "I'll have him climbing the wall."

"*Didja hear that?*" Eddie smacked his head with the palm of his hand.

Long after Eddie Berdowsky and Dolores had gone out to the parking lot, Howard Brouillette continued to sit forward in his chair, sweating freely and rubbing the flats of his hands between his clenched knees. He shivered from time to time. No one paid him any mind, though. Soon Emily had found her voice again, and it was apparent that her feelings of adulation toward Mr. Brouillette's call girl wife exceeded any rancor she might have felt over the fact that her name struck Mrs. Brouillette as being appropriate only for a piglet; and she joined Julie Marcotte in remarking on Howard Brouillette's good luck in finding such an accomplished and exciting wife.

"Isn't she something else?" Julie observed.

Mrs. Fitzgibbons nodded agreeably. "She's very attractive. Your wife is very pretty, Howard."

"Thank you." Howard's eyes twinkled moistly behind the fogged lenses of his glasses, and he continued to scrape his feet mechanically back and forth under the table.

Emily cupped her hands before her. "They stand up like this!" she said.

"That's vulgar," Julie chided her.

"You call that vulgar?" Emily retorted, not understanding. "If I were Mr. Hooton, I'd pay through the wazoo for something like that. He'll be begging for mercy. That's what I'd make him do. I'd make him beg for it. On his knees! He'd buy me diamonds and jewels until he was flat broke on his back, and I'd run over him with my five-speed Nissan Sentra!"

Mrs. Fitzgibbons tried to speak up, but Emily interrupted her passionately. "I wish I were a man. I'd like to buy something like that for an hour or two."

Swiftly, Mrs. Fitzgibbons reached and dealt Emily a noisy clout on the ear. "What's the matter with you?"

"What'd I do?" Emily howled in pain and jerked backward.

"Are you deaf?" said Mrs. Fitzgibbons.

"Mrs. Fitzgibbons was trying to talk," Julie chimed in.

"I was talking," said Mrs. Fitzgibbons.

Julie scolded Emily. "You'd better watch your mouth."

"*But I didn't mean it!*" Emily clutched her ear.

Mrs. Fitzgibbons was leaning forward with her hand in the air, contemplating the merits of a second slap. Emily cowered and held up her arm.

"The Chief was talking," Howard attested. At the sound of his voice, Emily burst into tears.

"How was I to know if I didn't hear her?" Emily whined.

Mrs. Fitzgibbons, who had not struck anyone in years, not since childhood, appeared fully prepared to continue to do so now. She looked angry.

"Please." Bruce pleaded for an end to the fighting. "What's going on?" The sudden violence at the table upset him.

"I'll never talk again!" Emily blurted tearfully.

"You'd better not," Julie said.

"People who insult me go to the hospital," said Mrs. Fitzgibbons.

"I love you more than any of them!" Emily protested.

"That's probably true," said Bruce, trying again to conciliate the dispute.

"It is," Emily cried.

"Finish your dessert," said Mrs. Fitzgibbons.

"I'd do anything for you. You know I would. There's nothing I wouldn't do. I'd commit murder. I'd rob and kill. I'd chain-saw somebody."

Mrs. Fitzgibbons continued to point at Emily's dessert, until Emily stopped talking and picked up her fork.

NIGHT OF DIRE RECKONINGS

FIFTEEN

The tension at the bank the following morning was palpable from the moment Mrs. Fitzgibbons came darting in at the front door and knifed her way through the lines of customers at the windows. No one on the job was insensible to the cold electricity she generated. Her features were drawn and masklike. She looked like someone who had agonized for days over a question of great consequence. The fact that Mrs. Fitzgibbons had not slept more than four hours a night for more than a week contributed to her edginess. She couldn't sit still at her desk for prolonged periods and often snapped at people in a way that intensified the spreading alarm, as when she interrupted Leonard Frye in midsentence and told him not to bore her with a detailed account of his Hartford business trip.

"It seemed to me a success," he protested politely.

"Summarize your views on paper. Prepare me a written report," she told him. "If I like the terms, I'll sign off on it. If I don't, I won't." She scowled at him then from behind her desk. To talk to her former boss in such a peremptory fashion sent a stab of sexual excitement up and down her legs. She shivered at the pleasure of it. "Do your homework, Leonard. Don't come to me un-prepared. You've been in this business long enough to know that."

Her rudeness pained Mr. Frye. "It could be a feather in your cap," he suggested softly.

"Please, spare me the blandishments." She patted her desk rhythmically then with the flat of her hand and repeated her instructions in the pedagogical style of a grade school teacher. "Type it on a sheet of paper and give it to my secretary."

Before departing, Mr. Frye lingered a moment, betraying his infatuation.

"Go along back to your work," she said. "You can beat off later."

This parting obscenity sent Mr. Frye twitching and blinking back to his desk. Mrs. Fitzgibbons couldn't help herself. In no time, she was exacerbating the general nervousness of the place by railing on the telephone about the competitor banks in the area. Her rising voice penetrated the surrounding quiet. Jack Greaney, making his way to Julie's desk, thought better of it and returned to his post.

At the same time, no one was indifferent to the steady surge of new business. The number of interest-bearing checking accounts had practically doubled in a week. Savings deposits mounted by the hour. No one on the staff could question seriously the triumphs of their new chief. If her manner was chilling, it only nourished the impression of her invincibility. However, to aggravate matters, it was during this same morning that Mrs. Fitzgibbons learned about the graffiti someone had scribbled in the men's room, a slanderous slogan to which she reacted with textbook paranoia. Mrs. Fitzgibbons summoned her guard and marched him straight in. There, above the porcelain urinals, was scrawled in black spray paint the legend: "Frankie Fitz Is a Fascist Pig!"

After dispatching Alec to the basement, to get someone from maintenance to eradicate the hateful words, Mrs. Fitzgibbons retreated to her office. No matter how fair or generous she tried to be, there were always those gutter rats and back-stabbers creeping about with murder in their hearts. Her flesh went cold at the thought that someone in their midst could perpetrate such a sordid act.

As it happened, though, the first extraordinary occurrence of the day did not originate with Mrs. Fitzgibbons. It started with a sudden shout from someone in the back offices. An instant later, Mr. Hooton was standing in the doorway of his office, waving a sheaf of papers in his hand and demanding an explanation. He was in a fury. The sight of the massively built man, his physical frame shaking with outrage, was not that of a displeased employee but of an infuriated boss. The shock of white hair on his head and his bushy white eyebrows made his face a brilliant red.

"What in God's name *is* this?" Mr. Hooton repeated himself in a belling, mooselike voice. He shook the paper in anger at the man sitting before him. The recipient of his thunderous demand was none other than Lionel Kim, his assistant.

Mr. Hooton hollered anew: "What do I have in my hand?"

Going quickly to her door, Mrs. Fitzgibbons forgot momentarily who she was and felt a stab of fright at the picture of Neil Hooton quivering in rage. No one at the bank had ever seen its like. Mr. Hooton, respected by all as the soul of smooth, managerial polish, stood forth in the doorway in an awesome light. Beneath his gaze, Mr. Lionel Kim cowered. He was speechless.

"I told you market level!" Mr. Hooton continued shouting. "That was two hours ago! Now, this security transaction has gotten away from me. It's down a point and an eighth!"

Turning, and waving the sheaf of papers like a traffic cop, Mr. Hooton ordered Lionel Kim into his office. There, the hollering persisted for a full minute, and ended abruptly. "You can just look for another job," he cried. "That's what you can do for me. You can *get out*."

By dismissing the slender, delicate young man from his employ, Mr. Hooton could not have created greater resentment or primitive fear in Mrs. Fitzgibbons's heart had he marched into her office and begun thrashing her with his fists. If there was one thing she had not anticipated, it was the possibility of Mr. Hooton stealing her fire. For several minutes, Mrs. Fitzgibbons had reason to wonder if the stout man in the yellow suspenders might not intensify the drama even further by firing some more people. After all, he had the authority to do so in his own department. Like any strategist who has committed the classic blunder of expecting his enemy to behave in accordance with his own schemes, Mrs. Fitzgibbons was left with her wings clipped. The man whom she reviled and dreaded most of all had disarmed her. The boldness of his act augured even worse things to come, being just the first step, that is, in an effort to usurp authority.

Presently, Mr. Hooton came bustling out of his office, only this time the target of his frustration was clearly Mrs. Fitzgibbons herself. He was vaporing away in a resonant voice, as he headed for the stairway leading up to Mr. Zabac's office. "These dilettantes who don't know bunkum!" he threw out. "Boiler room bimbos who don't know a bank note from a Band-Aid — who learned what they know about finance down at the Holy Rosary sisters' school on Mosher Street!"

For a split second, the neon glow of the copy machine painted Mr. Hooton's face green as he hurried by it. He continued spouting insults even as he shot past Julie's desk and Mrs. Fitzgibbons's open door. "Nobody takes advantage of me! Certainly not some psychoneurotic fish-snapper who's headed for the deep end. That's too laughable!" he shouted. "That's downright funny! That makes me laugh."

Unlike those at the bank, such as Felix Hohenberger, who attributed the big man's outburst to the pressures of the Wall Street crash, Mrs. Fitzgibbons knew better. His loss of control sprang from motives as desperate as her own. She knew what he wanted. He wanted to vilify and defame her. He wanted to drag her out of her office like a common criminal. He wanted to beat the life out of her. Mrs. Fitzgibbons snatched up her telephone and dialed the man upstairs. She was too late.

Jeannine Mielke deflected her attempt with a curt, precise response. "The chairman is talking to Mr. Hooton and is refusing all calls, Mrs. Fitzgibbons."

Mrs. Fitzgibbons hung up and shouted to Julie. "Get me Howard!"

By pure coincidence, though, just as Howard Brouillette came hurrying out of his office, an altercation of an entirely separate nature broke out in the bank. It took place in the open space in front of the tellers' windows. Three or four individuals were grappling with one another. Mr. Donachie was one of them. Depositors standing in line looked on in disbelief as the bank guard strove both to subdue the others and to disentangle himself from the struggling mass. The melee was a gratuitous occurrence, it was later established, and had arisen from the attempt by a rather burly customer to regain the place in line he had temporarily relinquished, and by the active resistance of two others to this effort. It eventuated in a noisy, scuffling, swaying knot of four men, lurching first toward the windows, then across the marble floor in the opposite direction.

If nothing else, the sudden crisis attested at once to Mrs. Fitzgibbons's own courage in an emergency. While the other employees looked on helplessly, she, arriving on the scene with Howard Brouillette at her heels, immediately took charge. She shouted for Howard to protect Mr. Donachie's revolver. "He's armed! Get it from him," she said.

In fact, the violence and danger worked an instantaneous tonic on her spirits, as did the sight of Mr. Brouillette emerging from the struggle clutching in hand Alec Donachie's immensely long, blue-black .38-caliber side arm. Had Howard Brouillette possessed any understanding of Mrs. Fitzgibbons's mental state, it is doubtful that he would have handed her the weapon.

The revolver in her hand looked like a cannon. "Who said banking was a dull business?" she exclaimed, to the delight and relief of those looking on. After Howard and Mr. Donachie had separated the other three men, Mrs. Fitzgibbons inspired a general outburst of laughter when she dealt Alec his pistol, saying, "This must be yours."

"You're one of a kind, Frankie!" a customer piped in admiration. Every time she opened her mouth, it brought an animated reaction, as when Mr. Donachie asked her if he should call the police.

"You are the police," she said.

"We love you, Mrs. Fitzgibbons," said a young woman.

Marcel Sullivan, the youth from the mailroom, was standing at her elbow. "You go back to work," she told him.

The boy was agog. "You were wonderful, Chief."

"What's your name?" She liked the fact that the young man called her Chief. He put her in mind of Terry Sugrue.

"I'm Marcel."

"Marcel what?"

Everyone looked on with interest as Mrs. Fitzgibbons, the supreme executive officer, devoted a moment of her time to question an employee of the lowest echelon. Mrs. Fitzgibbons's cheeks and eyes glowed in the aftermath of the violence.

"Marcel Sullivan," he replied.

"You do work for me?" she queried in a high-pitched voice, her chin raised interrogatively. Everything in Mrs. Fitzgibbons's bearing bespoke magnificence, but most especially the expression of condescending interest that pinched her lips and set her dark blue eyes aflare. Given her mood of exulting egoism, it was no wonder that the sight of Mr. Hooton returning down the back staircase from Mr. Zabac's office promoted powerful feelings of contempt for him. With Howard darting along at her side, Mrs. Fitzgibbons went out of her way now to put herself in the path of Mr. Hooton. Howard was by now thoroughly allied to Mrs. Fitzgibbons in the politics of the bank, especially as his wife, Dolores, had, in fact, fulfilled her assignment of the night before.

Mrs. Fitzgibbons flung her words out as soon as Mr. Hooton drew near: "Imagine entrusting your life savings to the likes of that!" she said. Howard laughed obediently at her side.

Mr. Hooton stopped in his tracks, then approached her. A rosy flush invaded his jowls. He reached with stubby fingers and took off his little gold eyeglasses. They confronted one another eye to eye. Mrs. Fitzgibbons looked quite splendid in her supercilious attitude, as she stood smiling before him. She mocked him. "Did you report me to the headmaster?" she said. Not only did Howard Brouillette laugh, but Julie, approaching from her desk, laughed also.

"Your days are numbered," said Mr. Hooton. His face shook with anger. "I'll be here when the men in the white coats come for you. You need psychiatric attention!" With that, Mr. Hooton marched past her, with his head high and his shoulders back. "Candidate for the loony bin!"

Mrs. Fitzgibbons clicked her fingers rudely at Howard. "Get into my office."

Howard was shaking his head sycophantically. "That man must have a death wish," he said, as he closed her office door behind him.

In a sudden tantrum, Mrs. Fitzgibbons picked up a tall stack of papers from her desk, and with both hands threw it at the wall. A nervous shiver ran the length of her body. "He insults me to my face. I have him in my hands."

"He doesn't understand who you are." Howard's moral descent was framed in his sallow cheeks and sickly smile.

"Mind you," she went on, "this pillar of the community is embroiled with a prostitute, a big-titted, hundred-dollar-an-hour whore from Lyman Street who looks like she could blow up the Goodyear blimp all by herself — and *she* works for me."

Howard was enthralled; he was sweating. "Dolores is the best. She'll do what's expected of her."

"If she doesn't," Mrs. Fitzgibbons retorted without skipping a breath, "you'll be working my rock-salt detail this winter. You'll be shoveling my driveway. I'll have you picked up. I'll have you booked. You'll go away, Howard."

Howard's lemony complexion admitted points of a red hue at the cheekbones. "Dolores's got him good, Chief. You'll see."

"Call her up! Tell her to start the ball rolling."

"Hooton expects her to call him at three o'clock."

"Now!" said Mrs. Fitzgibbons. "I want him out of here."

While Howard Brouillette spoke softly on the telephone to his wife, Mrs. Fitzgibbons paced the carpet, giving outlet to her nerves. "By midnight tonight," she vowed softly, "if somebody out there isn't floating in the water, I will be. Because I'll never stop now. Then we'll see how this organization ought to be run. They'll *never* get me out. They'll carry me out."

Howard was clutching the receiver to his head with both hands. His octagonal eyeglasses sparkled in the lamplight above Mrs. Fitzgibbons's desk. He was telling his wife what to do. "It's more important than that," he whispered. "My salary is riding on it, Dolores."

"Your head," said Mrs. Fitzgibbons.

"My head," said Howard.

"Tell her to talk dirty," said Mrs. Fitzgibbons.

"Talk dirty to him," Howard repeated dutifully, in a soft voice. "Do what you're told. Get him out of here. That's imperative. That's from the Chief, Dolores. Make sure you're in bed with him from five to seven. That's the *sine qua non*."

Mrs. Brouillette must have sought clarification of her husband's Latin locution, as he repeated his meanings. "That's the most important part. Just telephone us at the old German Club." Howard listened at length then, as Dolores repeated her instructions. He revealed a sudden vein of frustration, however. "It isn't just fun, Dolores!" he cried into the phone. "Does everything have to be fun?" He smiled sickishly then at Mrs. Fitzgibbons, who stood by her desk, watching him. He lowered his voice in warning: "The Chief can put you away, Dolores. You know what that would mean. No more satin sheets, no ostrich boots. No champagne weekends. No new boat."

"Cut that out," said Mrs. Fitzgibbons.

"No bikini waxes or pedicures at home. No more flights up to Bar Harbor to see Mr. What's-his-name."

"You're scaring the poor thing out of her wits."

Immediately after hanging up, Howard Brouillette returned hurriedly to his own office; from there, he could see across the consumer loan desks to Mr. Hooton's open door. Mrs. Fitzgibbons had Howard on the line, in advance of the incoming call. She wanted a description of what was happening. Within one minute, she heard the far-off tinkle of Neil Hooton's phone ringing.

"He's taking the call, Chief!" Howard's voice came over the phone excitedly.

"How does he look?" Mrs. Fitzgibbons asked.

"He looks happy, Mrs. Fitzgibbons!" Howard narrated what he saw. "He's put down his pen and taken off his glasses. "He's sitting way back in his chair."

"He looks happy, though," she said.

"Very happy. He has his hand over his forehead and is laughing at what Dolores is saying to him. . . . Look at him now!" Howard cried in a suppressed whisper. "He can't believe this is happening."

"She's talking dirty now."

"That's for sure. She's pouring it on, too! She's the best. Oh, Dolores!"

"You take it easy," Mrs. Fitzgibbons remarked.

"He's standing up! He's getting up! He's on his feet. He's looking up at the ceiling, he's laughing — he's listening —"

"She's talking dirty —"

"He's nodding. She's bringing it to a close. That's smart, Dolores. She's smart, Chief. She's not giving him too much. He's smiling — he's nodding — he's *nodding!*"

"You take it easy," said Mrs. Fitzgibbons.

"He can't believe his ears. He can't believe what Dolores is saying to him. She can do it all on the phone. She can do anything. She should be in Paris. She should be in Vegas. Dolores," Howard cried over the phone, "you're a dream. I wish I could hear you. He looks like a four-year-old. He's in heaven. He's rubbing his belly with the palm of his hand."

Mrs. Fitzgibbons had gravitated to her door, the phone at her ear extended the length of its cord. She could see Howard doubled over behind his desk.

"He's in ecstasy, Chief!"

"You sit up straight," Mrs. Fitzgibbons commanded. "I'm watching you."

Instantly, Howard's head snapped around. His glasses twinkled in the distance. Mrs. Fitzgibbons had determined that Howard's reactions to his wife were a species of behavior not fully understood by science.

"What are you doing over there?" she said. "Pulling your pudding? That's not David Rockefeller, you know."

"It could be," Howard attested in a chastened voice. "She's that good."

Not more than three minutes elapsed when Mr. Hooton came marching solidly out of his office, pulling on his venerable Irish-tweed overcoat and making for the front door. Mrs. Fitzgibbons watched the man depart with satisfaction. She remembered a time ten years ago when this powerful figure was her own ideal of successful manhood, and of how she had even encouraged Larry, her husband, to dress in the manner of Neil Hooton.

Mrs. Fitzgibbons dealt Julie the telephone to be hung up, and issued an order. "Tell Jacqueline Harvey to increase Marcel Sullivan's salary by twenty percent, effective today. Marcel is the youngster in the mailroom. And tell Marcel that the Chief likes his work and his respectful manner, and that I'd like him to start training in the home loan department after he graduates from school."

"Right, Chief." Julie reacted with military smartness.

This time, she didn't wait for the chairman to open their meeting with his usual recitation of compliments and recommendations, but started right in on him. "Here we have a man," she flung out, "who lost us a king's fortune in the markets overnight, and what has he done? He's dismissed the only person down there who had his head screwed on straight. This is what comes from allowing confusion in the chain of authority, over who has the power to eliminate undesirables. With the proper authorization from you, I could have prevented all of this! Now, it's too late. Mr. Kim has gone home, and we're rudderless down there. Well, it's not my fault." Mrs. Fitzgibbons crossed her legs. She was not unaware of the fetching, even formidable picture she presented to Mr. Zabac, as she rattled on in this same loquacious vein.

"I continue," she said, "to draw a world of new business in through the front door and over the wires, while others piddle it away by the tens of thousands behind my back. Matters are coming to a head, Louis." She hardened her mascaraed eyes. "I will not be sabotaged."

While he was growing used to Mrs. Fitzgibbons's increasingly truculent style, the speed and accusation in her voice appeared genuinely to upset Mr. Zabac's fabled calm.

"I don't like the firings," he admitted.

"We were through with the firings until today! . . . I had selectively singled out for elimination six or seven hard cases. I was satisfied. I was appeased." Mrs. Fitzgibbons felt an actual surge of anger in her breast. "I was happy." She shifted and straightened her torso meaningfully, as though each declaration were a physical eruption from within. "You have a tender heart, Louis. I can tolerate that. You don't want to hurt anyone. You prefer looking the other way. Et cetera, et cetera," she said, with a dismissing wave. "I was happy to do it. I threw them out. It was a tonic. Everyone feels better. The air is cleared. The deadbeats are gone. People who couldn't tie their own shoelaces" — Mr. Zabac winced painfully at Mrs. Fitzgibbons's reference to the one-armed Mr. Kane — "are scarcely qualified to cut the mustard in this new order."

"Mrs. Fitzgibbons," the chairman pleaded to be heard, "why are you so irritable today?"

"You don't run mongrels in a dog race," she added. "You use greyhounds."

"Discrimination is illegal."

"Please! Louis! We're both grown-ups. I fired a bunch of mutts." She laughed out loud as she recalled the air of innocence of Marshall Moriarty when she axed him. "I did it cleanly. The people I disposed of were either simpleminded, aging, or so inconsequential that if they dropped dead at the supper table their own families wouldn't notice."

"I have a fax right here —" He reached for a sheet of paper.

"Fax me no faxes." She held up a hand. "You're breaking my heart."

It was manifest by now that Mrs. Fitzgibbons's day-to-day triumphs, combined with her intransigent manner and rather brutal way of expressing herself, had worked a spell on Mr. Zabac. He sat motionless behind his enormous desk, his custom-tailored suit offset by a sky blue necktie, and strove to keep pace with her tongue. Now and again, his eyes dropped to the spectacle of her body. When she got worked up, as she was now, her body moved with a liquid grace that was a sight to behold.

"What will happen this afternoon if Elizabeth Wilson starts firing people?" she challenged. "Or Howard Brouillette? Or Jack Greaney? Or the man in maintenance? Or payroll?"

"Mr. Hooton has listened to my views," the chairman conceded, "and would not be opposed to our recalling Mr. Kim."

"I intend to recall him!" Mrs. Fitzgibbons seized instantly on the chairman's ameliorative attitude. "Did you think he wasn't coming back? I have plans for Lionel. He's a brilliant boy."

"Yes, I believe he is."

Without a clue, Mrs. Fitzgibbons threw out a lie. "It was Kim," she said, "who wanted that department to go into treasury notes and gold last summer. It was Kim who believed the market was too high and wanted to take corrective steps. I know that for a fact," Mrs. Fitzgibbons lied boldly, "because he told me so to my face."

"He's a very astute young man."

"Why, he's brilliant," she said. She sat back and recrossed her legs. "He was fired for being right."

Mrs. Fitzgibbons listened then as the chairman delivered a reasoned and well-meaning lecture on the importance of harmony in the workplace and of the need for her to help effect a reconciliation between herself and Neil Hooton. Looking exhaustedly bored, Mrs. Fitzgibbons waved her hand desultorily, as though such sentiments were too obvious to remark on. After that, Mr. Zabac spoke about the strong capital position of the Parish Bank, and of its future, and the important role it would continue to play in the region. To Mrs. Fitzgibbons, the man might have been addressing the local Lions Club; she breathed audibly and opened and closed her eyes many times.

"For six consecutive years," Mr. Zabac explained, "we have outperformed our competitors. The South Valley —"

"Outperform them? I'll tear them up, root and branch. The fighting has already begun. You can see it on the floor downstairs. Their depositors are coming to us by the hour. There's talk of insolvency, collapsed earnings, bank examiners, liquidation. What do you think I'm all about? I'm bleeding them. Everyone knows it. I promise you, on all that's holy," said Mrs. Fitzgibbons, "before winter is over, I'll be marching into their executive offices."

"The happy fact is —" Mr. Zabac sought to mollify her by confirming something of her optimism, but was cut short.

"When I go in there, watch out!"

"The happy fact is," Mr. Zabac tried again, "that we have had —"

"I'm not the forgiving person I once was," she said. "I'm not big-minded. I'm not a philosopher. I'm not Mother Teresa."

"I understand, Mrs. Fitzgibbons." For the third time, Mr. Zabac endeavored to soothe the figure sitting opposite him without rejecting the thrust of her assertions. "Truth is, we have received overtures this week from the Citizens Bank. Mr. Will Donnelly called me on Tuesday, and this morning, Mr. Lieber, one of their lawyers, telephoned Mr. Hooton."

"They did what?" Mrs. Fitzgibbons's reaction was predictable. She sat up. Her eyes dilated. She appeared thunderstruck.

For his part, while unable to suppress the enormous satisfaction he felt over this dramatic statement, Mr. Zabac maintained a grave, businesslike demeanor. He formed a steeple with his hands and regarded Mrs. Fitzgibbons over the tips of his fingers. "I believe they want an accommodation."

"They didn't talk to me?" Mrs. Fitzgibbons pictured Mr. Hooton earlier delivering this important news to the little chairman.

Louis Zabac made small of the matter. "Oh, pay no mind, Mrs. Fitzgibbons, to the manner they —"

"Are they psychotic?"

"It wasn't the president who called. It wasn't Mr. Schreffler. If Mr. Schreffler had called, I'm confident he would have telephoned you or me."

Mrs. Fitzgibbons pointed a long arm in the direction of the Citizens Bank. She couldn't credit her ears. "I could mail them their death warrants. I know every one of them. I went to school with half of them. Ralph Lieber called Hooton?" she repeated in astonishment. "So that I could do what? Nail him to his front door?"

"Now, now, let's don't get ahead of ourselves." Mr. Zabac made a calming gesture with both hands. "As I construe it, it was only an opening gambit."

"I have all the playing cards." She waved her hand illustratively over the surface of his desk. As often lately, Mrs. Fitzgibbons revealed her genius for targeting weakness in her opponents. "When this news leaks out, they won't have a leg under them."

The prudish chairman blanched instantly. "We are not to breathe a word about it."

That set Mrs. Fitzgibbons laughing. "Please."

"I've given my word. I am morally constrained to observe complete confidentiality. Otherwise —"

"Oh, I'll do the dirty work! But when I get there, it will be ugly. On that, they have Mrs. Fitzgibbons's word," she said.

Mr. Zabac's anxiety was visible. "We are to do nothing and say nothing."

"I'll give them confidentiality!" Suddenly, Mrs. Fitzgibbons gestured with her fist. "I'll give them the mother and father of confidentiality."

In her mind's eye, Mrs. Fitzgibbons had a vision of Dolores Brouillette — perhaps at that very instant — stepping off a curbstone and opening the passenger door of Neil Hooton's car.

"I've been running things for one week, and they're already folding their tents! Can you imagine where they'll be in a month?"

"You're an extraordinary resource," Mr. Zabac allowed with a sigh.

Mrs. Fitzgibbons didn't want to insult the man, but couldn't check herself at this moment. His fatuity embarrassed her. "What a mentality!" she said. She consulted her wristwatch and stood up.

"Before you go," Mr. Zabac insisted, while rising, "I want your word, Mrs. Fitzgibbons, that you will do all possible to patch up your differences here. I insist on that. I charge you with it. I'm going to be in Falmouth for the next three or four days, until Tuesday. I'm leaving within the hour. The contention and bitterness must come to an end."

"No problem." Mrs. Fitzgibbons waved a pretty hand.

"Fighting among superiors is demoralizing on the staff. I'm appealing to your wisdom. It must stop, and," he added, stressing his second worry, "the firings must stop."

Standing attractively before him, Mrs. Fitzgibbons let him look at her.

"There are reports of an early snow," he added, "and I want to get away before it starts."

Again, Mrs. Fitzgibbons said nothing.

"But I won't leave without an absolute assurance," he said, patting his palms softly for emphasis, "that my instructions will be obeyed."

Mrs. Fitzgibbons sighed with forbearance. "There'll be no firings."

"I need to know that," he continued doggedly.

"I swear it!"

SIXTEEN

At three minutes to three o'clock that same afternoon, Mrs. Fitzgibbons struck. Despite the day-long tension in the bank, her sudden appearance on the floor sent a shock wave among the employees. For one thing, Mrs. Fitzgibbons, who was not insensitive to the importance of her costuming at such a moment, was dressed for the street. She was wearing her gloves and dark, gun-metal leather coat. She came out of her office with great dispatch. There was murder in her face.

Behind Mrs. Fitzgibbons, Emily and Julie hurried to keep pace. The three of them came quickly along the big mahogany rail bordering the home loan department, with Mrs. Fitzgibbons leading the way energetically. Louis Zabac's departure for the airport minutes earlier had cleared the way for Mrs. Fitzgibbons to put an end to some unfinished business that had nagged her for days. All work came to a stop in the bank at the sight of the three of them moving in phalanx across the open space beneath the skylit dome. Mrs. Fitzgibbons's heels rang on the marble floor; her hair shook at every step; her face was bony and drawn.

When Mrs. Wilson's secretary, Patricia Quirk, saw them coming, she reacted with instinct. She spun impulsively and thrust open Mrs. Wilson's door, then danced out of the way. Mrs. Fitzgibbons shot past her and darted into Elizabeth Wilson's office. Emily and Julie were not a foot behind, the three of them forming a living wedge.

Mrs. Wilson gave a cry of alarm at the sudden hurly-burly entrance. She sat back in her chair. Elizabeth Wilson was a woman in her early sixties, a mother and grandmother, a living exemplum of the good citizen. Mrs. Fitzgibbons was shouting at her with great vehemence, leaning over the woman's desk, calling her names, castigating her. "What's happening?" Mrs. Wilson managed to bleat out. She was terrified, clearly fearful for her physical safety when Mrs. Fitzgibbons, while hollering at her, reached with her gloved hand and sent a mountainous pile of stacked papers and folders cascading to the floor. To worsen matters, Julie Marcotte and Emily Krok had instantly come round her desk on either side of her and appeared eager to commence striking her. Mrs. Wilson's voice was reedy with alarm. "What's going on? . . . What are you doing?"

Suddenly, unable to restrain herself any longer, and genuinely angered by the woman's bad manners toward Mrs. Fitzgibbons, Emily Krok reached out, grabbed the bow at the throat of Mrs. Wilson's white polyester blouse and pulled Mrs. Wilson up to her feet. "Stand up when the Chief talks to you!" she said.

To Mrs. Fitzgibbons, the sight of the tall, gray-haired lady trembling before her was a complete vindication of her willingness to deal resolutely with people who plotted behind her back. "Where are your friends now?" Mrs. Fitzgibbons was shouting, and waving a balled fist, as a spastic shiver of excitement darted the length of her body. She seized Elizabeth Wilson's telephone receiver from its cradle and threw it onto the desk. "Call them up! Tell them what's happening!" she taunted.

"I'd like to clock her one," said Emily, taking in hand a heavy Swingline staple gun. Seeing that, Mrs. Wilson pleaded anew not to be hurt.

"Your guard is here," Julie said.

Indeed, at that moment, Mr. Donachie was peeping into the

office. Mrs. Fitzgibbons did not look round at him, however. She was beginning by now to exult in the ease with which she was demolishing her detractors. It showed in her face. "This one couldn't keep her nose clean," she said. "It isn't enough for her to come in and mind her p's and q's. Not this one. This dried-out apricot wanted to see me on a slab." The contempt for the shaken woman rose in Mrs. Fitzgibbons's system like something indigestible. "Get her out of my sight."

Mrs. Wilson appeared all but ossified by now, managing barely to turn her head.

Emily pointed the staple gun. "Look at her! She can't move her feet."

Mrs. Fitzgibbons nodded sternly to her guard, and moments later, from one end of the bank to the other, the staff stared in awe as Alec Donachie marched a stupefied Mrs. Wilson across the great hall of the bank to the front doors.

Even before the woman was gone, however, Julie and Emily were circulating among the employees with an announcement that Mrs. Fitzgibbons intended to address the entire staff.

"I'm not going to bore you to death with a long speech," Mrs. Fitzgibbons started in without delay, in a voice that carried impressively from the locked front doors to the farthest reaches of the main floor. Marcel Sullivan had fetched a wooden chair for Mrs. Fitzgibbons; and no one who was present that day would not have conceded that the new chief executive formed an impressive picture standing upon it. The lights from above shone attractively on the collar and epaulets of her leather coat. Mrs. Fitzgibbons moved her torso decisively as she spoke, turning left and right, and pointing a gloved finger. The scores of faces looking up at her filled her with a warm, egoistic sense of personal accomplishment.

After the last employees had collected at the edges of the attentive throng, Mrs. Fitzgibbons lifted her face significantly, and the assembly grew still.

"This afternoon," she enunciated, in a clear, businesslike tone, "I completed the first phase of the new management. You were all here, and you know what happened. There's no need for me to talk myself blue in the face about the deceit and disloyalty of people who have been dismissed. I'll tell you what you need to know. It's enough to say that we are all the better off for the permanent removal of those who couldn't accept the changes that were inevitable under my administration, and who went skulking behind my back looking for ways to undermine me."

She noticed as she spoke that most of the bank's loan officers and middle management had unconsciously gravitated toward one another on the left side of the assembly, and that she instinctively was directing herself to the larger body of workers standing in the middle and on the right, the tellers, clerks, maintenance men, secretaries, and such.

"We're not going to face the future in a state of chaos. If I have to go out of town for three or four days, I can't be required to come rushing back each time to reestablish my authority. I want you to know that Mrs. Fitzgibbons knows how to take care of herself. I know it, and most of you know it. If you don't know it," she added pleasantly, and smiled, "you soon will."

This last quip brought a ripple of appreciative laughter from the people gathered directly in front of Mrs. Fitzgibbons and to her right.

"Because I'm not going to be replaced! I'm not your congressman. I'm not going to be voted out of office. If you oppose me," she said, "I'll know what to do with you. You could be a hundred and ten years old. You could be the imperial wizard of your local peewee league. If you abuse your trust, and go stealing off," she said, "to secret lunches, to plan my ruination — and I don't care if you're some slaphappy, psychotic automobile-loan woman with a rat's nest of gray hair on your head who's used to being bowed and kowtowed to — I'll look for you, I'll catch you," recited Mrs. Fitzgibbons, "and I'll break your bones."

Mrs. Fitzgibbons was interrupted by a second outburst of laughter, more enthusiastic than the first, initiated in large part by Marcel Sullivan and several young women from the clerical pool standing about him. Mrs. Fitzgibbons reacted with a toss of her head. "Mrs. Fitzgibbons is not your kid sister. She's not your mother, or your aunt, or the girl in the bathing suit next door. She is nobody other than the chief executive officer of this bank. That's not a mysterious proposition. It's not a twenty-letter word for something else. It's a statement of fact. And nobody," she added, rapidly, "downstairs or upstairs, living or dead, alone or with the help of others, is going to change that fact."

Several employees, located here and there in the crowd, hung on Mrs. Fitzgibbons's words with fixed, uncritical smiles attached to their lips. The bolder her words, the more startling was the effect it produced. Deborah Schwartzwald, standing in the rear, manifested on her pale, upturned face a similarly uncritical look of fanatical devotion; her lips were parted, her eyes locked on Mrs. Fitzgibbons. When those about her laughed, Deborah chimed in at once, laughing heartily, but without so much as blinking her eyes. She was mesmerized.

"Lately," Mrs. Fitzgibbons argued, "you may have noticed that we have experienced a surge in business. There are people who seem to forget that that's why we're here. We are not here to while away the hours of a pleasant October day. We're here to gather funds. So, if suddenly," she said, "we see the chart on our demand deposits going up like something from the national space program, and certain selfish, avaricious people out there want to cripple or remove from power the person who's responsible for this sudden boom — and I am the one responsible for it — obviously somebody is going to come to grief."

Mrs. Fitzgibbons raised her face to the glow of the dome above and revolved from the waist one way and then the other. Turning to her left and looking down on some of her more highly placed officers, such as Felix Hohenberger and Connie McElligot, she surveyed their faces in silence for a long moment while simultaneously pouting, as though daring anyone to register an objection. Without exception, the parties in question blushed, fidgeted, and looked away, especially when the silent glare of attention drew the interest of all the other workers, as well. Then she spotted Julie Marcotte making her way toward her through the throng. Julie was coming from the telephone in Mrs. Fitzgibbons's office, and bearing in hand a sheet of paper. Mrs. Fitzgibbons paused in her speech as Julie handed it to her.

On the face of it, the sheet of paper was an old letter, a September circular addressed to all banks in the region from the Federal Home Loan Bank Board. But on the back of the paper Julie had scribbled in pencil the essence of a telephone call from Dolores Brouillette.

While Mrs. Fitzgibbons perused the message, the assembled staff looked on with an air of suspense, as though the document, handed up in this way, must have had a critical bearing on all of them.

The handwritten note read: "*Mrs. B. and Mr. H. at the Show-boat. Drinks till dark. All O.K. No hitches.*" Mrs. Fitzgibbons crumpled the sheet and thrust it smugly into the pocket of her coat, and with no visible lapse went on.

"At first, there were only rumors," she was saying, as she turned to the matter of recent actions. "That's how it begins. Certain persons smiling behind their hands, snickering, cracking jokes, believing that what's new isn't going to last. One day, somebody else is going to take over, and, naturally, we'll revert to the same sleepy operation we used to be. Somebody else," Mrs. Fitzgibbons's voice grew huskier with irony, "will take over, and *reduce* our bonuses, and bring back that same collection of deadheads that fought me tooth and nail, and there go our promotions, our salary increases, our extended annual vacations, and we'll be the same old leaderless outfit we were — run by fat cats sitting behind closed doors who only wake themselves up to vote themselves big bonuses the end of every year — while the rest of us wait an eternity or two for someone else to stand up to them!" Mrs. Fitzgibbons raised a gloved hand to forestall the sympathetic reaction she sensed mounting. Again, the irony thickened in her voice.

"But they were just rumors. Just the whisperings of the malcontents. Of people who favored the old way of doing things, or who were beholden to those that were. I knew it was happening." Mrs. Fitzgibbons made a face to suggest the pathos of conspiracy in the face of wisdom and superior force. "I was kept abreast of it all. People loyal to me came to me and told me what was brewing. I could point you out, the loyal ones. Never mind!" she gloated. "I bided my time. I waited. I saw it the day I increased your bonuses! And, believe me," she added rapidly, "nobody on God's green earth is going to rescind them! That's why I'm here!"

She gestured impatiently as Marcel and those about him applauded.

"I'll share this thought with you," she cried. "If I were hatching a conspiracy, if I wanted to destroy a good person, I wouldn't do it over lunch down at Schermerhorn's Sea House. I wouldn't tell every Tom, Dick, and Harry about it. I'd watch my step! But never mind," she repeated and shrugged, showing her audience the patience of the just. "I waited. I gave them rope. I knew who they were. Every facet of the thing, every conversation, every meeting, was reported to me." With sudden inspiration, Mrs. Fitzgibbons pulled the crumpled letter from the pocket of her coat, and flourished it.

She laughed cheerily. "They were going to circulate a letter of protest. Look! Imagine the idiocy. This is it. This is the document. Look here." She ogled the paper at close range, and set her fingertip upon it. "They had begun signing their names to it. This work of genius was the total outcome of days upon days of their conspiracy to topple me. They were going to circulate it to other officers, to one and all, to put an end to me for good, and to the work I've done."

The people gazing up at Mrs. Fitzgibbons, with the exception of a grave handful, laughed in sympathy then, and glanced gaily at one another, as Mrs. Fitzgibbons ridiculed her invisible opponents. "If simplicity were brilliance," she said, "this plan was as ingenious as anything yet devised by man. An officer would receive this paper, unfold it, read the ugly things it says about me, sign his name to it — take out his pen and carefully write his signature upon it — then fold it up, and pass it along in secret to the next unhappy officer, and that figure would sign *his* name to it."

Mrs. Fitzgibbons was now holding the letter open in both hands and staring at it in an attitude of great incredulity. She rapped the paper with her knuckles. "It was so simple. They must have wondered why they hadn't thought of it sooner. I should send this to the Smithsonian Institute." The excitement of standing two feet higher than her assembled listeners, combined with the facility of her tongue and growing sympathy of her audience, encouraged her to deepen her attack upon the minority standing to her left.

She changed her appearance now. She put on the unhappy face of the disappointed tyrant.

"They would all sign it," she said, "and it would go on that way, as other fools would sign their names to it, until I — being of an agreeable nature — would quietly clean out my desk and go tiptoeing out. These are conspirators!" She waved the paper in triumph. "These are the people who detest me. These are the people who refer to the clerks, secretaries, and tellers as peons." She waved the sheet of paper illustratively. " 'The peons,' they say, 'are getting everything!' Officers of this bank — whose jobs depend from week to week upon my happiness with them, people whose families depend on a regular income — were going to affix their names to this piece of paper. Two of them actually signed it."

Lifting the letter, she turned sideways and pointed to the signature on the bottom of the innocuous bank-board letter. "This one," she said, pointing, "didn't seem to realize what it was she helped to create or what she was signing, because I just had her thrown out the front door! . . . I eliminated her!"

"That bitch," Emily spoke up from the first row.

The staff appeared a trifle relieved to discover the motive behind Mrs. Fitzgibbons's action that afternoon in Mrs. Wilson's private office. Many nodded and muttered approval. Clasping the letter before her, she carefully folded and creased it, while studying the effects of her revelation upon the expanse of upturned faces.

"We're not here to carp and complain," she said. "We're here to demolish the competition! There are institutions out there that have been competing with us since the Flood, but have no idea what's in store for them. You know who they are. You know who I'm talking about. They hate our insides." Mrs. Fitzgibbons balled her fist. "I could smash them at will! I could move upon them this afternoon. They loathe and fear us. Why? Because we're bigger than they are, and better, and getting bigger and better by the hour. Where do you think the surge in business is coming from? The moon?" Mrs. Fitzgibbons's eye went in turn from Mr. Donachie, to Deborah Schwartzwald at the rear, to the tellers on her right. "They're bleeding to death!"

Pauline Smith, the most elderly employee, shouted happily, "Take them over!"

"One of them is insolvent this instant." Mrs. Fitzgibbons's egoism gave a harsh thrill to her voice. "And I'm turning up the heat!"

"Take them over, Mrs. Fitzgibbons!" Deborah Schwartzwald couldn't restrain herself. Her eyes were as wide as saucers. "Do it!"

"I'll do more than that," said Mrs. Fitzgibbons. "I'll clip their wings good and proper. I'll replace every officer they've got with my own people, *my* experts, my friends. With you and you and you. One of them is courting me right now."

"Right on!" Marcel was in paradise.

"They're going to get a *new* chief," Emily sang out.

"When you see them in the streets," said Mrs. Fitzgibbons, with facetious generosity, "tell them to be patient. Tell them I am coming. '*Be patient! She is coming!*' " she said exultantly.

The response was one of stormy applause. Again, Mrs. Fitzgibbons raised a staying hand.

"We're in no hurry. The officers and help of the Citizens Bank will wait for us. The South Valley Bank will wait. I know what they're saying about us, I know they're worried, I know they're frightened. I have people in there. Please," Mrs. Fitzgibbons apostrophized, as in an appeal to the heavens, "let me finish putting my own house in order. *This morning*" — she imparted special moment to those two words, with a raised finger and a smirk on her lips — "one of our own loyal associates was treated with brutality. I don't mind telling you," she added, in a voice infused with sadness, "that Mr. Kim was a friend of mine."

She struck a pose, and waited as her remarks took effect.

"Some have said today that I was responsible for this action. For how could it have happened if I wasn't? And yet, oddly," she said, "I wasn't. Mr. Kim was a friend of mine, and now he's sitting at home, at the kitchen table, trying to explain to his puzzled wife and frightened little ones, the horrible thing, the atrocity, that befell him this morning. This pleasant man came to us a few years ago from over the sea, across the Atlantic or Pacific, or whatever ocean it was, for a new life here in America, and this morning he was struck down."

"Bring him back, Mrs. Fitzgibbons!"

Scarcely aware of the ironies contained in the sudden sympathy she felt for a discharged employee, Mrs. Fitzgibbons could feel her blood starting to boil. "That's what came of Mr. Kim's American dream. Without any justification under the sun, other than the fact that he was more competent than his superior and came to work on time every morning, our friend, Mr. Kim, was dealt the shock of his life. Why didn't the United States Navy just leave him thrashing about in the water? I'll tell you why. So that we could hire him, give him a post suitable to his talents, make wonderful use of his efforts, and then, one frosty fall morning, somebody here could up and throw him and his family into the street! Somebody who was afraid of him," said Mrs. Fitzgibbons. "Somebody who once had the balls to characterize Mr. Kim as a 'little slanty-eyed adding machine.' And who himself" — her voice rose in indignation — "lost more money for this bank in one day than the Third World can urinate in a month! You *know* who it was! You *see* what I'm up against. These are the people" — out came the folded letter — "who protest what I'm doing. Who want me, your chief executive, dead and buried."

Looking very righteous and in command, Mrs. Fitzgibbons made a little snapping noise with her fingers at Julie. "Get Mr. Kim on the telephone."

The sight of Mrs. Fitzgibbons standing on her chair, with the telephone to her ear, the light twinkling on her forehead, as she spoke affably to the dismissed employee, was a moment of inspired theater. Even the vice presidents and other officers, despite themselves, betrayed signs of hopeful expectancy as Mrs. Fitzgibbons recalled Lionel Kim to the ranks of his friends and fellow workers at the Parish Bank.

"He lacked the authority." She was addressing herself authoritatively to the ceiling, the black mouthpiece of the phone tilted upward. "We are all on your side. Everyone here is listening." She laughed pleasantly as though to quiet Mr. Kim's gentle, self-effacing doubts. "They're standing around me. Everyone is. We'd be heartbroken if you didn't come back. No one," said Mrs. Fitzgibbons, "gets discharged, or even seriously reprimanded around here, by anyone but me. You have," she stressed emphatically, after listening to him for a second, "a spectacular future with us. One of the best. I reward competence. I promote it, and I pay for it."

As Mrs. Fitzgibbons concluded what she judged to have been the most successful address of her career, and made her way through the milling employees toward her office, she could feel the love of all flowing upon her. They parted before her as if she were surrounded with a mystical aura that no one dared invade. Mrs. Fitzgibbons tossed out commands as she passed through them.

"You find out for me, Marcel, who was responsible for smearing on that graffiti in the men's room."

"I will, Mrs. Fitzgibbons, don't worry," he promised.

"Emily, tell Alec to lock up Hooton's office. Everything in there is impounded. Julie, I want Matthew outside the mall waiting for me at five o'clock, and tell Eddie to bring my own car for the rest of you to ride in.

"Did you hear," Julie whispered to her chief in a mortified voice at the first opportunity, "Mr. Hooton actually had the nerve to pick Dolores up in his car right in front of Mr. Brouillette's own house!"

"So?"

"In front of her house?"

"What did you expect her to do?" Mrs. Fitzgibbons snapped. "Walk over to *his* house?"

Julie appeared genuinely struck by the depravity and brazenness of it all. "Gosh, I'd've thought —"

"Mr. Brouillette's wife is expensive," Mrs. Fitzgibbons said. "She's not some tart that comes running across town for a quick buck or two. You saw her. Dolores is top of the line."

"She's beautiful."

"Use your skin." Mrs. Fitzgibbons strode into her office. "You're not a child. That's Dolores's M.O. She's pricey. She probably kept him waiting out there."

SEVENTEEN

Among her corps of followers, the only one who saw fit, or perhaps even dared by now, to question Mrs. Fitzgibbons on the wisdom of her plans to ruin her arch adversary was her most devoted admirer. Bruce had been apprised by his friend Matthew of the outline of Mrs. Fitzgibbons's intentions.

"It's important that I look my dramatic best," she explained, as Bruce toiled absorbedly on her eyelids and lashes. "Especially my eyes. Fix them up a little scary."

"Wouldn't it be as well," Bruce persisted worriedly, "to let fate take its course? After all, the poor thing has lost millions in his department. He hasn't a leg under him. The chairman and staff are behind you. Now, in addition, you've successfully overruled his dismissal of Mr. Kim."

She actually enjoyed having someone articulate the reasonable approach to a crisis of this kind, as it reinforced her pleasurable awareness of her opponent's defenselessness. Mrs. Fitzgibbons's motives in hounding Mr. Hooton to his ruin were no longer those of the aggressive competitor seeking power, but rather of the hate-filled victor determined to pour the full measure of her wrath on the head of one who had had the gall to oppose her in the first place. The mere thought of the man, with his big suspenders bulging, and his gold half spectacles balanced snootily on the tip of his nose, contemptuous and self-important, started her insides churning. The knowledge that the man was at her mercy imparted dark feelings of satisfaction.

"The man is going to fall," Bruce argued. "It can only be a matter of days."

"I appreciate your sensitive nature, Bruce. That's how you're built." She humored him while regarding herself in the wall mirror.

"It's illegal, as well."

That line touched Mrs. Fitzgibbons's fancy; she reacted mirthfully, while lifting her face to show Bruce a pitying glance. "Nothing's illegal when you win, pussycat. Please. The man is nothing more than an adulterous blowhard who had the bad luck of getting in the way." Words of this sort thrilled Mrs. Fitzgibbons. She clasped tightly the arms of her chair. "Besides," she added, referring to her associates, "I have to consider the needs of the others. They want action. They're in a fever state. They're champing at the bit. They're different from you, darling. I have to give them what they want."

"Ever since Matthew began driving for you," Bruce complained, "he's become a different person. He almost never cooks. He's out at all hours. He doesn't clean. He leaves his clothes and beer cans lying about."

Mrs. Fitzgibbons laughed.

"He talks like a thug," Bruce said.

"He is a thug," she cried. "What did you think he was?" Mrs. Fitzgibbons's wit carried clearly from one end of the salon to the other. "What on earth are you worried about? With your looks and brains and sex appeal, he's not going anyplace. If you can't control the affections of a measly city hall clerk who wants nothing more from life than to go out beer drinking and banging heads at night, you're not the artist I thought you were." Mrs. Fitzgibbons twisted around in her chair and looked him in the eye. "Slap his face!" she said. "Throw him out of bed. . . . Deny him!"

These jocular cracks set both the patrons and hairdressers in

Bruce Clayton's salon laughing aloud. Bruce blushed but chimed in laughing.

Mrs. Fitzgibbons concluded with a catalog of her driver's strong points. "He can drive a car, count to a hundred, and form an erection. Where is somebody like that going to find a lover who owns his own business and wears Italian silk boxer shorts at fifty bucks a throw?"

She was on her feet then, pulling on her coat. She was impressed with Bruce's artistry. Her hair and makeup were just what she wanted. Her features were beautified to perfection. Her eyes looked deep-set; they glittered brightly, lending a sinister quality to her appearance.

"I wasn't being critical." Bruce followed her to the front door. She was snapping on her gloves. She loved Bruce more than anyone on earth. That was a fact.

"You're supposed to be critical. That's your function."

"I would be willing to go, if you wanted and insisted. You know that."

"It wouldn't be fun for you," said Mrs. Fitzgibbons. "You stay home. Believe me, this is not your kind of outing."

Outdoors, Matthew was waiting behind the wheel of the Buick and came round in smart fashion to open the door for her. Pulled to the curb behind Matthew's sedan was Mrs. Fitzgibbons's own avocado green Honda, containing Eddie Berdowsky and Howard Brouillette up front, and Julie and Emily in back. They were all staring out at Mrs. Fitzgibbons as she emerged from the mall and strode briskly to the car. After Matthew closed her door, she didn't look back at Bruce, who watched worriedly from the sidewalk, but she was appreciative of his concern for her safety. She settled back in her seat. She was not smiling.

Mrs. Fitzgibbons snapped at Matthew. "Let's get started. Take me out the Rifle Range Road to the old German Club. Get moving. Step on it."

As the cars pulled smoothly out, one behind the other, accelerating in tandem, Bruce was left standing in dismay on the curb. He watched till the two cars were lost from view in the supper-hour traffic.

The wooded hills west of town, especially in the higher eleva-
tions, sustained the flimsy residue of an early snowfall. The two
cars slowed to a crawl on the unpaved gravel road leading a mile
up through the trees to the club. The whitened trees on either side
formed a glowing channel, illuminated by the headlights. It was
almost past twilight. The sky still presented patches of blue, dis-
cernible at intervals through the treetops, as darkness collected
under the hardwoods and pines. Soon they came in sight of the
old club. The green wooden structure looked more like a hunting
lodge than a gin mill. The only car parked under the pines was
that of the owner and bartender, Rudy Harnisch, as Matthew
brought his black sedan to a halt near the front door. Seconds
later, Mrs. Fitzgibbons's Honda pulled noiselessly alongside and
stopped. Getting out, Mrs. Fitzgibbons relished at once the feeling
of solitariness and suspense which the whitened forest greatly magnified. She paused to look about herself in a grave manner, as
though to impress upon the others collecting about her the gravity
of their actions. Mrs. Fitzgibbons motioned with two fingers for
Eddie and Matthew to precede her up the steps. Howard Brouillette
and the two young women followed at her heels. From somewhere
in the twilight, a shutter banged softly.

Inside, Howard went at once to see that the public telephone
was working, while Eddie checked out the rest rooms. The club
was empty, save for Mr. Harnisch, who folded up his newspaper and stepped behind the bar. Years ago, the club was headquarters for a local fraternal society called the Turn Verein. The
interior consisted of thick pine ceiling beams, planked paneling,
and an ornate walnut bar. Behind the bar, an immense but delicately frosted mirror reflected an array of neon-lighted beer signs.
Mrs. Fitzgibbons led the way to the big table by the window that
looked out on the summer beer garden, where metal chairs stood
stacked atop a dozen tables; strings of electric lights dangling in
the naked branches formed a visible tracery on the winter sky.
Mrs. Fitzgibbons permitted the members of her party to order
beer, but demanded a glass of mineral water with lime and ice for
herself.

While waiting for Dolores to telephone from Mr. Hooton's summer house at the lake, Mrs. Fitzgibbons maintained an edgy silence. Her face was colorless. From time to time, she turned her full attention onto one or the other of her followers and stared concentratedly. In fact, though, Mrs. Fitzgibbons's thinking during this waiting period was unusually disorganized. For a second or two, she confused Rudy Harnisch with a tomato-faced Sacred Heart priest named Lavelle, who had married her to Larry in 1962, and who was summoned to the hospital one summer evening three years ago to give her husband his last rites. Even more confusing, a little time after that, Mrs. Fitzgibbons suddenly heard the sound of her own voice, only to realize with a start that she had been talking aloud for some while; that that segment of her brain was functioning independently.

"With this shindy out of the way," she was saying, "I'll be in a position to work some useful changes around here. This region has everything." She gestured at the wilderness beyond the windows. "Beautiful countryside, good utilities, a professional work force, railroads, interstate highways, universities nearby, and the best of it, a half dozen little banks ripe for the picking." She listened to herself citing names. "The South Valley, the Citizens, the Smith's Ferry Institute. What do you think they'll do when I push my way in? They'll welcome me with open arms."

"They'll thank their stars it was you," said Matthew.

"With them in my pocket, I'll build myself a financial fortress, from Worcester to Albany, with the reins in these two hands. If those big-city metropolitan banks want a fight then, won't I give them a bloody nose!"

Eddie whooped and raised his glass mug. The others reacted noisily. Emily Krok, who didn't like the way the bartender was gazing over in fascination at Mrs. Fitzgibbons, spoke out to him in surly fashion. "Go back to work," she said.

"What's he doing?" said Howard.

"Looking funny at the Chief."

"Don't think that tonight won't be a lesson to everyone," Mrs. Fitzgibbons was declaiming. "Nobody's exempt. Not even you people. Everyone hews the line." Mrs. Fitzgibbons sat as straight as a ramrod, with her breasts up, her eyes fixed on Julie Marcotte.

Abruptly, Julie blurted out, "I'm so worried about Mrs. Brouillette."

"Pull yourself together!" Mrs. Fitzgibbons reprimanded the
young woman.

"I'm sure he's hurting her," Julie protested. "And I feel so bad
for Howard."

Here everyone looked at Howard Brouillette, whose long white
raincoat was, in fact, shaking to an extent that could not be explained by the draft coming from the windows. He showed his
friends a sickly smile. His shiny eyeglasses glittered like the eyes
of an insect.

"What if she can't *get* to a phone to call us?" Julie cried. "What
if she's trapped out there and being abused?"

"If you don't stop," said Mrs. Fitzgibbons, reiterating a threat
once leveled at her by a nun, "I'll have you taken from the room
and thrashed."

"Dolores is a professional," Matthew offered as solace to Julie.

"I'd like to have a wife like that," said Eddie.

"I can't believe she's really out here," Julie persisted.

"I'd like to be in her boots," Emily contributed. "Wouldn't I
like that!"

"That will never happen," Eddie said.

"Look at me." Julie showed her hands. "I'm shaking all over."

"The telephone is ringing," Eddie announced.

"Get that." Mrs. Fitzgibbons commanded Howard.

While Mr. Brouillette made a beeline for the pay phone, Eddie,
sitting in the chair next to Mrs. Fitzgibbons, capitalized on the
opportunity to compliment his mother-in-law. "You should see
yourself, Frankie," he whispered privately. "You look really scary.
You look like one of those Oriental Nazi dragon ladies in the
movies," he said. After a moment, he added, even more softly, "I
think Barbara is beginning to understand. She knows I work evenings for you now, and that you have our best interests at heart."

The gathering tensions had strung out Mrs. Fitzgibbons's nerves.
A hammer beat away on her brain; her presence of mind came
and went.

"I know she's your daughter," Eddie went on, covering his

mouth with his hand, "but ever since you took over at the bank, she's become like the walking dead." He leaned close to Mrs. Fitzgibbons, still whispering. "She knows she can't cut it. She knows that you're the kingpin."

"It's Dolores," Matthew spoke up to affirm.

Through the window of the telephone booth, Mr. Brouillette was flashing the high sign. Mrs. Fitzgibbons nodded austerely and got to her feet.

Eddie kept close to her ear. "She just wants a house," he said. "That's all she talks about. A little bungalow someplace. She doesn't suspect that I plan to get rid of her."

"What are you talking about?" Mrs. Fitzgibbons strode to the door, tying her belt. "Assert yourself." She showed Eddie a compact fist. "Give her a good drubbing."

"Oh, I couldn't do that," Eddie exclaimed hastily. "She's pregnant."

Emily Krok scooted in front of Mrs. Fitzgibbons and opened the door for her. Outdoors, night was falling fast. Although a light flurry of snowflakes was dropping softly, the sky to the east was clear and moonlit. Mrs. Fitzgibbons's troop of followers waited by their car doors as she paused on the porch and took her measure of the night. It was just the sort of icy, windless night, she imagined, on which significant events were meant to be settled. Descending the steps, she paced rigidly across the frozen ground. Mrs. Fitzgibbons enjoyed putting on a very stern look at such times, as she had discovered this week that it aroused an unholy fear in others.

Before entering the Buick, she paused in the snowfall and scrutinized Howard Brouillette at point-blank range. His chin was trembling. The man was a sight. "Get a grip on yourself," she ordered him.

For the next twenty minutes, the two cars, with only their dimmers burning, crept along at a sinister pace over the gravel roadbed, through the snow-cloaked trees, toward the lake. Their wipers were going. Eddie was leading the way in the Honda. Muffled by the snowfall, the two engines rumbled and droned like the echo of a lumber-camp saw. At last, to the right of the slowly moving automobiles, the dark expanse of the lake reached out into the night. A boarded-up summer cottage slid past in the dark. The snowfall was insignificant here. Eddie and Matthew killed their parking lights. The big black Buick gleamed ominously as it followed the battered Honda slowly beneath the whitened trees. Presently, the Honda came to a stop. "We're here," Matthew said over his shoulder.

Mrs. Fitzgibbons thrust open her door, clambered out, and started forward at once over the hard earth. That she was wearing high heels seemed not to impede her whatsoever. A hundred feet ahead, the gable and roofline of Mr. Hooton's year-round lake house loomed in silhouette. A softly lighted window in the gable shone forth like a portal to another world. The lake lapped icily against the boat dock. Mrs. Fitzgibbons stepped along in the dark as far as the crescent of slender pin oaks that stood like sentries around the flagstone terrace. The others came Indian file behind her. Halted, she surveyed the house and grounds. Mr. Hooton's BMW was parked between the dock and his front porch. A film of snow blanketed its roof, while the dock with its slatted planks jutted out in space like a skeleton. When Howard Brouillette drew abreast of her, his long white coat flapping, like the specter of death itself, she couldn't look at him. He was mumbling imprecations and shivering from head to toe.

Before forcibly entering Mr. Hooton's house, Mrs. Fitzgibbons took account of her charges. She studied them in the weak light. Of them all, Emily and Eddie were the most eager to begin. Emily was wringing her rough-skinned hands and licking her lips. Mrs. Fitzgibbons's own face was as pale as death. She spoke in undertones. "Mrs. Brouillette is being raped," she said.

"I want Dolores," Howard implored.

"You'll get Dolores," Mrs. Fitzgibbons scolded.

"It's too awful," said Julie, in pain.

Mrs. Fitzgibbons gestured then with a slow, mechanical wave for Eddie and Howard to precede the rest of them onto the porch. "You two," she said, "go first. Push it in."

The front door of Mr. Hooton's house swung in at the touch, however, and in less than a moment, Eddie and Howard vanished inside. The events to follow involved such tumult that Mrs. Fitzgibbons herself could scarcely perceive what was happening. Everyone began shouting, and there was a drumming of footsteps on the staircase to the upper storey. Just as Mrs. Fitzgibbons located the banister in the dark, Emily Krok pushed past her, with her elbows going, hollering encouragement to Dolores Brouillette in a raucous voice. Somewhere a vase shattered. Chairs went over in the hall. Eddie was yelling about "this fucking furniture up here," and in that same instant, just as Mrs. Fitzgibbons arrived on the upstairs landing, a bar of electric light shot slantwise across the corridor. Inside the bedroom, Dolores had leaped from the bed, pulling a long sail of a bed sheet behind her, and was shouting blue murder. "It's the man from the bank, Howard!" she yelled. "He tore off my dress! I couldn't get away! Look who it is!"

Dolores cowered in the corner of the room, with the sheet twirled about her. She looked paralyzed with fear.

"That's my wife! What have you done to my wife?" Howard was beside himself.

"It was awful, Howard. It was horrid. Look who it is." Dolores was worked up into an incantatory state.

Mr. Hooton in the meantime was sitting up in the middle of his bed. Under the glare of the ceiling light, his fleshy shoulders and fat pink arms created the impression of an inflated toy more than the solid bulk of a man. Atop his rubbery body, the sphere of his head flushed a bright crimson. If he had been sporting an erection at the moment his intruders banged the door in, there was nothing of it in evidence now beneath the roll of his stomach. With his mouth agape, Mr. Hooton stared up at the trim, vindictive figure of Mrs. Fitzgibbons standing over the foot of his bed. The ghastly intensity of her face and eyes expressed a tension born of causes not found in everyday stresses. Indeed, Mrs. Fitzgibbons's appearance and mannerisms would have worried anyone upon whom she looked.

"So, I was right," she cried, swinging her gloved fists this way and that in a show of suppressed fury.

Emily Krok was running back and forth in the room, like a ferocious dog.

Julie rushed to help Dolores. "He's torn her dress."

"Big cocksman from the bank," said Matthew.

Dolores Brouillette continued to grip the bed sheet to her throat, with only her face and fingers showing. "I thought he was a gentleman," she whined. "He said he was from my husband's bank. He acted so nice."

"It's okay, honey." Howard flapped his hand in reassurance. His breathing made pumplike suction sounds.

"He wanted to show me his home computer," Dolores explained pitifully. "He promised me a job at the bank. He lured me upstairs. We struggled. I told him who I was. He didn't care! He didn't care, he said. He didn't care who I was. He wanted me."

"He raped you?" Mrs. Fitzgibbons demanded matter-of-factly.

"Twice, Mrs. Fitzgibbons!"

"Lying bitch!" At last, Mr. Hooton found his voice. He swung about on the bed and endeavored to get up. "Get out of my house!" he bellowed.

As Mr. Hooton attempted to get his legs clear of the bed, Eddie gave him a magnificent shove that sent him sprawling. After that, the language got uglier.

"Break his balls!" Emily shouted, darting back and forth. "Shatter his balls!"

"That's Mrs. Brouillette!"

"Get out of my house!"

"Castrate him!" Emily actually doubled over in a paroxysm of rage; her face was livid.

"I'll have you arrested!" Mr. Hooton argued.

At a sign from Mrs. Fitzgibbons, her three male companions threw themselves on Mr. Hooton and commenced to haul him from his bed. Mr. Hooton bellowed at Dolores. "You fucking criminal. Deceitful, mendacious whore! I'll have you in court. I'll see you in jail. This is my house."

"I pleaded for my life," Dolores said.

Mrs. Fitzgibbons gestured perfunctorily. "Get him out of here."

In passing, Eddie Berdowsky scooped up Dolores's beaded red dress, which was, indeed, torn along the side seam, and waved it at Mrs. Fitzgibbons. "Look, Mom. Look what he did to her dress."

Mr. Hooton was throwing himself from side to side, expostulating roundly, but in no time began losing some of his fight. The spectacle of the fat, naked Mr. Hooton being alternately dragged and propelled to the door and stairway beyond aroused Mrs. Fitzgibbons's contempt. She followed importantly, as Eddie, Howard, and Matthew negotiated the great walruslike man along the corridor. She waved a hand at him. "This pompous windbag was going to boss me around. And I was supposed to wet my pants."

"Miserable honyocker," said Eddie, breathing hard.

Mrs. Fitzgibbons's eyes shone white and insensate in their sockets. "This sac of pus thought it all ended at the bank."

Dolores had pulled on her coat and was carrying her dress as she followed Mrs. Fitzgibbons into the hall. "I thought he was a gentleman."

"Well, he's not," said Mrs. Fitzgibbons. "He's an animal."

Julie was the last to leave the bedroom. "If it wasn't for the Chief," she sniffled, "he'd still be attacking her."

At the head of the stairs, Mr. Hooton must have gotten a second wind, or just better anticipated what was coming, because he resumed his noisy protestations. To the man's credit, he struggled with all his heart, throwing himself back and forth in a rage. It was to the credit of those grappling with him, as well, however, and of Mrs. Fitzgibbons's discipline over them, that no one actually struck the man a blow. The only exception occurred on the landing, when Mr. Hooton, roaring like a pig, dug in his heels and afforded Emily a clear shot at him. Mouthing a volley of curses, Emily thrust her way down between Howard and Matthew and dealt Mr. Hooton a resounding punch to the ear.

Mrs. Fitzgibbons followed the tangled mass of struggling bodies onto the porch. The night air, with the milk-colored moon shining beyond a bank of black storm clouds, heightened her omnipotent feelings, her ability to dominate events, as Howard Brouillette and the others compelled the naked man out across the snowy terrace. Mr. Hooton's flesh gleamed unnaturally in the cold air, like the skin of a flayed animal. In fact, amid the grunts and outcries, the quartet of men formed a frightening, primitive picture, as of prehistoric ritualists struggling with a recalcitrant beast. Dolores immediately banalized this awesome impression, however, with her remark on Mr. Hooton's sexual skills. "He fucks like a pizza," she said.

"Put him in my Honda," said Mrs. Fitzgibbons, "and drive him home to his wife. Dolores will drive the Buick."

Eddie called back jubilantly, "He's no big banker now!"

As Mr. Hooton was thrust into the car, his naked buttocks gleamed momentarily, a sight that took Mrs. Fitzgibbons's fancy. "That man was going to be president."

Julie opened the Buick door for her. Mrs. Fitzgibbons got in, and Dolores went round to take the wheel. Julie joined Mrs. Brouillette in the front seat. Mrs. Fitzgibbons continued to savor the ironies of it all, as Dolores pulled the sedan round into the narrow cart road and switched on the headlights. "He was going to get himself the biggest office," Mrs. Fitzgibbons cracked, "that mankind has ever seen, with a desk in it the size of an airfield, and sit there, with a little four-inch erection on him, and run my organization."

"The shoe's on the other foot now," Julie piped.

"He hasn't a shoe on either foot," said Mrs. Fitzgibbons, and Dolores laughed at that one.

"Mrs. Fitzgibbons is a woman who gets things done." Dolores was clearly impressed with the new head of the Parish Bank, of her pragmatism and shock tactics. She spoke respectfully. "Some people need a good scare."

During the drive back to the city, with the Honda close behind, and the snow coming down again in big, wet flakes, Mrs. Fitzgibbons grew jubilantly paranoid. She referred to Mr. Zabac as "that little Polish wonderwork with the manicured nails, who hides under his desk when I raise my voice."

She was sitting in the middle of the back seat, with the Honda's headlights illuminating her silhouette. She boasted that no one save herself possessed the cold-blooded virtues that were necessary to carry the hour.

From the top of the Apremont Highway, the lights of the city below vanished and reappeared many times through breaks in the snow squalls. Mrs. Fitzgibbons's thinking was so jumbled by this time, she scarcely knew where she was.

"Name me one person," she threw out in harsh accents, "who believed in me on the afternoon I went up to Zabac's office and seized power. Nobody! Not one living soul. Who but I would have known to bring in the newspapers? Who would have stuck at my side if somebody had rushed into my office that day and caved in my skull?"

Julie Marcotte looked round worriedly at Mrs. Fitzgibbons, who was gazing fixedly with bright, sparkling eyes at the road ahead.

"Who would have defended me? I didn't have one believer on the face of the earth. Leonard Frye?" She ridiculed the notion. "Felix Hohenberger? Jack Greaney? Why, if any one of them had a revolver in his desk, and the guts to use it, he'd have put a bullet in my head!"

Anxious to mitigate the frightening thrust of Mrs. Fitzgibbons's recital, Julie offered a plausible objection. "I don't think Jack Greaney would do you any harm."

"Those are my altar boys!" Mrs. Fitzgibbons exulted. "I could mash them to a pulp."

As Mrs. Fitzgibbons gloated over her triumphs and the severity of her treatment of enemies and critics, Dolores drove carefully through the city streets. The wipers were going. At each red light, Dolores slowed the Buick but did not stop, an illicit touch that added something sinister to the slow procession of the two cars. There was a great deal of shouting from inside the Honda, however, when they halted in front of Mr. Hooton's house on Princeton Street, and a second later Mr. Hooton was expelled into the open air.

Everyone reacted with revelry to the sight of Mr. Hooton wad-dling his way expeditiously across his frosty front lawn. The sight of his black footprints in the snow amused Mrs. Fitzgibbons. "You ought to wear shoes when you go out whoring," she called after him.

The two cars remained in place for several long minutes after the banker had entered his house and closed the door behind him, as Mrs. Fitzgibbons wished to show her disdain for the public at large. The snow fell in thick handfuls over the walks and hedges along the street. Before signaling Dolores to drive on, Mrs. Fitz-

gibbons surveyed the quiet scene before her with the air of a
military commander visiting a forward post. She told Julie to fetch
Howard Brouillette from the other car. "I want to talk to him."

To the surprise of all, Mrs. Fitzgibbons launched an attack upon
Howard. Dolores drove slowly, as the Chief castigated her husband. Mrs. Fitzgibbons's agitation had been mounting worrisomely all day long, but it was only now, when she sat back rigidly
in her seat, with cold blue flames in her eyes, and directed her
venom with manic force at those closest to her, that her friends
began to suspect the worst.

"No one thinks of me first," Mrs. Fitzgibbons scolded Howard.
"I pay you thousands and thousands of dollars above what you
deserve, and then I *increase* that amount by thousands more, only
to discover what?" Mrs. Fitzgibbons's stomach felt very jiggy, as
she leveled her invective at Mr. Brouillette in a manner that discouraged rebuttal. "That a secret communication took place today
between another bank and my own — a discussion that was un-
dertaken in secret — and what do you know about it? Nothing.
There I am," she ranted on, "sitting at my desk, tending to business,
devoting myself to the well-being of all and sundry, and secret
plans are being drawn up that will culminate in my lying in hell
with my back broken."

The sheer suddenness of her vituperative assault, especially in
the wake of her attack upon Mr. Hooton, fostered a stunned silence
in the car.

"I'm a trusting soul. I trust people. That's how I'm composed.
I trusted my parents. I trusted my husband. I trust everyone. When
I got married," said Mrs. Fitzgibbons, "I trusted the powers of
nature to give me a partner that would provide, if nothing else,
warm, intimate company on a winter's night. Someone to buck
me up when the going got rough. All right, so I was disappointed.
Not a lot, but enough to begin to question trust. I was going to
be a mother, anyhow, and trusted the Creator to give me a decent,
no-frills copy of what He's been doing with others for sixty-three
million years. If what I got wasn't a factory reject, you tell me.
Babies don't have to be Japanese to work."

As Mrs. Fitzgibbons spoke, she had the sensation of her mind expanding and contracting, while Dolores, Julie, and Howard stole surreptitious looks at her.

"So, I'm surrounded by morons. There isn't one of you I couldn't lambaste to within an inch of your life."

"I did learn something important," Howard spoke up, to apprise Mrs. Fitzgibbons of an extraordinary piece of intelligence he had come upon that day. "The Citizens Bank is stuck with a note —"

In that instant, the rear of the Buick slewed about on the snowy pavement and narrowly missed a parked car. Mrs. Fitzgibbons sat up excitedly. Her mood altered at once. "Go faster," she encouraged Dolores.

For the next ten minutes, Dolores raced the Buick through the downtown streets of Ireland Parish, with the Honda speeding along behind it. Emily, it turned out, was at the wheel of the rear car. Mrs. Fitzgibbons liked to drive fast and was laughing merrily and shouting as she exhorted the prostitute to ever riskier chances. "Do a U-turn! . . . Go up the hill! . . . Run the light! Up the hill!" At the corner of Maple and Sergeant streets, a woman with an umbrella stepped back quickly at the sight of the two cars hurtling into the intersection. "The puddle! The puddle!" Mrs. Fitzgibbons cried, and Dolores sent the big Buick in along the shoulder, spraying the woman from head to foot with gallons of muddy snow water.

The two cars ended up minutes later halted side by side at Maple and Main, stopped next to the low concrete barriers that prohibited automobile traffic from entering the brick-paved shopping district. Mrs. Fitzgibbons led the way in on foot, flinging invective as she went. Of her companions, only Eddie, clutching a beer can, was inebriated enough not to have anticipated something tragic. Near the ancient granite fountain in front of the city hall, Mrs. Fitzgibbons, while darting forward with some amusing word on her lips, lost her footing, and pitched head foremost onto the pavement. Falling, she sprained her arm. In a rage, she seized up something solid, a brick or a length of pipe, and rushed across the snowy outdoor mall with the object in her fist, and with a single blow, shattered the entire plate glass show window of the Walgreens pharmacy. The window exploded.

*   *   *

An hour after midnight, Mrs. Fitzgibbons was transferred by ambulance from the emergency room of the local hospital on Beech Street to the state installation some distance to the north in Smith's Ferry.

It was quite stormy by now, with a steady, snowy rain splashing down and the wind rocking the ambulance. The elms in the courtyard of the old Smith's Ferry institution groaned and swayed, as the driver turned in at the gate. One of the two emergency service workers opened a big umbrella, and with the two of them accompanying her, Mrs. Fitzgibbons climbed the front steps under her own power. Her right arm, throbbing painfully to the beat of her pulse, was supported under her coat by a sling. The caged overhead lights in the entranceway revealed Mrs. Fitzgibbons's exhausted state.

Forms from the local hospital detailing her condition were handed over at the registration desk, and within minutes Mrs. Fitzgibbons was being wheeled in a chair along the main corridor to the elevators. In the ward upstairs, she was helped into a hospital smock. The room had immensely tall windows on either side, and the ceiling was streaked with a dull yellowish light from the sodium-vapor lamps in the yard below. The snowy rain thrashed against the windows. The occupants of the room were all asleep, as, in a matter of minutes, was she.

EXILE AND RETURN

EIGHTEEN

If there was a single hour in the course of that entire autumn when Mrs. Fitzgibbons appeared to revert to the genial, self-effacing woman whom people had always known her to be — that is, the polite, attractive lady at the home-mortgage desk — it would have been during the discussion she had that Saturday morning with the psychiatrist on duty. She was perfectly lucid. She sat where she was told, and smiled, and thanked the nurse's aide who gave her a heavy knitted cardigan to put on over her smock. She directed herself concentratedly on the doctor. Inwardly, Mrs. Fitzgibbons was frightened out of her wits.

Sometimes the cold wave of dread that swept over her actually caused her tongue to loll. She sat beside his desk, with her mouth open, trying to react with conscious sanity to the appalling thrust of his interrogation. The physician's questions ranged from general inquiries concerning the health of members of her family to specific inquiries on the state and regularity of her menses. Had she ever been violent? Was there any history of thyroid problems? Was she under stress at work? — had she ever been diagnosed as compulsive? — had she ever been abused? — how well did she sleep? —

was there recent weight loss? The questions went on interminably. Was she allergic to any medications? Was she familiar with lithium? Was she depressed following her daughter's birth? Had she ever miscarried? Was her marriage a happy one?

"How old are you?" asked the psychiatrist, and he leafed back through the admission forms to locate her date of birth. He was a neat, clean-shaven individual, with a glassy head and long, pale hands.

"I'll be forty-six in December," she said. Every answer that Mrs. Fitzgibbons supplied seemed to her a further confirmation of something dreadful in the offing.

"An episode such as you suffered last night, Mrs. Fitzgibbons, might be even more worrisome in someone younger than yourself, because it often proves a prelude to serious disturbances of a similar kind. Which is not to say that a total loss of control like that isn't a very grave concern."

With her hands in her lap, Mrs. Fitzgibbons listened breathlessly as the doctor spoke.

"Frankly," he said, "I'm surprised by your placidity this morning, and by the obvious tightness of your thinking. Symptoms of that sort don't usually get remitted overnight. Maybe you're a medical phenomenon." A narrow smile split his face.

Mrs. Fitzgibbons breathed deeply now and again, and from time to time gave a long shudder. The name on the man's desk was Dr. Elton Cauley. His next remark also unsettled her.

"We've notified Barbara, your daughter," he said, "about what happened, and where you are, and expect her to come in early this afternoon."

Barbara's grim, bespectacled features appeared on the screen of Mrs. Fitzgibbons's mind. She put her fingers to her forehead.

"Have you been lonely lately?" Dr. Cauley went on exploratatively.

"No," she said. "I have not."

"You have been quite active, then."

"Yes, I have."

"Do you work long hours?"

"I do," said Mrs. Fitzgibbons, "yes."

"What, exactly, do you do at the bank?" he asked, glancing at a form.

Mrs. Fitzgibbons looked at the paper in his hand. "I run it," she said.

The odd crack of a smile that had parted Dr. Cauley's lips these past minutes vanished. "Really?"

To Mrs. Fitzgibbons herself, her response seemed no more significant nor less ordinary than any of her previous replies. "I'm chief executive officer," she said. "I took over recently."

Dr. Cauley was clearly impressed with that. "Jesus, that's wonderful," he said.

Mrs. Fitzgibbons smiled modestly and reached behind her cardigan sweater to rub her arm, which was still supported in its sling. Her air of modesty and self-effacement would have been an asset to a figure in holy orders.

The doctor laughed with artifice. "I should ask you about my adjustable-rate mortgage," he cracked. "I'm afraid I didn't read the small print."

"Who holds your mortgage?" said Mrs. Fitzgibbons, feeling a tiny stream of energy flowing into her nervous system.

"Citizens Bank."

"Oh," she said, and bit her lip. "They're undercapitalized." She delivered this intelligence in the same earnest, almost diffident manner that had characterized her work for many years. This manner came naturally to Mrs. Fitzgibbons, and engendered trust. The doctor was looking at her with intent.

"What does that mean to me?" he said.

"Well, they won't give you an inch. They haven't the depth to be as generous as they might have been in past years."

"I didn't know that."

"They're hard-pressed. They're looking to be taken over."

Dr. Cauley sat back in his chair. His new estimation of the woman before him was mirrored in his face. "That's a fact?" he asked in surprise.

"It's known to us. It's more than a rumor."

"Why, then," he inquired, in innocence, "don't you folks take them over?"

"I may," said Mrs. Fitzgibbons. "An officer of mine is putting together a profile on them."

The word *profile* had leaped unbidden from Mrs. Fitzgibbons's lips, even though she had never used the word in such a context before. She was reminded of the ease recently that she had experienced in making herself understood to others. She seemed to have been blessed with a gift for speech. This awareness was itself rather forceless, however, like a form dimly perceived on the horizon of the mind. She looked at him perplexedly.

"Am I medicated?" she said, finally.

"Well," he answered, "certainly, Mrs. Fitzgibbons. You were given a small dosage. You took it with juice at breakfast. You don't remember?"

Mrs. Fitzgibbons nodded embarrassedly. She recalled the tablets in the paper cup. "I do," she said.

Later, standing by the windows in the solarium at the end of the ward, to which she had retreated to avoid being pestered by the other patients — all women, pacing restlessly to and fro, chain-smoking, many talking obsessively to themselves — Mrs. Fitzgibbons spotted her daughter's car turning in at the front gate. The vision of Barbara's dirty gray hatchback, with its protruding headlights and slush-spattered grille, sent Mrs. Fitzgibbons's heart plummeting. For the first time, she was able to grasp the nature and implications of her circumstance, the shock of being incarcerated, the bleakness of what was to come.

At ten minutes past noon, Barbara came hurrying in, her big glasses sparkling. The first words out of her mouth were not consolatory.

"So, this is where it got you," she said hotly. "With your fancy mascara and thousand-dollar bras."

"What are you talking about?" Mrs. Fitzgibbons winced at her daughter's onslaught.

"Picked up in the street at two A.M. And didn't I know it was coming? Didn't I?" she wailed. "The big-shot la-di-da business executive who wouldn't even come to the telephone."

Mrs. Fitzgibbons, who had sometimes feared her daughter in the past, but never while imprisoned in a psychiatric ward, was sitting on a green plastic chair by the windows, trying to distill from her brain a mollifying response. She was long mystified by the combination in Barbara of a desire to safeguard various life forms in nature and a rancorous repressiveness toward others.

"Because of you," Barbara carped away in a thin voice, while glancing over her shoulder to ascertain their privacy, "I don't even know my own husband. Anyone would swear he was in love with my own mother. I'm a laughingstock in the street. You've belittled me. You've desecrated the memory of my father. You've done everything conceivable to stain and pollute my life. And for what?"

Mrs. Fitzgibbons's heart was thumping desperately as Barbara scolded.

"So that you, the big shot, could fire people at work. That's how Frankie Fitzgibbons gets her jollies. You're the talk of the city. People despise you! Whizzing around town in the back seat of a big Buick, and people like Eddie sucking up to it, just asking for it, *wanting* to be treated like dirt."

Mrs. Fitzgibbons objected softly. "It wasn't like that."

"That's your secret. Spit on people and they'll beg for more. Well, it just isn't like that. Because some people know better. . . . You're off your clock!"

A nurse interposed. "Your mother," she said, "will need toilet articles, a robe, slippers, underwear, that sort of thing. Did you bring anything?"

Barbara was too distracted to speak. Her lips drawn back in two thin lines, she stared blankly at the nurse.

"It's all right," Mrs. Fitzgibbons spoke up to dismiss the importance of Barbara's role. "Other people will do that."

Her reference to others, as to a devoted court, only fueled Barbara Berdowsky's bitterness, as, for many minutes without letup, she poured cold scorn on her mother's head.

"You won't even have a job now," she said, digging in her vinyl bag for a tissue.

"I always had a job," Mrs. Fitzgibbons replied with puzzlement.

"Please! Spare me!" Barbara mimicked her mother's most cutting manner. "After this farce? Who in their right mind would take you seriously? You're finished."

"But that doesn't make sense."

Suddenly, Barbara launched a scathing impersonation of Julie on the phone, in the way of ridiculing her mother's importance. " '*Mrs. Fitzgibbons can't speak to you now. Mrs. Fitzgibbons is in conference. Mrs. Fitzgibbons is with the press.*' It was for this obscene charade," Barbara said, "that I went to school, did my homework like a stupid little automaton, so that now, grown up, I would have you on my hands. What on earth did I do?" she cried out. "What will happen to me?"

By the time Bruce Clayton arrived on the fourth-floor ward at one o'clock, the start of the usual visiting hours, Barbara had left Mrs. Fitzgibbons in the solarium and was consulting with Dr. Salindra Singh, the Indian psychiatrist arriving on duty. The two of them were talking animatedly in Dr. Singh's glass-enclosed office behind the nurses' station. Barbara was pleading with the doctor in a loud voice. "She needs extensive care! I'll sign anything. Tell me what to do. This condition has been worsening by the week."

If Mrs. Fitzgibbons's behavior seemed suggestible to the behavior of others, as to Dr. Cauley and Barbara, her response to Bruce was no exception. That is, she responded to his fawning behavior and loving solicitude with the nodding, easygoing air of an established superior.

"I let myself into your house," he explained. He had in hand a shopping bag brimming over with articles of clothing and toiletries he had fetched from her bedroom.

"That was just the thing to do," Mrs. Fitzgibbons replied. Not strangely, while in Bruce's presence, Mrs. Fitzgibbons's perception of her daughter as a rather frightening, narrow-minded zealot altered smoothly into that of a hysterical nullity. Mrs. Fitzgibbons was frowning in the direction of Dr. Singh's office.

"Your daughter seems very upset."

"She's always been a little funny."

"I brought you a pair of flat shoes." Bruce was producing her belongings item by item from the bag. As he did so, Mrs. Fitzgibbons fell to studying him. He was crouched on his heels next to her chair. The look of his ears and the line of his hair awoke her loving instincts. She had the formless idea in mind that the category of her plight, its mystery and unknown prognosis, meant very little to him; he loved her. Her tongue lolled momentarily, and she shut and opened her eyes.

"That was wise," she said.

"Stockings," he went on, "brush, comb, some lotions."

Within minutes, Bruce had helped Mrs. Fitzgibbons on with a black turtleneck, skirt, and shoes. He adjusted the sling about her forearm, and then set about brushing her hair. The picture of the two of them, Mrs. Fitzgibbons gazing calmly out the window to the dismal wintry courtyard, Bruce standing impeccably behind her, handsome and formal, working the hairbrush with hypnotic movements, was altogether arresting. That evening, with the arrival of others, Mrs. Fitzgibbons's anxieties were further abated. Although she had taken the Haldol tablets prescribed for her by Dr. Cauley at supper hour, and the medication left her feeling a little slumbrous, the eagerness and sedulous attention of her young followers revived her spirits. Bruce had given the word out that Mrs. Fitzgibbons was in good fettle and would appreciate the solicitude of her friends. Only Eddie was missing. Howard, Dolores, and Matthew brought flowers. Emily Krok presented her with a box of chocolates. Julie, the most imaginative that day, arrived on the ward carrying a big, floral-printed envelope containing a dozen photographs of Mrs. Fitzgibbons herself; these were black-and-white prints of the full-length shot of Mrs. Fitzgibbons standing handsomely in front of her desk, which was published a week earlier in the *Ireland Parish Telegram* and had generated such interest.

To the nurses and attendants on duty, there was no mistaking the fact that the woman in the black turtleneck, toward whom such obeisance was being paid, was a figure of consequence. The impression was fortified when she was observed signing three or four of the photographs for her guests, while speaking to all in a softly instructive fashion. They stood about her chair with their hands behind their backs, laughing with polite restraint at her witticisms, and sometimes calling her Chief. In fact, Mrs. Fitzgibbons looked quite fit; her coloring was good, her hair lustrous and neat. At one point, when Howard Brouillette indicated a need to speak to Mrs. Fitzgibbons in private, Dolores turned to the others, and with a wave of her cigarette, led them away to a respectful distance.

Mrs. Fitzgibbons listened in silence for the next several minutes, while Howard, perched on a plastic chair drawn up to her side, delivered his report. The sight of Mrs. Fitzgibbons staring blankly in the direction of Matthew and the others, and of Howard in his long white coat, clutching a signed photo in his hands and going on and on at her ear, did confer on Mrs. Fitzgibbons more the look of a historic personage than of a patient in the hundred-year-old institution. From time to time, she frowned; she listened with an imposing expression; she nodded, frowned, and nodded again. She did not look at Howard as he spoke.

Mr. Zabac, he explained, who was attending a conference on Cape Cod, had learned about the firing of Mrs. Wilson and was fit to be tied. Julie had found this out through Deborah Schwartzwald, a friend of Patricia Quirk, Mrs. Wilson's secretary. Patricia Quirk had sworn Deborah Schwartzwald to silence because she lived in mortal fear, she said, of Mrs. Fitzgibbons, but Deborah wanted Mrs. Fitzgibbons notified at once, and would like Julie please to tell Mrs. Fitzgibbons what she, Deborah, had done for the cause.

Mrs. Fitzgibbons nodded sagaciously.

Mr. Zabac would be returning home on Monday instead of Tuesday. This information came from the horse's mouth, Howard said, and was absolutely reliable. Patricia Quirk had telephoned Jeannine Mielke at home today, instructing the latter to send the car service to Barnes Airport at noon Monday, a day earlier than planned. "Patricia Quirk is in this up to her neck," Howard said.

Mrs. Fitzgibbons grunted portentously but said nothing.

Dolores and the others stood as before, in the middle of the bright, expansive room, speaking subduedly among themselves.

"We spread the word," Howard went on, "that you had had a nasty fall and sprained your wrist, that the hospital was overcrowded, and you were sent elsewhere for treatment."

She nodded once more. She was gazing down at the dark fringe of trees that lay beyond the courtyard and driveway, beyond which lay the river.

"As for Hooton," Howard said, "I warned him last night that if he went to work Monday, I'd call the police."

Mr. Brouillette's views struck Mrs. Fitzgibbons as consonant with good sense. "Well, you should," she said. Her recollection of the dramatic undertaking of the night before was not particularly troublesome to her. "He's lucky not to be in jail."

"After what he did to my wife," Howard added for good measure. He scraped his feet back and forth on the floor. "He was lucky it was you who caught him, and not someone vindictive."

Mrs. Fitzgibbons's tranquilized thoughts harmonized with the other's sentiment, requiring just a modicum of mental energy. She allowed the remark to pass.

"The best news" — Howard pulled forward in his chair — "is that the Citizens Bank has a multimillion dollar note with the Mannox Apremont Development Company. It goes back three years, and the Mannox Company is taking a bath. This is not hearsay. Hooton mentioned it last night to Dolores. He was very, very excited about it, he said."

"It gave him a hard-on?"

Howard colored. "That's what she said, yes. It made him hard. He said it was his trump card. But that's not the best part. The Mannox Apremont Company —"

"We hold a note of theirs."

"That's the best part. Yes, we do. It's older and smaller and precedes theirs, and if you call it in, everything will come down."

For all her haziness of thought, Mrs. Fitzgibbons perceived the implications readily enough. "If I —"

"Exactly," said Howard. "Mannox will go under, and Citizens will be reduced to begging. They won't be able to go on. They'll be headed straight for receivership."

"Who told Hooton?"

"It came straight from the man himself."

"What man?" Straightening herself, Mrs. Fitzgibbons recovered something of her nervous irritability.

"The president of the place. Curtin Schreffler."

"Schreffler!" Mrs. Fitzgibbons turned this way and that, agitatedly, in her chair. Her exclamation had silenced the room. At such times, Mrs. Fitzgibbons's voice resonated with oratorical power. "Curtin Schreffler? With his Cuban heels and silver-headed umbrella? He didn't approach me?" She extended her good fist and appeared to be sighting along it. "I'll stand him on his patent-leather head," she promised.

In a setting where sudden commotions and flare-ups were the order of the day, somehow the commotion centering upon the ward's latest inhabitant evoked a more concerned reaction. Two nurses came running. By ten o'clock that evening, Mrs. Fitzgibbons, further medicated, lay deeply asleep in her bed. She created another minor crisis the next morning when she refused to take her prescribed dosage. She didn't want any pills, she said. Her refusal did not stem from any conscious resistance to the drug itself, or from any awareness of a need to clarify her mind. She was too drugged already to frame any such plan or rationale. The resistance was deeper, more psychotic: the pills in the cup were a poisonous yellow in color, and the cold rain striking the windows held evil omens. Later on, though, Mrs. Fitzgibbons's resistance to ministrations was more comprehensible; Matthew called her on the pay phone to inform her that she could not be held against her will at that (or any state) hospital for more than three days without a court order.

The change that came over Mrs. Fitzgibbons upon hanging up the phone seemed inspired by a powerful tonic. The mental revival was so thorough in its effect that she actually acknowledged the frightening character of her actions. She recalled demolishing an immense window with something solid in hand. She remembered crouching in terror behind the arbor vitae bushes by the city hall steps, hiding from the ambulance attendants. Her stockinged legs had been covered with muddy snow, her arm felt broken. Mrs. Fitzgibbons even remembered threatening the EMT men with death if either of them dared lay a hand on her person. (She had actually said that. "I'll have you executed.")

By coincidence, Mrs. Fitzgibbons hung up the phone at the same moment that her son-in-law, Eddie, paying his first visit, was being admitted through the locked doors.

"I brought you some tangerines, Mom," he said.

She was standing in her stockinged feet, her thoughts swinging back and forth in a mind grown almost worrisomely lucid. A split

second later, she caught sight of Dr. Singh emerging from behind
the nurses' desk, his swarthy head shining moistly in the fluorescent
light, and turned on him. "It was you," said Mrs. Fitzgibbons.
With her good arm, she thrust Eddie out of the way, knocking the
grocer's bag from his hand. Tangerines rolled on the floor. In a
thin, recriminatory voice, Mrs. Fitzgibbons started in on the psychiatrist. "You throw me into a general ward, with the dregs of
mankind, ask me a hundred thousand questions, feed me Styrofoam gruel, lock all the doors, and no one tells me my rights."

"Mrs. Fitzgibbons —" Motioning for patience, the doctor retreated a step. Mrs. Fitzgibbons closed the distance.

"I'm arrested against my will —" she started anew.

"You weren't arrested. Please," he protested.

"I'm picked up against my will, I'm taken in, I'm questioned,
I'm drugged. I'm transferred in the dead of night from one place
to another. Then," she said, showing him her navy blue eyes up
close, "I'm further interrogated, pumped up with more drugs,
locked into a ward with your usual assortment of nut cases, like
some Soviet dissident —"

"It is not like that. If you don't step away from me, I have the
authority to have you restrained and tranquilized."

Eddie spoke up from behind her in a surprisingly menacing tone.
"I wouldn't do that if I were you."

"I'm told what to do," she railed at him, "I'm told where to
sleep, I'm given an old rag of a sweater to wear, gruel three times
a day, some pills in a cup, and I'm supposed to be happy. I'm
supposed to start ovulating every time you walk into the room, I
suppose! You, an alien who ought to be locked up for what he
does to the English language."

In an aside, Eddie explained to Mrs. Huller, a nurse's aide, who
had stopped at his side to watch. "That's Mrs. Fitzgibbons," he
said. "She practically runs this town."

"I'm a Bombay street beggar!" said Mrs. Fitzgibbons.

"I'm going into my office," said Dr. Singh.

"*You'll stand here and take it,*" said Mrs. Fitzgibbons in a very
big voice. She was taller than he and backed him up to the glass
wall of his office.

"Do you work for her?" Mrs. Huller asked Eddie.

Eddie answered significantly. "Everybody works for her."

"I'm not asking for special treatment," Mrs. Fitzgibbons persisted. "I don't expect people to break a leg to go fetch what I need, or even strive to make a good impression on me." She pulled off the sling that supported her arm, and threw it down. "There was ice," she explained. "I slipped on it. I fell! I hurt my arm."

"You suffered a serious manic disorder, Mrs. Fitzgibbons. You lost control."

"*What if I did?*" she challenged him at close range, her head tilted to one side, her eyes drilling into his. "Do you want to pick a fight with me?"

"Somebody's cruising for a bruising," said Eddie.

"I could close this place down in a week."

"No one is holding you against your will, but you can't be released on a Sunday."

Twenty minutes later, before Bruce and the others arrived, Mrs. Fitzgibbons called Mr. Frye on the public telephone. She phoned him at home. Eddie stood beside her, holding her canvas tote bag in one hand and her address book in the other, while she dialed the number. Growing clearer in mind, Mrs. Fitzgibbons had recalled her scheduled luncheon appointment in Sturbridge the following day with the man from the Shawmut Bank in Boston.

"You'll go in my place, Leonard," she instructed the man on the other end.

"What happened?" he asked, suspiciously.

Surmising that news of her hospitalization had reached him, Mrs. Fitzgibbons raised her voice in a way designed to forestall skepticism. "Never mind about me. I fell on the ice. It's nothing."

"Where are you?" he persisted, insidiously.

"Listen," Mrs. Fitzgibbons stated, while gripping the phone to her ear and staring vacantly at her son-in-law, who was staring then at the soft contour of her bosom, "I didn't call to file a medical report. A car will come for you at noon."

"Will I see you before I go?" Mr. Frye's suspicions persisted in a maddening fashion. Had Mrs. Fitzgibbons been fully herself of recent days, she would have exploded. For now, she obeyed the urge to explain herself.

"No," she said, "you will not. Why are you asking me? Why should I see you? I've spoken to Zabac," she lied. "I've explained to him why I want this. You'll give Nate Solomon every encouragement. Do you understand?"

Still, the man on the other end of the line hemmed and hawed. She could picture him sitting in front of a televised football game, blinking and grimacing, a portrait in middle-aged pathos.

"I'm only worried that we're going off half-cocked," he said.

That did it for Mrs. Fitzgibbons. For the first time since the previous evening, when she lost her temper about Mr. Curtin Schreffler, she employed the big, thrilling voice that Providence had conferred on her a couple of weeks ago. "YOU'RE NOT PAID TO WORRY!" Her hand shook as she shouted.

Eddie stifled a laugh, clapping a hand to his temple and lurching to one side. Mrs. Fitzgibbons was white with fury. Patients, shuffling past, stopped and stared in wonder.

"I'll send Felix!" she bawled. "I'll send Mr. Kim! I'll send Connie McElligot! *Worry?* When you're licking stamps in the mailroom, you'll have reason to worry!"

"I wasn't disagreeing, Frankie," Mr. Frye objected ghostily.

"YOU BE READY AT NOON!" The voice was simply indescribable.

"Noon," Mr. Frye repeated.

"You be ready at twelve sharp, and sign anything that man puts in front of you. I don't expect you to understand me. I expect you to carry out my orders."

After hanging up, while still fulminating, she allowed Eddie to crouch before her and help her on with her heels.

"These Lilliputians!" she said.

She strode toward the sun room. Eddie came sniggering along behind her, carrying her tote, his eyes fixed on the vibration of Mrs. Fitzgibbons's calves.

"He'll do what you told him, Mom."

She gestured angrily. "Well, I'm going to be their big boogums from now on, mark my words."

NINETEEN

Mrs. Fitzgibbons was discharged from the hospital by Dr. Cauley late on Monday morning. At the time of her release, she was in an unexpectedly becalmed state of mind, however, despite her refusal these past forty-eight hours of her medication. By now, Mrs. Fitzgibbons's reputation among the hospital staff was such that her departure created a stir. She was looked upon by the help as something of a local force, a phenomenon, someone who had begun dominating the news in a way that portended even bigger things. Earlier, Mrs. Fitzgibbons had telephoned Julie at the bank, and instructed her to contact Mr. Curtin Schreffler and notify him that she wanted to see him in her office at one o'clock. She was not feeling especially resentful that morning toward the president of Citizens, but was acting on the information furnished her by Mr. Brouillette of her competitor's grave condition regarding the Mannox Apremont Company. That is to say, Mrs. Fitzgibbons saw nothing extraordinary in treating the president of a sovereign institution as though he were nothing more important than a book-keeper on her staff; in her quiet state of mind, she saw the matter in its essentials; in Felix Hohenberger's portfolio, she held a delinquent note on a company whose failure would prove ruinous to the other bank, and was therefore ordering its leader to report to her. If Mrs. Fitzgibbons had stopped to think about her rise to prominence, she would have seen this brash, theatrical rejection of protocol and of the social niceties as the hallmark of her success.

One of the nurses who was most admiring of Mrs. Fitzgibbons was Ellen Montcalm, a stoutish young woman with brilliant bottle-green eyes and frizzy hair. Nurse Montcalm had just heard a news item on her car radio. Mrs. Fitzgibbons, she said, had been selected over the weekend by the Massachusetts State Council of Women as recipient of one of its highest achievement awards, along with five other women from the state. Of everyone present, Bruce was demonstrably the most excited by the news; he hugged Mrs. Fitzgibbons. The nurse asked for her autograph.

After tying her scarf about her throat, Mrs. Fitzgibbons took the ballpoint and sheet of paper in hand. News of the award generated interest among staff members and patients alike.

"My father knew your husband," the nurse remarked.

"Knew Larry?"

"He knew him from their days at the Chestnut Street School. He said that when Larry Fitzgibbons died, it was the saddest day of his life."

Mrs. Fitzgibbons handed the woman the paper and pen. "Larry didn't die," she said. "He just slowed down terrifically."

Matthew and Dolores, who were standing by the door waiting to be joined by Bruce and Mrs. Fitzgibbons, shouted with laughter. Others joined in. Even Dr. Cauley could not restrain himself.

Mrs. Fitzgibbons and her friends waited then as Ellen unlocked the outer doors. Mrs. Fitzgibbons was not smiling, nor did she even look back from the elevators to acknowledge the salutations called to her from behind. The prospect of freedom and fresh air, and of her return to duty, set all else at naught. She waited solemnly on the gravel walk as Matthew Dean brought the car round. The sky above the distant river was the color of a wet bed sheet. As she did not invite anyone to join her in the back seat of Matthew's black sedan, Bruce and Matthew rode up front, with Dolores between them.

At the outskirts of the city, Eddie Berdowsky was spotted coming the other way in his mud-spattered hatchback. Eddie pumped his horn and swung around on the highway. He fell in behind them. The sight of the filthy compact following Matthew's gleaming, highly polished Buick down Dwight Street toward the business district was curious to the eye. It looked as though the Buick had snagged something under its wheels and was towing it to the city dump.

Mrs. Fitzgibbons's entry into the Parish Bank that morning produced a momentary hush, as she darted across the glassy floor toward her office. Had anyone credited the whispered rumors about her mysterious hospitalization Friday night, or wondered about her physical or emotional soundness, one look at her this morning put an end to it. In all her years at Parish, she had never looked more fit or adequate to her tasks.

"Look! It's the Chief!" Deborah Schwartzwald was the first to give voice to her feelings. Deborah's jewel-like eyes gleamed fanatically. "I knew it! I knew she'd come."

To Mrs. Fitzgibbons, the grand interior of the bank with its spectacular dome was more welcoming than home itself. Her spirits were bounding. Julie Marcotte came running to take her coat. "It was like death without you here this morning," she exclaimed. She carried Mrs. Fitzgibbons's coat like a sacred vestment to the closet.

"Get me Lionel Kim."

"Right away!" Julie snapped.

"I want coffee, the mail, the morning paper, any telephone messages —"

"Mr. Zabac called from Falmouth. He sounded really upset, I thought. He asked what time you were coming in."

Mrs. Fitzgibbons brushed Julie's remark into oblivion. "Get moving."

"He said that Mr. Hooton had resigned over the weekend. He was speaking in a loud, high-pitched tone of voice. He said he'd call you from the airport. Did you know that Mr. Hooton resigned?"

Mrs. Fitzgibbons had no patience for persons in responsible

positions who flew off to Cape Cod when a competitor was all but begging to be plucked from the bough. Mrs. Fitzgibbons worked on her feet. She tore open her mail.

"Call Maloney and Halpern," she said. "Tell them I want a preliminary agreement drawn up for the takeover of the Citizens Bank. You tell them I want a document on which a signature means something. And I want it in an hour!"

"I haven't heard back from Mr. Schreffler," Julie interjected, remarking on the president's failure so far to agree to Mrs. Fitzgibbons's summons.

Although she was eager to act, Mrs. Fitzgibbons's thinking was very agitated. It took Julie's remark to concentrate her mind. "You get them on the phone," she said.

Blanching, Julie hurried back to her desk.

"Because if I have to go over there," Mrs. Fitzgibbons called after her, "they won't like it. I want that man in my office." Mrs. Fitzgibbons's frustration escalated to the point where she rushed to the door to repeat her instructions about her lawyers. Julie, who wrote down everything, scratched away at her pad before picking up the telephone. "You tell Maloney and Halpern I want a binding document. A preliminary agreement with murderous penalties built in for welshers."

"Yes, Mrs. Fitzgibbons."

Coloring angrily, Mrs. Fitzgibbons returned to her desk. "He'll just be a number in my computers," she said.

She decided, at this point, that when Mr. Schreffler arrived, she would greet him not in her own office, but upstairs in the chairman's office. The decision came to her in an impulsive flash. Were Mr. Schreffler to come, he would be made to humble himself, first by climbing the narrow marble staircase to her office, like a schoolboy going up to the principal, then by being kept waiting in the outer office. By the time he was admitted into Mr. Zabac's spacious chamber, with its immense window looking out on the city hall, the president of the Citizens Bank would be softened up for the violent harangue to come.

There were those at the Parish Bank, however, who were not equally convinced that Mr. Schreffler would even appear that afternoon. Felix Hohenberger, for instance, merely shook his head, in puzzlement and disbelief, when word reached him that Mrs. Fitzgibbons had *ordered* the man to report to her. News of what was evolving on the executive level spread to the staff at large. When Mrs. Fitzgibbons went upstairs to occupy Louis Zabac's private office, and brought Julie Marcotte with her, she ordered Jeannine Mielke to vacate. Mr. Zabac's secretary resisted being replaced, saying that Mr. Zabac was due soon at the airport and would be upset to find her absent from her post. Jeannine sat behind her desk, looking pale and bloodless, her white-blond hair drawn back tight on her skull.

At that, Julie astonished even Mrs. Fitzgibbons herself with her reaction to the other secretary's obstinacy. "You'd better get moving!" she said, and advanced threateningly.

The expulsion of the Mielke woman from her desk was witnessed by Lionel Kim, who came in just as the anemic secretary departed. In his politeness, Mr. Kim gave no sign of having noticed the exchange or the drained face of Mr. Zabac's secretary as she hurried by him.

"I just received your message to report to you," he said. "I was at the Shearson office in the mall." He stood before Mrs. Fitzgibbons in his shirtsleeves. Mr. Kim was obviously in a guarded, if not suspicious, frame of mind. Mrs. Fitzgibbons didn't beat about the bush, however.

"You're my new treasurer," she said.

Mr. Kim looked in wonderment from Mrs. Fitzgibbons to Julie, while Julie flushed a pleasant pink color, thrilling to the way the Chief could confer happiness and good fortune on anyone she smiled upon.

"I am?" he said.

"You're in charge of my capital markets desk." Mrs. Fitzgibbons got a sexual kick from the way Mr. Kim's face mirrored, in quick succession, shock, thankfulness, and awe. Her nipples tingled. If Julie hadn't been present, Mrs. Fitzgibbons speculated that she might have grasped Mr. Kim between the legs. "I want a detailed report of four or five pages summarizing the condition of your department and all its accounts, and I want it by tomorrow."

"I can't thank you enough."

Mrs. Fitzgibbons touched her fingers in citing her prescription for success. "Work like the devil, watch the company you keep, and don't think you can fool me."

Appalled at the thought of deceit, Mr. Kim showed her a thunderstruck face. "I would never do that."

Smiling with seductive malice, Mrs. Fitzgibbons set a pretty fingernail to his nose in the way of a cordial warning. "I'd flatten you."

With her hand on his shoulder, Mrs. Fitzgibbons walked him out to the hallway, advancing a variety of views which all resolved to the importance of Mr. Kim realizing, now and forever, which side of the bread his butter was on.

On the floor below, however, no one was paying attention to what was transpiring at the top of the brass-banistered staircase at the back of the bank. For at that moment, at three minutes to one o'clock precisely, there emerged through the glittering revolving doors the figure of a beautifully postured man in an exquisite navy blue suit and burnished black shoes. The man entered the great well of the Parish Bank without once averting his eyes to the left or right. He carried an amber-handled umbrella as tightly rolled as a walking stick; his black hair was slicked down flat and gave a smooth anthracite sheen to his well-proportioned skull. Even the clocklike click of his built-up leather heels on the glassy surface of the floor, as he stepped along with elegant bearing, contributed to the impression of meticulosity that was evident in the dagger points of his pocket handkerchief, the immaculate white slash of his shirt cuffs, and the perfection of his tightly knotted red-and-blue-striped necktie. From the tellers' windows at the front, to the array of lamplit loan officers' desks situated athwart the marble columns, work came to a standstill, from stage to stage, as Mr. Curtin Schreffler, with his head up and shoulders back, came skimming by. To anyone who might have deplored the decline in formality in men's dress habits, not to say fastidious good taste, over the past generation, Mr. Curtin Schreffler of the Citizens Bank was a sight for sore eyes.

Emily, of all people, was assigned the task of intercepting and greeting the man upon his arrival. The instant he appeared to view, she came darting out of her corner, as quick as a rat, to lead him upstairs. The dark, wet-lipped smile on her face, joined to the dynamic forward hunch of her body and swift, crablike gait, created an unforgettable impression on all who saw. It was a picture of the inspired imbecile, of the lustful, grinning, happy-at-heart envoy of the Devil, leading an innocent mortal — a man of the world, vain and unsuspecting — up the narrow staircase to his destruction. The sublime touch, if there was one, was the big hole in the unraveling elbow of Emily's charcoal gray cardigan, out of which protruded a puffy swatch of her faded Indian-print dress.

Thankfully, Julie Marcotte offered an entirely different impression; she sat very straight in her chair behind Jeannine Mielke's desk, her hands clasped before her, her smooth temples and cheekbones shining like something phosphorous taken from the sea. Had anyone studied Julie this past week, they would have discerned a subtle, day-by-day progression in her appearance, from that of a casual but businesslike refinement in hair and dress, to something smarter and more severe. On this day, she wore a black tailored suit, with a double row of silver buttons that started at her lapels and converged slightly toward the waist; her hair was pulled back from her face. The effect was military. She did not rise to greet Mr. Schreffler but directed him with a terse remark and a tilt of her eyes to the deep leather sofa at the opposite wall. Emily Krok lingered in the room. She couldn't stop peering at Mr. Schreffler, staring lasciviously with glittering eyes, while standing awkwardly just inside the door. Mr. Schreffler seated himself at once, with a smooth, effortless folding of his body. He crossed his legs; the toe of his swinging shoe gleamed lustrously. Perfectly controlled, he glanced up, however, when Julie told Emily to leave. "Get out of here," Julie said.

A longish interval passed before Mr. Schreffler was actually summoned by Mrs. Fitzgibbons; but to the man's credit, he maintained a physical stillness and aura of imperturbability that would have dignified an ambassador to the Court of Saint James. When Mrs. Fitzgibbons finally buzzed Julie on the phone and told her to admit Mr. Schreffler, Julie conveyed word to him so brusquely, hanging up the receiver, and without even looking at him — "The Chief'll see you now" — coming round the desk to open Mrs. Fitzgibbons's door, that the man was unaware of the summons until, through the opened door, he actually spotted the silhouette of Mrs. Fitzgibbons herself, etched against the big fantail window of the inner office, waiting for him.

"My word," he said, upon entering," what an attractive view of city hall."

With her back to the sunlight, Mrs. Fitzgibbons's features were unsettlingly obscured. She answered in an inflectionless tone. "We're not here to discuss the view, or city hall, or the price of winter apples, Mr. Schreffler."

While it always came as a surprise, Mrs. Fitzgibbons still delighted each time she discovered herself capable of expressing herself in a smooth, spontaneous, loquacious way. Probably, in fact, nothing had given her greater pleasure the past fortnight than the facility of her tongue. She had never been so openly talkative, and guessed that it was an inborn talent that the world about her had stifled. Mrs. Fitzgibbons experienced momentary jubilation, a happy surge of energy. The fact that she cordially disliked the man only simplified the task at hand. Mrs. Fitzgibbons remembered Curtin Schreffler from the days of her parochial-school girlhood down on Mosher Street, in a district known as the Flats. Curtin and his chums were the favored ones, the sons and daughters of the old families on the hill; the youths who went away to smart boarding schools, who whiled away their summers playing tennis at the Canoe Club.

"We're here," she reminded him, "to talk about your bank."

"What puzzles me," said Mr. Schreffler, revolving on his heel as he looked about for a place to sit, once it was apparent that the chief officer of the Parish Bank had no wish to shake his hand in greeting, "is the suddenness of your interest in us, Mrs. Fitzgibbons. The air of emergency. The speed of it all. I hope that my telephone call of a day or two ago was not —"

"Please." She gestured him to a chair and paced importantly across the blue-and-cream Chinese carpet to Mr. Zabac's desk. She mocked him. " 'The speed. The air of emergency.' Your deposits are from money brokers. Your portfolio is packed with local mortgages. You can't meet your capital requirements." Going past his chair, she showed him the knowing frown of a schoolmaster ridiculing the protestations of a pupil. "What do you think we are," she put the matter more harshly, "simpletons?"

This last remark sent a pale flash of alarm through Curtin Schreffler's face. He was not used to being talked to in this way.

"A word from me," she added, "and the regional examiners will be crawling all over you." She shivered involuntarily, then felt a hardening of her leg muscles and an electrical impulse that left her fingertips tingling. In some indefinable way, she was even aware that her womanhood was itself a delicate bludgeon, an intimidating refinement, which, as the hour passed, would be employed with impunity.

Mr. Schreffler had no desire to argue. Seated opposite Mr. Zabac's desk, with a bar of sunlight suddenly igniting his shoe, he looked for all the world like a store-window mannequin. "We're just a small to moderate-sized bank, which," he began to admit, "recently —"

"You're nothing," said Mrs. Fitzgibbons, seating herself. Time and again, she strove to hold down the strain of exultant paranoia rising inside her. She saw herself clutching the knot of his necktie in her fist and elevating his head, while disabusing him of some very outdated ideas on banking theory, but held her temper in check by presenting him with a cool picture of the female executive.

"When you're insolvent, you're nothing. You're not *even* a bank. How is an insolvent bank different from an insolvent fast-food chain or some little company" — she gestured — "that makes choo choo trains?"

"I assure you on that point, Mrs. Fitzgibbons —"

"Of course, we all have our troubles." She struck an ameliorative note. "We swim in the same ocean. We dine on the same diet. We endure the same storms. No one is free from runs of bad luck. I am no different from you in that way." She conceded the man that, as she rocked back in Mr. Zabac's chair and employed one of her favorite lecturing devices, holding a long yellow pencil between the tips of her forefingers. "I'm not an idiot. I'm not unreasonable."

Mrs. Fitzgibbons paused to see if he would interrupt her, so that she could jump on him. As he remained silent, however, content just to sit and listen now as she waxed generous with maddening condescension, she adopted a more relevant line of thought.

"A smart-talking developer with promises of profits untold comes sashaying in the door and charms you out of millions of dollars. The rate spread narrows. The developer is a shyster. And you," she said, "are left sitting on an iceberg headed for the equator."

Both Mr. Schreffler and she laughed pleasantly over her witticism. If the expression emerging on Curtin Schreffler's face was an honest mirror of his emotions, he was a trifle relieved.

"The lending business is touch and go," he contributed lightly, with a sigh of modesty.

"I know the Mannox Apremont Company." She ignored his remark as she broached the name of the firm whose ill health threatened Curtin Schreffler's lending institution, if only to dispel any doubt as to her own secure position. "They're so far delinquent with us — with me — it would take an act of God to rescue them." Mrs. Fitzgibbons's egomania focused itself on the delinquent developer. "I'm tired to death of bothering with them."

The phone on her desk flashed. Guessing it was important, she picked it up. It was Julie. "Mr. Zabac called. I connected him with Jeannine Mielke," she whispered secretively. "He's at the airport."

"Thank you, darling." Mrs. Fitzgibbons hung up, and reiterated what she was saying. "I'm disgusted with them, with their wheedling and lying and making promises they can't keep. And I get nothing!"

Truth was, Mrs. Fitzgibbons knew precious little about the note in question. She had never dealt with a Mannox representative or even examined the account; but it pleased her to play the part of the patient, long-suffering creditor. "I wait, and I wait, and I wait," she said. "They know what their failure will do to you. They know the strength of my position. They know I'm sitting here behind the scenes with their fate in my hands." For the first time, Mrs. Fitzgibbons's voice achieved a penetrating timbre. She flung down her pencil. "I get nothing!" she shouted.

Startled by the woman's rancor, and the sight of the yellow

pencil rolling chaotically across the tulipwood desk, Mr. Schreffler
sought at once to salve her spirits. "Bert Mannox isn't a bad fellow.
You may have developed an unfair impression of the man. No one
has ever accused him of dishonesty." Mr. Schreffler went on with
growing confidence. "I have it from reliable experts that Bert needs
nothing more than six months to a year to stabilize his situation.
Frankly," Mr. Schreffler added on a rising tone, in the way of one
professional confiding in another, "I believe the man."

Mrs. Fitzgibbons was staring at him, gauging the peril of his
circumstance by his musical reaction to her sudden outburst. To
prolong the pleasure, she nodded coldly and expressed a reasonable
point of view. "I have my people to think about. I have my own
agenda, my own concerns and priorities." She sat far back in her
chair, her legs crossed, her knee pointing upward.

The man nodded with polite understanding. "Naturally," said
he.

"I have a duty to preserve us from the hungry wolves of the
world. I have every right to do this." Mrs. Fitzgibbons savored
her own words. "And I am expected to use every means at my
disposal. If I didn't, who would? I have had to deal with serious
challenges in my own house. With certain treacherous subordinates
who would sacrifice everything that is good and sound just for
personal enrichment, to put a little silver in their pockets. Or for
sicker reasons, for the perverse fun of making life impossible for
others. These are the people who urinate in the reservoirs." She
shrugged unconcernedly. "I knew who they were. I watched them
for a day or two. Everyone who is hardworking and sane was
behind me. I have their trust. They knew the sword would fall,
and now it has. Who would have thought," Mrs. Fitzgibbons
inquired shrewdly, "just two weeks ago, that I would have consoli-
dated my position this quickly? I'll tell you," she said. "No one."

"You've made striking gains."

"I acted," Mrs. Fitzgibbons agreed. "I didn't wait to be cudgeled
about the ears just because I wanted what was best for everyone.
Believe me," she came forward smoothly onto her feet and paced
to the big window, "I'm sustained by the devotion of my staff. To
them, I'm a blessing. I have their confidence and I have their love."

She might have gone on in this vein some while longer, but as she turned, the sight of the president of Citizens waiting impassively for her to reveal her intentions ignited her temper. An impulse to curse him out came and went. Color flashed into her face. She commenced marching to and fro. "I knew what you were up to," she snapped. "I'm told everything. Did you suppose that you could telephone someone in this bank without my knowing? You knew I was chief officer. You knew who I was. You saw me in all the newspapers, you saw me on television, you knew I was chief." Suddenly, Mrs. Fitzgibbons exploded in anger. The sight of the man sitting inertly on his chair inflamed her. "*Who do you think you are, Schreffler?* Lecturing me about Bertram Mannox. Where is your eleven million dollars? Where is my money?"

"I'm astonished by the extent of your unhappiness with us," he remarked.

Mrs. Fitzgibbons had stationed herself behind the big desk, her hands flat upon it, leaning forward angrily. "You have been a thorn in my side for years. I mean to be done with this!"

Evidently, Mr. Schreffler decided to make a clean breast of his troubles at this point, for the expression on his face altered. He showed her a patient hand. "It's not untrue, Mrs. Fitzgibbons, that we might not survive the failure of Mannox Apremont at this time, but it is true, nevertheless, given a period of six months at the outside, and not one day more than that, our survival and future health would no longer depend upon Mannox. That is not conjecture. I can satisfy your accountants and lawyers on that score, down to the last decimal point."

"You people." For the first time since his arrival, Mrs. Fitzgibbons paraded herself past him, conscious of the disdainful oiliness of her voice and the imposing lift of her breasts.

"If you will delay initiating any proceedings against Bert Mannox until the month of April, I can promise you —"

"Your whole history is one of shameless money grubbing. Every generation of you. Going all the way back. Seize their collateral! Padlock their doors! Carry off their sofas and refrigerators! Throw them into the street!" She made an annihilating sweep with her arm. "You have never done anything good or useful for the happiness of anyone, not in a century, not once or anywhere, not from Windsor Jambs to Nichewaug. Now, the shoe is on the other foot. Your depositors are coming to me in droves. Your capital is gone. You're on the brink of extinction!"

"I must correct you, Mrs. Fitzgibbons," he insisted, shocked by the sheer falsity of her charges. "Our contribution to the growth and welfare of this city and region is a long and distinguished one."

"It is nothing, do you hear me?"

"Our two institutions have lived side by side in harmony for decades."

"Last week," Mrs. Fitzgibbons moderated her manner in a quietly cynical fashion, "you and I might have sat down to a pleasant lunch together and discussed your crisis like two human beings. I would have listened to you. I would have sympathized and offered advice, and if push came to shove, I'd have helped you. There is no question about that," she cited categorically, as she strutted out from behind the desk. "I'm not unfeeling. I'm not a brute," she said. "I would have seen your side of things. I would have taken you at your word. I'd've extended the Mannox note, and it would have been business as usual. Now," said Mrs. Fitzgibbons, "all that has changed."

Mrs. Fitzgibbons picked up her phone and buzzed Julie. "Do you have the agreement from Maloney and Halpern?"

"It came two minutes ago," Julie said, then swiftly lowered her voice. "Chief," she said, "Mr. Zabac is on the other line."

Mrs. Fitzgibbons switched lines. "What is it, Louis?"

The chairman's voice on the wire was thin with anxiety. "Mrs. Fitzgibbons, I've heard news this morning that has distressed me more than I can say!"

"I'm in an important meeting, Louis." She gazed blankly at Mr. Schreffler, who was paying the most acute attention to the call.

"I insist," Mr. Zabac commanded with obvious stress, "that you do nothing further today until I arrive. Do you understand me? I'm going directly home, and from there straight to you. I can't believe that you dismissed Elizabeth Wilson. After all we said on the subject." He was beside himself with frustration. "You broke your word. I'm very, very unhappy."

"I'm talking to Curtin Schreffler, Louis. I haven't time for one of these chats. Leonard Frye is at a meeting in Sturbridge with Nate Solomon from the Shawmut in Boston, discussing the Worcester proposition — which is pure gold. While I," she said bitterly, her voice grown hoarse with determination, "am putting an end to a grievance that has me at my wit's end!"

This angry pronouncement left Mr. Zabac speechless. Mrs. Fitzgibbons held the receiver away from her ear, glanced at it bitterly, then hung up.

Witnessing the way that Mrs. Fitzgibbons had just treated the venerable Louis Zabac, Mr. Schreffler's face grew pale. After that, he sought to appease her. He complimented her on her successes and on the wealth of publicity she had won for herself and her institution. Cutting him short, Mrs. Fitzgibbons then launched into a fabulous description of several lucrative deals, all imaginary, into which she was steering her bank. She boasted of a February ground-breaking for a twenty-two storey office tower in Hartford in which the Parish Bank was a principal lender. Waving to the north, she cited an industrial park that she had on the planning boards with Wang Laboratories. Westinghouse, she said, was on the line over the weekend inquiring about the availability of skilled labor in the region. Mr. Schreffler listened to Mrs. Fitzgibbons's megalomaniacal boasting without stirring in his chair. There was not a grain of truth in what she was saying, and she knew it, but intuited correctly the usefulness of associating herself with stupendous projects. She was preparing the man for the savage onslaught to follow. When Julie came into the room with the preliminary takeover agreement hastily prepared by Maloney and Halpern, Mrs. Fitzgibbons was marching to and fro in front of the quiet, seated Citizens executive, who was holding forth magisterially. "We have the size, the weight, the assets. And I have the will. When I make up my mind to act, nobody on God's earth is going to stop me."

Mr. Schreffler was soon holding the ominous sheaf of papers from Maloney and Halpern in his hands, murmuring perplexedly as Mrs. Fitzgibbons paced before him. Sometimes she enjoyed uttering the man's name, the sound of which was like the gathering of a mouthful of saliva. "Nothing has been left to chance, Schreffler."

"Your achievements are the talk of the season. We all know that Mr. Zabac has the fullest confidence in you."

"Zabac?" That made her laugh. Mrs. Fitzgibbons ridiculed the chairman's importance. "You must be pulling my leg. I have the confidence of everyone, of every soul under this roof, as well as of the army of depositors rushing in to join us. What a mentality! You and Zabac. Who knows who you people are? Ask the man in the street."

"I concede you your popularity, Mrs. Fitzgibbons. All I am asking is that you set forth your specific complaints against us, so that we can correct them, and that we might then go on living side by side, just as always — our smaller bank," Mr. Schreffler conceded modestly, "next to yours."

Mrs. Fitzgibbons was wonderfully pleased with herself and could imagine a time very, very soon when Louis Zabac would be staying at home, in a sort of obligatory retirement, while she occupied this magnificent executive office. The room suited her vanity. The gray Gothic pile of the city hall looming ponderously before her, with its iron roof fence and towering spires, the somber walls of which deadened the power of sunlight itself, mirrored something equally grand within her soul.

"You must be feebleminded," she answered him rudely. "You're not listening to me. I intend to put an end to this charade. Do you suppose you could stop me? One day," she promised, lifting her voice musically, "I'll come blowing in at your front door like a winter wind. And then, Curtin Schreffler, you and your sleepy little staff will see what I've been talking about. I do not bluff. Trust me. It will be unpleasant!"

She stopped before him in imposing fashion. "I'm giving you this last opportunity to join your little bank to mine. I can promise that you will receive a respectable position in the resulting organization, and that everyone will know what an important part you played in the merger. I can promise you that. . . . I promise!"

As Mr. Schreffler appeared more confused than convinced by her words, Mrs. Fitzgibbons continued to cajole him.

"I swear it." She waved her hand as though to dismiss the contrary. "You have my solemn word. My sacred pledge. . . . You'll be happy here. I, personally, will look after your interests. I'll make the appointment on the six o'clock news!" she cried, showing her generosity. "We'll go on television together. I'll name you my executive vice president in charge of everything. Everyone will report to you. When you put your name on those papers, the Mannox Apremont nightmare will be over for you. Think of that. Think what it will mean, too, to be second in command here. You have my sacred word. May God strike me dead!" she shouted. "I'll look out for you."

"I'm not empowered to sign such an instrument as this," Mr. Schreffler objected finally, and looked down in dismay at the document on his lap.

Mrs. Fitzgibbons waved aside his remark as an irrelevancy and indicated the document. "Do as you're told."

"I will need to read it, then others, too, would have to read it. This is more than unusual."

"Turn to the last page," Mrs. Fitzgibbons instructed in a firm voice, "and sign your name."

"Also," Mr. Schreffler protested quietly, "if it should happen one day that we do merge, will the Citizens name be incorporated in the formal title of the surviving bank? My associates and family would be very curious on that point."

"What family?" said Mrs. Fitzgibbons. "What surviving bank?"

"The new bank," said he.

"What new bank?"

If Curtin Schreffler were a man who had ever experienced even a dash of fear while in the presence of an infuriated woman, the escapade to follow could only have frozen the blood in his veins. Her voice climbed to an incredible pitch. She was apoplectic.

"There is no new bank! At three o'clock this afternoon, you will cease to exist! I'm going to expunge," she hollered, "that name and everything it stands for from every wall and billboard in this city! I'll beat it into the mud! I'll obliterate it, so help me God. In the weeks to come, I promise you, Schreffler," she leveled at him, "as Providence guides my hand, there won't be as much as an envelope or letterhead left anywhere on the face of the earth to suggest that you and your family, and that sorry collection of yahoos working for you, ever sat together under one roof. I'm going to *smash* your bank!" Her voice soared out of control. Mr. Schreffler clasped the arms of his chair. "I'll smash it with my bare hands and scatter the bricks and mortar from here to Lake Champlain. *Julie!*" Mrs. Fitzgibbons ran to the door. "Get me my lawyers!"

At fifteen minutes to two o'clock, when Mrs. Fitzgibbons came out to the head of the stairs, Curtin Schreffler was left behind in Mr. Zabac's office to stew over the preliminary merger agreement. Mrs. Fitzgibbons had allotted him fifteen minutes to sign the formal instrument. Assured that he would do so, she called Howard Brouillette upstairs to witness the signature. If Mr. Schreffler failed to sign, Howard was to telephone their lawyers to start proceedings against the Mannox firm. Downstairs, Mrs. Fitzgibbons collected her coat, bag, and gloves, and signaled for Emily to join her. Jeannine Mielke was sitting at Julie's desk by Mrs. Fitzgibbons's door. She spoke up in a facetious tone as Mrs. Fitzgibbons came out.

"I spoke to Mr. Zabac," Jeannine let fall in a prim, gloating manner. "He instructed me to tell everyone that he's going to address the entire staff this afternoon at four o'clock."

Mrs. Fitzgibbons, pulling on her gloves, had already decided to put an end to Mr. Zabac's interference with her administration. "He did, did he?" she said.

"Everyone is to attend," Jeannine added, but the note of suppressed triumph faded at that moment, as Emily Krok appeared, pulling on her Navy pea coat and staring at Jeannine with a gap-toothed leer that was very unsettling to look at. (Twenty minutes earlier, in the ladies' lounge, Emily had startled the life out of Mrs. Jacqueline Harvey by suddenly assaulting the pink cinder-block walls with her fists, the knuckles of which were shredded and bruised.)

"Is Matthew outside?" said Mrs. Fitzgibbons.

"He'd better be," Emily said, pulling on her woolen watch cap.

The drive to Mr. Zabac's house was a pleasant six-mile tour up Route 116, over the hills of the Mount Holyoke Range, beyond the women's college, and north from there through farmland. There was an inch of snow on the high ground. Mrs. Fitzgibbons took Emily in the back seat with her this time. She had developed a liking for the hunched, pigeon-toed girl, especially for those occasions when vigorous steps were required. Emily's proclivity toward violence, combined with her doggish devotion, reinforced Mrs. Fitzgibbons's own appreciation of the felicity of settling problems in the most expeditious manner possible, with bold, blunt strokes. Since the Friday preceding, when Mrs. Fitzgibbons had invaded Neil Hooton's lake house, Emily had developed a low, ominous chuckle that persisted almost continuously whenever she was with the older woman. During the ride, Mrs. Fitzgibbons's speech was itself by now incessant. She talked every mile of the way. She hammered away on the subject of Mr. Zabac's constant questioning of her plans, policies, and actions. She was very resentful. She sat straight in her seat and aimed her invective at the road unfurling before her. The leafless trees on the roadside twisted past in a black, spidery maze; the afternoon sun was a white wafer in the sky. Matthew was behind the wheel, listening to her while driving.

"My computers are going round the clock," Mrs. Fitzgibbons went on and on, complaining, "my staff is competent and hard-working, everyone is doing his level best to perform his duty and discharge my orders, while he, the so-called chairman of this little enterprise, goes flying off to Falmouth. I've eliminated the last of the opposition. I have the Citizens Bank on its knees. The South Valley is headed for the same. I take the man on television and pass him off as a genius to an audience of five hundred thousand people, and when I need him to ratify a merger, or to sign a check — or just to *be* there when I want to address the staff — he's long-distance! He's gone. He's whining in my ear on the phone. He's worried. Moaning away like a little coward, telling me to wait — slow down — not so fast — do nothing." She stared fixedly through the front windshield, her face a cold tablet. "This is what the man does. He gives me the worst advice that anyone in history has ever given to another. Now, he wants to lecture my staff."

Matthew looked over his shoulder at Mrs. Fitzgibbons and chuckled amiably. "He's okay, Chief. He's supposed to worry. That's what chairmen are for."

"And what will I be doing while he's addressing everyone? I'll just stand there, like the rest of the galoots, just another face in the crowd, and grin and bear it, I suppose, while he delivers one of those sleeping-pill talks of his."

Matthew praised her indirectly. "Not everyone can talk, Chief."

"Well, he isn't going to address anybody!" Mrs. Fitzgibbons left no doubt on that point. She changed position then in her seat, her shoulders straight, her mouth set. "Little dwarf!"

Mr. Zabac's house, spotted through a cleft in the rolling farm country, was a sprawling picture-book affair, white with blue shutters and four white chimneys. The long asphalt driveway was flanked on the near side by a stand of bluish pines. Matthew halted the Buick by the front door. Mrs. Fitzgibbons ordered him to stay in the car and took Emily with her. She mounted the steps briskly and rapped on the window of the storm door. The raps of her knuckles echoed like gunshots. After a second, Mrs. Fitzgibbons opened the door impatiently and marched in. She was met almost at once by Amanda Zabac, the chairman's wife, who came rolling into view through a white doorway at the end of the foyer in a shiny, motorized wheelchair.

The invalided lady piped up at once. "Look who it is. You're Mrs. Fitzgibbons. I know you from the newspapers."

Mrs. Zabac immediately impressed her caller as a woman of delicate sensibility. She had a pretty face and a shapely head circled with babyish white curls. Her gown was trimmed with pink lace at the throat.

"I hope there are no problems at the bank," she said.

"None whatsoever." Mrs. Fitzgibbons reassured the lady in the wheelchair with a salute of her upraised hand. While she had long known about Mrs. Zabac's growing paralysis, Mrs. Fitzgibbons had never laid eyes on the woman, nor would have guessed her to be such a picture of sweet refinement.

Turning her battery-driven aluminum chair about, and piloting the way into the parlor, she spoke over her shoulder to Mrs. Fitzgibbons. "You will probably think me simple and naive," she exclaimed, "but I have been so encouraged by your promotion, and what it must mean to so many women, I've been just dying to meet you. As you know, Louis is due from the airport any minute, but what a stroke of good fortune his absence is for me."

Mrs. Fitzgibbons sauntered with unhurried footstep into the big parlor, glancing about herself at the crowded collection of yellow and pink chintz-covered armchairs and love seats, at the gracious array of shining tabletops, and canary draperies. Mrs. Zabac swiveled noiselessly about in her gleaming chair to look at Mrs. Fitzgibbons, who, in her muddied high heels and long, rather martial leather coat appeared to satisfy Mrs. Zabac's conception, not just of her husband's new CEO, but of a very capable and determined woman of the world. Her face was rosy with admiration. "Of course, I have no true quarrel with men," Mrs. Zabac conceded playfully, "but I think they've had things too much to themselves for too long."

As often lately, Mrs. Fitzgibbons underwent a pleasant physical reaction to the woman's honeyed words; her leg muscles tensed and a tremor flitted down her spine. Amanda Zabac was staring at her, eager to hear what Mrs. Fitzgibbons had to say on the question of the role of modern-day women. She took her eyes away just for a second, to glance curiously at Emily Krok, who hovered in the doorway in her pea coat and cap, leering.

Mrs. Fitzgibbons was not a disappointment. "Nothing comes without a fight. If I had waited around to be tapped on the shoulder, an eternity would have come and gone."

"My heavens." Mrs. Zabac liked that response very much. "You really are exciting." Seated in her wheelchair, amid the soft, beribboned folds of her flannel gown and lap blanket, Amanda Zabac looked as helpless as a newborn waiting to be fed. "I hadn't realized what a splendid figure you make. You ought to consider sometime a move into politics, Mrs. Fitzgibbons." With that, Mrs.

Zabac looked up once more at Emily for a response, but the latter was staring at her with an expression that could hardly be construed as corroborative.

"Just because I'm able to reach out and take what's there," Mrs. Fitzgibbons condescended a trifle, while completing her thought, "doesn't mean that somebody else wouldn't fail."

"I'm sure you're right. I'm hopelessly naive about such things. I admire what you've done. Ever since I saw you in the paper and on television, I've been one of your most outspoken champions. It's quite a pleasure to meet you in the flesh." While speaking, Mrs. Zabac activated her chair, turned ninety degrees to one side, and rolled soundlessly over the rug to a coffee table where she picked up a crystal candy dish of Canada mints. "I know a lot of influential people, well-to-do," she said, "earnest and civic-minded, particularly ladies who are very rights-minded, who would support a candidacy like yours."

Mrs. Fitzgibbons declined Mrs. Zabac's candy dish with a little waggle of her fingers and turned stiffly on her heel to Emily. "Get Julie on the line," she commanded. "Find out what's happening."

Mrs. Zabac watched fascinatedly as the strange, grinning girl in the dark coat darted past her wheelchair with the alacrity of an attack dog and picked up the phone.

"Tell her," Mrs. Fitzgibbons dictated in a bigger voice, "if Schreffler hasn't signed yet to notify my lawyers!"

"Is something important happening?" Mrs. Zabac set a chalky hand to her cheek. Her eyes sparkled; she couldn't take her eyes from the figure in the leather coat standing before her.

"I'm putting an end to the Citizens Bank," said Mrs. Fitzgibbons. "Their days of fraudulence and shady tricks, and of insulting me to my face, are coming to an end this afternoon."

Mrs. Zabac was stunned. "I can't believe what I'm hearing."

Mrs. Fitzgibbons's expression deprecated that. "If people like you knew what I was doing, I'd still be on first base."

Emily shot up her hand for attention. "He signed the papers," she said.

"Tell me again." Mrs. Fitzgibbons faced Emily.

"Mr. Schreffler has signed the papers. Mr. Brouillette and Julie witnessed the signature." Emily's pocked face shone darkly. "It's official! Julie says it's official, Chief. It's in black and white."

Mrs. Fitzgibbons laughed with her head back. "The little coward. Doesn't he know what I'm going to do to him?"

"The stupid yellow-belly," Emily chimed in.

"I have him in my pocket!"

Mrs. Fitzgibbons and her strange young companion were expressing themselves so boisterously that their spirits annihilated Mrs. Zabac's presence for the moment.

"Schreffler!" Mrs. Fitzgibbons tossed her head, then mimicked the man with a surprisingly accurate inflection. " '*I would like to remind you, Mrs. Fitzgibbons, that the Citizens Bank has a long and distinguished history —*' "

"Will someone tell me what's happening?" Mrs. Zabac begged.

"He must have boiled excrement for brains," said Mrs. Fitzgibbons. "Doesn't he know what I'll do to him?"

Emily Krok was beside herself with gaiety. She was doubled forward, clenching her two fists. "You let me at him."

"I'll tear him to bloody ribbons," said Mrs. Fitzgibbons.

Matthew blew his horn, signifying Mr. Zabac's arrival in the driveway. But Mrs. Fitzgibbons was too exultant to notice. The roof of the hired car winked in the sun as it drove in past the parlor windows.

Mrs. Fitzgibbons's heated mind gave a sudden redness to her temples. "He signed over an entire bank. I put the papers in front of him, and the man signed them. He took out his pen and signed them." She repeated herself with manic intensity. "I told him to do it, and he did it. I want your bank, I said, sign on the dotted line, and he did."

She was filled with such an adrenal rush that she could have snatched the dainty Zabac woman out of her wheelchair, and thrown her, lap robes and all, across the room.

"I have the document, I have the bank, and I have him." She gestured excitedly. "He gave it to me. Not his car, or his house, or a whole street of houses. No, he handed me the family bank. That," said Mrs. Fitzgibbons, "is the sort of cringing, gutless marvel that has been running this world for the past two hundred and fifty thousand years. 'Give me your bank,' I tell him, and he does. I would kill first."

"So would I," said Emily.

"What are we all talking about?" Mrs. Zabac pleaded to be heard.

There were moments in her triumphant fervor when Mrs. Fitzgibbons felt her thoughts slipping away from her. She could retrieve and hold them in place only through the device of repetition.

"If it were me, I would have shot him dead. I swear to God, I would put a bullet in any man, woman, or child that threatened to do to me what I did to him. With his Masonic Temple cuff links! His silk socks! That schoolboy necktie. I swear," said Mrs. Fitzgibbons, looking at her fist, "by Mary and Joseph and a skyful of angels, I'm going to choke off his fucking windpipe."

With that, Mrs. Fitzgibbons headed for the back door of the house. She was fit to take on an army. Her footsteps made booming sounds in the back hallway. Outdoors, she waited in the trellised breezeway for Louis Zabac to come to the door. Oddly, despite the light snow and lateness of the season, a considerable number of Mr. Zabac's rose blossoms clung tenaciously to life amid the climbers on the trellis. The rose garden itself, lying adjacent, with its gravel pathways and artificial dells and promontories, and a decorative gazebo, was covered with an evenly spread cloth of snow. As Mrs. Fitzgibbons awaited the chairman, Emily and Mrs. Zabac emerged behind her from the house. Mrs. Zabac stopped her motorized chair at the top of a low, specially built ramp that led into the garden. Clutching the handles of Mrs. Zabac's wheelchair, Emily hovered behind her, her watch cap pulled over her ears.

When Louis Zabac came stepping his way briskly up the path from the drive, the expressions on his and Mrs. Fitzgibbons's faces portended conflict. Both appeared determined, but of the two, Mrs. Fitzgibbons, being the taller and clearly the more angered in aspect, might well have been the wagering favorite, as she stood in the breezeway, blocking his way to the door. Notwithstanding her heated frame of mind, her thinking was not so disorganized as to obscure the fact that the prancing little man in the tweed overcoat had attempted to thwart her will on the telephone just as she was bearing down on her victim. Mr. Zabac had overstepped himself. It was time for him to swallow some strong-tasting medicine.

Mrs. Fitzgibbons spoke first.

"You look like you've seen the Holy Ghost," she said. "Where have you been?"

"I was delayed by the snow." At once, Mr. Zabac got to the point. "We're going to have a talk, Mrs. Fitzgibbons, and it's not going to be a pleasant one, I'm afraid."

He pushed past Mrs. Fitzgibbons, forcing her aside, and opened the back door to his house. He didn't trouble to greet his wife, or even indicate having seen her. Insulted, Mrs. Fitzgibbons turned on Emily.

"Take her for a ride in the garden," she ordered.

"Oh, no, it's too cold for that today," Amanda objected. She looked about in confusion. Mr. Zabac was already indoors.

"It's not too cold," Emily grumbled, and instantly started Mrs. Zabac's wheelchair rolling down the plywood incline.

"I'll be too cold," Amanda protested. "It's much too cold for me."

Hunched over the handles, Emily laughed nastily, and pushed Mrs. Zabac's wheelchair quickly onto the nearest path and headed out into the garden with her. The soft white curls on Mrs. Zabac's head trembled fluffily in the cold, windy air.

Inside the house, Louis Zabac was removing his overcoat. He was beside himself with vexation. Through the kitchen windows behind him, Mrs. Fitzgibbons could see the dark, crouched figure of Emily Krok thrusting Mrs. Zabac up the pathway toward the top of the garden. From where Mrs. Fitzgibbons stood, the featureless, gray-white horizon line of the garden looked like the final edge of the world.

"You knowingly and willfully deceived me," said Mr. Zabac. "You gave me your pledge that you would do nothing outrageous, nothing crude, sudden, or violent in my absence. No sooner had I gone," he flared up, "than you deliberately resumed your vicious, high-handed tactics." Mr. Zabac had hung his tweed overcoat on a wooden hanger and reached it into the closet. His face was pocked and mustardy, marked with a tiny wine spot of frustration on either cheekbone.

Mrs. Fitzgibbons was standing behind him in the vestibule, with her left hand hooked over the belt of her coat. Her scorn was apparent. The sight of Mr. Zabac's boy-sized overcoat, as he prepared to hang it up, and of his glassy little shoes, struck her as embarrassingly freakish. Mr. Zabac must have noticed the pained, disbelieving look on her face when he turned to speak to her, because his angry excitement mounted. Mrs. Fitzgibbons interrupted him.

"I didn't come out here to talk about Elizabeth Wilson."

"Mrs. Wilson," the chairman came right back at her, "has been a model employee of mine for twenty years. Longer than most. Longer than you, or Mr. Frye, or Mrs. Lecznar, or dozens of others. It was she who helped set up our money machines. I don't want to know your reasons. I am not asking for explanations. There is no excuse, Mrs. Fitzgibbons, for such an egregious exhibition of willful insubordination."

Mrs. Fitzgibbons's heart rate accelerated with the chairman's remonstrating manner. She stood, legs wide apart, in front of him, obstructing his emergence from the hall closet, glaring at him. She was too tongue-tied with frustration to speak right away.

"And where is Mr. Hooton?" he persisted. "He didn't come to work today. Where is he? Why doesn't he answer my calls at his residence? What have you done to him?" He worked himself into a lather. "Have you fired him, as well? What in God's name do you think you're doing? Have you gone mad?"

With a brisk forward movement then, Mr. Zabac bumped Mrs. Fitzgibbons to one side and strode forth into the vestibule. "Today," he said, gesturing, "I'll have my satisfaction."

In her charged state of mind, Mrs. Fitzgibbons's general inability to brook criticism was rapidly replacing any tolerance she might have possessed over the ravings of a pompous little figurehead. Her heart was thumping. When the chairman looked over his shoulder at her, he must have noted the truculent lift of her chin and flash of her frozen blue eyes, for a shadow of worry passed quickly through his face.

"Who do you think you're talking to?" she fired at him. She was striding along behind him in the corridor, her heels ringing solidly on the floor.

"I don't even know what you're doing here," he cried all of a sudden. "What are you doing in my house?"

If Mrs. Fitzgibbons knew nothing else, she knew that she could crush the man like a bug. She spoke to him now in the harshest manner. Her voice dropped a full octave. "How dare you speak to me that way?"

The walls of the prettily papered hallway that divided the ground floor were decorated with framed Norman Rockwell prints, ten or twelve of them, which Mrs. Fitzgibbons, in mounting indignation, would like to have gone about smashing with a hammer. Her voice was commanding.

"You're the one who reaps the profits from what I do. The little Midas!" she taunted. "Crying in his beer. 'You do my dirty work, and I'll sweep in the gold.' It was *I*," she exclaimed, "who brought Schreffler to the table. I did that! You're too kind and considerate to do that, you are. You're too nice. You're too namby-pamby." She had backed Mr. Zabac to the newel post of the front staircase and was letting him have it. The fact that she was a head taller than the chairman of the Parish Bank and had lately shown a disposition to take physical measures when feeling thwarted, contributed powerfully to the force of her reproaches.

"I bring him fresh game on a platter," she said. "Killed, cooked, and carved! A big fat roasting bird every week."

"You're going to have to leave." Mr. Zabac spoke up tonelessly, his back to the stairway, his face more sallow than ever. Like all creatures, wild or domestic, Louis Zabac obviously possessed an instinctive warning system that left him looking hypnotized in the face of impending violence. He stood stock still. He was staring into her eyes. "You're going to have to leave, Mrs. Fitzgibbons."

Her face was not six inches from his own. The scent of his Paco Rabanne shaving lotion dilated her nostrils. The man's ingratitude combined with his seeming self-assurance exasperated her. "*I* run things," she said, "you don't. You haven't in weeks. What does it take to penetrate that thick skull?" Mrs. Fitzgibbons's voice grew louder and harsher as she inched closer. "I attract deposits. I negotiate loans. I meet with the press. I fire whomever I please. What in God's name is the matter with you?" She gritted her teeth. She was shouting in his face. "Don't you understand? You're my rubber stamp. You're a title in a big office. You're a name printed on a piece of paper! I'm real. I do things. Things happen. Money comes in. People lose their jobs. People work harder."

Mrs. Fitzgibbons had raised a gray-gloved hand palm up and was striking it softly with the blade of the other hand, in rhythm with the points she was making.

"My computers make a noise, and a piece of paper comes out," she said, "with your name on top. Just read down the column of figures on the paper to see what you're worth. That's what you do. That's your job. And that's all you do. And I'll tell you something else. More is coming! There's going to be a bloodbath this week at Cabot and High. I know it, my staff knows it, and Schreffler knows it. *Put it from your mind!*" she cried facetiously. "Pretend it's not happening. Play with your rosebushes. Watch TV. Your hands will be clean. I'll be the one at Cabot and High. I'll be the one throwing bodies into the street."

Mr. Zabac couldn't even blink, let alone utter a word of exception.

"You'll be home sitting by the fire in your silk smoking jacket, with your wife and your hunting dogs and your cocktails, and I'll be cracking heads, and nobody," she shot a finger past his eyes, "will say boo. Not Schreffler, or the people under him, or your labor complaint boards, or the newspapers, or anybody. When I go into Citizens, and shut the doors behind me, not one fucker will lift a finger to stop me."

Her brain was churning; she couldn't believe that this diminutive person with his princely ways had had the temerity to speak up as he had.

"It wasn't enough for us to remain cordial and polite," she said, "to smile at each other like two jackasses and go on pretending that you were responsible for my victories. No," she lectured, "you call me on the telephone. You tell me to do nothing, and now come in here, pulling a long face, to show everybody how unhappy you are. I've got millions of new deposits in one pocket and an entire bank in the other, and he," she said, "is unhappy."

Mr. Zabac could bear the tension no longer. "Mrs. Fitzgibbons," he said, "you're fired."

Mrs. Fitzgibbons reached with her left hand and took hold of Mr. Zabac by his shirt collar and the knot of his necktie, thrusting two gloved fingers down behind his tightly buttoned collar in a way that immediately altered the flow of blood moving down from his head. Mr. Zabac's face darkened.

"He doesn't even want to hear about it," she said. "He wants to reproach somebody. I have my way of doing things — which is to get things done fast, and in a way that no one in his right mind will ever forget — and *he* has a better way. He flies off to Falmouth." While it was apparent in the way Louis Zabac's head was forced back, and by his rising color, that he was about to begin striking Mrs. Fitzgibbons with his fists, she betrayed no sign of alarm. "I have a man out in the car who would like nothing better than to come wading in here and break up the place, smash some furniture," she said.

Mr. Zabac was struggling. "Where is my wife?" he cried.

That made her laugh. She grabbed a fistful of Mr. Zabac's suit jacket just above the breast pocket with her right hand, and was simultaneously lifting and pushing him. "Your wife! That Grandma Moses?"

When at last the time came for Mr. Zabac to deliver the desperate retaliatory blow that he had been preparing, which was to have been a punch of considerable consequence to judge by the look on his face, the backs of his ankles came into contact with the lip of the bottom stair and instantly rearranged the gravitational axis of his body, with the result that the powerful forward delivery of his arm expended its force in space, rather like that of a frenzied schoolgirl. He toppled backward. Even as his spine collided with the fourth and fifth steps, Mrs. Fitzgibbons was upon him, unbelting her coat.

"Where have you been these past twenty years? On the planet Pluto? No," she mocked again, "he wants proof positive. He wants to be shown." Twice in rapid succession, Mr. Zabac strove to rise, each effort accompanied by a shout of outrage; but the natural downward pressure of Mrs. Fitzgibbons's own body weight redoubled the force of her rigid left arm upon his neck.

More than once, she actually bared her teeth, as she was using all her physical strength to pin him securely to the stairs. To anyone watching at this moment, it would have seemed that Mrs. Fitzgibbons was lifting him up and banging him down on the stairs, whereas in reality Louis was thrusting himself upward again and again, only to be met with superior force. The two of them were expressing themselves simultaneously.

"This is my house!" Mr. Zabac's face was the blood red of an overripe tomato. His breath was failing him. "What do you think you're doing?" he cried.

"Louis wants to be loved by everybody. Louis wants to be the boss." She mocked him in a sissified voice.

"You've gone insane. You're a madwoman!"

"He wants to see what I'm made of." She was tearing furiously now at Mr. Zabac's belt buckle. "He wants to see how much bilge I'll take. He wants to agitate me. He wants to fire my balls."

Flat against the stairs, with Mrs. Fitzgibbons full-length upon him, Mr. Zabac was not only disadvantaged physically, but was rendered additionally helpless by the growing recognition of what in fact was happening. For, of the many exigencies of life against which a man is expected to prepare himself, this was not one of them. Mr. Zabac was being raped.

Snapping his trousers and boxer shorts down free of his waist, Mrs. Fitzgibbons clapped her hand over his exposed sex. Mr. Zabac's eyes bulged scarily. He emitted a cry. "Come on," she yelled at him, "show us!"

Apart from her physical aggressiveness, Mrs. Fitzgibbons's moral leverage now precluded the likelihood of prolonged resistance. The hammers were going in her brain; her breathing was short. With her gloved fingertips under his testicles, she kneaded the hard ridge of flesh there with such force that it set her own torso rocking back and forth. She was still clutching him at the throat with her left fist. The amount of blood in his face was worrisome. "You and that gimpy little wife of yours. I should have given you the law weeks ago! I'm going to bang your brains out."

Unfortunately for Louis Zabac, whose eyes were flooded with tears, and who squirmed futilely from side to side, snapping his head this way and that, the reactions aroused in the genital area by Mrs. Fitzgibbons's violent rubbing and the imprecations streaming from her lips were not what she expected. Nothing was happening. With an astonishingly swift movement, Mrs. Fitzgibbons reached and swept back the sides of her gun-colored coat, hiked up her dress, and, with two or three deft jerks, yanked down her underpants. She was berating Mr. Zabac all the while. "You're going to sign what's put in front of you! You'll ratify my every wish."

At one point, Mr. Zabac twisted his head and cried for help, but the feebleness of his shout could only have revealed more acutely the thoroughness of his plight. The house was empty.

"You'll be Mrs. Fitzgibbons's helper. I'll put you in little overalls. You'll go to the store for me. *Come on!*" she hollered. "*Where is it?*"

What followed was so outrageous in nature, an occurrence so singular in the affront it paid to his maleness, that the expression on Mr. Zabac's face in the instant that Mrs. Fitzgibbons pushed herself forward and his head disappeared under her loins, was one of eye-popping horror. She was sitting atop him then, with her buttocks planted on his collarbone, her knees buried in the stair carpet. Mr. Zabac was being sodomized. Only his legs remained in view. From beneath the outspread hem of her leather coat, his legs flew straight up, thrashing and flailing the air, like a bicyclist pedaling furiously. He was being suffocated.

Mrs. Fitzgibbons, with the weight of her torso on his face, continued to apostrophize the fates that bedeviled her. "A woman could talk herself blue in the face. Nothing sinks in. Words aren't enough. He has to be shown. He has to be wrestled to the floor and shown. *I* run the bank!" She tightened the grip of her fist round the knot of his tie underneath her, while bouncing up and down atop him, and repeating this last assertion, over and over. Mr. Zabac's little glassy shoes jumped and twirled in the air behind

her back. "Mrs. Fitzgibbons runs the bank," she said. "Mrs. Fitzgibbons runs the bank."

Not surprisingly, Mrs. Fitzgibbons continued to ventilate her emotions during the long car ride back to town that afternoon. Even
Emily, who had often shown herself to be fearless, gave Mrs.
Fitzgibbons a wide berth; she sat against the back door on her
side of the Buick and stared with a dark, idiotic expression at her
boss. In truth, Mrs. Fitzgibbons did present an alarming aspect.
Her hair was disheveled, her makeup smeared, her coat thrown
wide. She lamented the extremity of circumstances that required
the taking of such extreme measures. Like many a rape artist, she
was experiencing powerful feelings of revulsion toward the victim,
in his want of appreciation, his ineptitude. She stared at her
upraised palms. "I could have strangled him with my bare hands."

By the time she reentered the bank at a few minutes before
closing, signs of the violence that had taken place at Mr. Zabac's
house were still evident upon her, not just in the disorder of her
clothes and hair, but in the mortal whiteness of her face. She pushed
her way rudely through lines of last-minute customers queued at
the windows. Unknown to her, hostile forces were already gathering against her, when she started up the back staircase to Mr.
Zabac's office. The first clear sign of trouble in the air came when
Jack Greaney, the head teller, ordered his staff to close their windows. He then buttonholed Emily Krok, who had followed Mrs.
Fitzgibbons into the bank by a few seconds, and had just returned
her pea coat to the ladies rest room, and let fall the news that
something in the nature of a descent upon the bank by a unit of
the local police was imminent. Emily was on her way upstairs,
when Jack told her to stay put. Of all those persons in the bank
that witnessed the events that were about to unfold and later
recounted them, none would have omitted as the starting point of
it all the quick, violent altercation that flared up between Emily
and Jack Greaney.

To begin with, Emily had probably grown frustrated in this past
week by her never being called on to show Mrs. Fitzgibbons her
love and loyalty in other than tacit, symbolic ways; Emily was a

hooligan at heart. For another thing, Jack Greaney made the mistake of laying his hand on Emily's arm while talking to her. This restraining gesture, to the mind of the stooped, churlish girl, was nothing less than a signal to combat. The brutality of what followed would haunt the young bank teller for a long time to come. The fact that she caught him off-balance, just as he was turning on his heel to point a finger at the staircase to the second floor, was likely noted by nobody. Not only did Emily sock him flush on the temple with all her might, but as Jack Greaney's foot caught on the leg of the desk behind him, and as he started to go down, she continued to slug away at his head with the most astonishing dexterity. As he was rolling sideways over the edge of the desk, Emily connected a left hook to the jaw that was so brilliant in execution — thrown with her head up and a sudden violent clockwise snap of her hips — had it been delivered at ten o'clock that night at Madison Square Garden, it would have brought ten thousand fight fans to their feet. Jack went down before her like a dead man.

As if the hideous sight of Jack Greaney's unconscious form stretched out on the marble floor (just his shoes sticking up from behind the desk) was not enough, the arrival of eight uniformed policemen, with Mr. Zabac himself walking along hurriedly in their midst, was more than sufficient to convince all who saw it of the magnitude of the drama unfolding before them. Mr. Zabac was so small amongst the strapping men in blue, as he darted his way forward, aiming them toward the staircase, that he was all but hidden from sight. The overall impression of the moving mass of sober policemen was one of great urgency. One of the onlookers, Felix Hohenberger of the home loan section, stated later that the dramatic rush of police, intent upon apprehending the woman upstairs, seemed less like the arrest of a small-town banker than the lightning seizure of a national leader. Others must have shared Mr. Hohenberger's impression, as scores of staff members and customers of the bank stood about the main floor in silence as the last of the police officers vanished up the staircase.

Notwithstanding her prescience up until now in anticipating the actions of others, Mrs. Fitzgibbons was nevertheless caught off guard. When she first heard the commotion from the foot of the stairs, she was brandishing in her right hand the sheaf of papers that Curtin Schreffler had earlier signed, and waving them in Julie Marcotte's face. She appeared insane as she stomped back and forth in a threatening manner. She had lost one of her gloves, and her shoes were badly muddied. Her eyes held a smoky glow. "I'm not an unreasonable person. I'm not an ogre. I have the right to expect obedience. I have the duty to expect it. Who will obey my lieutenants if my lieutenants disobey me? That's why I'm here," she chanted. "That's what I do. There are people out there who profit from being shouted at." She slammed the papers down on Mr. Zabac's desk. "A man who experiences terror will sign his name to anything you put in front of him — at any hour of the day — at any hour of the night — in any language —" She swept the air with her arm.

Led by Mr. Zabac, the police came bustling into the room. While the chairman had not specified the type of attack that Mrs. Fitzgibbons had perpetrated upon him in his house, or that his wife had been wheeled about outdoors in the frigid air for a quarter hour during the course of the debauchery transpiring indoors, his fear of the woman in the gray leather coat was writ on his face. It was clear that Louis Zabac's appreciation of human nature as something fundamentally decent had been dealt a devastating blow. "*That's* her," he cried, and skipped nimbly to one side as though to avoid a bullet.

Mrs. Fitzgibbons recoiled instinctively, certain in her paranoia that she was about to be murdered.

"That's the one!" Mr. Zabac repeated. "She's the one!"

Mrs. Fitzgibbons retreated to the windows. "You weasel!"

The sergeant in charge, Bill Daley, who answered to the odd nickname of Chandler Bill, was known in the department for his skills at defusing violent domestic fights. Employing an authoritative voice, Chandler Bill positioned himself at the center of things. "Now, there is no need to shout. That's why I'm here."

Mrs. Fitzgibbons's face was contorted. Her heart was going like mad. The room was full of policemen. Her brain dimmed and brightened. "I'm not leaving here," she said.

"She's a criminal!"

"Hold on, I said." Officer Daley reproached the small man behind him.

From time to time, Mrs. Fitzgibbons lost sight altogether of the chairman behind the mass of uniformed bodies, only, however, to see his head pop out once more. He was peeking at her round a policeman's elbow. "Get her out," he said.

Mrs. Fitzgibbons railed at him. "I'll see you in Hell with your back broke, you treacherous —"

Suddenly, Mrs. Fitzgibbons darted forward, her coattails flying, snaked past the astonished Officer Daley, and clubbed Mr. Zabac four times with the solid heel of her fist. The downward blows came thick and fast. "Fucking dwarf!"

A bright spurt of blood flashed in a scarlet jet from the chairman's nose, as the policemen grabbed Mrs. Fitzgibbons and wrestled her to one side. They were handling her roughly.

Mr. Zabac clutched his face with both hands, a dark thread of blood leaking over his knuckle.

Mrs. Fitzgibbons was shouting now in a tremendous voice, her arms pinned behind her back. "I'll chop his fucking spine off! I'm the Chief here! I'm —"

By the time the police got her into handcuffs, and started marching Mrs. Fitzgibbons through Jeannine Mielke's outer office to the stairs, the great rotunda of the bank below was packed with people. The four empty police cruisers, pulled up on the brick walks of the pedestrian mall, with their doors flung open and their roof lights still flashing, had created a sensation. Word spread so rapidly that shoppers from the mall were streaming curiously into the Parish Bank when Mrs. Fitzgibbons was brought to the stairtop. Her hands were cuffed in front of her waist. Chandler Bill Daley was gripping her arm.

Propelled forward through the crowd on the main floor, Mrs. Fitzgibbons looked at no one. She was deathly white. Her features manifested intense scorn. She marched with her head up. The manacles on her wrists glittered in plain sight. No one present, stranger or friend, could have gainsaid the presence behind that cold, milk white demeanor of a proud and resolute spirit.

She spoke only once, as the crowd parted to make way for the solid wedge of policemen surrounding her. "They wonder why banks are in trouble!" she flung out.

Two or three of Mrs. Fitzgibbons's most ardent, fanatical followers hurled encouragement at her as she was sped across the floor.

Deborah Schwartzwald was crying openly, beside herself with grief. "You'll be back, Mrs. Fitzgibbons!"

Mrs. Fitzgibbons maintained her self-control with heroic forbearance, a grim expression on her lips, till she was locked in the back seat of a cruiser. The police cars started up and seemed to be moving about in every direction possible. However, pictures of the most frightening nature were erupting in Mrs. Fitzgibbons's mind. She imagined her tongue being torn out. She had a vision of a severed head in her lap. She tore at her manacles. The naked trees flanking the road to Smith's Ferry offered a grotesque parody, with their frozen limbs, of a loving world. She was by then crying like a child and throwing herself against the Plexiglas barrier. "Don't take me to the hospital!" She beat on the glass with her fists. "Don't take me. Somebody help me."

TWENTY

From that Monday in November, Mrs. Fitzgibbons's days of glory were over. After this, there would be no return to prominence. There would be no subsequent struggles to wage against detractors or the status quo; no chauffeured car; no band of zealots to implement her will; no executive dicta to issue. She passed quietly into a shadowy region of featureless rooms and iron-screened windows. Her days that winter were spent in a quiet, narcotic stupor. The Thorazine, one of her medications, dried her out so badly that the skin on her fingers turned yellow and cracked open. Her hands and feet were a sight. She slept twelve to fourteen hours a day, ate tasteless meals from a Styrofoam tray, and gained several pounds. Her hair lost its luster. In behavior, she was reticent and thoughtful. The days melted one into the other.

At first, in the weeks before Christmas 1987, many of Mrs. Fitzgibbons's admirers and hangers-on visited her at the Smith's Ferry hospital, bringing flowers and candy, little mementos of their devotion to her during her season of triumph. However, the transformation of the vivacious leader into the smiling, acquiescent lady seated on her green plastic chair in the sun room was too shocking for most of them. They could not reconcile the distressing spectacle of Mrs. Fitzgibbons, looking wan and sedated, with the happy authoritarian figure they had known. If anything, she may have represented to them a living symbol of the darker side of their mortal hopes.

One of the most startling changes was the lack of curiosity she showed in matters concerning the Parish Bank. The fact, for example, that Mr. Hooton had never returned to his job, and that Lionel Kim had indeed succeeded to his post as treasurer, inspired no more of a response from Mrs. Fitzgibbons than an appreciative smile. She was pleased for Mr. Kim. She was confident, she said, that he would succeed brilliantly and be a credit to all. She was similarly indifferent a few days later to the front-page news of Mr. Louis Zabac's takeover of the Citizens Bank. Julie Marcotte brought the paper to the hospital and expressed indignation that Mrs. Fitzgibbons's name did not appear anywhere in the article. Mrs. Fitzgibbons, though, was blissfully indifferent to the omission. "I never wanted to be in the paper," she said. Julie was left shaken by the experience.

The only person capable of upsetting Mrs. Fitzgibbons's equanimity was her daughter, who was brimming over with sour feelings. Typically, Eddie stood behind Barbara, nodding sadly over his wife's wisdoms, a picture of the errant, penitential husband. He wore a big baseball cap covered with environmental patches and a new pair of rather lumpy machinist's shoes made of a synthetic material that shone like glass and squeaked when he walked. He jangled keys in his pocket nervously, while Barbara castigated her mother. At such times, Mrs. Fitzgibbons just stared into space and winced.

The happiest moment of her day was immediately after supper, every evening, without exception, when Bruce arrived in the ward like clockwork; he came striding to her, looking his fashionable best, and always bearing some precious trifle or other. He brought her a tiny radio, a scented handkerchief in a box, perfume, a tea rose, a pretty scarf. Besides being a picture to the eye, he was exuberant. He was the soul of good cheer. If Bruce's behavior was indicative, one might have surmised that Mrs. Fitzgibbons had suffered nothing more debilitating than a nagging head cold. It was Bruce, too, who telephoned Dr. Cauley and complained insistently about the dehydrating effects of Thorazine, which led to the painful but timely discovery that Mrs. Fitzgibbons's system was dangerously impacted. Bruce did everything for Mrs. Fitzgibbons that anyone who cherished her might conceivably have done, not to mention the way he fussed over her hair for an hour or so each evening. He also repeated candidly to her the doctor's description of her condition. Although Mrs. Fitzgibbons was not able to focus upon or grasp the larger significance of what he was saying, she was comforted by the way he said it. She had suffered a severe manic episode, triggered by psychological changes she was undergoing. That was how he put it. It was Dr. Cauley's informed guess, he said, that Mrs. Fitzgibbons would not remit her symptoms gradually, over an extended period, but rather all at once, virtually overnight, at some point in the weeks to come. "Then," said Bruce, "we'll take you home."

The only time that Mrs. Fitzgibbons caught a glimpse of Bruce's temper was the evening in December when he got into a shouting match with Barbara. It had been snowing, and he stood in the middle of the ward, with the snow on the collar of his winter coat and glistening in his hair, and commanded the younger woman to shut her mouth and leave the hospital. He was beside himself to such a degree that his voice actually cracked. After that, Bruce prevailed on both doctors on staff to prohibit Barbara from visiting her mother. Mrs. Fitzgibbons's daughter was only too happy to oblige.

At last, toward the end of January, Mrs. Fitzgibbons fulfilled Dr. Cauley's prognosis to the letter, when, literally overnight, her symptoms faded and vanished like the snow on the window sash. To Bruce, Mrs. Fitzgibbons's return to soundness was like a gift from the gods. She sat before him as a pale but thoroughly rational copy of the woman she had been. She was exhausted and weak, but the bond between her mind and realities external to it was clearly intact. She made perfect sense in everything she said, for the first time in twelve weeks. More puzzling than Mrs. Fitzgibbons's rejuvenation and return to lucidity, by then, was the depth and pertinacity of Bruce's devotion.

The sight of the two of them walking in the enclosed quadrangle outdoors, on sunny weekend afternoons, became a commonplace that winter. Weather allowing, Mrs. Fitzgibbons wore a big woolen sweater and an olive scarf; she held him by the arm. It was apparent to Mrs. Fitzgibbons herself by that time, in her rational under-standing of him, that Bruce was devoted to her in a way that went beyond conventional descriptions. Whether his love and stead-fastness were occasioned by some blind obstinacy in his makeup, or some hidden frailty — or by some equally recondite virtue in herself — she would probably never know. He allied himself to her to a degree impossible to comprehend. To Mrs. Fitzgibbons's mind, it was not dissimilar from the theological concept of grace, which, at one point in her school years, she had striven to com-prehend.

The pathways of the quadrangle were faintly derelict. The bricks underfoot were cracked and icy; patches of black snow lay beneath the ragged privet hedges like dirty newspapers. The sun over the hospital wing was a white wafer in the sky. During these interludes, Bruce entertained her with stories about persons of their acquaint-ance. By this time, Mrs. Fitzgibbons's exciting triumphs in the banking business, when she had lit up the local media with her flamboyance, her oratory, her good looks and indomitable will, were spoken of, when at all, with a mixture of humor and nos-talgia. To Mrs. Fitzgibbons herself, that short era was thoroughly anachronistic, as though the memory of it were just a facet of her troubled spirits in the hospital. Still, she couldn't help laughing, however embarrassedly, on learning that Dolores Brouillette had gone away to New York for the Christmas holiday, taking with her her new Oldsmobile Toronado and the balance of the Brouil-lette checking account, and had never come back. Also, since Bruce seemed not to care about it, the fact that Matthew had begun leading a brawling life, frequenting the most notorious bars in town, and had subsequently left Bruce and moved into a room of his own down by the Public Library, was nothing more than the stuff of delightful gossip.

The strangest anecdote that Bruce retailed that winter was his account of how Jack Greaney had been seen going into a movie house one Friday night with Emily Krok, and that they were seen again, a second time, not two days later, going side by side up Beech Street, looking for all the world like a fond young couple.

Mrs. Fitzgibbons took a surprisingly charitable view of this report, even after Bruce explained how Emily had knocked Jack out at the bank. Bruce found the story incredible. Mrs. Fitzgibbons thought otherwise.

"Jack's a very nice boy, delicate," she said, "and well behaved. He needs someone rough and ready. He's very bright. He hides his light under a bushel. Emily is a diamond in the rough."

"She talks about flattening him," Bruce said. "That's how she introduces him. 'This is Jack who I coldcocked.' "

Mrs. Fitzgibbons was not dissuaded. "I find no fault with that, if they're happy. I think they're lucky. The best thing to be in this world is lucky. If you're lucky, you'll be happy. You can't not be." She tightened her clasp on Bruce's arm. At the iron gate, they turned and started back. "The last thing I would want written on my gravestone would be, 'She was unlucky.' "

"You're right about that."

"So far," she said, "I've been lucky."

In fact, Mrs. Fitzgibbons was not quite the same anymore. That spring, after going to live with Bruce for several days, then returning to her home, her reticence and her indifference to the future were readily evident. She was accepting of everything, even to the point of apathy. Bruce managed her daily affairs and never ceased paying the most sedulous attention to her appearance. By midsummer, Mrs. Fitzgibbons's weight was in fact down to normal; her hair had regained its shine; she was still capable of fetching admiring glances in public. A memorable moment for Mrs. Fitzgibbons was when she asked Bruce if she might not help out at the salon, by looking after the cash register and handling the incoming calls of women seeking appointments. Bruce appeared genuinely appalled by the suggestion, so much so, in fact, that Mrs. Fitzgibbons was never so convinced of the depth and genuineness of his adulation of her as at that time. Even after he had acceded, and she had begun to spend her afternoons with him at the salon, the extent of his attachment continued to mystify her. Many months had gone by, and a thousand different instances of his

regard for her had come and gone, before Mrs. Fitzgibbons successfully grasped the whole of it. There was something in her that
he adored; something he worshiped. There was no other word for
it.

It showed in his dealings with her every minute of the day; he
leaped to open doors for her; waited at dinner till she was comfortably seated before seating himself; deferred instantaneously to
her preferences, whether in tuning a television channel or selecting
a jar of olives. Bruce was as close to perfection in consistency of
behavior as nature ever intended anyone should be. In time, Mrs.
Fitzgibbons accepted his passion, as it fueled and nourished an
ancient childhood narcissism within her, and she dealt with him
in the way that pleased him most; she showed him a gentle aloof-
ness, an air of certitude, the quality of a superior being that he
strove so hard to engender. On the summer day when he framed
the handsome gold-edged certificate of award that had been conferred on Mrs. Fitzgibbons by the Massachusetts State Council of
Women and insisted on hanging it in a prominent spot on the wall
in his salon, Mrs. Fitzgibbons was conscious of the thrill she imparted to him by showing him a trace of dissatisfaction. It was
closing time on a Saturday in August. They were alone in the salon.
Bruce had removed the paper and string and was holding the
framed document in his two hands.

Mrs. Fitzgibbons was standing at his side. She had just switched
off the air conditioning and cut the power in the cash register. The
only lights left burning were those above the several wall mirrors
behind him.

"I hope you like it," he said, and then looked at her question-
ingly. He wanted her to reject it, and she knew it. Currents of
concern rose and fell in her breast. She saw the color in his cheeks.
He was testing her.

Mrs. Fitzgibbons looked at the frame, conscious of the impressive purse of her lips and the expression of hopeful expectancy on
his face. Her reply, when it came, was as soft as a thought. "I
don't," she said. "You'll have to frame it differently."

Bruce nodded resignedly, as though her rejection of his choice
had confirmed his own better judgment. He looked up then into
the steely, dark blue eyes. "I'll bring it back."

"You do that," she said.

"I'll order the gold-leaf frame."

And that, on balance, was how it went, through the late days of summer and on into the fall of the year. In fact, from that time forward, the sight of Mrs. Fitzgibbons emerging from the downtown mall at closing time, with Bruce beside her, the two of them coming out the walkway past the darkened storefronts into the silent, lamplit street, was nothing more extraordinary than that of any two people anywhere on earth, coming out any door.

OTHER NEW YORK REVIEW CLASSICS

For a complete list of titles, visit www.nyrb.com or write to:
Catalog Requests, NYRB, 435 Hudson Street, New York, NY 10014

* *Also available as an electronic book.*